Sedu
Sy

FIONA MCARTHUR

CAROL MARINELLI

AMY ANDREWS

MILLS & BOON

First Published in Great Britain 2016
By Mills & Boon, an imprint of HarperCollins*Publishers*
1 London Bridge Street, London, SE1 9GF

SEDUCTION IN SYDNEY © 2016 Harlequin Books S. A.

Sydney Harbour Hospital: Marco's Temptation, *Sydney Harbour Hospital: Ava's Re-Awakening* and *Sydney Harbour Hospital: Evie's Bombshell* were first published in Great Britain by Harlequin (UK) Limited.

Sydney Harbour Hospital: Marco's Temptation © 2012 Harlequin Books S. A.
Sydney Harbour Hospital: Ava's Re-Awakening © 2012 Harlequin Books S. A.
Sydney Harbour Hospital: Evie's Bombshell © 2013 Harlequin Books S. A.

Special thanks and acknowledgement are given to Fiona McArthur, Carol Marinelli and Amy Andrews for her contribution to the *Sydney Harbour Hospital* series.

ISBN: 978-0-263-92061-1

05-0416

SYDNEY HARBOUR HOSPITAL: HOSPITAL: MARCO'S TEMPTATION

BY
FIONA MCARTHUR

A mother to five sons, **Fiona McArthur** is an Australian midwife who loves to write. Medical Romance gives Fiona the scope to write about all the wonderful aspects of adventure, romance, medicine and midwifery that she feels so passionate about—as well as an excuse to travel! Now that her boys are older, Fiona and her husband Ian are off to meet new people, see new places, and have wonderful adventures.

Fiona's website is at www.fionamcarthur.com.

To Flo, who went above and beyond
to help me do justice to Marco.
Looking forward to more journeys with glee, Fi. xx

CHAPTER ONE

MARCO D'ARVELLO paused in a pool of sunlight on the suspended walkway and watched the boats in Sydney Harbour. Not your usual view from a hospital corridor. He hoped to do more than just observe this country before he had to leave, but once this last client was seen he was booked up with all the surgery he could manage before he moved on.

That was how he liked it.

His attention returned to the consultant's referral in his hand. 'Foetal urinary obstruction.' Should be a fairly simple scope and shunt, he mused as he pushed open the door to his temporary rooms. The lack of waiting-room chairs meant his patients had to wait in his office. It wasn't really ideal but the view was worth it.

'*Buongiorno*, Marlise.'

His borrowed secretary blushed. 'Good morning, Dr D'Arvello.'

'Please, you must call me Marco.' He perched on the edge of her desk, oblivious to the flutter he caused, and peered across at her computer screen. 'Has Miss Cooper arrived?'

Marlise sucked in her stomach and pointed one manicured figure at the screen. 'Yes. About ten minutes ago.'

'Bene.' No time for dawdling. He hated tardiness himself.

When Marco strode through his door the view of the harbour and his nebulous thoughts of probable intra-uterine surgery paled into the background as Miss Cooper's smooth bob swung towards him.

Bellissima! The sun danced on the molten highlights of her hair like the boats on the waves outside, and emerald eyes, direct and calm against his suddenly dazed scrutiny, stared back at him as he crossed the room and held out his hand.

She shifted the big handbag on her lap and a smaller one as well, and stood up. Two bags? He forgot the bags, focussed on the slender hand in front of his, and remembered to breathe. Her fingers were cool and firm and he forced himself to let them slide from his grasp.

Her face. Serenity, wisdom, yet vulnerable? How could that be? She was older than he had expected, perhaps late twenties, maybe early thirties, the perfect age, and where she hid her baby he did not know, but she certainly had that gorgeous pregnant glow about her.

Marco consulted his notes to give time to assemble his scattered thoughts but he only grew more confused. Twenty-six weeks' gestation? 'You don't look very… um…pregnant.' Hell. Say something unprofessional, why don't you?

Emily Cooper blinked. They hadn't told her the new hotshot O and G consultant exuded raw magnetism like a roving gypsy king. Hair too long, too dark, windswept, and gorgeous velvety brown eyes that made her want to melt into the hospital carpet.

Her have another baby? If she could make her mouth work it'd better not laugh. 'I'm not pregnant.' Once was enough, she thought.

She hadn't had a relationship in who knew how long. Her shaky legs suggested she sit, but once safely down she felt like a sex-starved midget with him towering over her. But it wasn't only that, it was the whole broad-shouldered, 'span your waist with his big hands' thing that was happening. A random 'if I was going to have sex it would have to be with someone like him' thought that made her blink. Not her usual fantasy—that was more in line with 'wish I could sleep the clock around'.

Thankfully he stepped around the desk and she savoured the relief of increased space between them.

'But you're here for in-utero surgery…yes?' Such a delicious Italian accent. Emily tasted the sound like chocolate on her tongue.

Marco stared at the paper in his hand. He could easily grasp the most complicated sequences of micro-surgery but this he could not fathom. Not only the sudden misbehaviour of his rampant sex hormones but the concept of being inexplicably glad Miss Cooper was not pregnant. It was all very strange. Perhaps with the desk between them his brain would function.

Before she could answer, the sound of footsteps and a young woman appeared hurriedly at the door. Things fell quickly into place.

'How could you start without me, Mum?'

Fool. He felt like smacking his forehead. But excellent. He could see the similarities as the still barely pregnant-looking daughter came into his office with a mulish look to her rosebud mouth as she took the other handbag from her mother.

'My apologies, Miss Cooper.' He smiled and held out his hand. 'I am Marco D'Arvello.' Reluctantly the young woman shook his hand. 'We have yet to begin.' He extended his apology to Emily. 'And forgive me, too, Mrs Cooper.'

The daughter glowered and glanced at her mother. 'We're both Miss Cooper. Mum's Emily and I'm Annie. Illegitimacy runs in the family.'

Emily. Marco struggled to keep his face neutral when, in fact, he wanted to stand between this little virago and her poor mother. He was slightly relieved to see that Emily had ignored her daughter's outburst. Truly, family dynamics were none of his business, he didn't want them to ever be his business, so why did he feel so discomfited by what was going on here?

He forced himself to concentrate on the younger woman. 'Then let us discuss your child, Annie.' He gestured to the other chair. 'Please, be seated and we will begin.'

Emily held back the sigh along with the need to fan her face. Maybe she could disappear into the carpet until the air-conditioner cooled her cheeks. Why did her daughter's newly emergent evil twin have to appear here? The secretive one she didn't recognise. It was okay. Her daughter was emotional, scared for her baby and angry with the world since Gran had died.

Emily was pretty angry about that herself but really she just longed for the delightful girl child Annie had been up until the last two months.

Illegitimacy runs in the family. Cringeworthy at the very least. No chance of sex with him now.

The thought brought a reluctant whisper of ironic amusement and suddenly she didn't feel the need to sink into that scratchy hospital carpet; she could focus.

Which was lucky because they'd carried on without her.

'There are three types of foetal surgery. One we do only with a needle. Another is the opposite, and similar to a Caesarean section where we work directly on the anesthetised foetus, which we remove from the uterus and then return.'

Incredible what they could do. Emily watched his face. So intense and obviously passionate about something he knew so well. She couldn't imagine the tension in an operating theatre for such a procedure. It sounded easy. Too easy for reality.

'The risks of premature labour are greatest the larger the incision into the uterus, of course, until sometimes it is better to wait to deliver the baby and perform the surgery ex utero.'

Annie was chewing her lip. 'So can we wait for my baby?'

'Those cases depend on the foetal problem. Your baby is twenty-six weeks old, too young for the risk of premature labour or delivery, too old to be left much longer before damage cannot be reversed, and so we move on to the next alternative.'

He picked up the large envelope of ultrasounds and crossed to the light projector on the wall to clip up the dark images.

They all moved to fan around the light source.

'Foetoscopy would be my preferred option in your case. Or Fetendo—like the child's game—because the instruments are controlled while watching a screen and are less than a pencil width in diameter.'

'Neat.'

'*Si.*' He smiled, the room lit up, and Emily felt like grabbing her sunglasses from her bag. Probably just because working permanent nights made you sensitive to light.

Marco pointed with one longer finger. 'Your baby has a narrowing of the neck of the bladder.' He circled the darkness of the bladder on the film. 'In simple terms, the door to releasing urine from the bladder has closed almost completely and the kidneys are swelling with the retained fluid. I would have wished to perform this surgery at least four weeks ago for maximum protection of your baby's kidneys.'

Emily felt she had to explain. 'We've only just found out about my daughter's pregnancy. This is the first scan she's had. It's all been a bit of a shock.'

Understatement. And not just the pregnancy. Disbelief that her daughter had fallen into the same circumstances as herself had paled when they'd discovered Annie's baby was at risk.

Emily's fierce protective instinct embraced this tiny new member of their family wholeheartedly because already she loved this little dark gnome on the ultrasound films.

'*Si.* So we will schedule surgery as soon as possible. I believe the repair can be achieved by foetoscopy under ultrasound imaging.'

He smiled at Annie. 'The instruments are fine and

require a very small incision.' He glanced at them both under dark brows. 'Tomorrow?'

'Tomorrow?' Annie's squeak made Emily's hand slip across the distance between them to squeeze her daughter's cold fingers.

'It's okay. Better have it done as soon as possible for baby.' She looked at this man they were entrusting Annie and her baby's future to.

His strong profile and unwavering eyes somehow imbued the confidence she needed that these risks were worth it. 'Do you think much damage has been done to baby's kidneys already?'

He tactfully shrugged his broad shoulders and their eyes met and held. She could feel his compassion. His understanding of her fear.

They both glanced at Annie. 'We wait. It will be difficult to tell until after the operation. Hopefully the amniotic fluid volume will increase as the bladder is allowed to empty. That will be a good sign.'

He looked at them both. 'And in a few months, after the birth, there will be tests to give a true indication.'

Marco watched the young woman to see if she realised there was still doubt on the final outcome. They did not intrude on the dark sea of the foetal world without good reason. Annie's eyes, glistening green like her mother's, were glued to his face. 'So the procedure is safe for my baby?'

Ah. She began to comprehend and this part of it he could reassure her on. 'I have performed foetoscopies many times, and while you must be aware of the risks— your own anesthetic, your baby's analgesia, which we administer to prevent the procedure causing pain, and the risk of premature labour I spoke about before—to not perform this surgery would ensure a poor quality of life for your child, with extremely damaged kidneys.'

Annie gulped and nodded. 'Yes. I see.'

Perhaps he had been too blunt? 'I do not say these things to frighten you, but for you to know I believe this needs to be done, and as soon as possible.' He touched Annie's shoulder reassuringly. 'Do you understand?'

Annie glanced at her mother and nodded her head 'Okay. But I don't want to know any more. Let's just get it over with, then.'

'*Si.*' He moved to the door and they both stood up. 'I will arrange this now.' He glanced at the notes in his hand. 'I have your mobile phone number and will confirm the time Annie is to arrive tomorrow morning. You live together?'

'Yes.' Emily nodded. 'How long will she be in hospital?'

He pursed those sinfully chiselled lips and Emily diverted her glance quickly away to watch her daughter. 'The risk of premature birth is still present so at least forty-eight hours. My secretary will arrange for Annie to have an injection to help mature her baby's lungs should premature labour occur. This will be repeated tomorrow before surgery. If we have to open the uterus, her stay in hospital would be almost a week.'

Emily glanced back, careful to avoid looking at his face, stared instead at his collar and nodded. 'Thank you, Doctor.'

Marco looked at Annie. 'You are sure you have no other questions?' All mulishness and bravado had fallen away and Annie looked what she was. An apprehensive young woman scared for her baby.

'As long as my baby will be all right, Doctor?'

'Please, call me Marco. And your baby's wellness is our goal. *Bene.* I will see you tomorrow.'

Annie stiffened her shoulders and lifted her chin. 'Tomorrow.' She nodded, resolute. Now he admired her. No doubt her courage came from her mother. 'Thank you, Marco.'

The mother, Emily, just smiled and followed her daughter. No doubt this woman's whole life revolved around the girl, which would explain why there was an imbalance of power for the teenage years. He watched them walk away and readjusted his thinking. The daughter wasn't too bad. Just stressed. And if his child had required what hers did, he'd be stressed too.

He tried not to think about the mother. Because he really wanted to think about her. A lot.

But she did not look the kind of woman to have an affair, a liaison for just a month, while he worked in Sydney.

Unfortunately, after such brief exposure, her image was burned into his brain. Miss Cooper. Emily. Green eyes and vulnerable wisdom.

Emily went to work that night, like she had so many nights before over the last sixteen years, though times had changed in the last decade as she had progressed in her career. Now she was in charge of the ward at night, instead of being the junior nurse.

She could have risen higher but she chose night work

because night duty meant the only person who suffered was her.

Because Gran, dear Gran, the only one in her family who had unconditionally loved her, had supported her, and in the past had minded the sleeping Annie while Emily worked.

Gran was gone now, Annie was certainly old enough not to be minded, and though Emily had almost come to terms with having a grandchild, she hadn't really come to terms with the fact her daughter had had unprotected sex at sixteen.

Would that have happened if she hadn't worked nights? Who knew? After all those conversations!

The ward was quiet so far—unlike her mind. She set the scales beside the prepared bed for the impending transfer from a regional hospital and pulled the BP machine close to hand for when their patient arrived. Her thoughts roamed as she taped the name badge to the bed.

The new patient was under Marco D'Arvello as well. So they had an influx of foetal surgery now?

She shook her head.

'Is something wrong?' Lily, her colleague and friend, touched her arm and Emily gathered herself.

'No. I'm thinking about earlier today.'

'So how was Annie's appointment and the mysterious Dr D'Arvello?' Lily had recently met and fallen in love with the man of her dreams, a plastic surgeon, and she was keen for everyone else to be as happy as her. 'I hear he's a heartbreaker.'

Um. Gorgeous? Emily could feel the warmth creep up her neck. At least the dimness of night duty was good for hiding blushes. 'He seemed very nice. You tell me what you think when he comes to see the new admission.'

She didn't want to think about her visceral reaction at his office. 'Naturally it would have been better if Annie had had the ultrasound earlier. But I didn't find out until last week. How history repeats itself.'

Her young friend shook her head emphatically. 'From where I'm standing, history did not repeat itself. From what you've told me, your parents treated you with coldness and contempt. This time it's different. When you found out you didn't hesitate to support Annie. You're there for her and she knows it. Even if she won't tell you who the father is.'

Emily chewed her lip. 'She says it's over and he's not interested. I'm not pushing. But her life as a child will be gone. And now her baby might be sick.'

Lily might be young but she hadn't had an easy childhood. She was tough and could work anywhere in the hospital, used to be an agency nurse, but wards were vying for her shifts because she was so versatile. Luckily she loved Maternity and Theatres.

Lily knew how strong a woman could be if she had to be. 'Lots of girls manage beautifully. Even with sick babies. I survived. You survived. You took it on with your head high. She'll survive. And if her baby is like you two, she'll be tough, too.'

Emily breathed deeply. She would love to believe that. She squeezed her friend's shoulder. 'Thanks. I'm sorry. I shouldn't bring my worries to work.'

Lily shook her head emphatically. 'And where else do you go to unload? I'm glad to be here for you. Which reminds me, we should have coffee this week, and Evie wants to come.'

'And that's another thing.' Emily brushed her hair out of her eyes. 'Annie wants a baby shower.'

'Stop beating yourself up. You do a great job. It's been a hard year with your gran and now Annie's pregnancy.'

They both looked up at the sound of an approaching wheel chair. 'I'll try. Looks like our patient is here.'

The woman in the chair looked even younger than Annie and both women shared a sympathetic glance.

'Hello, there, June, is it?' Emily smiled down at the scared young woman. 'I hear you're having twins?'

June nodded. 'That's what the doctor said. Now I don't feel so bad I look like the side of a house.' Her smile dropped a little as her bravado faltered. 'My babies are going to be all right. Aren't they?'

'We'll be doing everything we can to stop your contractions and as my friend here is fond of saying, babies are tough little creatures.'

The porter wheeled her into the prepared room. June moved carefully, and her large abdomen became more obvious when she moved. She stopped for a moment and breathed through the next contraction and Emily rested her hand on June's belly to feel the muscles harden. 'The tightenings seemed strong. You're managing well with them.'

June breathed out a big sigh when the contraction had passed. 'I did one of those calming birth weekends. My friend's mum teaches them and it really does help.'

'I've heard they're excellent. Must get the number from you for my daughter later.' Emily helped June balance on the scales. 'With luck we'll weigh you and get you into bed and sitting up high before the next one.'

June swayed on the scales and she whistled at the numbers. 'I never knew babies were so heavy.'

Emily wrote down the weight with a smile. 'A lot of your tummy is fluid, not just babies.'

June glanced across at Emily. 'The ultrasound said one baby is bigger than the other.'

Not a good thing with twins, Emily agreed silently. 'That's why the new doctor is coming to see you. We'll get you settled and sorted before he arrives.'

June glanced at the clock on the wall. 'Is he coming tonight? It's after midnight.'

'Doctors work long hours. And this one is a specialist who's very experienced with twins that are different sized.'

'Oh.' June settled back in the bed and forced herself to breathe calmly through the next contraction.

'I've a tablet here for you that should help the contractions ease off while we wait. It's also used as a blood-pressure tablet so I need to check that before I give it to you.'

Emily wrapped the blood-pressure cuff around June's arm and pumped it up to check. Normal. Good. 'I'll check again in thirty minutes and if you're still having contractions we'll give you another then.'

June was well settled before the sound of voices drifted to her room. Emily completed her paperwork and put the chart in the tray at the end of the bed. 'Ah. Here's your doctor.' Lily brought Dr D'Arvello into June's room.

Lily winked from behind his shoulder and Emily chewed her lip to keep back the smile.

'Hello, there.' His eyebrows rose when he recognised Emily. He glanced at her badge. 'Sister Cooper?'

'Doctor.' He looked less immaculate than he had earlier today, with a subtle darkness of new growth over his strong chin and his hair unruly across his forehead as if he'd repeatedly pushed it back. Unfortunately he looked even more wickedly attractive.

'Ah.' She saw him file that away before he turned to their patient with a smile that had June relax back into the bed. Nearly as good as calming breaths, Emily thought, with a tinge of sardonic amusement.

'And this is June, who is expecting twins?' He shook June's hand. 'I am Marco D'Arvello. Congratulations.' He pulled the chair across and sat down as if it wasn't really midnight and he hadn't been at work all day.

Like he had all the time in the world to talk to June. Emily liked that. Not what she needed—to find something else she liked about this guy—but she was pleased for June.

June breathed through another contraction, though this one lasted less than twenty seconds. Marco frowned. 'She still threatens labour?'

'That one was shorter after just one dose of the Nifedipine.'

'Good.' He smiled at June. 'Your babies are better off inside at their age so we hope the contractions stop. I've looked at your ultrasounds, June, and your twins have a problem that I think I can help you with.'

June squared her shoulders. 'What sort of problem.'

He smiled. 'I like a woman who gets straight to the point.' Emily tried not to file that away.

'Because your babies share the one placenta, even though they use their own part of the placenta, it seems there's an extra blood vessel connecting their blood supply that shouldn't be there. The problem with that is one twin often gets the lion's share of oxygen and nutrients while the other can be quite disadvantaged.'

'Is it dangerous?' June was nothing if not focussed. Emily felt like hugging the girl.

'For the less fortunate foetus, it certainly can be.'

June turned to look at Emily and then back at Marco. 'You said you can help?'

He nodded. 'I offer you the option of an operation with a small instrument that enters your uterus through the abdomen and seals off the unwanted blood vessel between the twins. We use a tiny laser.'

June's eyes widened with distress? 'A laser? Near my babies? And you've done this before?'

'Dozens of times.' He smiled and Emily felt soothed just watching him. 'Believe me…' he smiled again '…I would do it very carefully but the risks are greater if I do not attempt this closure of the extra vessel.'

He was skilled with reassurance, too, Emily thought, but she could see June's apprehension so she tried to help with the little she knew. 'It sounds like science fiction, doesn't it?'

She gestured to Marco. 'Dr D'Arvello is consulting here on a secondment. Intrauterine surgery is his specialty and he's here to help our obstetric and paediatric surgeons increase their skills.'

June narrowed her gaze. 'So you're the expert?'

'*Si.*' Marco nodded.

'So you don't deliver babies, then?' June frowned. 'Just laser them?'

White teeth flashed as he grinned, and Emily could feel her own mouth curve because he just made her want to smile. 'But no. I am present for many births. Thankfully, only few babies need what I offer and a normal birth is always a joy.' He glanced at Emily. 'You would agree, Sister Cooper?'

'Of course.' Emily wondered if he did see many normal births. Nowadays, at Sydney Harbour Hospital anyway, obstetricians were usually only called when complications occurred. Or for hands-on service for their private patients, but perhaps it was different in Italy.

June had thought it through and now she nodded. 'So what happens now?'

'Tonight we give you the second injection to encourage your twins' lungs to mature in case premature labour cannot be stopped.' He glanced at Emily who inclined her head in agreement. 'And please, no more food or fluids until after we operate tomorrow morning.'

June chewed her lip as the closeness of the operation sank in. 'What time will they come for me?'

'It will be soon after breakfast.' He smiled. 'Which is not for you.'

She pretended to sigh at that and Emily wanted to hug her for being so brave, though the anxiety lay clearly behind her joking manner. 'Thank you, Doctor.'

Marco narrowed his eyes and studied her. 'You have a mother's courage. Would you like something to help you sleep? Sister could give you something to help you relax.'

'No. Thank you. I guess I won't be doing much tomorrow and I can catch up then.'

Marco stood up. '*Bene.* Goodnight, then.' He caught Emily's eye. 'May I have a word with you, Sister?'

Emily nodded. 'One minute.' And smiled at June. 'I'll be back soon. Would you like a drink of water before I take it away?'

June swallowed half a glass and Emily collected the water and followed him out to the desk, where he was writing up his orders for the night.

CHAPTER TWO

EMILY glanced at the clock. A quarter to one. Dr D'Arvello would have little sleep before his surgery day. She wondered if he was as used to lack of sleep as she was.

From her height above where he sat at the desk she couldn't help noticing the thickness of his dark hair. No sign of grey but he must be in his mid-thirties. A few years older than her and so much more experienced with the world. That deficit hadn't bothered her before. Why should it now? Silly. 'You wished to see me, Doctor?'

His dark eyes swept up from the notes and over her face. He smiled and she found herself grinning back like a goose before she could stop herself. 'I did not know you were a midwife at your daughter's visit this morning.'

It felt so long ago. 'It's not important?'

He frowned. 'But I would have offered more explanation if you wished. Is there more I can tell you?'

'No. Thank you.' She shrugged, a little embarrassed to admit it. 'Of course I have researched the internet and read what I can find. I think I understand the operation well enough.'

He nodded. 'Sometimes I wish my clients would not look up on the internet but I am sure you picked well with your sites. The procedure is fairly simple. Perhaps a little more complicated than June's surgery, but over almost as quickly.'

He stood up, towered over her again, and seemed to hesitate. 'And will you have to come to work tomorrow night after your daughter's operation?'

Her stomach dropped with a tinge of alarm. Was there bad news he hadn't mentioned? 'Actually, I'm not.' Did he think she would be too upset?

Still he frowned. 'So when will you sleep?'

'I'll go home as soon as Annie is out of surgery. So I will sleep when she does, afterwards.'

'You will be tired.' He handed her the completed notes and she took them and stared at the pages. Not really seeing his looping scrawl. Looked anywhere but his face. It had been a while since anyone had wondered if she was tired and his kindness made her feel strange. This whole conversation was surreal because she was so ridiculously conscious of him.

She risked a glance. 'I was just thinking the same for you.'

He shrugged his manly shoulders and she felt her stomach kick. This was crazy. She was way too aware of this man, this transient doctor. 'I sleep less than four hours a night. Always have done.'

'And I survive on about the same. I'm used to it.' She opened the folder at the medication page. She needed to get this injection for June happening. The last one had been given twelve hours ago at the regional hospital. 'So we have something in common.'

He wasn't ready to let her go. 'Perhaps we have more than that.'

She blinked. 'I don't know what you mean?'

He smiled but there was mischief that made her cheeks pink again. 'A concern and empathy for our patients.'

What had she thought he meant? 'Oh. Of course. Well, thank you for your concern. I'll just go for the hydrocortisone for June.'

'Perhaps one more thing?' He held up one finger. 'The reason I asked.'

She stopped. 'I'm sorry?'

'Tomorrow night. Because your daughter will be in the hospital. Perhaps you will need diversion from worry. It is Friday.'

She didn't get it. 'And?'

'A favour. I have promised myself a dinner on your so beautiful Sydney Harbour. I am only here for a month. It would be more pleasant to have company.'

Good grief. He was asking her out. On a date? 'I'm sure lots of ladies would love to be your company.'

He shrugged, as if aware what she said was true, not with conceit but with disinterest. 'I would prefer you.'

Normally he had no problem asking a beautiful woman to dinner. So why was this difficult? He just wanted to enjoy a diversion with this woman, not ask her to have his babies. Why stumble around like a callow youth when she obviously wanted to get on with her work?

It seemed his offer was the last thing she'd expected. He did not think shock was a good reaction and waited with unusual tension while she recovered.

'Well, I guess you won't run away because you find I have a teenage daughter.'

'This has happened?'

'Imagine.' She turned away. 'Anyway. Thank you. But, no, thank you. I don't date.'

'But this is not a date. Just kindness on your part.'

She raised her eyebrows. 'Really? Tricky. Then perhaps I could let you know tomorrow. In the mean time, you could keep looking. Now I must get back to June.'

'*Bene*. Of course. *Buonanotte*.'

'Goodnight.'

Marco left the ward with a smile on his face. It had seemed fortuitous to find the woman who had whispered through his brain at odd moments all day, unexpectedly, on this maternity ward.

A midwife, no less, and someone he would see a little of in the course of his work. And he had planned to dine on the harbour at some stage, though perhaps not tomorrow. And she intrigued him—though a conquest might not be easy. Always a challenge he could not resist.

But with sudden clarity he'd realised that Emily would be unlikely to leave her daughter unattended, except for work, when they lived together. So it had to be tomorrow or the next night or not at all. He smiled to himself. Perhaps her doctor could keep Annie in an extra night for rest. Bad doctor.

He didn't know why he was so sure there was no man in Emily's life, but she had the look of an untouched woman, and he trusted his instincts. She said she did not date. At least that instinct had been correct. A date would be good for her.

She hadn't said yes but that made it all more interesting. The degree of anticipation he could feel building already made him smile. He'd brushed off the need for appreciation and commitment, had had it leached out of him throughout his dark childhood, but a harmless dalliance could hurt no one and he would give much for Emily Cooper to look on his invitation with approval. But not until tomorrow would he find out.

Emily's night passed quickly and thankfully without time for the distraction of Marco D'Arvello's unexpected invitation. June's premature contractions settled, but the arrival of two women in labour, one after the other, left little time for her to work out how she was going to turn him down.

When Emily finished her shift the sun shone through the windshield straight into her eyes as she drove home to the little cottage above the pier at Balmain East she'd inherited from her gran.

On night duty public transport didn't work. Through the days she caught ferries. She couldn't actually see Sydney harbour from her windows but the swish of the wash on the shore from passing boats floated in her window at night as she dressed for work.

Annie was pacing the front veranda as she waited for her mother to arrive home.

'Why did you have to be late, today of all days?'

Emily carried her bag into the house and tried not to sigh. 'We've been busy. I didn't dawdle for the fun of it.'

Annie dropped her complaints and hugged her mother warmly. 'Sorry. I'm nervous…' she twisted her fingers '…and started to worry we'd be late.' She shook her head. 'And baby was awake and moving most of the night. It's almost as if she's nervous too.'

'I wouldn't be surprised if she was. Babies pick up on their mother's mood.'

Annie tilted her head and studied her mother. 'Well, I can see you need a cup of tea so maybe I can pick up yours too. I made you raisin toast!' It was a large statement. In case Emily didn't get the significance she added, 'Even though I'm starving myself because I have to fast.'

Emily was pleased to see after the initial stress Annie had calmed down. And was being nice. Though the last thing she wanted to do was eat. Her stomach was in knots about Annie's hospital visit and impending anaesthetic for both her and her tiny granddaughter. 'Thank you for that. Saves me a few minutes while I shower and dress.'

Three hours later Emily put down the crossword. The surgery seemed to be taking for ever. The waiting-room magazines needed to be tossed into the bin and replaced. Still, Emily had flicked through them all. She'd chewed her nails down to the quick. Now she was onto the edge of her finger. Come on!

At ten-thirty the theatre doors swung open and Marco D'Arvello strode through them. It seemed his focussed glance searched until he found her sitting along the wall.

She bolted upright off her chair as if on a spring. In seconds he was at her side. 'It is good. All went well.'

Emily sagged. Thank God. A strange buzzing began in her ears and her face felt funny, numb. The room began to tilt. His arms came up to steady her shoulders and he steered her back into a sitting position. His head dipped towards her with concern. 'Sit. Not so fast. Have you eaten?'

'What?' The room stopped its slow turn and the humming noises in her ears faded away. She closed and opened her eyes slowly.

'Emily? Have you eaten?'

His hands left her shoulders and she felt strangely bereft, almost tempted to catch them back. 'Must have got up too fast.'

'*Si.*'

Had she eaten? She couldn't remember. 'Um. Raisin toast three hours ago.'

'Come. We will go for a cocoa and some more of your raisin toast before you drive home and go to bed. Annie is not yet awake but will be back in the ward in about thirty minutes. I will return with you then to see her.'

Now she felt silly. Imagine if she'd fainted at his feet. 'I'm fine. Just stood too fast. I'm sure you have better things to do than drink cocoa with me.'

'I cannot think of one.' He shrugged with that Latin assurance Italian men seemed to have and her brain couldn't function enough to think of a good excuse to decline. She had to admit the thought of not being alone for another thirty minutes was attractive.

He went on. 'I believe the prognosis for both your Annie and our friend June's babies has improved significantly. I can do no more for the moment.' He searched her face and seemed satisfied. 'Your colour has improved. But another half an hour of waiting without food will not help.' He held out his hand. 'Come.'

Bossy man. Though she was feeling better. 'You say that a lot.'

He looked puzzled. 'What is that?'

She dropped her chin and deepened her voice in imitation. 'Come!'

He inclined his head. 'I will attempt to refrain.'

They smiled at each other. Such quaint speech patterns and it seemed he could cope with teasing. Luckily. What had got into her? She picked up her bag and glanced at her watch.

'Then thank you. A hot drink would be nice. I start to get cold when I need to sleep. Just twenty minutes and I'll come back.'

'*Si*. Your daughter should be back in the ward soon after that.'

They turned a few heads when they walked into the tea shop in the hospital grounds. Or Marco did, Emily thought as necks swivelled. She didn't actually know many of the staff, having worked in Maternity on nights most of her career, and not a frequent visitor to the kiosk either, but she'd bet someone would recognise them and spread the word.

This place was a minefield of gossip. Another reason she preferred nights.

There was Head of Surgery Finn Kennedy and Evie Lockheart, her friend she was to have coffee with later in the week with Lily. Evie was hospital royalty and heiress to the Lockheart fortune.

Evie and Finn sat, head to head, engrossed in a deep and meaningful conversation, and to her surprise Evie slid her hand across the table and gripped Finn's hand. Emily couldn't help wondering if something terrible had happened.

Evie's father had been kind to her all those years ago when she'd been a sixteen-year-old mother of an ill prem baby, and he'd been the one who'd suggested she would make a great nurse. He'd even provided the reference needed to start work as an unskilled nurse assistant until she could manage the extra burden of study. She liked Evie.

Finn, she was just happy to stay out of his way. He was a grouch. The hospital's most experienced surgeon, though rumours had begun to circulate that he suffered some kind of medical problem that was threatening his career.

Emily had enough on her plate. She didn't want to get anywhere near more drama and she steered Marco to the furthest corner of the kiosk.

More heads swivelled their way and instead of ducking her head she lifted her chin and smiled and nodded back.

Maybe she was sick of being boring. Ungossipworthy. Now she was the mother of a pregnant teenager, cavorting with the new Italian O and G consultant, and flaunting it all in the daylight hours, she may as well hold her head up.

Something had changed her. Marco sensed the stiffening of her shoulders and resisted the sudden urge to take her elbow. Surely she was used to people admiring her? Even bruised around the eyes from lack of sleep, she was a stunning woman.

He'd thought her attractive yesterday, but seeing her

this morning when he'd left Theatre, she'd reminded him of a fragile Madonna and a strange urge to protect her had welled uncomfortably in his throat. A sudden desire to cradle her worried face in his hands and re-assure her.

No doubt she would have something to say about him trying that and he shook off the uneasiness that feeling left him with. She stopped at a table that couldn't be described as secluded but it seemed it would do. Marco pulled out her chair.

'You are smiling? Something amuses you?'

'Gossip.'

He glanced around. 'In a hospital as large as this?'

'Especially in this hospital.' She followed his gaze. Tried not to look at Evie and Finn. 'I hate gossip. It lives and breathes other people's business. And here I am with the handsome Italian doctor who has operated on my daughter. I'm never seen with anyone.'

'At least you notice something about me.'

'You're a bit hard to miss.'

He looked around. 'I too despise gossip.' The memories tasted bitter in his mouth.

Emily heard the underlying resentment and wondered where that had come from. The waitress arrived as soon as they'd picked up the menu and Emily put it down again and smiled at the girl. 'We've only twenty minutes. Should we order food?'

'Sure. Promise I'll be quick. What would you like?'

She looked at Marco. 'Scones and cream?'

Marco smiled at the young girl and she blushed all the way to the roots of her hair. 'One hot chocolate, one

coffee black, and two scones and cream. *Per favore.*'
The girl nodded and sped off.

Well, that was that. She studied his face. He didn't
look tired. So maybe he really did manage on four
hours' sleep. She was beginning to droop. She stifled
a yawn. 'So tell me how it went.'

'Very well. No complications. A simple scope and
shunt away from the narrowed opening into the bladder. Initial ultrasound shows good drainage into the
bladder already.'

'Do you think my granddaughter's kidneys will be
very damaged?'

His face softened and he reached across to touch
her hand. Just that one stroke made her feel better.
Comforted. His hand moved back. 'This I cannot tell.
We will hope not.'

What did she expect? How could he know that? She
just wanted reassurance but wisely he had promised
nothing he couldn't give. Still, she appreciated his empathy. He was a kind man.

The hot drinks and scones arrived and they both
smiled at the waitress. 'So quick. *Grazie.*'

'Wow.' Emily too was impressed. 'Thank you.' The
girl grinned and hurried off and almost bumped into
Finn, who stood suddenly from his chair, almost knocking it over.

He growled something at their waitress and shook off
Evie's hand before he stormed towards the door. Evie's
face looked white and drawn and Emily looked away.
Maybe she could catch up with Evie later. Check she
was okay. There was no doubt she was in love with the

man who had just left her and Emily felt her heart go out
to the younger woman. She'd picked a hard road there.

'It seems our surgical chief is not happy.' Marco too
had seen.

She refocussed on the man beside her. 'I'm sorry?'

'Finn. We met in the States a few years ago. Got
on well.'

Of course Marco would know him. They were both
surgeons. She spread cream on the scone and then
dropped a dollop of jam in the middle. 'Evie's tough.
If anyone can bounce back from Finn's ill humour, Evie
can.'

'And who is she?'

'A medical officer here, a darned good one, but she's
more than that. Her father's the hospital's main benefactor, and the reason Sydney Harbour has so many
ground-breaking programs.'

'Lockheart?'

'Yes. If rumour is to be believed, she and Finn have
an on-again, off-again relationship that sometimes rat-
tles the windows around here. But if I needed medical
help, either of them would do fine by me.'

And you would do fine by me, he thought, and the
premonition that this woman could rock his stable skim-
the-surface world seeped into his bones with a wary
premonition. 'I realise you have a lot on your mind but
have you thought about dinner this evening?'

'No.' Not much anyway. 'I really can't think of anything until after I see Annie.'

'Of course. Forgive me.' He was not usually this
impatient.

They sipped their drinks and the silence became a

little strained. She broke it. 'So how long are you here? At Sydney Harbour?'

'A month. Then I fly out to the US for a consultancy in New York. Last month it was London.'

She sipped her cocoa and the heat seeped into her cold edges. His life sounded a little on the cool side too.

Suddenly she wasn't hungry. 'It sounds a glamorous life.' The creamy scone stared back at her. Like a red eye. She bet she had red eyes. Why on earth had this man asked her to breakfast? Kindness. That was all. Now she just needed to accept the favour and move on.

'*Si*. Glamorous.' He picked up his coffee and took a sip.

'So where is home?' At his frown she tried again. 'Your family.'

His expression didn't change but she felt stillness come over him. And the temperature dropped another two degrees. So he didn't like questions. 'I have no family. I rent when I need. Mostly I work.'

'I'm sorry. I didn't mean to pry.' She glanced at her watch and took another sip of her cocoa. 'I might see if Annie is back.'

He'd been abrupt. Closed her out like he always did when people asked about his family. No wonder she wanted to leave. What did he expect to happen? He never answered questions about himself. He'd learnt at a very young age when the police were eager for any news of his father. When neighbours had shunned his family as soon as they'd realised who they were.

But this woman would never do that. The voice came from nowhere. Just a whisper, like she'd whispered yesterday to his thoughts, and he closed his ears.

'I apologise.' He glanced down at her uneaten scone. 'Your food.'

'I'm not really hungry.' She yawned. 'Excuse me.' He wanted to pick her up and carry her to a big feather bed and tuck her in to sleep. Or not to sleep.

He glanced around for the waitress and managed to catch her eye. She nodded and started their way.

'We will go. See if Annie is back on the ward and then you must go home to bed.' There was that thought again. Emily in bed. He dragged his mind away from her golden bob of hair lying next to his on the pillow.

She dug into her bag for her wallet and he shook his head. 'Please. Allow me.' He laid a note on the table and stood up to help pull out her chair. The waitress arrived and he smiled and gestured with his hand that she keep the change.

Emily stood and he followed her out of the kiosk back towards the wards. He wanted to ask if she would come with him tonight but he would not ask again. Perhaps after she'd seen her daughter he would know.

CHAPTER THREE

'HI, MA,' Annie whispered sleepily. 'They said my baby's fine.' She lay in a twin-bed room and the other stood turned back, waiting for June to return to the ward. 'I'm gonna call her Rosebud.'

Emily ached with the thick swell of love in her throat. At the moment her daughter could call her daughter Medusa and she wouldn't mind. She was just glad Annie and her baby were okay. It was hard to realise her own baby was growing up. She didn't want to think about the time when she left her completely. And her little gnome granddaughter was safe from further harm too. 'That's wonderful, darling.' She squeezed the pale fingers on the sheet and stared mistily down at her daughter.

'It all went very well, Annie.' Marco's deep voice rumbled in her ear and his presence felt like a man they'd known a lot longer than twenty-four hours.

Emily stepped back to think about that, but he must have stepped forward at the same time.

His hands came up to rest on her shoulders and her shoulders fitted snugly up against a wall of chest she'd only dreamed about. It felt too good to move but Emily's attention flew to her daughter. Thankfully Annie's

long lashes rested on her pale cheeks as she drifted
in a post-anaesthetic haze and she couldn't see her
mother's weakness.

From the pillow Annie's eyelids didn't flicker as her
voice faded away. 'Thank you, Marco.' In her semi-
doze Annie's palm slid across the sheet to protect the
small mound of her stomach and Emily let herself relax
for a moment.

Just enjoy the sensation of being held.

Take the comfort he was no doubt offering. She
hadn't had a lot of that lately. Especially since Gran
had died.

But this was different from Gran's gentle love. This
was a virulent, protector of a man saying he was there
for her, if only for the duration of her daughter's recovery, and she'd be a fool to not accept it for what it was.
She didn't want to think about how some women had
this twenty-four seven. It felt too damn good.

But it wasn't reality. She stepped away. 'I'll visit this
afternoon, darling.'

Annie opened her eyes. 'Um. No. Don't. I'm just
gonna sleep. See me tomorrow, Mum. Have a rest.'

Emily winced. 'If that's what you want.' She chewed
her lip. 'You sure? I'll have my phone. Just leave a message on my phone and I'll come in.'

Annie nodded sleepily. 'Tomorrow. Love you.'

'Love you, baby.' She hesitated. Watched her daughter sink into a heavier sleep.

Marco steered her towards the door. 'Come.'

She flicked a glance at him and he grinned. 'I do
not know another word. Leave does not seem to work
the same.'

She smiled back. 'Come is fine.'

'Then—' he deepened his voice to a tease '—come.' They grinned at each other. 'She looks well, your Annie, and we can hope not too much damage is done. But for now, sleepyhead, are you going to go home to worry?'

'No. I don't think I will.' She'd try not to and think about leaning back into Marco's arms. 'I think I'll sleep well.'

'Good.'

Then she thought of tonight, of the empty house. Of waking this afternoon after the four hours' sleep she never seemed to be able to improve on, and wondering what it would have been like to go out with this handsome man, do something that would take her mind off the worry. Or she could sit at home and think about Annie. And maybe one day she could go on a dinner cruise on Sydney harbour on her own.

'I'm wondering…' She hesitated but he'd stopped and his attention was fully on her. 'Um. Dinner. What time?'

She had to guess he hadn't found anyone between hot chocolate and now.

So that was how she came to be dressed, waiting, scanning herself in the mirror. Wondering if the top was too old, should she wear a scarf? Could she still walk in high heels—it had been so long!

The doorbell drilled her like a cold knife and she glared at the mirror. Nerves. She was a big girl, dump the nerves, put on the smile and let the man take you out. You know you fancy him and he's only here for a month.

This would be good practice for the time when Annie

left for her own life. He'd said he'd pick her up so he had a car, must have hired one if he was only here for a month. She kept coming back to that. Just a month. Too short to lose her heart. She hoped.

She peeked out from behind the lace curtain. She hadn't expected an Aston Martin. Or the open-necked black shirt. He was standing at the door. Looking around. Waiting for her to answer, and she was watching him with nerves flapping like pelicans in her belly.

Marco breathed in. Was unexpectedly aware of the late afternoon light, as if he should remember this moment. The slosh of waves and chug of boats on the harbour a few houses away. The tang of salt and seaweed.

The drift of voices from homes close to Emily's. People who saw this woman every day. Probably had for years. How could she still be alone? How had some man not scooped her up and carried her and her daughter off?

When would she answer this door? He checked the number again just as the door opened.

His breath was expelled in a sigh. A woman with such style. *'Bellisima.'* Every time he saw her she captured more of his attention. Appeared more exquisite.

'Thank you. Come through.' She gestured to the quaint sitting area with the carved wooden archway between the rooms.

Emily smoothed her coral skirt, willing the heat in her cheeks to subside as she invited him in. He looked pretty hot himself in immaculate black trousers and a silk shirt that screamed Italian tailor.

If he only knew. She didn't spend money on clothes.

Only the occasional piece of underwear she still felt guilty about and hid from her daughter. Gran's skirt and antique lace blouse, even her lovely silver dancing shoes were sixty years old but fitted perfectly. She'd always been Gran's size since she'd had Annie.

Sixteen years the same size. Except for the last few months when the one loving person in her life had faded away to a wisp of her former self.

'The boat leaves at six. Forgive me if I rush you but it is to catch the sunset on the water.'

Not the time for sad memories.

Tonight she would embrace life and a handsome man.

She'd forgotten how good it felt to dress up and see her escort light up when he saw her. See his eyes smoulder, sweep over her, want her. Not that she was thinking that. But sixteen years was too long between attempted seductions so it would be nice to see if she still had feminine wiles.

He was waiting. 'I'll just get my purse.' She leant past him to the hall table and picked up her filmy wrap as well as her tiny clutch. 'A night on the harbour is worth the rush.'

He stepped forward and took the wrap from her hands. 'Allow me,' he said, and spread the floating silk over her shoulders. She tried not to shiver with the sensation. 'My car is downstairs.' She focussed on transport—much safer.

'Is it worth having a car when you work such long hours?' She was still gabbling as she pulled the door shut after him.

'*Si.*' He waited for her to precede him down the steps

and she could feel his presence solid behind her. It felt strange, to say the least. She felt strange. Like a teen. She really did need to get out more.

'I have rented an apartment across the bay near the clown's face and I am often called in.'

'Of course.' Not tonight, she hoped.

'Not tonight, though.'

She smiled as he answered her thought and glanced towards the harbour. Imagining the bright mouth of the amusement-park entrance. 'So you're near Luna Park. Do you look down on it? Can you hear the children screaming on the rides?'

Gran used to take her and Annie. For a few years it had been sadly neglected but she'd heard it had been renovated and new life breathed into the attractions.

'A little. It makes me smile. But my windows face mainly across the harbour and the bridge. The view is as good as anywhere I have travelled.'

'You could have caught the ferry from Milson's Point to me here. Just get off at Balmain East.'

'*Si*. Perhaps another day. But tonight I prefer the privacy of my own vehicle.'

He unlocked the car and waited for her to sit with her skirt straightened before he closed the door. Within seconds he was slipping in beside her and suddenly the car shrank to a tiny womb of warm air imbued with a faint tang of his aftershave.

She was really here. In a car with a gorgeous Italian man intent on sharing the evening with her. He'd said he only wanted her company. She couldn't remember the last time she'd been out with a man and felt like this.

Gran and her knitting buddies had nudged her into a

movie or two with men she'd met but each time they'd withdrawn when they'd realised how much time she needed to spend with Annie.

He gestured to the houses and trees around her home. 'You must love living here.'

'Yep. I walk around the bay to catch a ferry to the city on my days off. Or just walk around the harbour.'

He leaned forward and started the engine. 'Your harbour is incredible but I probably see more of it from the hospital windows.' He shrugged those lovely shoulders of his and she tried not to stare. 'Except at night before sleep.'

She didn't want to think of Marco sleeping, or maybe she did, because the picture came anyway. Black boxers? Or those hipster undies the male models wore that clung. Also in black. No shirt. Silk sheets. Stretched out across the mattress. Whoa.

What on earth had they been talking about before her mind had gone AWOL? View watching? 'Perhaps you should do less work hours.'

He grinned at her. All white teeth and vibrant male who scorned the thought of taking things easy. 'For what reason? I like to give my job everything.'

'Um. Life just might speed by.'

He glanced at her as they waited to turn onto a busy road. 'Has life sped by for you, Emily?'

'I'm thinking the last sixteen years have.' She loved the way he drawled her name. Emerrrleee.

The way it rolled from his lips with that sexy undertone. She'd never really felt she'd arrived in the sexy department but, hey, there was a first for everything, and Gran's blouse was firm across her breasts. Must be why she was so conscious of her curves tonight.

Conversation remained desultory until they arrived. She'd expected a shiny white mini cruise ship like she saw most times ablaze with lights and four decks high with tuxedoed waiters. Five star, sit behind glass, no nasty breeze to muck up your hair. She didn't get that.

What she got was a hundred-year-old tall ship, three masted and dark polished wood. He ushered her up the wooden gangway on the side of the ship and they were met by a very official-looking captain with a feathered hat.

His staff was dressed in period costume, sailors and maidservants from a bygone era, the few tables grouped in secluded areas of the deck set with lace and crystal and the dull glint of genuine silverware.

Marco watched her. Enjoyed her reaction. Her eyes widened with wonder and she turned to look up at him. 'Wow…' The word was soft but his heart warmed at the genuine delight he could see in her face.

'How did you find out about this? I thought they were only privately hired.'

'Your Dr Finn. He's been very helpful.'

Finn helpful? He must have read her face because he smiled and said, 'He is a man's man, perhaps.'

She thought of Evie. Or a strong woman's man. Grumpy Finn even knowing about something like this was hard to take in but she didn't care.

She much preferred a man who had gentleness and a way that made her feel at ease. Though a little sexual attraction wasn't going astray. Like Marco? What was wrong with her tonight? She needed to remember where fact lay and fantastic fiction fell. She rested her hand on his arm. 'This is great. I love it. Thank you.'

His hand came up to cover hers. 'And I am glad.' The captain gestured to their table and helped her sit.

The best seats. They were seated at the stern and she could glance behind her to the water slapping gently against the hull. The masts soared into the sky in front of her.

They hadn't made it with much time to spare. The rattle of the wooden gangplank echoed across the water as it was pulled in. The scurry of sailors as mooring ropes were untied and the boat drifted quietly away from the wharf. She glanced up with amazement as figures overhead leant on cross spars to pull ropes and loosen the smaller topsails.

'This is incredible.' Suddenly she was aware she hadn't eaten since her nibble at the scones that morning.

'Yes,' he said, but he was watching her face. A tiny smile on his lips as her gaze darted about, each new sight making her eyes widen and her mouth open.

Champagne appeared on a tray and he took two glasses and offered her one. Absently she smiled and sipped and he could barely contain his amusement to see her so involved in the business of preparing the ship.

'You really love this.'

Her eyes were shining. 'Yes.'

He'd thought he had his walls up, solid, impenetrable walls around his heart, around his desire to even acknowledge his heart. He was doing all right on his own, had been on his own since he'd left home not long after his mother had died, but watching Emily, savouring her pleasure, this was different. Different from anything he'd felt before. And it was not possible. *Non e'possibile.*

'Aren't you?'

He'd lost the train of conversation. *'Scusi?'*

'Aren't you enjoying this too?' She tilted her head and her cap of golden hair swung across her cheek. His fingers itched to reach out and brush it back from her face. It looked like silk. It would feel like silk. Such a caring face for one so beautiful.

This was outside his experience. Usually the more beautiful the woman the more shallow the water. Emily was not such a person. She waited for his answer with anticipation clear in her eyes.

'Si, the night is very special. You are very special.'

She blushed again and glanced out over the water. 'I wasn't fishing.'

'Of course not.' This he did not understand. 'You have no rod.' He glanced around. 'You wish to fish?'

She laughed. A throaty, infectious giggle she tried to hide behind her hand. Now, why would she try to hide such a thing of joy?

The waiter came. 'Evenin', all.' Dressed like an English officer, he took their orders and refilled their glasses. Emily grinned at him and the waiter grinned back. Marco frowned.

She looked back at him. 'I mean I wasn't looking for a compliment. I don't want to catch a fish.' She laughed again and he had to smile back at her.

Her face glowed. Like the first time he'd seen her. 'I see. A colloquialism. You Australians have many of them. Like the English.'

'My gran married an Englishman. She told me he

always said "give me a butcher's hook" instead of "give me a look". It was funny when she said it.' She smiled at the memory. He'd never seen a woman smile so much. It warmed his cold soul.

'Tell me about your family. Your parents. Your gran.'

She put her glass down and rested her chin in her hands. 'My parents? They're both dead. But they were very strict, traditional, not at all suited to having an unwed pregnant teenager for a daughter.'

He nodded. 'I see.' She could tell he did.

'My gran? She loved me unconditionally. Like I love my daughter. One day I hope to find a relationship like that.'

From a man who could lay down roots and be there for her. One who didn't immerse himself in his work for a limited time and then pack bags and leave without looking back. Not like him. 'But not the father of your Annie?'

She shrugged. 'His family were wealthy. Too good for me. Once the scandal broke he was packed off. We never saw him again.'

He could not comprehend this. 'Never?' Then no doubt she was too good for him. *Bastardo*. 'He has never seen his daughter?'

'Never.' She broke her bread roll, picked up her knife and stabbed the butter. He flinched. She looked up and grinned at his expression.

'I got over his lack of interest years ago. Though for Annie's sake I'd have liked him to have made some contact. His parents send money every year on her birthday and I put it in trust. When she's twenty-one she can do what she likes with it.'

She spread her butter and took a bite with her tiny white teeth just as the entrée arrived. He thought with amusement it was good she'd put the knife down or the sailor could have been frightened.

'Ooh. Calamari. I love calamari. What's the Italian word for calamari?' She made short work of her few pieces and he held back his smile. He liked a woman who didn't play with her food.

'I'm sorry.' He grinned. 'The same. Calamari.' He glanced down at his tiny fillets of fish on the bed of lettuce. 'But the word for fish is *pesce*.'

'*Pesce*,' she repeated. 'It almost sounds like fishee.' She grinned and watched him put the last one in his mouth and he was very conscious of the direction of her eyes. 'Your English is very good. Much better than my Italian.'

He swallowed the delicious fillet in his mouth without tasting it, his appetite elsewhere. 'I have spent a lot of time out of Italy.' He changed the subject back to her. 'So you went into nursing after your Annie was born?'

She patted her coral lips with her napkin and his attention, again, was caught. It took him a moment to catch up when she spoke. 'Annie was in Neonatal Intensive Care. She was four weeks early. A prem that took a long time to feed.'

She glanced up at him. 'I never missed a feed in the three weeks she was there and I fell in love with the midwives. With the special-care nursery. With tiny babies. I'd found what I wanted to do. And Gran, not my parents, supported me.'

He could see her. A vigilant young teen mum with her tiny baby. Turning up, night and day, to be there for her daughter. Incredible. The more he found out, the more she intrigued him.

'Enough about me.' So Emily didn't want to think of the early years. Perhaps what she'd missed out on in her younger days.

She glanced around the ship. 'They must have engines as well because I don't think they have enough sail on to make it move this fast. Can we walk around? Check out the other side of the ship?' She glanced towards the thick mast. 'Touch things?'

She could touch him. 'You wish to touch something?' She picked up on his double meaning and flicked him a warning glance. He was glad the knife was on her plate. She amused him.

'Si. Of course.' He stood and helped pull out her chair. Then he crooked his arm and to his delight she slid her hand through and he savoured the feel of her fingers against his skin.

They strolled the deck and the magic of the night fell over them like the soft wrap she wore around her shoulders.

The lights of the harbour twinkled and shone across the water, ferries and paddle-wheel dinner cruisers floated past, and occasionally the sound of a band floated across from a party barge filled with revellers.

This was so much better, to have Emily quietly beside him. Few couples were walking, and the awareness between them grew with the unexpected privacy a bulkhead or a thick mast could provide.

Always the Sydney Harbour Bridge dominated the skyline, they passed under it, the soaring iron structure a thing of great beauty lit like a golden arch, and it receded and became even more magical with distance.

He wished he could hold onto this moment so that he could pack it away in his suitcase when he left here. Perhaps to remove and examine one lonely night in a hotel room on the other side of the world. *Stupido*.

This would all be over too quickly.

CHAPTER FOUR

Two hours later Emily held his hand as they stepped off the gangplank of the tall ship and sighed as she stepped back onto terra firma. 'A wonderful dinner. Thank you.'

'The night does not have to be over yet.' He squeezed her fingers.

They watched a ferry come in and there was something vibrant about the noisy reverse of the engines that churned up the water and the delayed slap of heavier waves on the pier as the deckhand jumped off and secured the vessel to a wharfside cleat.

'That's my ferry,' Emily pointed. 'It docks two minutes from my door and goes on to Luna Park jetty. You could have taken the ferry and walked up the hill to your apartment.'

He glanced across the water as other ferries did their business. 'Would you like to take it now? I can return for my car tomorrow. It is safe. We could have more time on the water. Perhaps stroll around your Luna Park, eat an ice cream?'

'Or fairy floss?'

He squeezed her hand. 'Fairy floss?'

'Pink balls of spun sugar. A dreadfully evil sweet.'

A wicked look. 'Dreadfully evil is good.'

It would be silly to leave his car in the car park. Mad to jump on a ferry just because of a whim and walk around an amusement park at nine at night. She so wanted to do that.

She gave in to the child within. 'Let's.'

So they did. She explained how the vending machines spat out the ferry tickets, dragged him up to the front of the boat so they could get blown to pieces on the deserted bow, and they lifted their faces to the spray. 'This is much faster than our sailing boat.'

She looked back at their beautiful three-masted vessel. 'Not quite as romantic.'

His arm slipped around her shoulders and he turned her to face him. 'We could change that?'

She stood on tiptoe as he bent. Met his smiling mouth with hers with a light-hearted press of lips that never intended to be anything else—except for that second farewell light press that deepened just a touch and invited a third quick kiss, which deepened just a little more…

What magic was this? What spell had she cast? Lust slammed into him like their ferry had hit a solid wave and it was Marco who stepped back. If he didn't stop he'd have crushed Emily into him and who knew what might have happened?

Always he had control, was the master of his own desires, but this Emily's sweet innocence gripped him with more power than the most experienced woman and forced him to pull back while he still could.

He wrapped her in his arms and stared over her head at the lights on the edge of the harbour. What was he doing?

He would leave in three weeks. Began to realise she might not know the rules by which he played and did not need the complication he offered. A darker voice within disagreed. Perhaps she did?

Emily snuggled into the warmth of solid muscle. Lo-o-ovely kisses. Mmmmmm. Shame he'd stopped but that was good. She needed to be sensible. She could remember her mother's cold voice very clearly even after all these years. 'Your father and I don't deserve this shame. You're a tramp!' Though how one fumbled night and a broken condom made her a tramp she didn't know. And Gran had shooshed her and said it wasn't true.

Well, she hadn't tramped at all for the last sixteen years. A few pathetic-in-hindsight kisses and a meal or two. No wonder she hadn't been tempted to chase those men. They didn't kiss like this. She felt Marco's arms loosen from the after hug and she guessed it was time to step away.

His hands slid down her shoulders with a lingering reluctance and dropped right away, and she pushed the hair from her eyes so she could see his face. He looked serious. Too serious.

'Is everything okay?' Crikey. Maybe she'd been a hopeless kisser and he was embarrassed.

'You kiss like an angel.'

Her cheeks flamed. Had she said that out loud? He went on with a twisted smile. 'And it seemed prudent to stop.'

Not quite sure how to take that but maybe with sincere gratitude because it wasn't unreasonable to think that kiss could have led to an embarrassing incident.

'Oh. Well.' She brushed the hair out of her eyes again. 'You're pretty good yourself.'

The ferry pulled into Balmain East, tied up then untied and chugged across the harbour to McMahon's Point. They both watched the busy deckhand with an intensity born of diversion from what they wanted to really do. Marco squeezed her hand and she squeezed back.

When the ferry pulled into Milson's Point wharf, at least they had a purpose as they stepped across the walkway to the pier.

The laughing-clown mouth of the entrance invited them to join the milling crowd and Marco couldn't help looking up at the squealing victims spinning above their heads on a swirling circular ride. His stomach contracted at the thought.

'You like these rides?'

Emily laughed. 'Not those ones. Though I am partial to the view from the Ferris wheel and a trip on the Wild Mouse.'

'A wild mouse?'

She pointed. 'Up there. It's a mini roller-coaster that makes you think you're going to fly out over the harbour and instead turns the corner suddenly. It's Annie's favourite.'

'It sounds like your favourite. Not Annie's.' This one didn't look too bad. At least it didn't turn upside down.

He crossed to the payment window and purchased a wrist-banded ride pass for both of them.

'Come.' He lingered over the word until she grinned. 'We will see who is the most frightened.'

They jogged up the gaily painted steps hand in hand

and Emily turned to him. 'Can't you feel the infectious enthusiasm from the young crowd?'

He wasn't sure if he was infected yet. The teens were having a ball on this Friday night and her smiling face turned from side to side as she caught glimpses of the screaming occupants…and perhaps seeping some foolishness into him.

A battered little red car on rails trundled across and stopped in front of them with a clang. 'Jump in,' the laconic ride attendant drawled, 'man at the back, lady between his legs. I do the seat belt.' Marco could tell he'd said the same a million times.

This idea improved with time, Marco thought with satisfaction, as Emily snuggled into the space between his legs with her skirt smoothed out in front of her. Nice. Warm and soft and in need of protection during this coming adventure. It was a very small car.

She had to lean back into his chest and his arms came along the outside of hers to grip the same handle. Snug. The car shunted off with an unexpected jerk and Emily was forced back into his chest with a bump. He tightened his hands and prepared to enjoy the ride.

They rolled down the first hill and jolted onto a runner to be pulled up the next and then gathered speed. It blurred after that.

The first sharp corner loomed as they rocketed towards it and he read the sign just before they turned.

'Brace Yourself!'

He braced and Emily slammed into him and he slammed into the side of the car, she laughed and he had to laugh as the next corner came up and it seemed they would sail out over the harbour, but the trusty wheels remained hooked to the track as they flew around that one.

Emily laughed again and he could feel the spread of a huge smile across his face as the ride rocketed on. Up and down steep little hills that lifted them out of their seats as they bounced at the bottom, still stuck together, and he decided then they would repeat this experience before they went home.

The car rolled to a stop. It was over. Shame, that.

'Lady out first. Then the gent. Keep to the left and down the stairs.'

Emily waited for him to climb out, not as elegantly as he could have wished but that smile seemed glued to his face and she laughed at his expression. 'You'd think you'd never been to an amusement park before.'

The laughter fell away. No.

He tried not to think of his lonely childhood, his family moving towns in the dead of night, and those periods of abject poverty when his father had been in gaol.

'Oh!' She was not slow. The smile she threw him would have lit the whole harbour in a power failure. 'In that case, we need to really make a night of it.'

She grabbed his hand and dragged him down the stairs. 'It's Coney Island for you. I want to see you in the rolling pipes and if you don't get motion sickness I'm going to stick you to the wall in the Rotor.'

And the darkness was gone. Lifted from him by the light of her joy. He followed her, soaking in her delight in silly games, ridiculous rides and fairy floss. Her hand in his, laughing and looking at him to be sure he too enjoyed the night. A strange feeling to savour that she cared so much that he was the happy one.

He kissed her as she reached the end of the wacky walkway, kissed her after the slippery slide, and leant her back into the wall and kissed her thoroughly after another ride on the wild mouse.

The most memorable kiss—though not the most successful—was upside down in the centrifugal chamber where the forces glued them to the wall while the floor fell away. They only just made it back to upright before the floor came back and gravity returned.

From there it seemed natural to walk her back to his flat, hold her as they ascended the lift, and lean her against his outside wall while he opened the door.

Emily was in a fairy floss coloured daze. She hadn't laughed so much for years. She knew it wasn't real, it was all an illusion like the wacky mirrors that made you first fat and then thin. She was happy at this moment and she refused to look into the future and see the end of this night.

She'd never felt so silly, so beautiful, so protected. But she hadn't intended to come back to his flat. Tomorrow was a little too close for that.

And then they were inside and the door was shut. 'Now, how did I end up here?'

He watched her indulgently. Like she was a child. She may have behaved like one but so had he. Make no mistake, though, she was a woman.

Marco said, 'It is your fault. You and your amusement parks exposing me to the testosterone of teenage boys and the flirtatiousness of a woman who could be a teenager herself.'

'I did not flirt.'

'Did you not? Then you were yourself. Incredible, whimsical, amazing self, and I am enthralled.'

She turned her back on him. Stared through the glass across the room at the harbour and thought of stopping this right here. Not taking this to the logical conclusion for a man of the world and a woman who had always wondered what good sex would be like.

She had to remember this man was heading off to the other side of the world very shortly. But maybe that was a good thing.

His arm dropped around her shoulders. 'Let us view the harbour.'

She glanced at his face. 'You didn't say come.'

'Perhaps later.'

CHAPTER FIVE

HE OPENED the sliding glass door and she went ahead to stand out on his terrace. A soft sea breeze ruffled her hair and he smoothed it with his hand.

The last few hours had tilted his axis. Twirled his thoughts like the rides had twirled their bodies, shifted his plans from conquest to surrender, made him see that taking this woman to bed when they had no future could harm her, and he didn't want to do that.

Soon he would move on to the next city. Needed to. Was unable to form a trusting relationship because so much trust had been broken in the past and the scars were deep. Had crippled him for the emotional agility a relationship needed.

But he wanted her badly.

She leaned back into his body, her slender neck enticing his mouth, and he dropped a kiss under her ear. She tasted so good, felt like silk, and her body pressed back into him so that they both felt his hardness rise.

She wriggled some more and he bit back a groan as he strove to speak normally. 'Perhaps we should go in. Would you like coffee?'

'It's not coffee I was thinking about.'

'Really?' His mind was lost to conversation. Was fixated on the woman in his arms. The need to create distance fading as the heat built between them.

He spoke into her hair. Desperate for one of them to be sensible. 'I leave in a few weeks. I may not return.'

She spun in his arms and looked up at him. Unflinching. So courageous. Her head up. Green eyes burning like the starboard lights of ships in the night and he'd never wanted another woman more than at this moment when she offered herself to him.

Then unexpectedly she said, 'I'm a little rusty so you'd better be good.'

And his heart cracked open just a little more. He couldn't help the smile that pulled his cheeks and made him shake his head in wonder. Feel the pound of his heart and the jump in his groin.

'I am good.' Marco closed his arms around her and Emily's silver shoes left the ground.

Suddenly she was trembling with her own audacity but it felt so good. So different from going home alone tonight and regret and an empty bed.

He spun her like she'd been spun so many times in the last two hours and the lights of the harbour blurred as he swept through the doors with her hard against his chest, carried like a child, placed her like a princess in the middle of a gorgeously pillowed bed.

She watched him and he watched her. Pulled off his shoes and socks, unbuttoned his shirt, never taking his eyes from her face, until the shirt fell open to reveal the breadth of his chest, undid his trousers so that they flapped open to reveal the curling hairs that snaked down, slid them off to reveal his black briefs. Then he stopped.

She moistened her lips. Oh, my goodness. He was the most beautiful man she'd ever seen. In black shorts, just like she'd imagined. Her throat closed and she swallowed to moisten her dry mouth. 'I had hoped you might wear those black trunk things.'

'So you wondered.' He smiled at her and never had he looked more like the gypsy king as he did then with his dark chocolate eyes burning down at her. Just one word as he held out his hand.

'Come.'

And suddenly it was easy. To reach and take his hand. To stand in front of him as he undid the covered buttons on her blouse until it too hung open. Allow his big hands to slowly slide over her hips until she stood before him in her underwear. The only indulgence she allowed herself.

The tip of one long finger slid slowly from her throat, between her lace-covered breasts, to the top of her ribboned bikini. 'What is this delight?'

She blushed. Her secret was out but she doubted he'd be telling anybody. He'd better not.

'Such beautiful underclothes.' He brushed her face with his lips and bent to breathe his way down between her breasts. Tasting and murmuring. 'Such a beautiful body.' He looked up at her. 'You are exquisite.'

She should be doing something. Touching him, but she didn't know where to start. Shouldn't be just having all the fun. Tried not to look at the bulge in the dark briefs in front of her. She hadn't thought this far. To her inexperience. Her shortcomings as a lover. She could feel the beginnings of shame, left over from her rigid upbringing, left over from the horror of coldness and disgust from her parents the last time she'd lived with them.

She turned her head. She didn't want to think of that. Especially now.

Marco felt the change come over her. Looked swiftly at her face, straightened and drew her against him.

'What is it, *innamorata*? Sweetheart?'

'Nothing. Kiss me.'

It was not nothing. But he would kiss her. Hold her and show her how much he wanted her. And that was all for the moment. It would be no good for him if she was not also transported.

Emily sat in the pre-dawn light on the ferry huddled into her thin wrap, lost and confused, unable to believe she'd slept with him. While her daughter lay in hospital.

She'd woken at five, spooned by a strong man's body, the curve of her hips tucked into his heat, her lower body pleasantly aware of a new set of muscles she hadn't used in a while and her face had flamed as erotic snapshots of their night had blown on the embers low in her belly and urged her to arch back into him.

His arm had lain heavy across her shoulders as the panic had flared. Somewhere behind the panic a little voice had whispered that no wonder this golden man was sleeping like the dead. He was right. He was good.

She'd fought to keep her movements smooth as she'd eased out from under his hand and away from his body.

He'd murmured something in his sleep and she'd

pushed a pillow into his seeking hand and he'd drifted off again.

Scooped her bra from the floor and clipped it, she remembered that spot, had picked up her panties from the chair and pulled them on, and then her skirt and blouse. She'd glanced away from the chair, remembered Marco pulling her down onto his lap, and hurriedly scooped her shoes from under the bed—she certainly remembered the bed—and then she was dressed and couldn't think past the concept that she'd been the easiest conquest in the world.

So she'd let herself out, putting her silver shoes on in the hallway, and had tapped the lift button impatiently in case he opened the door.

Now here she was. Alone, shivering, pulling into her wharf in the early morning for the first time in her life that wasn't because of work.

An awful thought jolted as the ferry bumped the wharf and she checked her phone. No missed calls from Annie or the hospital. She sighed and thought self-mockingly, How lucky, because she suspected there had been some moments there when the whole apartment block could have come down around their ears and neither would have noticed. Would have thought it just part of the impact of making love together. Oh, my goodness, she wasn't sure how she could regret that!

Marco woke to an empty bed. Like he did every morning, because he never asked a woman to stay. Today he had expected it to be different.

He'd heard the door shut and he opened his eyes as he sighed, slapped his forehead, and groaned. What had he done? What had she done to him? His hand slid across the remaining warmth where her head had lain and he wanted to run. He just wasn't sure if it was as far as he could get from Sydney or after Emily.

He did neither. He sat on his terrace and nursed his espresso as he looked over the waking harbour. Imagined her hunched in the ferry on her way home, but by the time he realised she would be cold in her thin wrap it was too late to do anything but abuse his own stupidity.

Obviously she didn't want to face him this morning, which was a damn shame because already he missed her. Missed her in more ways than he should. Regretted, of course, they had not made love one more time—because he was afraid he hadn't quite got her out of his system. In fact, he regretted he hadn't the chance to share breakfast, drink coffee, watch boats together.

He missed her. Missed Emily. And this was bad for a man who did not wish to stay in one place.

CHAPTER SIX

'HI, MUM.' It was ten o'clock and Annie looked rosy cheeked and relaxed.

Unlike Emily, who could barely meet her daughter's eyes. 'You look good. How's your tummy this morning?'

'Not sore at all.' Annie stroked her little belly mound. 'And she's moving well. You look a little stressed. Stop worrying about us. We'll be fine.'

Oh, goodness. 'It's hard not to.' More guilt. 'But I'll try.' Emily looked across at June, because she didn't know what else to say. This was ridiculous. She needed to get a grip. No one was going to know and she could just push last night to the back of her head and forget it. Ha!

'Hi, there, June. How are you?'

'I'm good, thanks, Emily. How cool that Annie and I are roommates.'

'I know. That's great. You'll have to tell her about the calm breathing course you did.'

'I will.' June's mobile phone buzzed and Emily smiled and turned back to her daughter.

Annie whispered, 'She knows you're not going to go

mad on her for the mobile phone. We try not to let the other staff see us use them.'

Emily lowered her own voice. 'Maternity's fine. We're separate from the rest of the hospital over the sky bridge and the high-tech equipment. It's easier for the staff too rather than running portable phones everywhere. They won't mind.'

Of course Annie had never been on this part of the hospital as a patient and her mother hadn't thought to explain yesterday. Was that because she'd been thinking of other things? Other people? A particular person?

Annie looked relieved. 'Oh, good. I'm almost out of credit. Can you get some, please?'

'I think they sell phone credit at the kiosk. I'll ask.'

'Goodie.' A word that reminded her how young Annie was. 'Do you know if Dr D'Arvello is coming in this morning?

'It's Saturday.' Crikey, I hope not. Her neck heated. That was the reason she was here so early. It wasn't even visiting hours. 'Not sure. I'll just get that credit.'

She needed to get away for a minute and get her head together. She was a mess and she didn't like it. This was not how she did things. She was known for her calm and serene manner, famous for it over the hospital, and at the moment she couldn't even recognise herself.

Ten minutes later after her quick trip to the kiosk she was feeling calmer. Head down, she waited at the main lift as her mind sorted reasonable strategies for what she was going to say to Marco when she met him again.

Someone called her name. Twice. She looked up. Evie Lockheart stood next to her with a quizzical smile on her face. 'Earth to Emily?'

'Oh. Sorry. Hi, Evie. How are you?' She hadn't made that date for afternoon tea yet.

'So-so.' Evie frowned. 'You okay?'

'Yes.' Earth to Emily was right. She needed to plug into her surroundings. 'Of course. I'm visiting Annie. Her baby had intrauterine surgery yesterday.'

'Ah. I heard it all went well. Marco D'Arvello. Lucky we've got someone of his calibre here, even if it's for a short time.'

Emily nodded with her head down. 'He said Finn arranged his visit.'

'Finn likes him.'

Emily remembered yesterday in the cafeteria. 'Everything okay between you guys? I saw you in the kiosk yesterday.'

Evie shrugged. 'Ah. Yes. Well. He's a stubborn man.'

'I've heard men often are.'

Evie laughed. 'About time you did more than just hear that, isn't it?' Evie studied her face. 'Shouldn't you be retraining a stubborn man yourself?'

Marco wasn't stubborn. But she didn't say it. 'I'm a little snowed under with a pregnant daughter at the moment.'

'Of course. Though that's the funny thing about falling in love. It doesn't always pick the perfect moment to happen.'

Emily thought about that and didn't like the direction. 'Well, I'll be careful, then. This really isn't a good time for me to be sidetracked.' It wasn't too late!

The lift doors opened and they moved in. Emily pressed sky bridge level and Evie leaned forward and pressed the button for Administration. The doors almost shut and then opened again.

Marco took two long strides from the left as the lift doors began to close. Stabbed the button. He'd seen Emily get in there. The doors reopened and he stepped inside.

Her eyes widened and she stepped away from him back into the corner. This woman who had left his bed that morning. As if afraid of him?

A slice of pain he didn't expect. Did she feel she needed to do that? Peripherally he was aware there was another woman in the elevator so he leant against the side wall and nodded. It was the woman with Finn yesterday in the cafeteria.

The other woman smiled at him. 'We were just talking about you.' Vaguely he realised she was pretty but he only had eyes for Emily.

Then her words sank in. That wasn't what he expected to hear. Gossip? He felt the air still in his lungs. Memories from his childhood as always the people whispered behind his back as he walked. Trust issues reared their ugly head. His father's words, 'Never trust anyone.' So already she was boasting. He had not expected that.

She held out her hand. 'I'm Evie Lockheart. So you operated on Annie yesterday.'

Ah. *'Si.'* They shook hands. 'Dr Lockheart. You must thank Finn for me. Last night we dined on the brig.' Then Evie's last words penetrated the haze of hurt. She'd only said he'd operated on her daughter.

Evie's face lit up. 'The three-master? Lovely. And the weather was great last night. Who'd you go with?'

Emily's face was pink and already he felt guilt for his thoughts—let alone the indiscretion he had started in retaliation. 'A friend.'

The lift stopped and the doors opened. Evie turned to Emily, saw her red face and frowned, but Marco had his hand across the doors, waiting for her to exit. 'Is this you?'

She turned to look at him. Glanced at Emily again and stepped out. 'Thanks. See you later, Emily.'

'Bye, Evie.' Emily didn't step away from the corner as the lift doors closed.

Evie Lockheart watched the lift doors shut. Frowned. Stared at the doors a minute longer and then smiled. There just might be something going on there.

Nice if someone had a normal relationship. Emily deserved it. She turned and headed down to Finn's office. She hoped to hell he'd calmed down since yesterday.

Sometimes she felt as if she was just another conquest to him and at others she thought she glimpsed their unwilling connection. But, damn it, she cared.

He'd point blank refused to talk to her about his problem. Like the future of his career wasn't worrying him. She only wanted to help.

She'd been shocked by the depth of emotional turmoil she'd seen in his eyes. Finn the invincible looking just for a moment anything but invincible and it had stayed with her. Of course it had stayed with her. She'd barely slept. But then again she hadn't slept well since the day she'd gone to his flat and discovered a side to herself she hadn't realised existed. A wanton, wild and womanly side she'd only shown to Finn.

A side that he had mocked—and here she was, back for more.

But today wasn't about that—or even them as a couple, if that was what they were. It was to talk about the possibility of a cure. Again.

Yesterday's discussion hadn't worked. From the little he had let drop, the experimental surgery—despite the huge risk—offered a chance Finn could continue the work he lived for and take away the pain he tried to hide. If it was a success.

Even odds. Fifty per cent he might be able to operate or fifty per cent he might never operate again.

All this was constantly going over in her mind and how she could broach the subject when he obviously wanted no interference from her, and it was driving her bonkers. Unfortunately, she couldn't leave it alone.

Wouldn't leave Finn to go through this alone. She had to believe they had a connection and he was the one pretending they didn't.

She paused outside his office door and drew a deep breath. 'Gird your loins, girl,' she mocked herself. She knocked.

No answer. So she knocked again. 'Finn?'

Silence. She pushed open the door and the room was empty. Damn. She circled the empty room, frustration keeping her moving as she realised she'd have to psych herself up all over again. Then her gaze fell on his desk.

The research papers he'd mentioned. Explanations of the experimental surgery. So he had considered it, despite his horror of the risks. She could understand that, see his abhorrence of life without his work, but he had to do it. You couldn't live with increasing pain for ever. The time was past when he could do nothing.

'What are you doing here?' Finn stood tall and menacing in the doorway with blue ice shooting from his arctic eyes.

I'm not scared, she told herself, but she swallowed. Guess he was still seething from yesterday, then. 'Waiting for you.'

'Why are you rifling my desk?'

She raised her eyebrows, outwardly calm. 'Hardly rifling when it was all open for me to see.'

He stepped into the room and the space around her shrank to a quarter of the size. Funny what the aura of some people could do. 'Not for you to see.'

Evie stood her ground. 'Afraid I might suggest you consider it again?' She paused. 'So at least you've read it?'

He ignored that. 'I've read it. And I don't want to talk about it.'

She stepped around the desk until she was standing beside him. This man who infuriated and inspired and drove her insane with frustration and, she had to admit, a growing love and need to see him happy.

'It's a choice, Finn. One you're going to have to consider.'

His voice grated harshly. His face was set like stone. 'Now you want to look after me? One episode of good sex is all it took?'

She ignored that. Ignored the splinter of pain that festered inside from his contempt. Banished the pictures of him showing her the door afterwards.

'Hippocratic oath,' he mocked. 'Save your patient.'

'You're not my patient.' She met his eyes. Chin up. 'Just think about it.'

His eyes narrowed further. 'Why should you care?'

'Because I do.' She touched his arm and the muscles were bunched and taut beneath her fingers. 'Is that so hard to believe?'

He shook her off. 'I look after myself. Had to all my life and it's never going to change.'

She took his hand and held it firmly. Looked into his face. 'Tell me.'

He looked down but this time he didn't pull away. 'Tell you what?'

She shook his arm. 'Finn. For God's sake, let me in.' Finally he seemed to get it. A glimmer of understanding of what she wanted to know. Why she wanted to know.

'What?' A scornful laugh not directed at her for a change. 'The whole sob story?'

Evie didn't move. 'Yes. Please.'

He sighed. Her hand fell away as he turned and stared out over the harbour and when he started his voice was flat, emotionless, daring her to be interested in his boring tale. 'Why would you want this? You probably know most of it. Orphan. Unstable foster-homes. The army was my best parenting experience and they don't do affection or connection.'

A sardonic laugh that grated on her ears. 'Maybe that's why I fitted so well.'

She wanted to hug him. 'You did connection okay the other night.'

She saw his frown from across the room. 'Don't go there, Evie.' She flinched and he sighed. 'Do you want to hear or not?'

She held up her hands. 'Please.'

This time he turned to look at her fully and she watched the muscle jerk in his cheek as he held emotion rigidly in check. She wanted to cradle his head in her hands but she was too scared to interrupt him. Too scared she'd stop the flow she'd waited so long for him to start.

'You know about Isaac. I had to watch my brother die. The same bomb that tore into me, which is wrecking my career now, took his life. The day Isaac died I died too, Evie. Since then, what little ability I had to love, I lost. And with Isaac gone I lost the only person who really cared what happened to me.' He shrugged. 'That's why I am what I am. I don't want to be around someone when I feel like that.'

She took a step towards him. Aware how much it would hurt if at this moment he rebuffed her. 'You don't have to feel like that, Finn.'

Sardonic sweep of eyebrows. Daring her to contradict him. 'Don't I?'

'No.' Closer.

'Why's that, Evie?' The biting sarcasm was back but she refused to be put off by it. Toughened herself because she would never be cowed by this angry man who frightened others to keep them at bay.

Another step. 'I care what happens to you, Finn.'

Vehement shake of his head. 'Don't pity me, Evie.'

She almost laughed. 'You're not a man anyone can pity, Finn. You won't allow it. You alienate people so they don't. But unfortunately I feel so much more for you than that.'

She swallowed, tossed caution to the winds, stepped

closer and stared into his face so he couldn't ignore her words. 'I love you, Finn Kennedy. And there's not a lot of reward for that at the moment.'

A more subtle shake of the head. 'How can you love me?'

Now she was in front of him again. 'How can I not, you stupid man? I think about you every minute of every day, wondering when you're going to care for yourself like you should.'

He sidestepped her, crossed the room to shut the door, shut out the hospital for probably the first time since he'd started here, and then came back. Put himself in her space deliberately.

'What are you saying, Evie?'

'I love you. Foul temper and all.'

His hands slid around her waist. 'I didn't ask for that.' Something in his voice had changed. Gave her a glimmer of hope.

'You didn't ask for it?' She stared into the harsh and haunted face she loved so much. 'Neither did I. But there's not a lot we can do about it now.'

His face softened just a little. 'So you weren't just after sex the other day?'

This was what she dreaded. 'What do you think, Finn? Did it feel like that to you?' She'd laid herself open, exposed her soft underbelly of caring, and he could mortally wound her, even worse than he had after she'd given herself to him.

He lifted his hand and stroked the hair out of her eyes. 'No.' He sighed. 'Though God knows why you bother. What I felt the other day scared the hell out of me, Evie. And that's not all I'm scared of. I'm scared I'm not the man you think I am.'

'Well, seeing that I don't want to be without you, Finn, we'll just have to take that chance. Whatever happens, I'm here for you. And always will be.'

He shook his head. Couldn't accept that. 'I might not just be an emotional cripple, Evie. I could be in a wheelchair.'

She leaned towards him. 'Or it could be the answer to all your medical problems. You could get full control back. You have to take that chance.'

'I don't think it's an option.' He sighed. 'But I'll think about it.' An air of finality.

She had to be satisfied with that. It was better than they'd had before today.

CHAPTER SEVEN

THE lift doors closed after Evie left and the silence deepened with Marco and Emily alone in the lift.

Finally. 'I'm sorry.' Marco sighed as the elevator began its ascent. 'I thought you had spoken about our evening out with her.'

And, boy, were you unhappy! 'I gathered that.' So he was that embarrassed to say he'd taken her out. Not that she wanted to be the centre of a gossip storm.

She went on, 'You were pretty quick to retaliate.' Like a cobra, and a big warning for the future. Or their lack of it.

'My apologies. Again.' His face stayed frozen and even his words seemed to have difficulty leaving his mouth. 'It is how I am.'

He must have an interesting history—but she wasn't going there. Emily sighed. So he hated gossip. She did too.

But they were both mad if they thought the whole hospital wouldn't find out anyway. It always happened. She'd seen it time and again over the last sixteen years.

Somebody's son would be a waiter on the boat or a deckhand on the ferry. A woman thought nobody knew and usually she was the last to figure out everyone had been talking about her for a week. Now she'd be one of those. Thanks, Marco.

And a bit of ill feeling might help keep him at bay. Maybe cultivating that wasn't a bad idea. 'As long as we don't repeat the experience, I'm sure we'll both be fine.'

He stepped across to her. 'And yet I'd hoped to see you again, spend more time with you before I spoiled my chance.'

'No. Thank you, Marco. You're not my favourite person at the moment.'

The lift stopped and he moved back as the doors opened. Emily didn't look at him as she left but she could feel him behind her as she walked towards the nurses' station.

Then he was gone as she went on to Annie's room.

When he walked in five minutes later Emily had herself well in hand. She smiled distantly at his left shoulder, watched her daughter's face the whole time, and agreed that tomorrow morning would be a good time to pick Annie up.

Then he was behind the curtain, talking to June, and she could drop the silly smile from her face and get on with life.

'You okay, Mum?'

She jumped. Annie was staring at her. 'Sorry? Oh. Yes. Fine. I'm tired.'

'Didn't you sleep last night?'

There was silence from behind the curtain. Maybe he was just feeling June's tummy. 'Oh. Um. Not as well as I'd hoped.'

Conversation started behind the curtain and she frowned at herself. Stop it.

'Why don't you stay home this afternoon? Just chill. I'm fine. Some friends are coming in to see me in visiting hours and I have my phone credit now. I can ring if I want anything.'

And do what? Mope? 'No. Don't be silly. I'll come back this afternoon.'

'Seriously, Mum. I'm just as happy if you don't.'

She looked at Annie. Hurt. Stung and embarrassed that everyone else in the room would have heard it too.

'Oh. Okay. That sounds fine, then.' Ridiculous stinging in her eyes and she'd be mortified if she cried. 'I'll catch up on all the things I've been meaning to do.' Forced brightness. 'Lovely.'

She leant over and kissed her daughter's cheek. Avoided her eyes but, then, Annie seemed to be avoiding hers too. Maybe she realised she'd been an ungrateful little wretch. Wishful thinking probably. She had her friends coming. She didn't need a mother. 'See you tomorrow.'

She walked hurriedly away but not hurriedly enough. Marco caught up with her in four strides. 'Are you okay?'

She paused, turned and stared at his tie. 'Fine. I'm sorry. Perhaps we were both rude in the lift. Thanks for last night.'

Then she walked away. Thanks for last night? She winced. What did she mean? Dinner. Great sex. Today was a difficult day but she'd got through others.

She could feel his eyes on her back.

She wasn't surprised when he turned up at her house two hours later. He was bearing gifts. Well, food anyway.

She stood back to let him enter. 'I guess we do need to talk.' A lingering trail of subtle exotic herbs and spices followed him.

'And I wish to apologise again.'

What was in that bag? 'For what?'

'For my comment in the elevator. For doubting you.'

She forgot food and studied him. He had his mask face on again and she wondered where the smiling Italian gypsy had gone. But, then, again the smiling Emily seemed a tad AWOL at the moment as well. 'Why are you here, Marco?' Because I don't want to fall for you.

'To see you. To ask why you left this morning. To see if you are all right because I have been worried I made you unhappy.'

'You don't have to worry about me. I'm a big girl.' Better on my own.

'Last night at the fair you worried about my happiness.'

'Last night was an illusion.' She sighed. 'A really fun one but still an illusion. Look, Marco. You're a great guy. Too great. And I haven't got the best track record in not falling for the wrong guys. You're leaving in three weeks and I don't want to get any more used to you being around. It's too good. So there won't be any repeats.'

'What about lunch?' He glanced at his parcel.

'No.'

'Please?'

She couldn't throw him out. 'Lunch I could probably manage but only because I need to know what that incredible smell is coming from those bags.'

He obliged in relief. 'Let me show you.'

'That's what you said last night.' She flicked a look at him from under her lashes and the other man was back.

Emily sighed because she knew she was in trouble. 'Come through to the kitchen.' It was just too hard to maintain distance when he was grinning and producing delicacies like rabbits from a hat.

'*Si*. The rolls are crusty, the butter fresh churned, and many cheeses.' He pulled out some plastic takeaway containers and she realised the aroma came from there.

'Fresh sage?'

'No festive Tuscan meal would be complete without chicken liver crostini.'

'We're not having a party.'

'It is Saturday. We should. *Crostini di Fegatini di Pollo*.' Emily wasn't really sure she could eat liver.

As if he'd read her mind. 'Even those who dislike liver enjoy this on thinly cut crusty bread. Trust me.'

That was what it all boiled down to, she thought glumly. Trust him. Or trust herself. If either of them dropped control, she doubted trust would have a look in.

He pulled out a dish of pasta. She could see mushrooms and red peppers, could smell the provolone cheese and the basil. It made her mouth water and he saw. He smiled.

'We will have a picnic in your tiny back yard. Perhaps you could lay the table and I will serve these.'

So now he was ordering her around in her own kitchen. Was opening and shutting Gran's cupboards as he looked for dishes to serve from. She couldn't take it all in. Was bemused by his energy and sudden good humour and becoming fixated on the way his shoulders moved and his biceps flexed as he reached for highly placed articles.

Might be best to leave him to it and grab a checked tablecloth and some cutlery and bolt outside.

The air cooled her cheeks. It was a glorious day. Funny she hadn't noticed that this morning. Not too hot. Outside anyway.

She glanced over her shoulder and he was singing in her kitchen. She'd never heard a man singing baritone in her kitchen before and she paused as the sound teased her. Made her smile. Chased away caution again because, darn it, it was good to have so much fun.

She set the table with new vigour, wondered about that bottle of cold Chablis she had in the fridge, and a rainbow lorikeet flew down and scratched in the empty bird feeder and then glared at her.

'Okay. Okay. I'll get some.' Gran had always fed the lorikeets. It was a bit early in the afternoon for this bloke but maybe he was having a bad day. She could relate to that.

She almost walked into Marco and he put his hands out to steady her. 'Who are you talking to?'

'The lorikeet is complaining there's no seed.' She tried not to stare at his chest but it filled her vision. She wanted to bury her nose in him. 'Do you need something?'

'Glasses. I brought Lambrusca.'

All she could think of was how good his hands felt on her arms. 'Aren't you driving?' No matter she'd been going to offer him white wine.

'Not yet, and we can have a glass. You keep the rest.'

'Trying to loosen my morals again?' She stepped past him and his hands fell.

'There is nothing wrong with your morals, Emily. I look forward to sharing your lunch.'

That had been rude. She turned back. 'Sorry. I'm not good at this.' Then she disappeared into the kitchen.

Marco watched her go. She was very good at this. He was a mess.

He didn't follow. Gave her a moment to gather her composure. He should not have come but had been unable to stay away. He should know better.

He stared at the brilliantly coloured bird on the steel feeder, iridescent red and lime green and vibrant yellow all mixed in the lorikeet's plumage as if painted by a colour-hungry child. So much of this country was bright and brash and brilliant so it hurt your eyes.

There might be more pain in store for him here. Seeing Emily's pain hurt his eyes and his heart when she was upset and his stomach when she was away from him. He should go in and help her bring the food out.

She reappeared before he could move. 'I've brought the wine out. It looks good.'

'And for after… Limoncello.' He wondered if she'd like the liqueur and looked forward to her reaction. 'Nectar of the gods. I will help you carry the rest.'

Soon they were seated, shaded by the tree that hung over the fence from next door, and Marco felt a peace settle over him that defied description and warned him to be careful.

'Gran always said that tree was the best of both worlds. The trunk didn't take up any room in our yard and we got the shade.'

He glanced up at the thick, glistening foliage. Little brown birds flitted around in it. 'Tell me about your gran. Was she a widow?'

'My grandfather died in the Vietnam War. His family owned this whole block all the way down to the water. There's a magnificent old home over that fence and this was the dower house. The big house left the family years ago and this little house was left to my gran, and I always think of her here.'

He glanced around and the feeling of peace deepened. 'No doubt she is here.'

'I'd like to think so.'

He smiled. 'My grandmother came from a long line of gypsies and we can tell these things. This tiny house is very beautiful and full of character. Like its mistress now, and no doubt also the one from the past.'

'Thank you, Marco. That's a lovely thing to say.' She tilted her head. 'So tell me about the gypsies?'

His peace seeped away. Serve him right. 'There's not much to tell. My father was not one, yet still we moved a lot.'

She put her chin in her hands. A willing listener eager to hear his exotic tales. 'It sounds very romantic.'

She would be disappointed. 'I can assure you it was not.'

'So what made you want to become a doctor?'

Marco shook his head and realised it would take more to daunt this woman or her curiosity. He owed her a little more than he usually gave.

Why had he become a doctor? Many reasons, but the need had been strong enough to drive him along the hard road his career had carried him. He tried to verbalise it. 'To help others? To stretch my brain. To find solutions to pain. Perhaps a need to feel worthwhile.'

She frowned. Stretched her hand across and took

his. Lifted his palm and placed a kiss in his hand as a gift. 'Worthwhile doesn't even begin to describe you and your work.'

Her words made his heart ache and he tried to harden himself against her. As if she knew, she shook her head. 'All those babies, parents, grandparents who needed your help. Families like us. Like June.'

He shrugged. 'Everyone does their part.'

She squeezed his hand and then let him go. 'And some strive to achieve the impossible when others fear to push boundaries.' She shrugged and smiled at her seriousness.

'But I see this isn't helping your mood so instead we will toast.'

She glanced around for inspiration and he watched her eyes light up with amusement. Up went his own spirits.

'To lorikeets, and harbour boats and wild mice.'

'Especially wild mice.' She captivated him. 'I will certainly toast that.' He smiled. 'And I am partial to the idea of your rotor. Cannot help but wonder what could be achieved without the benefit of gravity.'

She blushed and concentrated on her antipasto. 'See. No fear to push boundaries.'

He laughed and they ate and sipped and laughed again until the afternoon shade brought a chill and they cleared up their picnic together.

The kitchen was small, and smaller still as Marco dried the dishes while she washed, and Emily tried hard not to bump into him. Every time she did, awareness grew, every 'Excuse me' made her mouth dry as she reached past, and gradually the laughter of the lunch changed to a slowly rising tension that burned in the pit of her belly and warned her of imminent danger.

Glances collided, hands brushed, and as the last dish dried Emily's nerves screamed to create some distance or give in.

In the end, Marco took her shoulders and held her. Stared down with those dark eyes, like the coffee she'd made that still sat on the bench. 'It is not coffee I want, Emily.'

Emerrrleee. She savoured the sound of her name on his lips again. Relished the power in his hands as he held her. Acknowledged the lust that rose like a wraith inside her. She wanted him too.

His hand brushed her cheek. She stepped closer. That was all the permission he needed and once more she was swept up. Spun in the confines of the kitchen, carried across and under the arch into the hall, and in through the door to her bedroom.

She let her head fall back. Closed her eyes. Acknowledged the surge of power she felt to ignite his passion and accept her femininity. She was a woman. She did have needs. And she wanted Marco so badly the centre of her being ached with that need.

Then he placed her on her bed. Gently. And stepped back. 'Perhaps this time you would like to undress me?'

She raised her eyebrows. 'Mmm.' She crawled off the bed, accentuating the wiggle of her bottom, and his voice deepened with amusement and definite intent.

'Although if you persist with that movement, you will not have the chance.'

She stood up. Sidled up to him. Ran her finger down

his chest and he laughed with delight. 'I have created a monster.'

'You have no idea.'

Marco was dazed. Stunned and enthralled by the sexy innocent who had suddenly shed her shyness and had taken control. It was dream and fantasy and to think that she could trust him enough to allow her playful side to surface when she had been so hurt in the past.

She ran her hands down each side of the buttons on his shirt, feeling his chest, until they dipped under his belt. Deftly undoing the buckle, she opened the top button of his trousers and he couldn't help the sigh of relief at the extra room afforded.

Then she flitted back to the neck of his shirt. Skipping from button to button, a kiss for each opening, a kiss down his chest until the last button ended back at his trousers. She looked up at him. Mischief, and still that tiny hint of vulnerability, and suddenly he could not take any more of this.

He captured her face in his hands. Drew her up until he could reach those perfect lips, hugged her against him, then in a flurry their clothes were slipping from their bodies with minds of their own. He could only see Emily. Her face, her mouth and her truth shining out at him.

He thanked her in the only way he knew how. With reverence at first and then with mounting passion, mutual need creating a maelstrom that seemed to intensify each time he joined with this woman.

CHAPTER EIGHT

THIS time when she woke she knew her survival depended on not seeing this man again. But she had the horrible feeling it was too late.

And this time it was Marco who was leaving. He turned when she stirred. Strode back to the bed fully dressed. Kissed her one last time, thoroughly, and stroked her face. 'I must go. *Ciao, bella.*' And left.

'*Ciao.* Bye.' She didn't ask why he had to go. She had an idea. This connection, rapport, infatuation, whatever they were going to call it, had been more than either of them had expected. And he was leaving at the end of the month. Not the most sensible thing to continue.

She rose, wandered into the shower, dressed again and tidied the wreckage of her bedroom. She had to smile. With a slightly embarrassed smugness. He'd said he was good. Judging by his response, she was a fast learner.

Marco had had to get out. He'd been a fool. Did he think that reciting the reasons he was a loner would be good enough to insulate him from falling for Emily? He was no long-term prospect for any woman, let alone one as special as this woman, and his gut had told him that from the first day.

He needed to leave. Move on. Needed to keep presenting his best side to the world and avoid the chance others would find out that he was irrevocably tainted by his dubious background and should never be trusted. He didn't trust himself.

Look what he had done to Emily.

He had seen the light in her eyes when she'd looked at him. No doubt that same light had shone from his own stupid face. *Bastardo.* He was as bad as her daughter's father. But he had been unable to back away when he should have. Had been seduced when he was the one who normally did the seducing. She was incredible.

He parked his car in the garage and took the stairs to his unit, changed quickly, and left again. He needed exercise. He needed to drive himself to exhaustion. He needed to run until he dropped. Run until his legs ached and his head drooped. Run until he could forget that he was tempted to risk all and even think about a life that existed in one city with one woman.

Emily had to get out of the house. She stared at herself in the hall mirror. Her eyes shone, her face gently glowed and a small smile tilted her mouth even when she tried to look serious. 'I'm falling in love and I can't. He's transient,' she told the mirror. 'He's going to leave me, like Annie's father left me. Though, to be fair, Marco had always said he wasn't planning on staying.'

She sighed. 'What is it about me that men don't want to stay around?'

Maybe Annie would welcome her for a short time.

She winced at this morning's hurt at her daughter's dismissal. Well, she was always there for Annie and right at this moment her mother needed her.

She glanced at the grandmother clock on the wall. It was almost the end of visiting hours. She could take an ice cream, sit with her daughter for the last fifteen minutes. Then maybe she would be able to come home and settle for an early night. She started her week of night duty again tomorrow night so it was important she feel refreshed before the new week began.

Refreshed? She felt like she'd been plugged into a power source. 'If that's what sex does for you, my battery must have been low for years,' she muttered to herself as she locked the door behind her.

When Emily walked into Annie's room in the hospital a little later, at first glance she thought she'd taken the wrong doorway. The woman on the bed was wrapped in the arms of a dark-haired tattooed boy and their absorption in each other forcibly reminded her of what she'd been doing earlier in the day.

'Ahem…' She cleared her throat, and the couple on the bed jumped apart. No mistake on the room number, then.

'Mum!'

'Annie.' She waited.

'Um. This is Rodney.' Annie looked at the young man and lifted her chin. 'My baby's father.'

Tattoos. Undernourished. Torn jeans. Emily tried not to cry. 'Hello, Rodney. Nice to meet you.' She paused. 'At last.' Very dry.

Rodney stood up awkwardly. Wiped his palms on his jeans and held out his hand.

Emily forced a smile and shook. 'So is this an un-expected reunion or the reason I wasn't supposed to visit today?'

'Um. Hello, Mrs…Miss…' He glanced agonisingly at Annie, and then struggled on manfully, 'Emily. I'm sorry we haven't met before.' He sent one last agonising look at Annie. 'I—I have to go.' And hurried from the room.

Marco stepped out of the lift as a young man, his face painfully red from embarrassment, hurried past. *Christo.* He remembered that feeling. Unworthy. Scorned by someone he wanted to impress. Too many times this had happened to him at his age. He wanted to take the boy aside and tell him he must love himself before others could love him. But for all his efforts he had never learned that lesson. He shook his head and walked on to the nurses' station, the memories circling like bats around his head. Work. He needed work.

In Annie's room the young girl sat higher in the bed. 'Look what you did.' She adjusted her pyjamas and glared at her mother.

Good grief, times had changed, Emily thought. Imagine if she'd said that to *her* mother. 'I'm sorry. I don't understand? What I did?'

Annie crossed her arms over her chest. 'You made him leave.'

'Not guilty.' Emily held up her hands. 'I did no such thing. Not my fault Rodney didn't want to stay while I was here.'

Annie fumed. 'You shouldn't have been here. I asked you not to come.'

Emily took a step closer to the bed. The idea of a

cosy chat with her daughter, a mutual salve for unstable times, lay in tatters around her feet. 'You said friends. When were you going tell me you were seeing your baby's father again? You went behind my back. Sneakily. Annie? Where has all this come from?'

Annie glanced away. 'I knew you'd judge him just because he doesn't come from a good family.'

Emily shook her head. 'That's unfair. Since when have I *ever*—' she stressed the 'ever' '—tried to influence your choice of friends?'

'I know what you're thinking, Mum!' Annie's voice rose.

Marco paused outside the room. Unwilling to interrupt when he was obviously not wanted but unable to avoid the conversation.

'I know how you looked at Rodney. As if he's not good enough for me.'

Emily's voice. Quieter. Calm. 'That's unfair.'

'He's tainted by a family that doesn't live in the best part of Sydney. Doesn't work all day.' A bitter pause then a little softer and Marco tried not to strain his ears. 'Or all night, like you.' Ouch.

Annie went on, 'I know it's going to be because his brother's done time.' Marco straightened as if stung.

'Jail?' The horror in Emily's voice said it all. Did it all. Sealed it all. Marco sighed. Pictured that boy's face. Empathised. Felt the whoosh of time, of scornful villagers, of police questioning. He winced and walked away. And to think he had considered telling Emily about his past. About his reasons for choosing not to settle. Why? Did he hope she would not care? Fool.

He knew exactly what she was thinking. Of course.

And he didn't blame her. Marco kept walking. Each step to the lift more final with his decision. He would stay away. Not seek out Emily. He had done enough damage. He would just do his work and then leave.

He pressed the lift button. Stepped inside, saw little, had trouble deciding on the floor he wanted and totally oblivious to the other occupant.

'What are you doing here today?' A gruff masculine voice.

He looked up. Hard blue eyes scrutinised him. Finn Kennedy. He was rubbing his shoulder.

'Just checking on my patients. You?' Ball back in Finn's court because his mind wasn't working real well at the moment. He'd been delusional to think he could just have fun with Emily.

'Same.' Finn nodded. 'Want a drink?'

Emily was trying to make sense of it all. Of this woman who was and yet wasn't her daughter. 'What do you mean done time? Rodney?'

'See. I knew it. It's not Rodney's fault his brother made mistakes. Rodney's had a difficult life but he is still a good man.'

'Annie.' She sat on the edge of the bed. 'I don't care what Rodney's family have done. What Rodney's background is. It's what he himself is doing with his life now and that he makes you happy that I care about. That he loves you and your baby. Treats you both right. Every woman and every child deserves that.'

Annie's lip quivered. 'I thought you'd look down on him because of his brother's past; you think I'd be tied for ever to a family of trouble.'

'Why? How could I do that?' She shook her head. 'Your father was from a very well-to-do family. An upstanding future citizen. Once a year his parents send money, sure—but he dropped me, and you, like a hot potato.'

She patted Annie's hand. 'Your father never visited me in hospital like Rodney has visited you. Why would you think I'd look down on that?' Her voice firmed. 'But if Rodney ever treated you badly then he'd have me after him.'

Annie shrugged. 'If he treated me badly, I wouldn't be there.'

'That's my girl.'

They looked at each other and then Annie held out her arms for a hug. 'I'm sorry, Mum. I should have told you.'

Emily hugged her and Annie squeezed back. 'Is this why we've been fighting the last few months?'

Annie nodded. 'I hated having a secret and I should have known you'd understand.'

Emily swallowed the thickness in her throat. Maybe she'd have her normal daughter back now. She glanced down at the plastic bag on the table. 'Now I have two melted ice creams we were going to share because I got lonely and needed my baby's company.'

She pulled out a droopy ice cream and gave it to Annie. Annie looked at it, took it gingerly and stripped it of its wrapper. She grinned. It didn't quite fall off the stick. 'I'm sorry.'

'That's fine.' Emily pulled hers out and it looked worse. They both giggled.

Emily pulled the towel off the end of the bed and

spread it between them as a safety net for dripping ice cream. 'I guess I have to realise you won't be there for ever. You have your own life. But when you're ready I need you to tell me about Rodney and what your plans are.'

'There's not much to tell. I love him.'

Emily's brows went up. 'Really. Where did you meet him? How long have you known him? Though I'm guessing more than twenty-six weeks?'

'Mum!'

Emily raised her brows and glanced at Annie's belly. 'Well?'

'I met him in a chat room. Just after Gran died. And before you go, "Oh, Annie", it's okay. We'd been chatting for about three months before I met him, and we can talk all night. He understands me, likes the same things—music, books, movies. We laugh. A lot. And when I met him...' Annie rolled her eyes '...it was just right.'

'Okay. I can understand that.' Boy, could she understand that. 'But did you mean to have a baby with Rodney? I mean, how old is he?'

'Eighteen. And no. We only did it once. And we weren't going to do it again until I went on the Pill. But when I finally went to the doctor he told me I was pregnant.'

Oh, my poor baby. 'We must be very fertile women.' That thought came with a shudder of relief that she'd started the Pill after Annie's birth and never missed it. So she could banish the horrible vision of the two of them eating ice creams with pregnant bellies. And Marco had been careful too.

Emily accepted how it had happened. 'Though for the record, if you like a boy enough to want to have sex, it would be good to let me into the secret so I could at least meet him. When all this is over, we're going to discuss contraception again.'

Annie blushed. 'It's a bit late now.'

'Not for the next one it's not.' And if she could cover herself for the last sixteen years and not use it, her daughter would be doubly covered. 'And condoms.'

'Mu-u-um.' Annie rolled her eyes again.

She grinned. 'Sorry. Having a belated stress attack. This has all happened pretty fast, you know.'

Annie's fingers crept across and squeezed her mother's hand. 'I know. And I'm sorry. I've been crabby because I was hiding Rodney and it felt rotten to be sneaky.'

'You didn't need to do that. You can always tell me anything. I may not like it but I'll always love you.'

Annie sighed. 'Rodney wanted to. He wanted to drive around to home and be with me when I told you. But I didn't want you to meet him for the first time then.'

Emily felt her heart squeeze. Wished for a different scenario, but it was all too late now. 'You'll have to grow up too fast. But we'll talk more about that later.' She glanced at her watch. 'Visiting hours are over. I'd better go.'

Annie reached out her hand. 'Mum?'

Emily stopped. 'Yes?' She caught her daughter's hand and held it.

'Can we put your birthday decorations up when I come home?'

Emily squeezed Annie's hand. 'Sure. I'd like that.'

Annie hung on for another second. 'And thanks for the ice cream.'

'Thanks for the conversation.' Their hands dropped apart. 'I've missed having them with you.'

They hugged again because they were both a little teary as they waved goodbye.

Marco hunched over his beer at Pete's Bar, a watering place across the road from the hospital where most of the staff drifted if they didn't want to be alone—or wanted to be alone in a section Pete called Off Limits.

The aroma of beef pie permeated the walls and Pete himself remembered every name he was told. He had twenty years of hospital names stored in his head.

Finn ordered the pie. 'You should try it. To die for.'

Marco looked at it consideringly. 'I have eaten but maybe I could manage one. I think I ran that off.' And some other exercise, he reminded himself sardonically.

'Evie says you're seeing Emily Cooper.'

His appetite disappeared. So she had told her in the lift. And he'd apologised. Before he could say anything, Finn went on. 'Good woman. Good midwife in an emergency too. Not the kind I would have thought up for a fling.'

'We went out once.' And slept together twice.

Finn looked at him under his brows. Must have seen something in his face. 'Emily hasn't said anything. Evie said she was in the lift with you two and could've cut the air with a knife.'

He'd got it wrong, again. Suspicion would kill him

one day. 'Very observant of her. I think I will have the pie.' He stood up and walked over to the bar to order.

Man after his own heart. 'Use your staff card. It's half price,' Finn called out, suddenly in a good humour because he'd found some other poor bastard who didn't understand women either.

There was a lot of Marco D'Arvello that reminded Finn of Isaac. His brother had had that same kindness and warm exterior, and Finn wondered if Marco hid a similar feeling of homelessness. Thankfully Isaac had found happiness for the time he'd had with his wife, Lydia, something Finn had never allowed himself to find. The closest he'd come had been when he and Lydia had comforted each other after Isaac's death. Lydia had been smart enough to know there was no future with Finn.

But now there was Evie. The reason he'd decided to come across here and think. That and the pain that was eating him alive.

Headstrong, defiant, warm-hearted Evie who for some incomprehensible reason said she loved him and he couldn't quite believe it.

That was the problem. He didn't want to risk becoming a quadriplegic—or worse—if she was going to hang her future on him. But there was the chance this surgery could remove the shrapnel and give him back full control of his hands.

Did he owe it to Evie to try? Or owe it to Evie to be half a man instead of just a shell? If he chose the surgery he'd just have to make a back-up plan to get away if it all went wrong.

'You okay? You look worried. What's up?' Marco

was back and he could see Finn was in pain. He set the pie down.

'Nothing.' Subject change. 'So you're leaving in a couple of weeks?'

'Is it that close?' Marco shrugged. 'Doesn't matter. You want to roster me on?' He tried not to think of Emily. Of her character-filled house. Her family. He didn't do families.

Of course Finn jumped at the offer. 'The O and G guys would be thrilled. It's always a pain getting cover.'

'Fine.' So this was penance. He could have left Sydney in fourteen days. 'But I wish to be gone by the twentieth.'

'Planning something special?'

He said the first thing that appeared in his mind. 'Times Square.' He'd be in New York for the new contract but it was unlikely he'd be out partying.

'So, you going out with Emily again?' Finn's curiosity surprised him. Marco had never known him to be interested in someone else's social life. Perhaps his friend was becoming more human.

'I doubt it. She has a lot on her mind with her daughter.'

'It's a big responsibility. She does seem fairly consumed by her. I wouldn't like to have a teenage daughter. Especially a pregnant one.'

'Emily is a good mother.'

'No doubt about that but she wouldn't know squat about teenage boys and that's how their life is going to change.'

Marco thought about that. Thought about the young man he'd seen. Emily's natural reservations. About who was going to help her? And maybe the boy?

CHAPTER NINE

EMILY walked onto the ward Monday morning to collect Annie and the dull ache behind her eyes wasn't helped when she saw Marco was still there.

'Ah. Here is your mother.' His glance swept over her. No doubt he could see the bags under her eyes. What did he expect if she'd been awake most of the night, reaching out for his hand in the bed beside her, or, worse still, scared she was falling in love?

His voice seemed to soften—or was it just her imagination? 'Good morning, Emily.'

Cautiously Emily returned the greeting. 'Marco.' She could see Annie's glance from one to the other and she prayed her daughter would hold her questions till later.

She made an effort to forestall her. 'Dr D'Arvello has been very good when I was worried.'

'*Si*. But today you look worried again.' He smiled at Annie and then back at Emily. She wanted to look away but couldn't because it felt too damn good to bask in the light. 'All is good. Annie's baby has increased the amount of liquid in the uterus quite substantially, which is a good sign of kidney function. I am very pleased.'

Emily felt one burden ease. 'That's wonderful news. So we can go?'

'*Si*. But Annie must rest. I have clinics for another two weeks and I would like Annie to have another ultrasound at the end of this week and see me Friday morning in the rooms here.'

She glanced at Annie, who nodded. 'Fine. We can do that.' That meant one more definite time she would see Marco and the occasional ward sighting. She could handle that. Just.

'So you'll be here for a while?' Annie was on a different track, a mission of her own, and Emily's neck prickled.

'*Si*. I have said I will work and do the on-call before I leave for the States.'

Annie looked so sweet and Emily's trepidation grew. She knew that look. 'So you have no family here, do you?'

Emily froze, wanted to put her hand out or even over her daughter's mouth as she sensed what was coming.

'No.' Marco wasn't stupid either and Emily held her breath.

So innocent Annie. 'Would you like to come to my baby shower?'

'Annie!' Emily's voice came out strangled.

'I'll see.' Marco's smile was crooked. 'Perhaps your mother would prefer if I didn't?'

Annie feigned horror. 'Mum!'

Emily knew she was trapped. 'What?'

Annie cajoled, 'Well, I'd like to invite Rodney and his friends and maybe you could invite Dr D'Arvello and yours?'

Emily's face reddened. 'We'll see. I'm sure Dr D'Arvello has other plans.' She hoped.

Marco didn't offer anything and she glared at him as she was obliged to fill the gap. 'But of course he's welcome.'

Annie was full of mischief. 'You could even come home this afternoon and help us put up the decorations for Mum's birthday.'

Emily blinked in shock. It got worse. 'Annie! That's enough.'

He looked at Emily. 'It is your birthday?'

'Not until Friday.'

Annie sighed. Rolled her eyes. 'Okay. I've already invited Rodney.' She grinned at Marco. 'If you get bored you can get the address from my notes.'

Marco smiled at her. 'Strangely, I know where you live.'

Annie nodded as if he had just confirmed her suspicions. 'I thought you might.' She glanced at her mother's red cheeks.

Going down in the lift Emily fumed. She gripped the handle of Annie's overnight bag and squeezed it until the plastic bit into her fingers. She'd kill her. The little witch had planned that.

She speared a look at her daughter and Annie was innocently staring at the numbers on the console. Avoiding her, as well she should.

Emily stopped grinding her teeth. 'Please don't invite any more people without asking me, Annie.'

Annie swung to face her. Mischief clear and bold. 'Oh, come on. You two can't keep your eyes off each other.' Annie raised her brows and for a moment she looked like her grandmother and Emily felt her anger drain away like water from a leaky pipe.

Until her daughter said, 'And for the record, who was it who said if you like a boy enough to want to have sex, it would be good to let me into the secret?' She grinned cheekily. 'I hope I don't have to discuss contraception with you, Mum.'

It was that obvious? Emily buried the fingers of her free hand into her forehead. This was all too much. She felt like the daughter here. 'Touché.' She huffed her breathe out. 'He is a nice man but he's leaving soon.'

'Come off it, Mum. The guy's gorgeous and he's smitten with you. Even more reason to have some fun, for goodness' sake. And Friday is your birthday.'

Who was this young woman? Then again, Annie had no idea how much fun her mother had already had. Her ears heated. 'I'll think about it.'

By the time she'd driven home and Annie was settled into the big squishy living room chair with her feet up, Emily had calmed down. She even whipped up a batch of date scones to set on the table with butter and jam. Men were always hungry. She couldn't help feeling it would be a bit of an anticlimax if Marco didn't turn up along with Rodney.

She glanced out the window. A black Aston Martin stopped across the road.

Marco turned off the engine. He'd been kidding himself that he wouldn't come. He was glad now because he could see Rodney sitting in his car, staring at the front gate. He'd bet the young man tried to build up the courage to knock on the door.

Marco crossed the street and knocked on Rodney's car roof. 'Hello?'

'Oh. Hi.' Rodney drooped in his seat.

Marco bent down. 'You are coming in?'

Rodney poked his finger down his T-shirt. 'I don't think Annie's mother likes me.'

Marco opened his door. 'Annie's mother will like anyone who makes her daughter happy. You can come with me. We will go in together. Your lady will be glad to see you.'

Marco wasn't real sure about his own lady but he could understand her reluctance to become more involved when he had stated his intention to leave.

Today he was going to help Rodney.

It would be cathartic to help. To help an insecure boy like Marco had been all those years ago. He certainly would have benefited from some advice from another man.

To Emily it must have seemed as if Marco and Rodney had arrived at the same time and she opened the door with a smile that welcomed.

She greeted them both warmly and he couldn't help his relief. Though why he was surprised was a measure of his own insecurity because she had always been polite.

'Come in. Welcome. Annie will be pleased to see you and we have scones ready.'

The house floated on the aroma of fresh baking, Emily's cheeks were flushed, and Annie lorded over them all from her chair.

It felt like a family. He swallowed the fear in his throat.

Or how he imagined a family would feel. He shouldn't be here. Only when his father had been in jail had he had any idea of a stable life with his mother and he'd been ready to leave home by then. Was there any chance one day his life might come to this?

'Marco, can you help, please?' Perhaps Emily had sensed his ambivalence because she didn't leave him to ponder too deeply for long.

Within minutes industry ensued as Emily directed and he could see where her daughter had inherited her organisational skills from.

A doting Rodney carried buttered scones across to his lady and Marco lifted down the heavy box of decorations that overflowed with a family history he could only imagine. Even at a glance he could tell some of them were very old.

'Thanks.' Emily peered in. 'That's the hardest part—getting that box down from the top of the cupboard.'

She lifted a handful of paper chains from the box, some of them falling apart, and set them on the table ready to hang or repair.

'Annie and I make these every year with the greeting cards from her birthday we saved from the year. So there's lots of them. It's a family tradition. We usually put them up a week before someone's birthday so that they can really soak in the lead-up.'

'A birthday that lasts for a week?' Marco had very few memories of any celebrations for his birthday.

Emily looked a little embarrassed. 'It was really for Annie and Gran more than me. Some of these are from when Annie was only a toddler and just started to play with paper. See, that strip has part of her fourth birthday card on it.'

Marco shook his head and tried to imagine a home that stayed still long enough to hoard such things.

Rodney carried the ladder inside and they discussed their plan of attack.

Emily grinned at him. 'You'll be sorry you came. By the time you've finished blowing up the balloons—and they're big ones that Annie loves—you'll be exhausted. I've been dreading that job.'

Marco's first sight of the balloons confirmed the reason she'd dreaded the thought.

'They're huge.' Rodney was wide eyed.

Emily shook her head sadly. 'I know. I had a pump but it broke and I've never got around to buying a new one.'

She frowned at the bag of hand-sized balloons. 'I should insist on the little ones, these ones kill me.' She looked up. 'But Annie loves these.'

'Maybe we could just do a couple?' Rodney was looking dubiously at the balloon in his hand.

'Not this year,' Marco said with finality and a sideways look at Emily. 'In these matters a woman's wish is law. Perhaps if we do them one at a time, we will survive.'

They achieved the impossible, twelve enormous balloons, and all stood around admiringly at the colourful clump on the floor.

'Rodney looks sick.' Annie squinted worriedly at her beau.

'It's just a little headache,' Rodney said gallantly, and Marco patted his shoulder.

'Just.' Emily smiled at Marco and Rodney was given a kiss by Annie. 'We could not have done that without your big lungs. Thank you, both.'

Rodney blushed and Marco whispered in an aside, 'That is why we do what they want. Worth it?' Rodney nodded carefully.

'So, Annie, if you tell Rodney where to hang the chains, Marco and I will sort the balloons. We'll have it all finished by lunch.'

Much hilarity ensued as every time Rodney stretched the chains the loop broke and they had to strengthen the strips until Marco demanded a stapler and they began to staple the links together.

'Some are older than others and fragile.' Annie defended their chain and Marco shook his head. 'Next birthday perhaps you could start with the stapler and then hang them.' He glanced across and Emily was watching him.

Her face was quietly thoughtful. He saw her acknowledge that he would not be here for the next birthday. Or the one after that, because he had no continuity like these women and their years of family traditions epitomised by this handmade diary of life.

Suddenly he needed fresh air and a cold breeze on his face to snap him out of melancholy. He pulled his phone from his pocket. Pretended to glance at it. 'Excuse me. I need to make a call.'

He left her standing in the middle of the room and Emily watched him go. She couldn't help but wonder about his childhood. What had formed the man who froze at the idea of permanence? She crossed to the kitchen and looked out the window. He wasn't on the phone. He was staring at the empty bird feeder and the silhouette of his face made her ache for the loneliness she saw in his usually smiling face.

She turned, picked up the seeds for the birds, and followed him out. 'The lorikeet isn't here today.'

'I should not have come.'

'Why? Because you don't think you're welcome?'

'Because I cannot have a healthy future with any woman.' He turned to face her squarely. Lifted his head. 'I cannot be the man you deserve, Emily.'

Emerrrlee. Yes, it would have been nice. More than nice to have a normal, evolving relationship with Marco. One with a future and stability and new excitement every day. But in reality life wasn't like that, she of all people knew that, and from this last hour she'd discovered she was still glad she'd connected with Marco D'Arvello and really believed she always would be.

She wished she knew what had him running so scared from forming relationships. 'We don't have to be intensely involved in each other, Marco. The last couple of days were just a mirage for both of us.

'But if you want a family to join for the next couple of weeks before you head off on your next high-powered assignment, please join mine.'

She spread her hands. 'We'd love to have you. Anyone who blows up my balloons is welcome at my door any time.'

He smiled but the humour was missing. 'I worry that it will be difficult for you when I leave.'

Maybe it would be difficult for him too? She shrugged. 'My problem, not yours. I'm single, free to have what friends I choose, and I think regret for time we could have spent together could be worse than being safe with no friendship at all.'

She touched his arm. 'But it's up to you.'

That night at work Emily couldn't help thinking about the day. How it hadn't been as awkward as she'd expected it would be. How Marco had been unobtrusively supportive of Rodney and Annie, and circumspect with her. Maybe too circumspect, according to Annie's view of her mother's love life.

But the idea of just getting to know Marco without actually touching him could be a good idea, could help her see that a globetrotting, super-specialist was not in the realms of reality for her life. The problem was she really did like the caring man she could see beneath the handsome exterior.

Today she'd been glad he'd come back inside. Stayed another hour and helped. Had steadied her while she'd climbed the ladder and precariously placed the last balloon on the lightshade so that everyone clapped when it was done.

The phone rang and she blinked her way back to on-duty. 'Maternity, Emily.'

'Emergency Department. We're sending up a thirty-four-weeker in prem labour. Helen Roberts. She's a booked Caesarean for foetal abnormality and we have the team coming in for that if you can get her ready. We're up to our ears down here.'

She knew Helen from the antenatal clinic. 'No problem. Thanks.' Emily put the phone down and scooted over to the cupboard with all the pre-admission notes for the women booked to have their babies with Sydney Harbour Hospital.

She pulled Helen's notes and flipped them open on her way back to the desk. 'Prem labour coming in.' Helen would be stressing.

'Must be the month for it.' Lily reappeared from her ward round with a torch.

'Helen was a booked Caesarean for next month. Baby has an oomphaceal picked up on late ultrasound. I'll grab the IV stuff and theatre clothes if you set up the catheter trolley.'

'Who's going to Theatre with them?' Lily was an experienced plastic surgery nurse and Emily was the more experienced with Caesareans.

'I'll go this time because I know her, and you hold the ward.'

Lily nodded as they hurried together to the sterile storeroom and loaded their trolleys.

Lily was frowning. 'That's a weakness in the skin around the navel, isn't it?'

'Yep. So part of the baby's intestines and sometimes organs are not zipped inside.' Emily grabbed an IV pole with one hand and pushed the trolley with the other. 'The good thing about oomphaceals are the tummy contents are protected by the same membrane that covers the cord. So they're usually safe and can be replaced over time as the skin grows and makes room until it can be replaced inside the abdomen. Or they can have surgery earlier.'

'Imagine the mum.' Lily shook her head. 'It must be hard to be told your baby has something like that.

You'd want to see your baby's face in your mind but you'd have to be thinking about his tummy.'

Emily glanced at Lily as they hurried down to an empty room, set up their work areas and turned down the bed. 'That's very true. Helen's amazing, though. I do wonder if sometimes the imagination is much worse than the actual reality.' She grinned. 'You and Luke not getting clucky, are you?'

'Us?' Lily shook her head but she did blush. Emily let it go with a smile. Lily changed the subject. 'I'll bet this mum will be looking forward to seeing her baby. Then she can stop imagining so much.'

They heard the lift doors open and Lily went out to direct them down the hall. Emily leaned over, stuck the name badge to the wall and shifted the bed across so the trolley could come in easily.

She was surprised to see Marco accompany the trolley but he'd said he was on call tonight. Apparently he'd offered to do call for the rest of the week so there'd be no more Limoncello for him when he got home from work.

CHAPTER TEN

HE SMILED at her and it was crazy, but just for that split second she felt the room light up and her heart swell. Then it was gone. She greeted her patient as she arrived at the door.

'Hello, there, Helen. Your baby decided to do this in a rush?'

'Hi, Emily. It started all of a sudden.' Helen looked pale and anxious and Emily touched her hand in sympathy.

She gestured to Helen's belly. 'Maybe she decided it was time she called the shots? Where's Ned?'

Helen grimaced. 'Minding the kids. We couldn't get anyone at such short notice.'

Emily nodded. 'I'll stay with you until he can get here.' She glanced up at Marco. 'It will take us about ten minutes to get Helen ready. Then I'll come down with her.'

Marco leaned down and smiled at Helen. 'I'll see you in Theatre.' He patted her shoulder and sent one last look Emily's way before he was gone.

Emily glanced at the porter who'd helped Marco push the trolley. 'So you'll come back here for us as soon as you drop the baby resuscitation trolley in Theatre?'

'Okeydoke.' The man smiled at their patient. 'See you in a minute.'

The next seven minutes saw Helen admitted, changed into a gown and hat, and an IV cannula inserted for the fluids she'd need before the epidural anaesthetic.

Emily and Lily worked steadily and Helen breathed quietly through the contractions as they finished each task.

'One thing to go,' Emily said. 'I know we've been attacking you from both sides, but now I have to pop a catheter into your bladder before the surgery. When they reach the uterus, if the bladder isn't completely empty and flat, there's a small risk it could be damaged.'

Helen nodded. 'The sooner it's done, the sooner we go. I read the book you gave me on Caesareans, so I've got a bit of an idea what's happening.'

Emily ticked off the last of the list. 'Lovely. But just ask if you need to.'

Within minutes everything was done. The orderly came back, Emily handed over the keys for the ward to Lily, and they were on their way.

After the epidural was inserted in the anaesthetic bay they pushed Helen through into Theatre and the first person Emily saw inside was Marco—but that may have been because he towered over the others.

He had his head back and was chuckling at something he'd said to the attractive theatre sister. The sight sent an unfamiliar ache through her chest and she glanced back at her patient. 'You okay there?'

When she looked up Marco was by their side and he introduced the man who'd followed their trolley in.

Marco gestured. 'This is our head of paediatrics, Teo

Kauri, Helen. Teo's standing by for the arrival of your daughter and he's brought Dr Luke Williams, our plastic surgeon, and a bevy of neonatal nurse specialists so your baby will be in very good hands.'

Helen nodded, a little tearfully, and Marco squeezed her shoulder. Emily thought briefly of Lily back on the ward. Luke and Lily were such a perfect couple, and Luke was introducing himself to Helen with that special smile that Lily raved about.

She was in very good hands, Emily thought to herself, and couldn't help the tiny prayer she sent for her own little granddaughter, who had already benefited from these amazing people. After transfer to the operating table Emily held Helen's hand as the next twenty minutes crept by. Marco gently incised his way down to the uterus, a little more slowly than usual because of the fragile oomphaceal, but still Emily wished it was over. No doubt Helen was a hundred times more impatient than she was.

Emily heard the sound of the suction as the amniotic fluid surrounding baby gushed out, to be captured and removed by the suction tubing. So they'd reached the amniotic sac.

'Not long now.' She squeezed Helen's fingers and watched the neonatal specialists prepare to receive her baby.

The oomphaceal, a greyish-looking balloon on the front of the baby's tummy, wasn't quite as big as Emily had imagined but still it was shocking in weirdness.

Helen's eyes were darting as her imagination tried to make sense of the quiet conversations that were going on. Then Marco's voice. 'Your baby is breathing well and—' He was interrupted by a lusty wail as Helen's baby decided she didn't like being handled by these people.

Everyone laughed with relief and Emily blinked away her own tears. She didn't have a hope of not being affected by the moment. Distantly she heard Marco murmur quietly, 'This is good.'

'Our baby is okay?' Helen was craning her neck. 'Charlotte. We're calling her Charlotte. Charlotte is okay?' Her voice quivered and then the team pushed the neonatal trolley closer and Emily moved out of the way so Mum could reach out and touch her daughter's hand. From the angle she was lying Helen could see the big unfocussed eyes of her daughter as she blinked at the bright lights. The tiny hand closed over her mother's finger and held on tightly.

These were the moments Marco savoured. The naming of a baby. The beginning of a life. Despite the bizarreness of the protruding balloon of organs, this baby would be okay. The mother's fears would be allayed over the coming days, and all would be well.

He saw Emily wipe her eyes and then scoot around the edge of the crowd and snap photos for Helen, and he had to smile at her concentration. But, then, to look at Emily was to smile—and he would do better to put his head down and get on with his work.

But this was a moment he'd always doubted he would ever share with a woman. Many times he had been the outsider but this time he felt closer to the baby than usual. Perhaps it was the fact he had shared the moment with Emily.

Helen's baby was whisked off to the neonatal intensive care unit and Emily and Helen left Theatre an hour later via the NICU. Helen's husband, Ned, arrived just in time to accompany them, and Helen burst into tears with relief.

Teo came across as the trolley was wheeled in. 'Hello, there, again.'

'This is Ned, Charlotte's dad.' Emily introduced the anxious father and Teo shook his hand. Then he bent closer to Helen. 'Congratulations, you two.' He grinned. 'Except for her decision to wear her tummy on the outside, Charlotte looks great.'

They all smiled at that and Helen almost sagged into the bed with relief. Teo went on. 'Because she's four weeks early as well as the tests she needed to undergo, she'll be there for at least a week or two—maybe a little longer if anything crops up. But from our early examinations and tests Charlotte looks good.'

Such a relief. Emily felt her shoulders loosen and she sighed as she smiled. Ned reached down and kissed his wife and Emily turned away to give them some privacy. Such a different birth to experience but so fortunate the team had everything well under control.

'This is good!' Marco had appeared beside her and she looked up at him. This time she didn't care about the tears in her eyes as she shared her joy.

'It's great news.' She turned to Helen's husband. 'Ned, this is Dr D'Arvello. He's the obstetrician who operated on your wife.'

The two men shook hands. 'Thank you, Doctor.'

'My pleasure. It is very rewarding when there is such a good outcome as there is with Charlotte.' He glanced at Emily. Suddenly the impact of not being a part of any family slammed into him. Was he happy with that? Not having what this man in front of him had? What even Emily had with Annie. For ever?

'I will leave you in the very capable hands of the sister and see you later on the ward,' he said, and walked away.

The night passed swiftly after that. Marco came back briefly to check to see his patient was settled and comfortable and to impart the information that despite Charlotte's IV running well she was sucking happily on her fist.

Emily glanced at the clock and wondered again at how he managed with such a full schedule. She'd just happened to look for his next theatre list and saw it commenced in six hours. She left him to his conversation and went back to the desk to clear up the paperwork involved with the birth and there was a mountain of forms to keep her mind occupied.

She didn't hear him approach and Marco took a moment to just soak her in. Her cap of hair was across her face, her shoulders bent over her work, and he could see the curve of her neck that continued to entrance him. His obsession was becoming troublesome.

She brushed back her hair and held it away with her hand and he could see the frown across her forehead. 'You look worried. Anything I can help with?'

Emily jumped. Looked up and tried not to let him completely destroy her concentration. 'You could go to bed.'

He opened his mouth to say the obvious thing, smiled

instead, and they both knew what he'd been going to say.

'Well stopped,' Emily said primly.

'But still thought of.' His smile melted any resistance to loss of concentration. She was a basket case.

'Goodnight, Emily.' He turned and walked away and she watched his broad back disappear up the corridor.

She sighed.

'What was that sigh for?' Lily plonked the torch up on the shelf after another ward round.

'Nothing.' Emily changed the subject. 'Luke was in Theatre with Marco.'

'Yep. He's on call. I try to do nights when he's on call because most of the time he does come in and that means we can have the days off together. But you changed the subject. Were you sighing after the gorgeous Dr D'Arvello?'

Lily glanced up the hallway as the lift swallowed Marco. A hint of concern in her friend's voice. 'He's going soon, isn't he?'

Like she needed to be reminded of that. Lily cared and was always discreet. Maybe it would help to tell someone. 'I'll stay sensible but I can't help wishing he'd open up a little. Why is it so hard for men to talk about themselves?' She glanced at Lily and smiled ruefully. 'I'm pretty happy to chat about myself if someone asks.'

'Women are used to connecting with people. But he's not different. Luke was like a clam.' She tilted her head and studied Emily's face. 'You really like him, don't you?'

'I don't have any illusions. He'll be gone by the end

of the month, but Annie likes him as well. But, then, he did do a lifesaving operation on my grandchild.'

'Always a good reason to like someone.' They both grinned. 'But I think it's more than that. You look at him like I look at Luke. Or Evie looks at Finn. That worried, "are you okay, I care," look that women get when they've chosen their mate.'

'No, I don't.' She stared at her friend. 'I hope I don't. Do I? Lily?'

Lily laughed at the lack of choice people had when they met their match. 'Yeah. I can see you're trying to keep your head free but that must be hard when your daughter invites him to put up decorations and come to her baby shower.'

Emily put her head in her hands. 'It was probably too late anyway.'

Lily's eyes opened wide. 'You've slept with him!'

Emily sighed. 'I could tell you but then I'd have to kill you.'

'Oh.' Lily hugged her. 'He's a very cool guy.'

Emily nodded. Ridiculously proud of him. 'He's amazing. But he has issues. In fact, I have issues. Like he's leaving in a couple of weeks and the more I see of him the harder it's going to be when he leaves. I should stop now.'

Lily laughed and stood up. 'If only it was that easy. And they all have issues. Look at Finn.'

They looked at each other and shook their heads. 'Wouldn't be Evie for quids.'

CHAPTER ELEVEN

EVIE wouldn't have agreed. It wasn't easy but she'd chosen her man and she would make it work. She'd tracked Finn to his office again and this time she shut the door behind her when she went in.

He'd been working on some papers and his eyebrows lifted mockingly. 'Come to take advantage of my previous weakness?'

She was over him pretending they didn't have a mutual attraction. 'I've decided to stake my claim.'

'Claim on what?' He glanced down at himself. 'A broken-down quack with a penchant for princesses?'

She so didn't see him like that. 'I think you're the most amazing surgeon I've ever met.' She gave him a hard stare. 'And I'm trying to keep you away from barmaids.'

He shook his head. 'I never slept with her, Evie.'

He hadn't? So all that angst had been for nothing. She could feel her temper rise. 'Well, thanks for putting me out of my misery.'

He stood up. Stared at her and then crossed the floor. She held her ground despite the unnerving stare he kept her pinned with. 'Misery is my middle name. You wanna play with me then get used to it.'

'Well, Pollyanna is mine so expect some disagreements.'

He laughed, short and sharp, and to her relief his face softened. 'Why on earth would a gorgeous girl like you want me? How long do you seriously think this is going to last?'

'I was hoping for ever.'

He pulled her in and held her against him and she knew this was where she wanted to be. She knew how hard it must have been for him to make the decision to let her into his very private world and she still couldn't believe her luck. She hugged him and even the tiny easing of his tension made her feel hopeful.

'I love you, Finn.'

This time he crushed her against his chest but it was over too soon. She tried not to be disappointed he couldn't bring himself to return the declaration.

Her whole damn childhood had been like that. Cold emotions, brick walls between her parents—she didn't want that with Finn. Surely she hadn't chosen a man that would freeze her out like her father had frozen her mother out?

But she wasn't as easily bowed as her mother. She'd make him join the human race if it killed her. Or him.

'A little bit of feedback wouldn't go astray here, Finn.'

Finn strangled back a laugh. Not a sound she heard nearly enough but it was so good to hear it now. 'Evie, you are some woman.'

'I know. It's about time you appreciated me.' She needed to hear this.

His hard blue eyes softened further. 'Oh, I do. Don't you worry.'

Like blood from a stone. 'I repeat. Some feedback would be good.'

'I didn't realise you were so needy.' The old Finn was back.

Ohh. She could strangle him. 'You don't realise much at all do you, Finn, that isn't directly related to Sydney Harbour Hospital? You live and breathe this place and I'm asking that you cut yourself a little slack to think about the outside world.'

'Why?' He shot her hard look. 'Because you think I might have to give it up? Is that it, Evie? Is this another discussion leading to that experimental surgery?' As if he was surprised she'd brought it up again.

Well, yes. 'If I don't have that discussion with you, who will?' She pointed her finger at him. 'You'll shut down any of your few friends that dare to bring it up.'

He shrugged and turned away.

'You'll block out your doctor's recommendations.'

Finn laughed again but this time Evie didn't like the sound. 'It's been done before. Happens to me with my patients all the time.'

She wasn't listening to excuses. 'I might be your only chance, Finn. And I'm going to push until you face the reality. There is no choice.'

'There is a choice, Evie!' He turned and faced her and this time she saw, way at the back of his eyes, the fear of being less than a man. 'At least if I don't have the operation I can walk away. If I have it I might be flat on my back without that choice.'

She stepped up to him. Wrapped her arms around him and he stood stiff in her embrace. 'You can't put up with this pain for ever, Finn.'

Still he wouldn't lean into her. 'I'm putting up with it now.'

She stepped back so she could see his face. Plead her case. 'You're drinking too much. Your analgesia is becoming ineffective, the exercise that used to help isn't doing its job any more.'

He glared at her. Building barriers faster than she could break them down. 'If you can't stand the way I am then get out, Evie.'

She shook her head. Glared right back. 'You'd like that, wouldn't you? That way you could just go back to drowning out life along with the pain and self-destruct in your own time.'

He didn't deny it.

'Well.' She put her hands on her hips. 'I reiterate, I love you, Finn Kennedy, and I'm going to fight tooth and nail for you and the life we could have together. It's your job to make that decision.'

Still no response. She took a deep breath and dived in where very few had dared. 'You need to take the step to stop suffering physically and emotionally from the explosion that killed your brother, Finn.'

His eyes blazed. 'That's enough.'

She nodded. Not surprised, and sorry she'd had to hurt him, but he needed to break through the barrier. 'It probably is.'

She stepped away. Physically and mentally. 'I'm too frustrated to talk to you any more today, Finn.'

Finn watched her go. Damn her. Well, he wasn't chasing her every time she got the huffs.

* * *

By Wednesday Finn was looking for Evie. He'd had three horrendous nights' sleep, the pain was getting worse and he'd dropped his keys beside his car this morning and they'd almost gone down a manhole. Maybe he did need to consider the op.

Now, for the first time in his life, he wanted to share his thoughts with another person. Apparently that was what she wanted, but Evie was giving him the cold shoulder, and now he couldn't find her. Maybe he'd driven her away with his disgusting temper but he'd thought she had more staying power than that.

'There you are.' She was suturing a boy's hand in the emergency room theatre and she looked amazing. He felt like hell.

'I've been here on and off for the last three days, Finn. What can I do for you?'

Well, she couldn't do much for him while she had that laceration to fix. 'Lunch. At one. At Pete's. Talk about that thing we talked about. That suit you?'

Evie didn't smile but he had the suspicion she was having trouble keeping it in. That made him smile. 'Don't be late.'

Emily, Evie and Lily finally made it to coffee.

Emily invited them all to the baby shower and then stopped and reached across and squeezed Evie's hand. 'So how is Finn?'

'I can tell you girls because I know you don't gossip.' Evie lifted her head and they could see she was okay. Emily was glad. 'Cranky as a cut snake but I actually think I'm finally getting through.'

Lily grinned. 'If anyone can—you can!'

Evie smiled. 'Early days yet, but I'm quietly confident. How are you and Luke going, Lily?'

Lily's face lit up and there really wasn't a need for her words. 'I'm in seventh heaven.'

They both looked at Emily. 'And what about you and Marco?'

'It's complicated.'

'It always is.'

Emily sighed. 'I'm just going with the flow but I'm scared of getting too close. It's not long till he leaves.'

Evie nodded. 'At least he's here for your birthday on Friday.'

Emily sighed again. 'Annie's been onto you. And I don't even know if he'll come.'

Lily grinned. 'We discussed it while she was in hospital and of course he'll come.'

'I hope nobody spends money on me!'

Lily shook her head. 'I know you hate that. Just friends for tea. I told Annie I didn't think it was a good idea to surprise someone who's just come off nights. So she knows I was going to tell you.'

'Finn's coming.' The other two girls looked at Evie.

'No wonder you're quietly confident,' Lily said.

The next two days flew by. Emily didn't see Marco as the theatres were particularly busy, and she knew she would see him on Friday for Annie's appointment.

Then there was the looming non-surprise party but she couldn't worry about that. She had no doubt that Lily and Evie would have her best interests at heart even if it was the last thing she wanted. Inside a little voice whispered plaintively and wondered if Marco would come.

* * *

Emily's birthday started on Friday with a busy shift in the early hours and Annie's post-ultrasound appointment was scheduled before Emily could have her after-work sleep.

Happy birthday just didn't seem the same when you wanted your bed.

So when Marco and Annie decided to talk about her, not to her, during the appointment, Emily's sense of humour was far from tickled.

Annie lay on the examination couch as Marco palpated her abdomen. Ah, Marco thought. Even abdominally they could tell Annie's baby was growing. 'So this baby of yours is feeling better. See the height of your belly has come up to here, that is more than a centimetre.'

'That's what the ultrasonographer said. It's great.' Annie sat up. 'So when are you taking my mother out?'

Marco helped her step down and studiously avoided looking at Emily. 'Do you think I should?'

Annie tilted her head and for a moment she looked older than her sixteen years. 'How many more days do you have to waste?'

She was correct. Marco could not resist a glance across the room. Emily had turned and walked over to the window to look out over the harbour. A delightful pink tide had risen to her ears. He had always admired that soft curve of her neck. He lowered his voice. 'Not many. But perhaps your mother has seen enough of me.'

He saw Annie glance at her mother's back. Mischief danced in those green eyes so like Emily's. 'She likes you.' She shrugged and grinned at him. 'I like you.

And she doesn't have much fun. She seems to think that apart from work she's bad if she's away from me.'

'That's enough, you two. I'm not some charity that needs supporting.' She glared at her daughter then at Marco, and he had to smile at the fire in her eyes. He knew she was a passionate woman. He'd seen what she could do to butter with a knife.

'I think your mother needs to rest so she can enjoy her day. We are *finito* here. Your baby is doing as well as I hoped.'

'Will we see you tonight at Mum's party?' It seemed nothing would suppress Annie's intention to meddle.

'I have a very long theatre list but as soon as it is over it would be my pleasure to come.' He looked across at Emily. 'Is this fine with you?

Emily sighed and nodded. Her weary smile reminded him of the day of Annie's surgery and how he'd wished then to tuck her into a feather bed. And that had been before Emily had shown him a world he hadn't believed existed. His heart squeezed painfully in his chest as he acknowledged he'd become drawn into the magic world of the Cooper women. It would be hard to leave.

'Of course.' She crossed the room and held out her hand like she had the first day he'd met her. He took it and lifted it to his lips. '*Buon compleanno*. Happy birthday, Emily.'

Emily slept surprisingly well—perhaps because of the news Annie's baby was better, or maybe because of the truce between her and Marco. Or the fact she would see him tonight.

When she woke Lily and Annie and Rodney had

quietly done all the work and she could just sit back and enjoy.

Emily's party was a huge success. Pete's Bar had catered and he'd outdone himself with mini beef pies and brilliant entrées that melted in the mouth and kept coming so that the little alcohol imbibed was soaked up nearly as fast as it went down.

Annie's portable music system belted out songs everyone knew and a few of Annie's strange modern ones she couldn't resist, though Rodney kept a firm eye on the content in honour of Emily's advancing age and delicate sensibilities.

The girls, unbeknownst to Emily, had requested gifts but set with a price limit to two dollars. That guaranteed some hilarious choices.

The paediatrican, Teo, had declared himself fairy godfather and handed out the gift-wrapped surprises one by one to Emily. There was something about a wide and mischievious Polynesian grin and a man with a pink wand that made everyone smile.

His new wife, Zoe, kept slipping up for a sit on the fairy godfather's knee whenever there was a vacancy and Emily shared the envious glances from other single women at the blatant happiness that shone from Zoe's face.

Finn was there, not scowling quite as hard as usual, and when Evie handed their gift to Emily, a flashing faux bejewelled tiara, she looked more relaxed than she had for a while.

Lily and Luke were cuddled up in the corner discreetly, chuckling over the pair of his-and-hers shower caps they'd given Emily, and Annie and Rodney had splashed out on a weather vane for the back yard that they thought Emily would laugh at.

Emily smiled and thanked everyone and had a good time, but she couldn't help wonder if Marco would manage to slip across for half an hour before it all ended. Teo had said he'd finished his operating list late but at least it was finished. Not that she should be getting in any deeper with a man who was leaving but it was so hard not to look forward to just seeing him. Even feeling his presence and basking a little in the unmistakable pleasure he seemed to have in her company was worth it.

Someone touched her on the shoulder and as she turned slowly she knew even from that light caress whose hand it was. She couldn't help the pleasure that welled. 'Well, hello, there. You made it.'

His eyes crinkled as he smiled down at her. 'I heard there was a particularly delightful princess coming tonight.'

He tweaked the silver crown Emily had forgotten she wore and she grinned up at him. 'All the best princesses wear jewels like this.'

'And *buon compleannao*. Happy birthday, again, beautiful Emily.' He handed her his present.

She felt the package with her eyes shut then opened them still mystified. 'You know it can't be worth more than two dollars?'

He grinned. 'Of course.'

She undid the wrapping and then she smiled with a wobble of her lip because suddenly she wanted to cry. 'It's beautiful.' She looked up at him mistily. 'Thank you.'

'Let me see!' Annie had dragged Rodney across to

welcome Marco and she looked down at the little pink mouse with wheels. 'Huh? So what does it do?'

Marco took the mouse from Emily and wound the key. Then he bent down and pointed it towards the wall. It zipped along in erratic directions until finally it hit the skirting board. Emily got the giggles and her daughter looked at her.

Annie tugged Rodney's hand to go back to the music. 'That's a weird present,' Emily heard her say, and the giggles came back.

Marco watched her indulgently. 'Did you sleep today after Annie's appointment?'

'Of course. My usual four hours. It's been a big week for you, too.'

'Unlike you, I at least go back to my bed at night. Do you still have to do this night shift? Your daughter is old enough now to not need you to work such abnormal hours.'

She shrugged. 'It's what I do. One day I will stop but someone has to pay the bills.'

Marco frowned. He could understand that. And it was none of his business. He needed to remember that. In fact, he was mad even turning up here, but he did hate it that Emily was as tired as she'd looked that morning. Had worried about her all day at the back of his mind during his surgery list.

For the last few years his financial concerns had improved so much they'd been delegated to a financial planner. A very good one. Never again would he worry where his next meal came from, or even his next house should he wish to purchase one, but he didn't like the idea that Emily had such concerns.

Emily frowned at him and he realised he'd over-stepped the boundaries of their relationship. Again. He didn't even know why he'd started that conversation and she had every right to look at him strangely. He changed topic abruptly. 'I was pleased with Annie's ultrasound today.'

'She's happy. She asked when you were coming over again for a barbecue.'

'Is that an invitation?' He had become so needy it sickened him.

'You know you're welcome any time.'

But would he see her alone? He had his other gift to give. Annie he enjoyed, she made him smile, but it seemed like a year since he'd had Emily to himself. 'It's a shame I can't run you home after the party.'

She smiled and in her beautiful eyes he saw the acknowledgement that she too missed their time together but accepted the reality of no future. 'That would be hard when I live here.'

'I could drive you around the block. Then drop you home.' It seemed his heart was not yet ready to listen to reason.

'Or you could just stay back when everyone goes.' Perhaps her heart wasn't ready, either. She tilted her head. 'But I don't know if night-time is a good time to be alone with you, Marco.'

Now he could not give in. 'It could be a very good time.'

'That's what I mean.' Wistful perhaps. He hoped.

'Afraid?' Always a trump card with Emily. The dare.

'Of you?' She arched her brows. 'Not likely. I've been stuck to a wall upside down in a ride with you.'

He laughed. Could feel the lightness of heart that he had come to realise was how he felt whenever he was with Emily. 'So may I stay?'

She glanced around. Everyone was starting to leave. The party was almost over and what mischief could they get into when Annie was here? What harm could be done with sharing his company just a little longer? 'Of course. But you can explain to Annie. I'll just say goodbye to people. Do you want to come?'

Not really. Was it wise to advertise the fact they were together? Perhaps he needed to get over this aversion to being paired with one woman. Paired with Emily. He had never worried about parading a beautiful woman on his arm before. He would be gone and forgotten in another couple of weeks. So why was this different?

'As you wish.' There must have been the remains of his discomfort in his voice because she swivelled back to face him.

'Is there a problem?'

'No.' He thought about it. Tasted his reasoning. Fear? Fear of what? 'No, there isn't. I'm sorry. Let us say goodbye together.'

She looked at him strangely, as well she might, but he'd had an epiphany. He realised he was proud to be seen with Emily. Even if it was for a few short weeks he would carry the memories with him for a long time and he was far from ashamed that she enjoyed his company.

He held out his hand and smiled at her. 'Come.'

She took his hand. Grinned at his word choice. 'It's just Evie and Finn and Lily and Luke mostly. They organised this with Annie.'

When he shook hands Finn grinned and Marco acknowledged the satire behind the smile. Evie hugged him but he was not sure why and Luke and Lily smiled warmly when Emily said Marco was staying for a while.

Maybe it wasn't so bad to face the world with someone you were proud of. He realised he was proud of Emily. Proud of the amazing woman she was. He just hoped she felt the same. But he would like at least a few moments alone with her.

'Would you like to go for a walk?'

'With a big strong man as my escort? Why not? I don't usually walk around here at night on my own.'

The thought sent a shiver of disquiet through him. Emily alone at night. 'I should hope not.'

Emily heard the possessiveness in his voice. Couldn't help but smile at it. A woman could get used to a man who wished to ensure her safety. Wanted to protect her. A woman could—but Emily wouldn't have that opportunity. Marco would be gone and she would be travelling alone again shortly. 'I could walk at night if wanted to.'

He laughed. 'And if you had a butterknife, any man would be afraid.'

She called out to Annie to say they'd be down at the wharf and they walked out into the street together.

They walked with purpose, hand in hand, neither quite relaxed enough to dawdle—perhaps the idea of time marching on kept their pace fast, as if they could squeeze as much distance covered into the short time they had together.

The sensation of walking with Marco by her side seemed bitter-sweet for Emily until they came to the pier where the ferries came in.

He reached into his pocket for the gift box that had arrived by courier from the airport. More notice of her birthday would have been good. 'I have something else for your birthday. Something from Italy to remember me by.'

It didn't sound as good as he'd hoped when he said it like that.

She took the box hesitantly and he shook his head. 'I do not buy much. It will give me pleasure to give you this.'

She nodded, smiled up at him, and he savoured her reluctance to tear the paper. Finally it was open and the brilliantly hued heart-shaped pendant shimmered in the streetlight. Such brilliant greens that matched her eyes. Exactly as he'd wished.

'It is Murano crystal. Made in Venice.' He took it from her and indicated he would help her fasten it. 'May I?'

'Of course.' She turned and exposed her nape and his stupid fingers shook as he fastened it.

'It's beautiful. Thank you.' She leant up and kissed his cheek. 'I will treasure it.'

And I will treasure the memories of you, she thought, and turned away to hide her face from him.

She pointed out the big old house on the water. 'So my little house is tucked in behind there.'

Marco stared thoughtfully at the huge white mansion. 'And that was your grandfather's childhood home?'

'Yes.' They both looked at the untidy lawn that ran down to the water's edge. 'But it was sold well before he met Gran to pay his father's debts.'

A ferry glided in, churned the water, and reversed

away again as they leant on the rail and gazed over Sydney harbour.

There was a certain melancholy in their comfortable silence. 'Would you like to catch the next ferry to Luna Park for an hour?'

She smiled and shook her head. 'I have my mouse now.'

He lifted her hand to his mouth and kissed her palm. The movement drew her towards him and she stepped in closer. By the light of the streetlamp his chiselled features stood out starkly and she lifted her other hand to stroke his cheek. 'Thank you for coming to my party.'

'I needed to see those decorations in all their glory.' She was going to joke back when he broke in again.

'Already I miss you, Emily.'

Her brows drew together and she looked across at him. 'We must be sensible.' And then he kissed her and neither felt very sensible at all as he pulled her into the shadows away from the pool of yellow light cast by the streetlamp.

Marco's mouth trailed her throat and she slipped her fingers in between the buttons of his shirt. Splayed them across his chest because who knew if she would ever feel this chest again? The warmth of reality, so firm and strong beneath her palm. She turned her head so she could hear his heart beat like a drum against her ear. Then his mouth came down again and he lifted her, spun her in the way she loved, and she wrapped her arms around his shoulders as she stared down into his face. A face she saw so often now in her dreams. A face that would soon be gone, and the added fuel of that thought deepened her response as she lost herself in his embrace.

Rodney's running footsteps penetrated and Marco lowered her until her feet touched down as the kiss broke. His arm steadied them as they turned.

'Here you are!' The relief on Rodney's face sent a shiver of alarm through Emily's whole body. 'You have to come home. She's got pains.'

Emily could feel the fear balloon in her chest. She should have noticed something was wrong. And she hadn't been there. She'd been out kissing Marco in the shadows. What sort of mother was she?

The three of them jogged up the hill until they reached the house and then Marco followed more slowly. This was not good. 'What time did the pains start?' he asked Rodney.

'Just after you left. But she didn't tell me till just now. I was going to ring Emily but she wouldn't let me.'

Stupido. 'Afraid of the false alarm. Next time you tell her she must. Do not take no.'

Rodney nodded but he looked alarmed that he might have done the wrong thing. Marco patted his shoulder. 'It is good you are here and that you came for us. Wait. I will see what is happening.'

Before he could make his way to Annie's room Emily was back. 'Her waters have broken. She's in full labour.'

So. As he'd feared. 'Take your car. It will be faster than an ambulance and we both have the experience. I will phone ahead and they will meet us with a trolley.'

Emily's eyes were anguished and he wanted to pull her in close and comfort her. But there would be time later.

'What if the baby comes?'

He squeezed her shoulder. 'Then we will manage. It is our work. We are minutes from the hospital. Get the car and I will carry her out.'

Emily couldn't remember the drive. Just that this was real and it was happening. And she hadn't been there. Rodney held Annie's hand and Emily tried desperately to pretend her daughter was a woman she didn't know. Her voice was calm, steady, matter-of-fact when Annie started to panic, was this transition stage already, and deep inside Emily wanted to scream and beat her chest and say '*No!* I'm sorry.'

They arrived in the ambulance bay within minutes and, thanks to Marco's call, were transported immediately to the birthing suite where others were already assembled.

Teo was there, and his team from the NICU was there, even one who had been here when Annie herself had been born.

And always Marco. Calm, organised, directing the administration of drugs, acknowledging there was little they could do to halt the birth of Annie's baby but secure in the knowledge the best of neonatal care was waiting.

Twenty-seven weeks. Thirteen weeks early. Emily was transported back through the years to the day her own baby had been born. To the strangeness of the NICU, to the fragility of her own newborn. But that would be nothing to what Annie would go through.

Her granddaughter would be tiny. Like a doll in a man's palm, wrinkled and skinny and bright pink with blood too close to the surface through too few layers of skin. Little eyes barely able to open. Too tiny to fight any infection, would forget to breathe, struggle to eat. It would go on for months. And always the risk she would get sick and not see the next day.

Why? Why had this happened? How could she have prevented it? She should never have left the house with Marco.

Marco saw the fears cross Emily's face. Wave after wave. Battered but never beaten. He wanted to stride across the room and shelter her. Calm her storm of fears, but he couldn't. Tell her it would be all right but he wasn't so sure it would.

In his mind he reassured himself. She was strong, she didn't need him. Not someone who would be leaving before this whole drama had played out.

All he knew was this baby was coming. Then Annie's baby arrived.

The next hour was fraught as Rosebud fought for life.

They all moved down to the NICU. Annie, shaking with the hormones of labour, in a wheelchair, Rodney holding her hand, his eyes red from emotion, Emily hovering, explaining, supporting… And Marco…stood apart.

Teo orchestrated the recovery of a perilously ill neonate with his team of intensivists. Men and women who worked like clockwork, a day in their lives pretty much like another, but not for the Cooper family.

Check tube, intubation, the sound of mechanical lungs breathing such minimal breaths for tiny lungs. Rhythmic, relentless, a breath even if she didn't want to. IV lines in veins like patterns drawn by ballpoint, incredibly thin and fragile vessels captured and taped.

Skin dots attached to cardiac monitors. Murmured voices discussing the life of your child in equations and gradients and percentages of oxygen for the very prem.

Marco had seen it all many times before. Had done his time in NICU as a registrar, had chosen the maternal side of birth in preference to this very prem duelling dance with death. Standing there, he knew why.

For Emily, as she eased back away from the open crib until her spine was against the cold nursery wall, suddenly she felt disconnected. Unable to believe this was happening.

It took her back sixteen years. Even though Annie had never been as fragile as this baby, the feelings were the same.

Fear, helplessness and such a sense of loss for the beautiful, tranquil birth and introduction her tiny granddaughter should have had if she'd stayed where she should have.

She sucked in another breath. But she would stay strong for Annie, strong for little Rosebud, even strong for Rodney, who had surprised her with his caring, his inability to hide how much he adored Annie and looked up to her, and his absolute devotion to his tiny daughter.

She wiped a disobedient tear away. She wasn't going to cry. Not here. Not now.

God, she was so sick of being strong.

Sixteen years ago she'd stood against her parents and their wish that she should have her baby adopted, had refused their attempt to sweep her pregnancy and their granddaughter under the mat of public scrutiny.

Her parents had come once to see Annie after the

birth, and had refused to even hold her, and that had been when Emily had decided her daughter wouldn't grow up in such a house of disapproval.

On discharge from hospital she'd packed her school things, the few pieces of baby clothes she'd managed to collect and headed to Gran's, where she had been welcomed with open arms.

Emily had been determined, had begun to plan the future for her daughter and herself, but still inside she'd needed to prove to everyone that she was not just a good mother but the best mother anywhere.

Now she needed to be strong again. She saw Marco watching her. Saw his concern, and for a moment she was tempted to ask for help, pass some of her load across to those broad shoulders, but what if she did? What if she weakened and then suddenly he was gone? What would she do then?

What if having to deal with Marco's departure eroded the well of strength she'd always relied on? She didn't go to anyone when she struggled with life. She just got on with it. The thought terrified her. Soon he'd be gone. If she took strength from him she'd have to start being alone all over again.

And she didn't have the emotional fortitude to spare. Annie and Rosebud needed her. She wouldn't let them down again. It was better she carried the load alone, like she would have to when Marco was gone.

This was family pain of a different sort. Marco watched from across the room.

He ached for Annie, for her tiny baby and especially for Emily, but he could not become involved. Could not cross the floor to stand by her side, no matter how much he wanted to.

She needed someone strong, someone who would always be there for her. He glanced around the room and still she stood alone.

But who would that be?

Such isolation. Suddenly he saw that she was like him. Alone. Isolated. Yet she had not let it affect her ability to welcome people into her circle of caring, like she had admitted him. She made friends, stood by them, opened herself to risk. This he could not do, had never learned, but maybe, one day slowly, he could absorb the rudiments he'd learned from Emily. If he crossed the room, what could he do? He felt so helpless.

Did she blame him? Could he have foreseen Annie would go into prem labour? What if he had kept her in hospital longer? But he knew any other hospital would have done the same. And the speed that she'd laboured would never have been successfully stopped. He had to go to her.

'Emily?' He touched Emily's shoulder. Brushed the hair back from her eyes. 'It is good Rosebud had already had her hydrocortisone and this will stand the lungs in good stead.'

She looked at him but he wasn't sure she could see him. 'I know. But still she's so fragile.'

His hand fell and then he lifted it again. He'd pushed through his fear of becoming too involved with this family. She would not push him away now. 'What can I do? How can I help you?'

She looked at him. Stepped back a pace out of range of his hand. 'I'm fine. We'll get through this. It's what we do. It's what I do. I'm sorry, Marco. I need space. I need to be here for my daughter. For Rosebud.'

No. He could not accept that. Finally a moment that was not about him or his past. This was about Emily, who needed to take his help. He would fight to help her; for the first time in his life he would fight for a woman, he would find a way.

She thought she did not need him. But she did. 'Let me be here for you. Be here for Annie and for her Rosebud. I can be a shoulder to lean on. Perhaps you should learn to share the load.'

'With who, Marco? With you? A man who has already turned my life upside down. Already made me yearn for things I can't have. What we had was good. But it's finished. I don't have time for me right now.' She glanced at her granddaughter. 'Look at her. She's as fragile as a butterfly on her little open cot.' She shook her head. 'I don't have time for you.'

Appropriate for a man passing though. The pain sliced through him like it had in the lift when she'd stepped away from him. Perhaps he should get used to that pain. There was a greater one coming when he flew from Sydney. Marco nodded. He wasn't sure he was finished, but at this moment he wasn't helping. So he walked away.

What did he expect? The doubts eased in as the distance between he and Emily grew. Why should someone want and need him? Nobody ever had. Except for his work. Always he had his work. So back to work and then he would finish here before he caused himself, or Emily, more pain.

But it was much harder than he expected to walk away from the Coopers. Even more reason to run. He passed Finn and Evie as they came in but he didn't stop.

CHAPTER TWELVE

'I HOPE Emily's granddaughter is okay.' Evie and Finn stood outside the door to Finn's penthouse after visiting the Coopers in the NICU. This was the first time Evie had been back to his flat because they'd both been absolutely snowed under with work—and to be honest she was a little nervous.

'Born on her grandmother's birthday. So I guess if she has as much guts as Emily, she'll make it.'

Finn opened the door and gestured for Evie to precede him. She couldn't help a sliding glance at the wall in his apartment she'd become very acquainted with the last time she was here.

Finn saw the pink in her cheeks and raised his eyebrows mockingly. She walked swiftly across the room and perched on the edge of the leather lounge. 'I think that's the nicest thing I've ever heard you say, Finn. You sound almost human.'

'Hmph.' He shut the door with a click. She remembered that from last time too. Goose-bumps feathered along her arms. 'Don't tell anybody.' He crooked his finger. 'Come here.'

She raised her own brows. 'You come here.' Actually,

she didn't think her legs would carry her with the way he was looking at her now.

'Okay.' He was across the room in three longs strides and his hand came down and captured hers. He guided her up until she stood hard against his body. 'Let's not talk.'

He was so solid against her. She'd never get used to being this close to Finn. She never wanted to stop being this close to Finn. But she needed to know his decision. 'You said you had something to tell me.'

'In a minute.' His finger lifted her chin and slowly his face came down. 'I need something first.' His mouth took hers with an aching need that grew more searching, more demanding of her strength, exposed her aching love for this embittered man, tried her by the fire of his fears and her own, and the finality of his decision brought tears to her eyes.

He stepped back but she followed him. Thrust her hips against him to anchor him. 'Tell me what you've decided about the operation.'

'It's booked for next Monday.'

The words fell into the quiet room like drips of water in a cave, yet the impact was a ripple of emotion she didn't know how to ride.

She shivered and for a moment she wanted him to change his mind. Not risk the worst-case scenarios of mobility loss or even death. But the alternative was never going to be an option. His pain would continue to spiral upwards as the shrapnel buried deeper, the motor loss in his hands and arms would grow more unpredictable, and the medications would become more useless.

Her arms crept around his waist. 'Then we should make the most of the time we have.'

Finn looked down at her and imperceptibly his face softened. 'Always to the point, Dr Lockheart.'

'The point is, Dr Kennedy, I love you and always will.'

'Always?' Mockingly again but there was a thread of uncertainty in Finn's voice that brought the tears to her eyes.

'It's terminal.'

'Thanks for bringing that up.'

'For God's sake, Finn. Take me to bed.'

He laughed, threaded his fingers through hers, and drew her through to his room.

A week later the NICU was quiet when Emily called in on the Friday morning after her shift. The lights were dim and it seemed more peaceful than usual. 'All the babies must be behaving,' Emily murmured to herself.

It had been a slow couple of nights and sometimes she wished for the craziness of a busy ward that made the wee small hours fly and the sun come up before she knew it was on its way. Especially when she wanted to divert her mind from drifting to a tall, dark Italian who made her toes curl for what might have been.

Her eyes ached with tiredness, that was all, and the dull headache was because it was nearly time for bed and she hadn't been sleeping as well as she usually did. It was probably all the worry of Rosebud.

She was getting used to her name.

There was an empty chair beside her crib and Emily sank down into it. When she put her chin on her hand she could just sit and soak in the regular in and out of little lungs growing stronger every day. So tiny. So amazingly tough.

She realised that her granddaughter was growing and unfurling like a little blossom. A bud. A rosebud? Emily smiled. Okay. She liked the name.

She looked sturdier, less translucent, and while Emily sat there Rosebud's little arms flexed and her eyelids flickered.

'Hello there, little one.' Emily said softly, and held her breath as Rosebud turned her head and opened her eyes. Emily bit her lip. 'Hello.' Such a tiny little pixie face yet so like her mother's. The little eyelids fluttered and then shut again and Emily sighed back into the chair. 'Wow. Thank you.'

Marco watched Emily from the corner of the room. He carried the coffee he'd taken to drinking with his *piccola rosa*, his little rose, before he started his day. He enjoyed the few moments with his tiny friend but was always careful to be absent when her grandmother was due.

He did not wish to cause Emily pain, though often he stayed, as now, just to catch a glimpse.

He saw her smile from across the room and it pierced his heart. He did not know how much more of this he could stand.

He'd added cases every day to the end of his list so that he could shorten the time he was in Sydney. Perhaps he had done enough. He would look for flights tonight.

Something made Emily glance across the room. Marco stood silently in the corner. How long had he been there? She really didn't think she could do this right now. Every day she had to remind herself he was leaving. Less than a week now.

Perhaps by then this aching wound he'd left in her life would have begun to heal but she was afraid that it hadn't yet ripped all the way to the bone like it would when he flew out.

Now he knew she'd seen him. He was walking towards her. Tall and solemn he still filled her with that fluttery awareness, the intrinsic magnetism she could barely hold out against, and her heart begged her to reach out and touch him.

Emily tucked her hands into her lap. 'I didn't expect to see you here.'

He inclined his head and spoke quietly so as not to startle their baby. 'I visit Rosebud when I can. We are old friends.'

So he came when he was sure he would not run into her. Well, that was what she'd asked for. Unfortunately she could imagine the early mornings or late evenings with Marco and Rosebud in the quiet nursery, communing in the semi-darkness, and she felt the pain of exclusion.

The image of her and Marco, sitting together at those times, the seductive concept this tiny infant could have been shared as a grandchild. She looked up and the spasm that crossed his face told her he was thinking the same. She tried to hold back the tears that prickled behind her eyes as her wounded heart gaped a little wider. 'You make friends easily.'

'But not keep them.' He tried to catch her eye again but this time she wouldn't let him.

She studied her granddaughter intently, checked

the readings on the machines, examined the make and model of the open cot, looked anywhere but at him. 'Perhaps they feel you cannot be relied on.'

He stepped closer and she could feel the hairs on her arms rise in anticipation. Couldn't help the deeper breath she took to inhale the subtle tang of his after-shave, the intrinsic masculine scent of Marco, that she would recognise anywhere. 'I would be here if you let me, Emily.' The words settled over her like a hug she couldn't touch.

Emily stood up. Picked up the bag she had for Annie. This was survival because if she didn't move now she'd throw herself onto his chest. 'It's called a short-term fix, Marco. The cure is worse than the disease.'

'How come Marco leaves every time you arrive to visit me?' Annie was straight to the point.

Emily tried not to wince. 'Do you think he does?' She knew he did. But that was what she'd asked for, space. It was hard enough without Annie on her case. Their bitter-sweet encounter in the NICU—bitter on her side and sweet on his—had almost done her in. The guilt for her harsh words ate away at her compo-sure and she wasn't sure if she could take Annie's cen-sure as well.

'I hadn't noticed.' Liar. Emily looked up. 'I thought Rosebud looked amazing this morning when I went across to the NICU after my shift.' Emily adjusted some flowers in a vase as she smiled brightly. 'She even turned her head and opened her eyes for a few seconds.'

Instantly diverted Annie smiled and nodded. 'I know. She did it when I went down. Dr Teo is very happy with her progress and she's tolerating the tiny bit of milk from me down the tube really well.'

Emily's day brightened a little. 'That's wonderful, darling. A week being stable makes a big difference to a prem baby.'

Annie's eyes shone. 'Rodney's coming in early because they think we'll be able to have her naked against my skin for a while today.'

Emily smiled mistily. 'Kangaroo care. If it's after my sleep, can you ring me? I'd love to see her snuggle up to you.'

'You do look tired. Are you sleeping okay without me at home?'

'I'm fine.' She smiled and then nodded at Annie's magnificent cleavage. 'I see your milk's come in.'

Annie poked her chest out and looked down with a smug smile. 'Did you know that my breasts make milk that suits the exact premature age my baby is?'

'Yep. Mother nature knows best.'

'That is so cool.' Then she fanned herself. 'Actually, my boobs are quite hot and sore but I'm telling myself I'd be more upset if they weren't working.'

Emily pulled a brown paper parcel from her bag. 'I have a present for you.'

'More presents?' Annie clapped her hands and Emily shook her head.

'You're spoilt but I think you'll appreciate these.' Emily laughed and tipped two opened disposable nappies out of her bag onto the bedside table and they rocked like little cradles. 'They're frozen. I poured some water on them and put them in the freezer and now you can open them out and wrap them around your breasts. It's just for the next twenty-four hours while you're engorged.'

'That's crazy.' Annie wasn't sure she was convinced this would be a good idea.

'Try them and see.' Emily helped Annie ease the crunchy nappies down into her bra and wrapped the cold netting around her hot breasts.

Her mouth pursed as she looked at her mother. 'Oh. Wow. That feels so-o-o good.'

'Excellent. And you just put them back into this plastic bag and pop them back in the freezer to re-freeze.'

'Awesome.'

'I bring the coolest gifts.' Mother and daughter grinned at each other.

Annie patted her chest and sighed blissfully. Then she sat up. 'Speaking of cool gifts, Marco brought me a card and more phone credit so I could ring Rodney whenever I wanted.'

Emily struggled to keep the smile on her face. 'That was nice of him.'

Annie's attention sharpened. 'Which brings me back to my original question. Have you two stopped seeing each other?'

Emily studied her fingers as she screwed up the brown paper bag on the bench. 'We were never really seeing each other. Did he say something?'

'Oh. Pleeease, Mum. You guys are hotter than my boobs for each other. And, no, he didn't say anything. He's a clam, like you.'

A clam. Where had she heard that? Emily drew a deep breath and faced her daughter with the truth.

'Look. He's going soon, Emily. You and Rosebud are my priorities.'

She slowed her words even more. 'I need to concentrate on what's important in my life and at this moment you and Rosebud top that list. I don't have space in my life for a doomed love affair.'

Annie wasn't having that. 'Why not?'

Emily closed her eyes and opened them again. 'Because I want to spend time with you. And my granddaughter. And be here for you both.'

Annie stared at her thoughtfully, chewed her lip, and finally sighed. 'I don't want you to take this the wrong way, Mum, but…' She reached out and took her mother's hand. Squeezed it. 'I'll always want your support and your love, it's just…maybe it's time you should think about your own life. Your own happiness.'

Annie drew a deep breath and began to speak faster, as if afraid her mother wouldn't understand if she didn't get the whole concept out before she was interrupted. 'Heck—even embrace being the wonderful, gorgeous woman you are and not just be a mum to me. Rodney's here for us, Mum. He's Rosebud's father. She has us and I have him. You deserve a man who cares too.'

Emily gulped, felt the sting of tears, and she forced them back with iron control, but she didn't know how she was going to get the words out. Her throat had closed and another dull ache opened in her chest. Imagine if she lost both Marco *and* Annie!

She squeezed the words out. 'I see.'

'No, you don't.' Annie climbed out from under the covers, took Emily's hand and pulled her down until they were sitting side by side on the edge of the bed.

'You look devastated. Don't be. You're my mum, my hero, for goodness' sake, there is nobody in this world who can do what you do, make things happen like you can.' Annie squeezed her hand again. 'You're amazing.'

Annie shrugged. Patted her mother's hand like she was the mentor here. 'I just think you might have found an awesome guy who actually has an inkling how cool you really are, and you're beating him off with a stick.'

Annie hugged her mother carefully, and the ice in her bra crackled between them, until Emily gave a watery smile. 'Please don't be hurt because I'm actually thinking of you for a change.'

A lone tear trickled annoyingly down her cheek and Emily brushed it away impatiently. Tried to take in her daughter's words and the sense behind them, but the flicker of fear hovered in her throat. What if she did lose both of them? And it was already too late for Marco. 'But he's going.'

Annie snorted and for a moment there she sounded like Gran. 'Well, for goodness' sake, do something about that. If anybody can, you're the one.' She looked at her mother. 'But you'd better go home and go to bed for a couple of hours before you take on the weekend. You look tired. We have the baby shower tomorrow afternoon in the NICU.'

It was only an afternoon tea but Rosebud nearly missed it. Her see-through skin tinged yellow like a baby banana with jaundice. Not surprising really. Her tiny liver was so immature it couldn't handle the breaking down of her unneeded blood cells now that she was in the outside world.

It just meant Rosebud couldn't watch with her painted blindfold sunglasses on as she lay under phototherapy. But the air was warm, and love and caring drifted her way from her family and their friends, and the purple light that shone on her was doing the job her liver couldn't.

'Never mind,' Rodney said. 'She sleeps a lot anyway, like her mother.' And everyone smiled.

The original baby shower had been planned for today at Emily and Annie's home.

For obvious reasons that wasn't possible but the NICU girls who'd helped look after Annie during those first few difficult weeks sixteen years ago had decided Annie's own daughter held a special place in their hearts and they wanted to be a part of Rosebud's baby shower.

Along with the fact that most of the guest list worked in the hospital, it was a crowded but well-behaved affair.

Rodney brought one friend, Jack, a big, blond, punk-haired and pierced bouncer, who turned out to be a favourite once they could stop him washing his hands and making sure he was clean enough to come in.

Jack kept punching Rodney in the shoulder and telling him, 'You're so lucky, man.' And Rodney just nodded and glowed and hugged Annie.

Rodney had brought Annie a gift-wrapped box with tiny rosebud earrings and for his daughter the smallest bracelet with her name engraved on it and a little pink rabbit.

Emily had found the softest little pink lace cap for Rosebud to wear. She would have liked to show it to Marco but he wasn't there. She'd have liked to show Marco lots of things but she had driven him away. Teo and Zoe brought exquisite tiny doll's clothes and Lily and Luke brought a doll to dress up after Rosebud grew out of them.

Even Finn and Evie showed and chose a magnificent pink shawl to take Rosebud home in when the time came.

Annie floated graciously around, thanking people.

Emily passed around fairy bread and tiny scones and jam and cream and held onto her pride for the maturity of her own daughter while she kept the tears at the back of her throat.

And Marco should be here. Even Annie had commented sadly that he must be very busy. Emily knew their last conversation had driven him away. Not surprisingly.

She couldn't deny his absence left an aching sense of loss she hoped nobody else saw, and she only had herself to blame.

All the while Rosebud slept on in her little sun bed, oblivious to the subdued good wishes from her departing guests.

When all was eaten, when presents were stored and everyone but the NICU staff had drifted away, Emily sat in the chair beside her granddaughter. Annie had gone out for the afternoon with Rodney instead of going back to the accommodation put aside for mothers with sick babies, so Emily was alone.

She gazed unseeingly at the open crib, tried to let the beeps of the machines wash over her, but seemed only able to replay her conversation with Marco from the previous morning.

Emily turned her head and stared with stinging eyes

at the little determined chin that poked out from under the eye protection. 'You're so like your mother.'

Her daughter's words circled around and around in her head. Even Annie's words in Marco's office came back to haunt her. Yes—she had tried to be everything for Annie. Had chosen the night shift so nobody could say she was leaving her baby for her gran to rear. Had pushed any thought of a relationship away because someone might say—or she might feel—she wasn't doing the job well enough. Perhaps it hadn't been those few men who had been lacking—but her. She just didn't have what it took for a man to fight for her. Or was it she that lacked the fight?

Footsteps and then Marco's voice came from behind her as his hand rested lightly on her shoulder. 'Did you have a nice party?'

She put her fingers up and over his hand. Felt the strength in those fingers that could be so gentle. Fingers that could caress her so eloquently they almost sang against her skin. So he had come. The overwhelming relief and comfort made her shoulders drop. Without turning, she said, 'Annie was sorry you couldn't make it.'

His hand tightened. 'Only Annie?'

CHAPTER THIRTEEN

'RODNEY missed you too,' Emily said, with the first tinge of humour she'd felt all day.

'Ah, my friend Rodney.' He stood behind her for a moment longer and then lifted his hand. She missed it already but he'd stepped away to bring a chair.

'May I?' When she nodded he placed it beside her so that they both faced Rosebud's open crib. 'You are very good to Rodney.'

Was she? 'Rodney is very good with Annie. If he wasn't, it would be a different story.'

'I can see that.' He smiled and she had to smile back because they both knew how protective she was of her daughter. 'But you do not hold his family history against him.'

She heard the dark taste of bitterness in his voice. Frowned at it as she tried to imagine where it had come from. 'Why would I do that?'

'Forgive me.' He shrugged. 'The first day you met Rodney, I too saw him, and overheard Annie tell you his brother was in jail. Your distress was clear.'

Emily had no idea where he was a going with this

but something warned her that was very important to Marco and therefore it was important to her.

She needed to be careful how she answered so she watched his face. Tried not to be distracted by how much she enjoyed just looking at him. 'That's got nothing to do with Rodney.'

He shrugged. 'How is this nothing to do with Rodney?'

'Why would it be? I didn't ask him to, but he explained how his brother became involved in a bad crowd, and now pays the price for that. I try to take people how I find them. Rodney is not the one in trouble and cannot be held accountable. He has a good heart and genuinely loves Annie and Rosebud.'

She shrugged. 'Still, they are very young and it will be hard to grow up at the same pace from this age—but that's for them to decide and discover for themselves.'

He raised his brows and she could see that he was surprised. 'So you expect them to move in together?'

She supposed that was liberal from an Italian male's point of view. 'I haven't come to that conclusion yet. Maybe not for a long time. But Rodney doesn't have a satisfactory place to stay and he wants to carry some of the load in caring for Rosebud when she comes home. We'll see. Maybe he'll stay weekends.'

'You are a very understanding person.'

Except to him. He should know she could be better at that. 'I'd be the pot calling the kettle black.'

He frowned. 'This is like fishing?'

'A colloquialism. Yes.' She smiled. 'I will miss you. And I'm sorry I pushed you away the other day.' There, she'd said it. She went on in a bright little voice that only just cracked. 'So, when do you leave?'

Marco heard the tiny element of distress and told himself he'd imagined it. 'Tomorrow. I have come to say goodbye.'

'Tomorrow.' More brightness. 'You didn't give yourself much down time to see Sydney.'

He glanced across at Rosebud. 'I've seen the important parts.' Glanced back at her and smiled and something in his expression made her eyes sting with emotion. 'I have been on the important rides.'

She turned to face him. Touched his sleeve and tried to smile. 'We had a lovely time. Thank you.'

So it ended, Marco thought. He looked across at her. Held his hand back forcibly so that he didn't caress her hair or run his finger down her cheek despite the overwhelming urge to do so. 'I will miss everyone here.' He was surprised how much. This was what happened when you opened your heart. The pain soaked in. As he deserved.

'And we will miss you.'

Perhaps they would. For a brief while until he was forgotten. He glanced at the baby girl with her sunglasses on. He would miss seeing Rosebud grow stronger, grow more alert and active, start to make noises. Cry louder. Demand food. Recognise her mother. Recognise her grandmother.

The impact of his next thought vibrated in his head. Now this tiny infant would never recognise him. He had to leave this woman and this baby and this family, and that tore his heart into tiny strips.

He stood up. Lifted his chair and put it against the wall and then he came back to her for the last time. 'Goodbye, Emily.'

Emerrrlee! Emily watched him turn, take two steps. Had she not thought Marco was worth the same fighting spirit she'd always found for Annie? Was the chance of happiness with Marco and perhaps his happiness with her as well at stake and she was willing to let him fly away? For ever?

'Marco?'

He stopped and she stood and crossed the space to him. 'Why do you have to go?'

He squared his shoulders and did not meet her eyes. 'Because that is what I do.'

She wanted him to look at her. 'Why?'

'Because I learnt this during my childhood.' Even with his chin averted she saw the pain cross his face. Felt his anguish. She so wanted to understand.

He went on. 'My childhood was a series of uprootings in the night. My earliest memories of hurriedly dressing, told to be silent, hide before questions were asked. Such memories burn holes in the psyche that I have not yet filled. Now my parents are dead and at most I have vowed never to return to the place I felt so branded by disgust. As a boy I learnt to accept that I am not good enough for any parent's daughter.' He lifted his head. 'Not good enough for you.'

No. That wasn't how she wanted him to leave. 'I think you're amazing!'

'Ah. The amazing Dr D'Arvello. My work is good.' Simple truth. 'You do not know of my family.'

She reached out and touched his sleeve. Felt the tension in his shoulder even through the fabric.

Marco wanted to squeeze her hand against his arm with his fingers so that she was welded to him. So he couldn't lose her. He could not believe he had told her some of his past. Never had this happened with a woman.

'Your family do not matter to me.' He heard her words but did not believe them. She went on. 'I know about you. The Marco we all care about. Of how much my family love you. Of your kindness and your strength and your amazing heart.'

Her words unmanned him. He shook his head. She had no concept. Could not know. 'My father.'

She lifted her fingers and stopped his words at his lips. Such gentle insistence. 'And you felt tainted by him. Like Rodney did.' Her words seeped into the wall he had guarded for all these years. Washed away the mud that had stuck to him for so long. Exposed his need to the daylight of her caring.

He hadn't thought of it like that but, yes, and the voice inside his head insisted, she had accepted Rodney for who he was.

She went on in that calm and almost steady voice, 'So if you didn't seek a relationship, nobody could say no?' She gave a strangled laugh. 'Imagine that. You and I are not dissimilar, you know.'

And the light cracked through like the peep of sunlight through one broken slat of a fastened shutter.

She felt that way too? Was this why no man had carried her off?

She lifted her chin high. Drew a breath and stared up into his eyes, and he could not look away, could feel the physical embrace though she wasn't touching him, such intimate connection as he stared into the depth of his Emily's green soul.

'I wish you could stay. Please don't go.' He shook his head and he saw she thought he was saying no. But it was in wonder of this woman. How did she have that strength? Risk all and stand before him so resolutely? Ask the question he hadn't realised he'd longed to hear. How could he have arrived at this moment in life and suddenly seen the light?

A light that blinded him. The light that was Emily.

'And if I stayed, would you share yourself with me? Share your family? Your heart?' He grinned and suddenly joy bubbled from within. Swept away the years of bitterness and fizzed in his bloodstream. 'Share your house?'

She pretended to frown at him but he was not fooled, could see a little of that joy in her face too now. 'That would depend on how long you were staying.'

'Ah,' he teased. 'That would depend on how long you would have me.'

She smiled slowly, with such tenderness and warmth he blinked. 'A long, long time.'

A sudden vision of her grandfather's family home. Renovations. Perhaps even extensions for all the children or grandchildren they would have. Little girls and boys running on the freshly mown grass. Perhaps another baby shower with tents and tiny pink cakes and women with sunshades all watching the children and the boats on the harbour. And Emily. Always Emily. 'Then in that case I have seen a house I wish to buy.'

She frowned. 'You've been looking at houses?'

'I didn't mean to.' He could do nothing but smile at her. Loving her confusion, loving her bravery, loving her. 'Someone I know has a house near you and I have grown very fond of your ferries and your harbour. And if I bought it, restored it to its former glory, perhaps you would move there with me. Make a gate in the side fence to join your grandmother's house. We would know our neighbours very well.' He could see Annie swinging Rosebud as she came through the gate to visit her mother. His daughter, his granddaughter, his family.

Emily's nerves were settling. She didn't know what he was talking about but there were more important things going on here than houses.

She couldn't believe she'd dared to ask. Dared to dream and give that dream a chance. Fought for him and very possibly, judging by the adoring look on his face, perhaps won. 'Do you think you'd be able to find work?' she teased.

'I am sure.' He smiled that smile that lifted her feet off the ground then whispered almost to himself, 'Never did I think I would say these words.'

He glanced at Rosebud, almost as if to ask permission, then back at Emily. Stared into her eyes and the love that shone from his face took her breath away. *'Amore mio, per favour, sposami.'* Then more strongly, again in English, as if something had been set free with the words in his native tongue. 'My love. Please. Be my wife.'

Emily stared into his beloved face. His wife! This man who had turned her life upside down, whose strength and kindness and skills had saved her family, and whose passion and warmth and caring had saved her.

She reached up, cradled his face and gently kissed his lips. 'With all my heart, my love.'

* * *

Three months later, at sunset, a three-masted brig drifted away from the wharf at Darling Harbour.

It seemed the captain was a real captain and could marry those aboard his ship once outside the heads.

At the bow of the ship, with his hands clenched behind his back, a tall, dark man stood anxiously, magnificently dressed in coat and tails, and waited for the ship to sail out to sea.

Marco drew in the salt-laden air and savoured the breeze at his back as he stared down the length of the ship, past the guests seated on the chairs arranged under the masts, all craning for a glimpse of Emily. His life had changed so much in the last precious months and it was all because of the woman he waited for.

As they'd arrived for the wedding Emily had decided each guest should be given a wristband that entitled them to free rides for the rest of the night at Luna Park after the wedding reception. They wanted to share their love and excitement with all of their friends, and what better way than at a funfair?

At the stern of the ship the bride, in an exquisite sixty-year-old lace wedding dress, with her beautiful daughter as her bridesmaid, stood framed against the sunset as the ship passed under the Sydney Harbour Bridge under sail.

Annie held Emily's posy of pale pink rosebuds, in honour of the bride's granddaughter, too young to be flower girl but old enough to be held by her father as they waited in readiness for the ceremony.

The bride's hands shook slightly as she imagined the time when she would walk the length of the ship and bind herself for ever to the man she loved, and her fingers shook so much that her engagement rings, one old that had belonged to her grandmother and the new, a magnificent emerald, caught every ray of light from the pinkening sky.

Finally it was time. The music drifted towards her on the afternoon breeze and Annie leaned across and kissed her mother's cheek. 'You look beautiful. Good luck.' She handed her the posy.

'Good luck?' Emily laughed and her fingers relaxed as the movement stilled. She lifted her face to the breeze. 'I don't need luck. I have Marco!'

* * * * *

SYDNEY HARBOUR HOSPITAL: AVA'S RE-AWAKENING

BY
CAROL MARINELLI

Carol Marinelli recently filled in a form where she was asked for her job title and was thrilled, after all these years, to be able to put down her answer as "writer". Then it asked what Carol did for relaxation. After chewing her pen for a moment Carol put down the truth—"writing". The third question asked—"What are your hobbies?" Well, not wanting to look obsessed or, worse still, boring, she crossed the fingers on her free hand and answered "swimming and tennis". But, given that the chlorine in the pool does terrible things to her highlights, and the closest she's got to a tennis racket in the last couple of years is watching the Australian Open, I'm sure you can guess the real answer!

For Anne Gracie.
Thank you for your friendship and support.
It means a lot. Carol x

PROLOGUE

SHE would call him.

Ava Carmichael sat in her office at Sydney Harbour Hospital and stared at her phone, willing herself to pick it up and call her husband. She had just spent the best part of the last hour counselling a couple—telling them to talk, to open up to each other, that if they just forged ahead with communication then things would begin to improve.

As a sexual dysfunction specialist—or sex therapist, as everyone called her—Ava got to say those lines an awful lot.

Well, it was time for the doctor to take her own medicine, Ava decided, reaching out and picking up the phone and dialling in his mobile number. At the last moment she changed her mind, and hung up. She went back to twisting her long dark hair around her fingers— just unsure what it was she should say to him.

That she missed him?

That she was sorry?

Ava didn't know where to start.

Her husband, James, had been away for three months

in Brisbane. He had taken a temporary teaching placement at a school of medicine there, which was ridiculous. James was an oncologist and completely hands-on in his work. He loved being with his patients more than anything. Had it been three months of research, it might have made some sense—Sydney Harbour Hospital was cutting-edge and James kept himself right up to date, but James liked reading about findings rather than discovering them. He liked being with his patients and James, her James, wasn't a teacher.

She smiled at the very thought.

The medical students got on his nerves.

He hated explaining his decisions.

He was a man's man, a gorgeous man, her big honest bear of a man who would come home and flake on the sofa sometimes and moan because he wanted it to only be him in the room with his patient, especially when giving bad news.

'It's a teaching hospital,' Ava would point out, lying on the floor, doing her Pilates. 'They have to learn.'

'Yeah, well, how would you like to have a couple of students sitting there watching when you're trying to talk to someone about their bits not working?' There was rather more to her work than that but he'd made a very good point, and he had made her smile too, especially when he checked his own bits were there for a moment, indignant at the very thought.

Well, there *had* been conversations like that one, lovely evenings that had been shared, talking easily about their day, their thoughts, *them*, but those evenings seemed like an awfully long time ago.

Yes, he loved his patients and they loved him back, and the real reason he had taken the position, they both knew, even if they hadn't voiced it, had been because they'd needed space from each other—they'd needed those three months to hopefully sort out their heads.

James and Ava had been married for seven years, but had been together for ever. They had met at university and, quite simply, at the age of eighteen the awkward and rather shy Ava Marwood had discovered love. James had been twenty-one, good-looking, funny and the first person in her life, it seemed, who actually wanted to spend time with her. Like James, she was an only child, but unlike James, who had grown up with parents who adored him, Ava's parents had made no secret she'd been an accident, an inconvenience really. It had been a parade of young nannies who had raised Ava—her parents had been far too busy with their lives, their careers, their endless extra-marital trysts, which, they'd both agreed, kept their relationship alive.

It had been a confusing, lonely childhood and then she had met James and her world had changed. Ava had found a whole new definition for love. It had been completely unexpected, thoroughly reciprocated and though they had their own friends and lives, there was no doubt they had met their match. Everyone thought them the golden couple and it had been golden for a very long while. A thirty-six-year-old James still made her toes curl just looking at him, and he had always made her laugh. And even if he wasn't particularly romantic, it was a love that went so deep Ava had considered it invincible. But over the last two years their marriage had slowly unravelled. With each miscarriage Ava had suffered, they had grown further and further apart and now they were barely talking. In fact, if it weren't for email they would hardly be corresponding at all.

Still fiddling with her hair, she looked at her computer and then went and reread the last email he had sent her.

It was just his flight details really, and all so impersonal it might just as well have come from Admin.

And then, loathing herself, she did it again—checked their bank account with suspicious eyes.

She saw the boutiques he had visited and couldn't quite envision it—James, of all people, in male boutiques!

James, who got a wardrobe update each Christmas and birthday when she went and did it for him, had taken himself off to several trendy shops these past few weeks and from the amount spent he had been having quite a good time of it.

And what was it with all the cash withdrawals?

James never used cash or rarely, but now it was a couple of hundred dollars here, another couple of hundred there, and what was this weekly transfer? A few minutes' research later she found out.

Her husband, who liked nothing better than to lie on the sofa and laugh at her doing her exercises, had, a couple of months ago, gone and joined a gym.

She didn't know if she was being practical or being a fool to believe that James wouldn't cheat. And things must be bad because she was even thinking of turning to her mother for advice!

Call him, Ava counselled herself. *Call him now from your office.* Because each night at home she went to call but couldn't, and each night was spent in tears. Perhaps she could be more upbeat, logical and truthful if she sat at her desk.

More direct.

'Hi.' She kept her voice bright when he answered the phone.

'Ava?' He sounded surprised, well, he would be, she told herself, it was six-twenty in the evening and so rarely did she ring. 'Is everything okay?'

'Of course it is. Does there have to be a problem to ring for a chat?'

'Er…no.'

She could feel his wariness, but she forged on. 'Look, James, I know things haven't been—'

'Ava, can I call you back?' He sounded awkward and James was never awkward. She'd timed the call carefully, knew that he wouldn't be teaching now.

'Is someone there?' she asked, and there was a long silence.

'I'll call you back in ten.'

She sat trying to ignore the unsettled feeling in her stomach that was permanently there these days—he might have a colleague with him, she told herself, but that had never stopped him talking before. They were a very open couple, or had been; he wouldn't give a damn if someone was around—and he wasn't seeing patients so it couldn't be that.

'Sorry about that.' He had called her back five minutes later.

'Why couldn't you talk?'

'Just…' She could almost see his wide shoulders shrugging the way they did when he closed off. 'What did you ring for?'

'Just…' She shrugged her shoulders too.

'Ava.' She could hear his irritation. 'I'm sorry I couldn't talk before, but I can now—you just called at a bad time.'

'Well, when's a good time?' she snapped. 'I called you the other morning and you couldn't talk then either…' He had hardly been able to breathe. More to the point, he'd hardly been able to breathe! She'd rung him at seven and he hadn't answered and she'd called him straight back, and he'd picked up then, trying to pretend he'd been asleep, but he'd been breathless. She knew he was having an affair, except she didn't want to know it. Ava had always thought that their marriage ending was just about them—a private affair, not a real one.

She wasn't stupid. They hadn't slept together since God knows when, more than a year at the very least. As if James wasn't having the time of his life in Brisbane. She was mad to think otherwise.

'Do you want me to order a cake for your mum's birthday?' she asked instead.

'Please.'

'What about a present?'

'I don't know…just think of something.' And that annoyed her too. Veronica Carmichael was a difficult woman; she and Ava had never really got on. A widow, James was her only child, and she was never going to like the woman who, in her eyes, had taken him away and, worse, a woman who couldn't give her grandchildren. Ava had organised a small family gathering for Veronica's sixtieth, which was next weekend, and would on Saturday go out and buy her something lovely for her birthday, something really beautiful. And she'd wrap it too, and then Veronica would unwrap it and thank James, and would go on and on about what a thoughtful son he had when, had it been left to him, there would have been a card bought on the way to her house and no party.

So she and James chatted for another thirty seconds about his flight home on Monday and then she hung up and stared at the view she loved. SHH looked out over Sydney Harbour and the sexual dysfunction centre was on one of the higher floors—the floor was shared with Psychology and Family Counselling. Nobody would ever get out of the lift otherwise, James sometimes joked when he came up to visit her some lunchtimes, though again, that hadn't happened in a while. Still, every morning that she came into work Ava pinched herself at the view from her window, and she gazed out at it now, to the opera house and the Harbour Bridge, the blue of the ocean and the white sails that dotted it, and she waited for the view to soothe her.

Unfailingly it worked.

It really was a wonderful perk of her job.

It was the same view she looked at the next morning after another tear-filled night when Ginny, her receptionist, came in carrying a huge bunch of flowers from James.

'Ahh…' Ginny beamed and handed her the bouquet. 'He's so romantic.'

Ava *knew* at that point that he was having an affair. Knew that she wasn't simply being paranoid.

Not once in the seven years they had been married and not even when dating had James sent flowers, not one single time. It just wasn't him. *What do I need to send flowers for?* He'd shrug. *I've done nothing wrong.*

She read the card.

Miss you.

See you on Monday

James x

And she remembered a time, took it out from the back of her memory and polished it till she could clearly see.

It had been two, maybe three years ago.

Yes, three years ago and it had been their wedding anniversary and they'd both decided they were ready to try for a baby. Ava's career had been in a really good place and she'd felt confident she could juggle work and motherhood far better than her mother had. James had bought her a ring, the large amber ring that she was wearing now, because, he'd said, it matched her eyes.

And he'd taken her out for dinner, the perfect night, and they'd had the same old good-natured joke as they'd got back to the apartment and she'd moaned about the lack of flowers.

It hurt to remember and she tried not to, but the memory was out there, all polished and gleaming and allowing for total recall.

Tumbling in bed together, making love as they once had.

His big body over hers, his chin all stubbly, those gorgeous green eyes looking down, and she saw in that image what she hadn't seen in a very long time. James was smiling. 'Men only send flowers when they've something to feel guilty about.'

'In your own words, James,' Ava said, and looked at the flowers and wanted to bin them. If her window had opened she would have tossed them out there and then, except her window was sealed closed, and then in came Ginny with a huge vase.

'Put them out in the waiting room,' Ava suggested. 'Let the patients enjoy them.'

'Don't be daft,' Ginny said, and plonked them right there on her desk. 'He sent them for you.'

And there they sat, for appearances sake, their sweet, sickly fragrance filling her nostrils, the violent colours perpetually in her line of vision. She wished they'd just wilt and fade.

Like her marriage.

CHAPTER ONE

'THEY'VE cancelled the surgery.' Ava said nothing for a moment, just stood quietly as her colleague Evie Lockheart leant against the corridor wall, her eyes closed as she struggled to keep in the tears, utterly defeated by what had happened. Ava had seen her walking dazed along the hospital corridor. Even if she didn't know Evie particularly well, she liked her—they had shared the odd conversation and everyone in the hospital knew that Finn Kennedy was having his surgery today.

Complicated surgery that was extremely risky. Ava already knew his operation had been called off—news spread fast around SHH and she couldn't even hazard how Finn must be feeling to have been told an hour before such major surgery that it wasn't going to go ahead.

'It hasn't been cancelled,' Ava said, her voice practical. 'It's been postponed.'

'Well, it might just as well have been cancelled,' Evie said. 'He just told them not to bother booking it again, then he told me to get the hell out.' Evie shook her head. 'I shouldn't be troubling you with this.' She was clearly

in distress and not used to sharing her private life, and
Ava was more than used to situations like that.

'Come back to my office,' Ava suggested. She could
see a couple of nurses turning their heads as they
walked past—Evie and Finn were hot topics indeed.
Finn was the chief of surgery and a formidable man
at best, well known for his filthy attitude and ability
to upset the staff, but no one could question his brilliance. His voice could be as cutting as the scalpel he
so skilfully wielded, except lately he hadn't been operating and it had done nothing to improve his mood,
and today poor Evie was wearing it. 'We can get a coffee there. I'm sure you might like a bit of privacy now.'
She walked Evie back along the corridor and to the left
and then up in the lifts they went without a word. She
walked along the corridor, nodded good morning to
Donald, one of the therapists, and then through to her
own centre and shook her head when Ginny told her
she had a message from the spinal unit.

'I'll call back later,' Ava said. 'I'm not to be disturbed.'

She and Evie entered her office—well, it was more a
room. Yes, she had a desk, though it was terribly messy,
but the room had a couple of couches and a coffee table,
and a small kitchenette where Ava would make her clients a drink, or herself one, if they needed a moment to
pause, and she gave Evie that moment now as she went
over to make them a drink.

'Finn would never forgive me, you know…' Evie
gave a pale smile as she sat down on one of the com-

fortable couches 'If he knew I was stepping into a sex therapist's office to talk about him.'

'I'd be patronising you if I laughed.' Ava turned around and smiled. 'I hear the same thing I don't know how many times a day. She put on a gruff male voice. "'Well, I never thought I'd find myself here. I really don't need to be here…"' Ava rolled her eyes and poured coffee, taking a little longer than perhaps she needed to, to give Evie a chance to collect herself.

'Well.' Evie gave a wry laugh. 'At least we know that's one type of therapy that Finn doesn't need.'

Ava chose not to correct her—Finn had been using women as sticky plasters for a very long while, there was certainly something going on in that brilliant head of his. Still, that wasn't what Evie needed to hear today. Finn's and her on-again, off-again relationship was clearly taking its toll on her.

'What a view…' Evie noticed her surroundings for the first time. 'Maybe I could ask them to consider moving Emergency up here.'

'The paramedics would never forgive you,' Ava said. 'Do you want me to leave you?' she offered, handing Evie a steaming mug of coffee—Ava wasn't a nosy person at all and she certainly never gossiped. It was why, perhaps, she often found herself in situations such as this one. 'The cleaners have already been in.' She glanced at the desk, wished those blasted flowers were gone, but apart from a couple of wilting roses that the cleaner had removed, they were still there and still taunting her. 'I haven't got any patients for another hour, so you won't be disturbed.'

'No.' Evie shook her head. 'You don't have to go. It's actually nice to talk, just to be up here and away from the prying eyes.'

'It must be an extra pressure on Finn,' Ava mused. 'Having to have his operation where he's the chief of surgery. Still, there's no better place.' SHH was the best hospital for this sort of procedure, there was no question that it might be done elsewhere. It was experimental and even with the best surgery, the best equipment, there were no guarantees that Finn's ability to operate again could be saved. Indeed, there was a good chance that he would be left a quadriplegic.

Ava knew that, not because of the gossip that was flying around the hospital but because, unbeknown to Evie, Finn had actually been in for mandatory counselling prior to surgery. The team had discussed who should see him and Ava had immediately declined. She didn't know Finn particularly well, but they lived in the same apartment block, Kirribilli Views—his penthouse apartment was directly above hers—and though they barely greeted each other if they met on the stairs or in the lift, still, it could surely only make things more awkward for Finn.

He'd seen Donald instead.

And even though Donald was terribly experienced—he did both family counselling and sexual dysfunction and his patients adored him—Ava wondered if his brusque approach would mesh with Finn in such a delicate matter.

Ava dealt with spinal patients a lot. Her work gave her much pleasure, seeing relationships saved, helping people to learn that there could be life, a satisfying sex life even, after such catastrophic events. Her work was, in fact, moving more towards trauma and post-traumatic stress disorder patients, it was how she and Evie had first started talking. Evie worked in Accident and Emergency and had dropped by for a chat about a 'patient'. Ava was sure, quite sure, that the person they had been discussing was Finn. Finn's brother had been a soldier like Finn. His brother had died in Finn's arms and shrapnel from the bomb that had killed his brother was still lodged in Finn's neck, and it was that that was causing his health issues.

Sometimes Ava wondered if Finn had ever heard the rows between her and James, not that there had been many, really, before he'd gone away to Brisbane. They had been so deep into injury time by then that she and James hadn't talked much at all, but Finn had never intruded, there had been no chatting on the stairs or anything, just a very occasional 'Good morning'. And not once had Finn questioned her about her red, swollen eyes, neither had he done the neighbourly thing and popped around to see if she was okay when she'd lost the last baby. Ava cringed at the memory—Finn had been in the lift that day—the cramping had started on her way home and she had just wanted to get into her apartment, to call her doctor, to lie down, but there had been this awful sudden gush and then a crippling, bend-over pain and, terribly practical, Finn had helped her to her door, had taken her inside and had then called James. They'd never discussed it further—instead it had been a brief nod in passing and Ava had been grateful for that. Grateful now that Finn never stopped to ask when James was returning, or how she was getting on.

No, they just shared the same brief nod and greeting.

Grief recognising grief perhaps.

Respecting it.

Avoiding it.

'I can't believe we're going to have to go through all this again.' Evie broke into her thoughts. 'I really don't think he'll consent to surgery a second time.'

'Why did they cancel the operation?' Ava asked. 'I thought they had everyone on board, it's been planned for weeks.'

'This piece of equipment they need,' Evie explained, 'they're having trouble calibrating it. There's a technician coming over from America so it looks like it will be another week before the surgery can go ahead. They just can't risk even a single mistake.'

'What did he say when they told him?'

'Not much—a few choice words and then he took out his drip, put on his suit, told me where to go, and not very nicely either, and now he's back at work—he's doing a ward round as we speak, no doubt chewing out everybody in his path. Ava…' Evie's eyes were anguished '…the thing is, with Finn and I, I know it's very on-and-off, I know how appalling he can be, but

in the last few days we've been close. Last night we…'
She let out a startled half-laugh. 'I can't believe I'm
discussing this.'

'You won't make me blush,' Ava said.

'We had a really nice night.' Evie was awkward. 'I
mean, it was really intimate, amazing. It wasn't just
sex, it was so tender, we were so close.' Ava said nothing, reminded herself she was thinking as a friend, not
a therapist, and she let Evie continue. 'And now, just
like that, he's told me to get out, that he doesn't want
me around.'

'Give him some time,' Ava said. 'He would have
been building himself up for this surgery, and to have
it cancelled at the last minute—'

'But cancellations happen all the time and you don't
see couples breaking up over it,' Evie interrupted. 'He
said that now he knows a bit how the patients feel when
we cancel them at the last minute.'

'Ooh, are we going to get a new, compassionate
Finn?' Ava was pleased to see Evie smile. A cheerful
person, Ava found that a little dose of humour helped
in most situations.

Most, not all.

'Finn compassionate?' Evie rolled her eyes, and then
sat quietly as she finished her drink. Ava sat in silence
too, a comfortable silence that was perhaps needed by
Evie before she headed back out there, but after a moment or two in their own worlds it was time to resume
appearances, to play their parts. Evie drained her drink
and stood. 'Thanks so much, Ava.'

'Any time,' Ava said.

'Oh.' Evie suddenly remembered. 'That gorgeous husband of yours comes back today, doesn't he?'

'This morning.' Ava nodded. 'He's heading straight in to work. That's James.'

'Well, you can see him tonight,' Evie said. 'He's the luckiest guy in the world, isn't he? Married to a sex therapist...'

Ava grinned. 'Again, I'd be patronising you if I laughed, if you had any idea of the amount of times I hear that each day...'

She was *sick* of hearing it.

So too must James be.

The assumption that they must have most amazing sex life and wonderful relationship was a pressure in itself. As if people thought her job followed her home, as if the smiling, cheerful, practical Ava, who was open to discuss everything, who managed to deal with the most sensitive subjects with barely a blink, translated to the Ava at home.

Finn would never say such a thing, Ava thought as she saw Evie out.

Or maybe he would, she mused—nervous, embarrassed, new to a wheelchair, maybe Finn would crack the same old jokes if she offered her help.

She stood alone in her office and looked out the window at the glittering view and wondered if she could stand to leave it, not so much the view but her work here. She didn't want to start over at another hospital or open a private practice. Because SHH was so cutting-edge she got the patients in her office that she was most interested in helping. It was no doubt the same reason James would remain here, but how hard would it be to work in the same hospital, to see your ex-husband most days?

Ex-husband.

There, she'd said it and she didn't like how it sounded. More than that, she didn't want to be James's ex-wife.

CHAPTER TWO

'LOVELY flowers.' Elise was a bit flustered but George was friendlier this time. 'From your husband?'

'They are.' Ava smiled. 'Come in, take a seat.'

She had been seeing them for a few months now. For George and Elise it was a complicated process and not as simple as writing a prescription. George had been in an accident at work last year, an appalling accident where he'd seen a colleague die. It wasn't just George's physical injuries that had caused him pain. Over and over he had relived the moment of the accident and the depression and anxiety had been all-engulfing. He'd seen his GP but the medication for the depression had affected his libido, which had increased his anxiety, and by the time they had arrived at Ava's, the pair had all but given up, not just on their sex life but on themselves.

She was seeing them monthly as a couple and George was also having one-on-one counselling with Ava, but more about the accident and the flashbacks he was getting and his appalling guilt that the colleague who had died had been so much younger than him.

'How have you two been?' Ava asked.

'We're doing fine,' George said, handing over a folder. 'I've done my homework.'

Ava grinned and checked off their sheets. Her methods were a bit flaky at times, and with some couples she made things a bit more fun. With George and Elise she had them playing Scrabble, taking walks, doing little quizzes to find out more about each other, just little things, and she looked through the sheets.

'Elise?' She saw the woman's worried expression as she handed over a folder. She looked as if she was about to start to cry. 'Elise, the homework's for fun…'

'It's not that.' She was really flustered, Ava realised. 'You know you said we weren't to…' She could hardly say it.

'I suggested that you didn't try to have sex.'

To take the pressure off George Ava had suggested a sex ban, kissing and holding hands only—which apparently they hadn't done for decades.

'Oh, we haven't,' Elise assured her.

'Okay.'

'We did get a bit carried away, though,' George admitted.

Quite a bit carried away, it turned out! By the time their hour was up, they were all smiling. 'I'll see you again next month and, George, you in two weeks,' she said to the couple. 'And follow the rules this time.'

She grinned at her own success. Okay, they had a long way to go, but they were both determined to get there, and with a couple as lovely as them, they would, Ava was quite sure.

'Ava?' She heard a knock at the same time she heard her name, Elise and George had left the door open. She felt her stomach tighten at the sound of her husband's voice, and she turned round.

'James.' There he stood, tall, strong, gorgeous and *different*. His light brown hair, which usually fell rumpled and messy, now had a modern cut, and usually his chin was crying out for a razor, but he was clean-shaven today. Generally James wore jeans and a T-shirt or jumper, depending on the season. His patients, he'd explain, had more on their minds than whether or not the doctor was wearing a suit—but now and then he donned one and when he did, he quite simply took her breath away.

He wasn't wearing a suit today but, dressed in grey linen trousers and a black fitted shirt, he was a mixture between the two versions of James she adored and it almost killed her to see it. James never bought himself new clothes; they simply didn't interest him. Her heart stopped in her chest for a moment, seeing him in new attire, wondering who had bought them for him, or who James had bought them to impress. She had a horrible glimpse into her future if they both worked at SHH, watching the man she loved and knew so well change before her eyes.

'You've lost weight,' she said, because he had. He was a big man, and had never been *that* overweight, but he'd lost a lot and now stood broad, lean and toned.

'A bit.' He shrugged.

'How was your flight?' How stilted and formal she

sounded when really she wanted to run to him, to rest her head on his chest, to welcome him home, to say how much she had missed him, except she greeted him like a colleague and clearly it was noticed, because he didn't even answer the question, just shot her a slightly incredulous look that that was all she had to say after his three months away.

'I'll see you tonight,' James said instead, and then as he turned to go, he stopped. 'Ava, we need to talk.'

He'd been saying that for months—no, years—as more and more she'd shut him out, only this time it was a different conversation to be had. 'I know we do.'

'I'll speak to you tonight.' He didn't come over and kiss her, he just turned and walked away and headed out to work, to involve himself in his patients. Only it wasn't his familiar scent that lingered. Instead she smelt cologne. Ava wished she had patients scheduled this morning, that she could think about someone else's problems instead of her own.

Instead, she was giving a lecture.

She had her little case packed, filled with aids that would make the student nurses laugh at first, but she would push through it, hoping to get her message across, hoping that one day in the future her words would be recalled and a sensitive, informed word might be had by one of them to a patient, that there was help available.

Except she felt a fraud as she stood there, this cheerful, laughing, sexual dysfunction specialist married to the gorgeous James.

She couldn't remember the last time that they had

slept together and wasn't stupid enough to think in the three months he'd been away, in the years they'd been away from each other physically, that James wouldn't have seen someone else.

Someone he liked enough to lose weight for, to tone up for, to buy new clothes for and splash on cologne for—it wasn't the James she knew. She knew that she'd lost him long ago.

Lost them.

CHAPTER THREE

'Look at you!'

The reception that greeted him as he walked onto the unit for the first time in three months was far more friendly and receptive than Ava's had been.

'Where did you disappear to?' Carla, the unit manager on the day ward, asked.

'Brisbane,' James said.

'She meant this.' Harriet gave a friendly sort of pat to his stomach as she walked past and, yes, he'd forgotten that Harriet had been getting a bit too friendly before he'd gone away.

'Ava's got herself a whole new man,' Carla said, and winked at him, and he grinned back, because Carla would soon have a word if needed. 'Bet she's delighted to have you back.'

'She is,' James said, and as Harriet pulled on her gloves he watched her cheeks flood with colour as he made things clear. 'And I'm really glad to be back—I've just been up to see her.'

He'd read through files and results and it really was good to be back—at least on the unit. He tried not to think about Ava's lukewarm—or, rather, stone-cold—reception. A long breath came out of his nose as he tried not to think about it but, hell, he'd thought she might be at the airport, he'd even emailed his flight times as a prompt, and then when she hadn't been he had stopped by the flat, just in case she'd taken the morning off, but of course she was at work.

'We've a new patient this morning.' Carla handed him a file. 'Richard Edwards. He was supposed to be in on Friday for his first round of chemotherapy but he cancelled. I wondered if you could have a word with him as he's ever so anxious. Wouldn't be surprised if he refuses again.'

'Sure.' James read through the file and his colleague Blake's meticulous notes. Richard was nineteen and had been recently diagnosed with testicular cancer. He was stage one and all his markers were good, but after discussion with Blake he had decided to go ahead with chemotherapy, though he was clearly wavering on that decision now.

'Where is he?'

'He's in the coffee room. Do you want me to bring him through to your office?'

'I'll find him.'

James headed down to the patients' and relatives' coffee room and met with the young man and his worried parents. 'I'll have a chat with Richard...'

'We'll come,' his anxious parents said, but James shook his head.

'I'll speak with you all shortly, but first I'd like to speak with Richard himself.'

'He gets overwhelmed—'

'I'm sure he does,' James said. 'That's why I'll go through everything again afterwards.'

'Thanks for that,' Richard said as they took a seat in James's office. 'They've been great and everything, but…' He struggled to finish his sentence and James tried for him.

'They're not the ones going through it?'

Richard nodded. 'They don't understand why I wouldn't want the chemotherapy if it gives you more chance that it won't come back. Blake seemed to think it was the better option, but he did speak about waiting and watching,' Richard said. 'I've just started a new job, I've got a new girlfriend and she's been great and everything, but I just can't imagine…' He closed his eyes for a moment and James didn't interrupt. 'I always look after myself. I'm a vegetarian. I just think I might be able to take care of this myself. I've been looking into things…'

'It's called watchful waiting,' James said. 'There's no evidence your cancer has spread so if you adopt that approach then you'll come back regularly for tests— and if it does come back the treatment is still there for you. Some people prefer that, whereas others find it far more stressful and just want the treatment straight away.' He spent time with Richard, going through everything, giving him pointers to do his own research, and it was good to be back at work with real patients.

He liked informing his patients, liked them informed, and Richard was. He didn't, at this stage, want to go ahead with the treatment, but as they wound up the discussion, along came the question, the one he was asked so many times. 'What would you do if it was you?' There were variations to the question, of course—if it was your wife, your mother, your daughter, your son. So often James was asked what he would do in their place, and normally he answered it easily, but maybe he was out of practice, because he hesitated a moment before answering.

'What you're doing,' James said. 'I'd weigh up my options. Do you want to make another appointment so we can talk again in a couple of weeks?

'That would be great,' Richard said. 'Will you speak with my parents?'

'Sure.'

It didn't go down very well, but James took his time with them too, assuring them that it was a valid option, that Richard wasn't closing any doors—and sometimes, James thought as he headed back to the treatment area, it was the relatives who had the hardest time dealing with things.

'No go?' Carla asked.

'Not at this stage,' James said. 'I've given him some decent sites to look at and some reading material.'

As he wrote in Richard's notes James could fully understand Richard's decision. He was fortunate that he did have options, and chemotherapy wasn't a decision to be made lightly, or pressured into. He looked through the glass screen at the patients in for treatment this morning and recognised a couple of them.

There was Georgia, back to do battle again, her headphones on. She gave him a smile as she caught him looking over and James returned it, and then he let her be because she closed her eyes and went back to the affirmations she played through the headphones each time her treatment was delivered. Then he looked over at Heath, who didn't look over or up. He was still too busy controlling the world from his laptop, still insisting the world wouldn't survive without him for a couple of days...

It just might have to, though.

James must have dropped his suitcase off on his way to the hospital because when Ava walked into the apartment, laden with bags, there it was in the lounge.

She could smell that blasted cologne in the air, just a trace that lingered, and she opened a window to let in some fresh air. They had a two-bedroom apartment at Kirribilli Views. It was the perfect place for a young professional couple and several other medical staff from the hospital lived there. One of the bedrooms was used as James's study. Many times while he had been away Ava had found herself in there and she found herself in there now. It was always messy. James had forbidden her from tidying it, insisting he knew where everything was. There was their wedding photo on the desk and Ava couldn't help but think how young and happy they looked. She wandered into their bedroom—well, for the last year or so it had been her bedroom. She kept her home far neater than she kept her office, though it was hard to keep anything tidy with James around, even though they had Gladys, the cleaner, coming once a week. Really, for the last three months Gladys must've thought herself on holiday—well, she'd get a shock when she came in this week now that James was back.

She wandered into their en suite. Gladys would have a fit when she saw it, because for the last three months it had been spotless. Ava routinely wiped down the shower after use and folded towels and put them back. James left his clothes where they dropped and his towels too. Funny, that even though he slept on the sofa, he always used the en suite. There was a small bathroom in the hallway, a guest bathroom, and James probably didn't want to be a guest in his own home.

God, she was nervous, and she jumped when her phone bleeped a text from James telling her he'd be home about seven.

Well, he wasn't exactly racing home his first night back.

So she put the shopping away and marinated some chicken and tried to tell herself it was ridiculous to feel so nervous. It was just James coming home.

'Sorry about that.' She jumped as she heard James's key in the door. 'I dropped into Mum's.' He was balancing containers of food from Veronica, who seemed to think he needed rations to fortify him. He gave her a kiss but he was still holding the containers, so it was rather hit-and-miss.

'No problem.' Ava was used to him being late, so she didn't put the vegetable steamer on till she heard him come through the door. 'Dinner won't be long.' It felt strange to be cooking for two again. The last three months she'd been eating mainly frozen meals, healthy ones, though, and with extra steamed vegetables, and she'd taken up exercising again and lost a little bit of weight too. Still, cooking for two really meant cooking for two in this house. James liked jacket potatoes and butter with *everything* and he hated steamed vegetables, which were what Ava liked. She'd started eating really healthily when she'd lost the first baby, and she couldn't quite let go of it, but she *was* trying to get her old self back.

'Do you want veggies?' she asked as she served up, and he gave her the oddest look. 'I mean, you've lost weight, I thought maybe you're on a diet.'

'I joined a gym.' James shrugged. 'I can eat what I want now,' he said. 'It's great.'

No, she wanted to correct him, because it wasn't just about that, but she didn't want to start the night with nagging. She'd already pursed her lips when he'd come home with cartons of chicken and stir-fried rice from his mum's.

'You look like you've lost weight too.' James followed her into the living area and they sat down at the table for the first time in a very long time. She felt more awkward than one of her patients on their first visit. 'I've been riding,' Ava said, 'and swimming.'

'That's good,' James said. 'That's good, Ava.'

It was good, except she felt as if she was giving up on her dream... She'd given up so many things trying to hold on to their baby. Their first pregnancy the doctor had said that of course she could ride, given that she regularly did, and she was incredibly fit after all. So she'd carried on riding and swimming each morning and they had made love lots, as they always had.

The second pregnancy, she'd given up riding, figuring that it seemed stupid to risk a fall.

The third pregnancy, she had felt as if she were on a tightrope and had given up swimming, and by the fourth she had given up James.

And when she'd lost that one, Ava simply knew she couldn't go through it again. It had been a relief to go on the Pill, to decide that children weren't going to happen for them, to get on with their lives.

Except they hadn't.

She sliced her grilled chicken, tried not to think about it. She didn't want to think about babies. It was hard not to, though. She never had any problems getting pregnant. It was staying pregnant that had proved impossible. Six weeks, nine weeks, seven weeks and then ten weeks once...

She remembered Finn dragging her to the door.

Remembered his voice as he'd called her husband, but by then it had already been too late.

'So what did you get up to in Brisbane?'

'Not much. The teaching was pretty full on.'

'You seemed pretty busy.'

He stood to get another bottle of water.

'Might treat myself to sparkling,' James said, and she knew it was a dig, because after three months apart they should be popping corks.

'Can you check I turned the oven off?' She watched his shoulders stiffen, knew it drove him crazy when once it had made him laugh, but she was forever checking things like that.

'Well?'

'It's off,' he said, cracking open the sparkling water, filling his glass and then raising it. 'Cheers!'

She was quite sure he hadn't checked but didn't say so, very determined not to start a row.

Or face *that* conversation.

'I got you Mum's present for her birthday.' God, but it was awkward. They hadn't seen each other for three months so they should be at it over the table right now, completely unable to keep their hands off each other. Instead, there had been no contact and, worse, the conversation was strained. They simply had nothing to say to each other—it was worse than a first date.

'How's your work?' James asked.

'Busy.'

'I heard about Finn's operation being cancelled.'

'Postponed.'

'Ava.' He'd finished his chicken and she had barely started hers. 'While I've been away, I've been—'

'I had a chat with Evie…' They didn't speak at the

same time. James started and she interrupted and then stopped. 'Sorry.' She knew she had to face it. 'You were saying?'

'It can wait,' James said, because he didn't want to face it either. 'How was Evie?'

They watched a movie, or tried to, but it was a crime one and she hated those, so midway through Ava gave up and went on her computer, writing up patient notes, fixing other people's lives instead of her own.

'I'm going to bed.' She didn't bend her head to kiss him and James hardly looked up, neither quite brave enough to have *that* talk.

He sat in the semi-darkness, teeth gritted, and tried to concentrate on the film, because if he didn't he might just march into that bedroom and say something he'd regret.

Some welcome home.

He was a night person, and once Ava had been. She'd been a morning person too—up at the crack of dawn and swimming on weekdays, riding at weekends, and he was glad she was doing that again. It was the early nights he couldn't stand and she was going to bed even earlier. Now it was lights down at ten, like some school trip.

James hauled himself from the sofa and wandered into his study, saw the wedding photo on the desk and he barely recognised them so he closed the door, went back into the living room, opened up his case then headed to the cupboard and took out a blanket and pillow and tossed them down.

God, but he hated that sofa.

There was a small bathroom in the hall and he was quite sure she'd prefer that he use it, but he refused to, so he took out his toiletry bag from the case and walked into the bedroom where she lay pretending to be asleep as he went into the en suite.

James took off the shirt and discarded the linen pants on the floor, then he rinsed off the cologne and looked at her make-up bag, saw the little packet of pills that was supposed to have been the solution. He thought about having a shower, but decided that it could wait till morning. There was a show he liked starting soon, so he put a towel around his hips and walked past her bed on the way to the sofa. They'd talk tomorrow, he decided, or maybe they should wait till after his mum's birthday. He was starving. One piece of grilled chicken and a baby potato with a tiny knob of low-fat sour cream— there hadn't been butter in the apartment for years, another thing that was banned. Maybe he should ring for a pizza; that would really get under her skin...

And then he stopped.

He just stopped.

Because he could do this no longer, because it had come to *this*. He was sick of the sofa and sick of not wanting to come home—and, as hard as it was, he had to say it—he was an oncologist after all, should be able to stand by a bed and deliver a grim diagnosis.

'Ava.' He stood by the bed. 'I need to talk to you.'

Her eyes were still closed but he carried on. 'These last months while I've been away in Brisbane, I've been doing a lot of thinking.'

'James.' She turned on her side. 'It's late, can we talk tomorrow? At the weekend maybe?' She didn't want to hear it.

'No,' James said. 'We're going to talk now. You know how we agreed about no children, that we weren't going to have babies…'

She didn't want this conversation, just didn't want to have it, but James pressed on regardless. 'When you went on the Pill, I thought it was supposed to take the pressure off, supposed to be a relief, but if anything it's made things worse.' She could feel him standing over her, could feel tears building behind her eyes, and then as he carried on, she grew angry. 'I mean, even if we only had sex because you wanted to get pregnant, at least we did it…'

'Oh, poor James.' She opened her eyes now—angry eyes that met his. Three months apart and a whole lot of thinking and that was all he could come up with, that they weren't doing *it* any more. 'So you're not getting enough!'

'I know I'm not good at this.' James hissed his frustration. 'I know that I say the wrong thing, but will you just hear me out? Every day you tell your patients to talk things through,' James said. 'Every night you come home and refuse to.'

'What do you want to talk about, James? That we're not doing *it*? Well, sorry…' And she stopped. She just didn't have the energy to argue any more, couldn't drag up any more excuses, and she sat up in the bed and looked at the face she had always loved, and he was looking at her as if he didn't even know who she was.

'We're finished, aren't we?' James said it for them and it made her want to retch, but instead she just sat there as he answered the question for them. 'I mean, how much more finished can you be if after being away for three months I'm automatically heading for the sofa?'

'Some sex therapist!' She made the stupid joke for him, the one he must hear every day, when no doubt people nudged him and said how lucky he was. If only they knew. She wanted to reach out to him but she didn't know how. She'd tried so many times to have the conversations that ran in her head with him, to mourn the loss of their babies together. She had tried to tell him how she was feeling, that it wasn't just the baby she grieved for but the chance to be a mother, to fix what had been broken with her own mum. She really had tried. At first she'd cried on him. James all big and strong, telling her things would be fine, that there would be other babies, except that wasn't what she had wanted him to say.

Neither had it helped when he'd told her that they'd try again soon because she hadn't wanted him to say that either.

He was an oncologist, for God's sake; he should know how to handle grief!

She could remember how excited he had been the

first time she had been pregnant. He'd told her how much he wanted children, how much he was looking forward to being a dad. He'd shared his dreams with her and she felt like she'd ended them.

'What happens now?' She looked over at him.

'I don't know,' James admitted. 'I guess we both get a lawyer.'

'We don't need lawyers.'

'That's what everyone says, isn't it?' James said. 'Let's just get a lawyer and get it done.'

He headed out to the sofa and she called him back. 'It's your mum's birthday next weekend—should we do it after that?'

He gave a short nod. 'I'll go to a hotel tomorrow. I'll tell her after, well, not straight after...'

'Okay.' She couldn't stand it—she couldn't stand to look at what she was losing so she moved to turn out the bedside light. 'Night, then.'

That incensed him. He strode over, his face suddenly livid, and as she plunged them into darkness he turned the light back on and stood over her. 'You can't even squeeze out a tear, can you?' James accused.

'Don't say that.' Because if she started crying she thought she might never stop.

'You're just glad it's done, aren't you?' James said. 'Well, you know what? So am I. It's been hell...'

'It wasn't all bad.'

'No, Ava, it wasn't all bad,' James said, his voice rising, 'but it wasn't all good either, so don't try and sugarcoat the situation. This last year has been hell and I just want done with it.' She winced at his anger, at the hurt that was there, and then he stopped shouting. 'Sorry.' he ran a hand through his hair. 'I'm sorry, okay? I don't want to fight.' He sat down on the bed and took her hand. 'We'll do this civilly. I don't want any more rows, we'll finish things nicely… You're right, it wasn't all bad.' And he looked at her. 'There was an awful lot of good.'

'I don't want to fight,' she begged, because she hated fights, she hated rows, they made her feel ill, and James knew that.

'We won't,' he promised. 'We'll just…' He gave a shrug. She could see all his muscles, he'd really toned up, he looked amazing, he felt amazing on her skin as his hand met her arm. 'We'll remember the good times,' James said. 'We don't want to end up like Donna and Neil.'

And they both shared a pale laugh, because they'd had Donna and Neil over many times, at first together and then, when their marriage had broken up, separately, where they'd sat bitching and moaning about their exes—and James and Ava had shared many cross-eyed looks in the kitchen as they'd topped up drinks or put out dips…

'"He makes out he's so easygoing…"' She put on Donna's voice.

'"Don't know what she spends it on."' He put on Neil's.

'"He was crap in bed…"' She was still Donna.

'Well, you won't be saying that,' James said, but in his own voice now.

'No,' she admitted. 'Though you might.'

'No,' James said, and he smiled. ''Cos when we were good…' She knew what was happening as he leant over, she knew what she was doing as she put her hand to the chest that was so very close, and she didn't push him away this time, but felt his skin beneath her fingers, and her fingers lingered as she returned his kiss. She knew it wasn't a last-ditch effort to save a relationship, it was a kiss goodbye, and sex because you never would again.

She thought about it quite logically as for the first time in a year their mouths met properly, so logically for a moment that she knew it had been the same for Finn and Evie, the wonderful night Evie had recalled had been goodbye sex from Finn—while he still could.

Goodbye sex where you tried to imprint every detail as you kissed the other goodbye.

And logic went then.

His mouth was the same as the one she'd first kissed at uni, and his chin was a little stubbly now, not smooth as it had been this morning. God, but she'd loved his mouth. His shoulders were broader too, she thought as her fingers traced them, and she loved the solidness of him, loved the new toned James beneath her hands, and she pulled him further into her. And even if they hadn't been together in a very long time, still their bodies knew and recognised each other, still they matched the other's wants, a delicious familiarity, and she didn't care if he'd been with another, because she'd got to love him first.

She'd started wearing pyjamas in their year apart, big, baggy things that were buttoned to the neck, and James very slowly took them off. He looked at her body, which was way too slender now, but he had loved it for more than its shape and he kissed her ever harder.

Even if he'd lost weight he was still big, big and strong. He pressed her into the pillow and pulled the sheet down as he kissed her deeper till his towel was long gone and he was over her and here she could cry, his mouth on her salty cheeks as he slipped inside and moved inside where only he had ever been. She remembered the first time as their bodies meshed for the last time. She remembered so many times. Their first kiss on the beach, the night in his room when they had first made love, a carousel of images that flashed through her mind, and they flashed through his too—the first time, how many hours, days, weeks it had taken her to unbend, to give in to him, and the bliss he had felt when she had. He told her with words and with moans how good it felt to be there. They had always been noisy, James the most, just a delicious, uninhibited lover, and she'd miss their sounds, miss the one she was making now as her body throbbed its admission as to how much she had missed him. He moaned as he came—a deep, loud moan with her name on the end of it—and she'd miss that too, and then they lay there, conjoined, neither speaking for a while, till he rolled off and lay looking up at the ceiling, waiting for the carousel to slow down.

'Well,' Ava said finally, 'that was very civil.'

'Yeah, I can be sometimes.'

She curled up into a ball and faced away from him, wondered if he would head to the couch now, but he pulled her over to him, tucked her right into him and shielded her through their last night.

She woke to the dark, as she often did, and wriggled from his arms and lay on her back, trying to sort out problems in her head—sometimes she laughed out loud as she sorted them, but she wasn't laughing this morning; instead, she lay there fearing the dawn.

He hated the clock. He hit the snooze button, then thought better of it, leant over and turned it off. He climbed out of bed and headed to the shower. His toiletry bag from his time away was still unpacked and he went to get the razor, but couldn't be bothered. He'd only have to pack it again, so he went into the shower instead.

Maybe they could make it. Maybe after last night now they could somehow talk. He was supposed to be packing a bag and leaving for a hotel, except for the first time in more than a year there was a glimmer of hope. Yes, he knew last night hadn't been about rekindling them but somehow it felt as if they had. He thought of her body and how it had responded to him as he washed himself, thought of her warm and half-asleep in the bed just a few steps away from him, wondered about going back to her, just sliding in beside her still wet from the shower. He was hardening just thinking of her. Maybe, James thought, they should just talk; maybe they should just get angry and have a row. He knew how much she hated them, but maybe they should just shout it out, or maybe he should go in and just… He decided other-wise. It wouldn't be particularly sensitive to go in there and try to save his marriage with a throbbing hard-on, so instead of shower gel he picked up her conditioner and lathered himself with the scent of her, because that was what he often did, then bit down on his lip so as not to call out to her—when a couple of years ago he would have.

'Hey, sex therapist,' he'd used to call out from the shower, 'I've got a bit of a problem here…'

He leant his head on his arm against the shower wall as he recalled it, how she'd slipped into to the shower to 'take a closer look'. He remembered the time, be-fore babies and miscarriages and depression and hell, his hand moving faster and the carousel was back and spinning faster now. He backed against the wall, using both hands now, remembering her hands cupping… And then he stopped.

Everything just stopped for a moment.

Even the water seemed to, because it all just seemed to go still and silent till his senses returned again and he could hear the cascade of the water, and could feel the lump in his hand. He tried to detach, to examine it clinically, and he almost managed to—could feel the lump that was certainly suspicious, except now there was no clinical detachment, he could feel sweat run-ning down his head too, running down his back, and it wasn't the water…it was the cold sweat of fear.

'James?' He heard her voice and looked up. He heard

the concern in her voice too, and Ava was far too open-minded to care what he got up to in the shower, and in that moment she knew.

CHAPTER FOUR

'I DON'T need to leave a specimen,' James said. 'I'm not exactly in the mood.'

'Well, you'd better get yourself in the mood,' Donald said brusquely. 'Of course you will still have one testicle, but if you need chemotherapy…'

'We both decided ages ago that we're not having children.'

'James.' Donald was always blunt. He had a completely different approach from Ava. She sat there beside James for the counselling session that the surgical oncologist had insisted on, and she didn't like being on the other end of it. Ava wanted to get the hell out. 'Your marriage is over.' He looked over at Ava, who sat with her face rigid. 'You've pretty much said that you're just together for appearances' sake.'

'We didn't say that,' Ava snapped. In fact, it had been James who had said it almost the moment they'd sat down, had told Donald straight that their marriage was finished, had said up front that he didn't even know why Ava was in there with him.

'You wouldn't be here if I didn't have cancer,' James said. 'I'd be in a lawyer's office now and so would you.'

'Well, in here you can forget appearances' sake. You wanted to put off this operation so you didn't ruin your mother's birthday—for God's sake, man!'

It was Thursday. James had already had a battery of tests and there were more still to come. Blake was the oncologist that James had chosen for his treatment, thought it would be the surgical oncologist doing the operation tomorrow. He would have his testicle out, and a nice prosthetic one put in. There was one on Donald's desk now, like a strange worry ball, and she was sorely tempted to squeeze it now, though she had handed it straight to James like a hot coal when Donald had first passed it, like some bizarre game of pass the parcel. James had given it a very cursory squeeze and put it back on the desk and they both sat trying to ignore that little saline-filled ball. Ava stared out the window instead, at a view that had once soothed, as Donald spoke on.

'It's often a very treatable cancer. You may well re-cover from this—have the two of you thought about that? Have you, James?' Donald asked. 'Have you even let yourself consider a wonderful future, one in which you're well—where you meet someone else and fall in love and you both want to have children?'

Ava felt as if she was choking. She had this sud-den vision of James running around the garden in the house they'd intended to buy when they had children.

They'd wanted a weatherboard and hopefully one with a massive garden.

'Three bedrooms,' she'd said as they'd looked through the real-estate pages.

'No, four.' He'd kissed her, patting her belly because they'd wanted loads of kids. They'd put the flat at Kirribilli on the market when she'd first got pregnant and had then wandered around homes trying to choose the one that would suit their family. She could see it in her mind's eye now, a gorgeous old weatherboard and loads of white iceberg roses and wisteria too—could see James running around the garden, clearly at one with his saline ball, children hanging off him as she trudged past on her way back from the shops, with her frozen healthy meals for one and a tin of cat food.

She hated it that he took the specimen jar.

They walked down the long corridor, James with the jar and pathology slip, and he was shown to a room. She didn't kiss his rigid, tense face, neither did she offer him a *hand*. Instead, she just stood there.

'I'll be in in the morning to see you.'

'There's no need to come in,' James said. 'It's a very simple procedure...'

'Your mum will be there,' Ava said. 'It will look strange if I'm not.' She wanted to be there, she wanted him home with her tonight, not checked into the hospital because he was first on the list and he wanted the bliss of a sleeping pill.

'James, please,' Ava said, 'please, can we talk?'

'Talk?' He gave an incredulous laugh, 'That's the

one thing we don't do, remember? Or rather one of the many things we don't do.'

And he walked into the room with the specimen jar that would soon hold his future and it terrified her that he might have one. Of course she wanted a future for James but she wanted it to be with her. Ava wanted to walk into the room and be with him now, wanted to make this hell somehow easier for him, but instead she had to head for home.

Her head was pounding, it really was.

Every root in her scalp throbbed a pulse. They'd been together so long every step was a memory.

It was here she'd started to lose the last pregnancy. That first low cramp that she'd tried to ignore and pretend hadn't happened and then a block later she'd got the next.

The sun was hot and her blouse clung to her and home just seemed too far, and she didn't want to retrace her footsteps so she walked into Pete's instead, but it was a place she and James had often gone together, and it had been ages since Ava had been there. She sat at a table and ordered a glass of sparkling water and rummaged in her bag for some headache pills, but of course she had none.

'Ava!' She heard her name called but she ignored it, and there must have been something on her face that told people to stay away, because no one came over. Pete's was filled with hospital personnel. It was a place where many met. She couldn't face going up to the bar and seeing anyone so she sat alone at her table and looked out of the window, watching all the people walking past, just getting on with their day as if it was just another day, except her marriage was ending and James had cancer and she wanted to be with her husband so badly that even the phone ringing felt like an invasion.

She answered her phone. 'He's fine, Veronica. He said he doesn't want visitors tonight.' She did her best to answer her mother-in-law's endless questions, but Veronica wasn't just a nosy old boot, she was a perceptive one too.

'It's because he's a doctor,' Ava said, when Veronica pointed out that these days people went in in the morning and James had told her it was a day-case procedure and nothing to worry about. 'They're just doing him a favour so he can get a bit more sleep. He'll have a sleeping tablet and be knocked out. It's better than him being at home, stressing.'

Except James didn't stress.

It was one of the things she had so loved about him. Arrogant, some said; male chauvinist, a few others, but he wasn't—he was just this big bull of a male and she loved him for it. This man who didn't sweat the small stuff, who didn't care about clothes and flowers, and it wasn't that he expected her to do the washing-up: he'd happily leave it undone.

'Can I get you anything else?' She blinked as she saw the waiter taking away her empty glass. She couldn't remember even drinking the sparkling water.

'A glass of wine,' Ava replied, and then she had to go through whether she wanted red or white. She stabbed her finger at a random one on the menu. She didn't care what she had, she simply couldn't face going back to the flat, to lie in bed without him.

But they had been sleeping apart for months, Ava reminded herself as the waiter came back. She sipped on her drink.

'Ava!' It was Mia and Luca walking into the bar, friends they had often shared a drink and a meal with, but they were so in love, so together, it made Ava want to weep.

'We heard about James.' And they were a nice couple, just up front, and she should be grateful that they faced it, that they didn't pretend that they didn't know. Except she was starting to cry—she was sitting in the middle of Pete's and starting to cry.

'Ava,' Mia put her arm on her shoulder but she pushed it off and stood.

'Leave me, please...' She didn't even pay for her wine, just stood up and walked out. She saw Mia's eyes close in regret for her handling of things, except they hadn't been insensitive, they were doing what everyone said you should: facing it, bringing it out in the open, talking about it.

She never wanted to hear those words again.

She walked home, thinking of the babies James would have with another. She had so often blended their features—amber-eyed babies with light brown hair, or green-eyed babies with their hair dark—but now she had to take herself out of the picture.

Her blouse was sticking to her again, and as she

stepped into the air-conditioned lobby at Kirribilli she shivered as she waited for the lift. Tears were really starting to come and she didn't know how to stop them. She pressed the lift button again, relieved when the doors opened. As she stood inside, pressing the button for her floor, someone raced to catch it, and she was quietly relieved that it was only Finn.

And because it was Finn, of course he ignored her.

He was having surgery first thing tomorrow too, but unlike James he was spending his last night at home.

Ava glanced at the bottle he must have gone out to purchase, figured a sleeping pill would be the safer option, but it was none of her business.

Neither nodded.

Neither bothered pretending it was a good evening.

They just both wished the lift would start moving. She was holding on to her tears for dear life, but they kept slipping out and her breath was coming out in little shudders and she just wished the lift would move.

'Looks like we're walking.' Finn broke the tense silence after several of Ava's frantic attempts at pushing buttons.

'Looks like it,' Ava said through gritted teeth.

She pushed open the stairwell door, and didn't hold it open, which was maybe a bit mean with his crippled arm, but she was past caring and started climbing. She could hear Finn behind her, determined to keep up with her, probably to prove he wasn't in pain.

She wanted to start running.

She just wanted to be in her flat so the tears could

fall more readily, but even if she wanted to run her legs seemed to be turning to lead. She gripped the hand rail, moved one foot in front of the other, could hear Finn catching up, and she couldn't move a step further. She was doubled up in pain, not bleeding this time as Finn came up behind her. The pain wasn't physical, but it paralysed her just the same.

'Leave me,' she sobbed as he walked past her and she sat on the stairs, grateful that if someone had to see her like this it was Finn, because he was perhaps the only man who would walk straight past, because no doubt he just wanted to get up to his flat too. It was a relief to hear his footsteps pass, to just sit with her face buried in her hands and to weep, to give in to the tears and just let them fall. Later she would try to summon the energy to move.

She didn't hear him come back down, as she was crying too hard to notice his about-turn. She just sort of felt him on the stairs beside her, but she was too far gone to stop.

She hadn't cried like this in years.

Oh, there had been nightly tears for a long time now, but she hadn't actually broken down, not since she'd had the second miscarriage.

She hadn't sobbed so hard she thought she might vomit, that she might never again be able to breathe, in ages, but she did it now, sat on the stairs with Finn beside her and shuddered her pain out, and it seemed to echo through the stairwell. Surely people would come

soon and tell her to shut the hell up, but she was shutting up anyway. Somehow the sobs were slowing down.

'Do you want some?' She glanced over as he opened
the bottle.

'I really wish you'd just kept walking.'

'Believe me, I tried.' He handed her the bottle and
she took a sip. She hadn't had whisky in years, hadn't
had a glass of wine in years either. She had just kept on
giving up everything she liked in the hope of keeping a
baby inside her, and never going back to them again—
just giving up all the things that made her her. And she
didn't like who she was any more.

She didn't like the nitpicking, low-carb, healthy version of herself.

And she cried some more, but not so violently now.
Finn just sat there and let her, and she took another
swig of his drink.

'I don't want to talk,' Ava said.

'Good,' Finn answered. 'Because neither do I.'

They sat, him in silence, Ava still catching her breath
as the tears started to slow, her body shuddering with
little hiccoughs as it slowly calmed. Then she remembered it was his drink and Ava handed the bottle back
to him. 'Should you be…?' And then she stopped herself because it wasn't her business and he too wanted
silence and she was surprisingly grateful that he was
there, but he declined when she offered him his drink.

'I think you need it more than me.'

She didn't. She took the lid and put it back on. They
sat a while longer, her tears slowing down, the hic-

coughs silencing, and it had actually been better here than alone. Finally, she could think about moving those last steps to her door as she sat there, still catching her breath from her crying marathon.

'I think the chivalrous thing to do would be to put my arm around you,' said Finn, 'except I can hardly feel it.'

She turned and gave him a very watery smile and after a moment's pause he returned it.

She'd never really looked at him, never really understood what Evie saw in him. James was macho, but Finn could be a bastard at times, yet he'd always been quietly nice to her and he was being quietly nice to her now.

And Finn looked at Ava. He'd never really been able to work her out. He liked James a lot, he was a bloke's bloke, and they'd shared more than a few nights at Pete's. But Ava—she was a funny little thing. At times he'd heard their rows, but she was always so prim and guarded when they met in the corridor. Even when she'd had the miscarriage, she'd hardly said a word, just 'Call James,' but surely she wasn't so prim and guarded? He knew what she did for a job. 'Lucky guy,' he'd ribbed James at times when they'd shared a drink at Pete's. 'Married to a sex therapist.'

Except he knew now how stupid those words had been. He'd had to see that Donald a couple of weeks ago, a requirement for the surgery he was having, and hadn't liked one bit the details that Donald had gone into. He had firmly decided he wouldn't be seeing him again.

His smile turned wry as both sat on the steps, staring at the other, and it was Finn who broke the strange silence. 'You know, we could really mess things up here,' Finn said, removing his gaze from her and looking at their surroundings. 'We could have drunken sex on the stairwell…'

And she actually found herself laughing.

'Except I'd hate myself even more in the morning,' Finn said.

'Hate yourself?' Ava frowned.

'Guilt.'

'I didn't know you possessed such a thing.'

'Neither did I. But it'd be there tomorrow—you know, when Evie tries to come and see me to wish me well for the operation.'

She doubted a man like Finn had ever felt guilty before, had ever felt so loyal to a woman before, and he looked at her for a very long moment and she looked back at him. And then he spoke. 'And I'd hazard a guess that the only person you want to have sex with is your husband…'

It was true, so very true.

He stood up; he'd done enough sentiment for one night.

'Here.' She handed him the bottle, but he shook his head.

'Better not. Better still that the lift isn't working and I'll have to climb up these stairs again if I change my mind.'

He headed back up towards his penthouse suite as she sat on the step. 'Hey, Ava?'

'The answer is no.' She turned and smiled as

she hauled herself up to go home, except his face was serious.

'If I end up in a chair…if I…' He closed his eyes. 'I don't want Evie and I coming in to see you for help, don't want to be sitting in your office being told… I don't want to do that to her.'

Ava went over to him. 'Let her in, Finn.'

She saw the conflict knit his face closed, knew then how badly he wanted Evie there and understood too why he was pushing her away.

'And I'd help you,' she said, and wondered how she would deal with such a complicated, private man, because there was something about Finn, something about his brilliance that was intimidating. But she knew that if it came to it, and if he let her, she would help him.

'I don't want all that for her.' He shook his head. 'I saw that Donald…'

'You'd see me,' she said firmly. 'And *I* would help you, I would help both of you,' Ava promised as he shook his head to decline. Sometimes a bit of humour *was* needed. 'On the condition that you promise not to make one of those awful jokes.'

'What one's that?' Finn asked.

'Well, I never thought I'd end up in here.' She put on a macho male voice.

'You'll need the biggest one!' Finn gruffed back.

'They all say that.' Ava laughed.

'I *would* help you,' Ava said, joking over now, and her voice was kind as she did what she never thought she would to this dark, moody man—gave him a cuddle. And he put his good arm around her and they stood and held each other for a moment.

'We'll go back to ignoring each other tomorrow,' Ava assured him.

'I'm back to ignoring you now,' Finn said, but as he let her go, as he turned to go, he paused. 'Ring him,' Finn said, because he knew how cold and lonely James must be feeling tonight.

'Ring her,' Ava said, except she knew Finn wasn't going to take her advice. Was she going to take his?

Ava had a shower and washed her hair. It would be dry and frizzy tomorrow because there was never any conditioner in this place. She pulled on her robe and went through to the lounge and looked out of the window to the hospital where tonight James lay. She scanned the windows and tried to work out which was his room, wondered if he was looking out now towards their home.

She should be with him, Ava realised.

They should be in bed right now, making love—because she loved him and she had to tell him, and it was pure need that drove her impulse to pick up the phone.

'James.'

'Ava.' he sounded in no mood to talk. 'They've just given me a sleeping tablet.'

'I love you.'

'Look.' He was very practical, had anticipated that she must be feeling as guilty as hell by the timing of everything. 'We'll talk about this another time. We're over, Ava. You don't have to—'

'I want you here.'

James frowned as he heard her carefully formed words. 'Have you been drinking?'

'Yes.'

'How much?'

She looked at the bottle. 'Not much, but I haven't had anything for ages.' And then she remembered. 'Oh, and I had some wine too...'

'You lush!' She could picture his smile.

'God, James, I wanted to come to that room and help you...'

'You really have been drinking!' He grinned, remembered the times in their marriage when they would share a bottle of wine, and she carried on talking, told him she loved him, and even if they weren't going to make it, it was nice to hear it tonight, to talk to her, to hear her voice.

She wandered as she spoke, walked into the bedroom and then to the en suite, where there were towels all over the floor, and about four razors because there was no way a nurse was shaving him.

'Are you bald?'

She should have shaved him and she said what she was thinking.

'I should have shaved you.'

'Ava.'

'No, I should have...' And she told him how she would have.

'Hell, Ava.' His hand was under the sheets. 'I'm

going to have to press the bell and get them to bring in another specimen jar soon.'

They were both laughing.

'My wife the sex therapist.'

CHAPTER FIVE

'WE NEED you over on the trolley.'

Ava stood outside with Veronica as James was transferred to the trolley that would take him to Theatre. The warmth from last night had gone and she wasn't so shallow as to try and rekindle it. This morning wasn't about them, it was about James. He had been gruff and impatient when Lily the nurse had come in to take his obs and was equally gruff with his responses as she checked off the theatre list. Not that she seemed to mind. Lily was a friend of theirs—or rather Lily's husband Luke was a friend of James's and she and Lily always said they must catch up—they'd been to Luke and Lily's wedding. It just made it all the more awkward, though, but apparently not for Lily—she smiled over to where Veronica and Ava stood and Ava tried not to look at Lily's pregnancy bump. 'Just one of you can come down to Theatre with him.'

'I'll be fine,' James said.

'Don't be ridiculous,' Ava said, and Veronica said she might go for a wander, but, as she walked alongside him, she wondered if James actually wanted her there, if she was just making this harder than it had to be. James stared up at the ceiling as she walked alongside the trolley to Theatre and his responses were just as curt as the theatre nurse now checked off the list.

'Two crowns,' he said for perhaps the tenth time since last night. 'Front two,' he said again. And Ava could not help but remember the rugby accident when he'd been at uni where he had lost his two front teeth and broken his nose. A few days later his father, Edward, had died, and he'd had temporary crowns for the funeral...

There was so much of their history in each box the nurse ticked.

'No,' he snapped when she asked if he had any allergies, though he was, in fact, allergic to Play-Doh. Veronica had told her that he'd had came home from school when he was five, all covered in welts—not that the nurses needed to know that. Maybe it was good that she'd come up with him after all—she could just imagine Veronica chiming in, which wouldn't have been the best with James in this mood!

Still, all too soon he was all checked off to their satisfaction and was ready to be wheeled through, and it was time to say goodbye.

'Say goodbye, have a kiss,' the cheerful theatre nurse said. 'He'll be out soon. The operation usually takes about an hour, sometimes a bit more, but we'll page when he's in Recovery and about to head back to the ward.'

Ava leant over him and stared into those green eyes.

'Good luck.' How paltry those words sounded. She

went to kiss him but he turned his face so all she got was the edge of his mouth and his cheek and then he closed his eyes and said nothing, and she wanted five minutes away from everyone, just five minutes of his time, but since he'd found that awful lump they'd had none.

That dreadful morning was burned into her brain.

'James?' She could hear her question that morning, knew in an instant what he'd found.

She'd sort of dragged him to the bed, all sensible and reassuring, with her heart hammering in her chest. She'd felt for the lump and, yes, there was one, and she'd been all practical and agreed that, yes, he should get it seen to, except James had snapped into action by then—had been off the bed and ringing a colleague, and from that moment on it had been round after round of tests and scans.

And because it was James it had all been rushed through. They didn't do biopsies for testicular cancer—instead, it was ultrasounds and blood tests and CTs and counselling. And then he'd had to go round and tell his mother and then his mother had told the rest of his family and of course there had been uncles and cousins and just too many people coming over at night.

And when they went, so too did James's smile.

He was back on the sofa—his choice now, and using her own excuses against her.

'I'm tired, Ava.' That was one of them. 'I need space.' The other.

So she stood for a moment, watching him being wheeled away behind the black plastic doors, and as she turned around to go she saw Evie standing next to Finn. She was trying to talk to Finn, but his face was as closed as James's, staring over her shoulder, and then Finn's eyes met Ava's for a very brief moment and maybe last night had affected them both because she watched as he did turn to Evie.

As he let her kiss him.

'I'll always be there for you, Finn.'

And she wanted to step in.

Wanted to tell Evie just to kiss him.

Wanted to somehow explain that her saying she would always be there for him was what terrified Finn most.

But as she looked at the black plastic doors, she wanted to run to her husband, wanted to say the same words to him.

Except he'd assume he was being given the sympathy vote.

Even though Ava's heart and mind were consumed with James, she couldn't help but feel for Evie as Finn was wheeled off. She felt for Finn too and, based on their conversation last night, the best she could do for Finn was to go over as Evie stopped trying to be strong. She felt the other woman almost implode beneath her fingers as she put her hand on her shoulder.

'Come on,' Ava said. 'We'll go to my office.'

Evie held it together till they were there but once away from the sympathetic stares and curious eyes, she broke down. 'I'm sorry,' she sobbed. 'It's your *hus-*

band that's having surgery and I'm not being much help at all.'

'It's fine,' Ava said, because she'd had her tears yesterday and could at times be terribly, terribly practical, and also because she did not want to think of the paltry last words she and James had exchanged, did not want to spend the next couple of hours going over what was happening in Theatre, because she could not stand to think of him being operated on now. As complicated as Evie and Finn's relationship was, right now their problems were easier for Ava to deal with than her own. 'This is the easy bit for James. It's going to be hell waiting for the results and then finding out what's going to happen in the way of treatment, but today's really quite straightforward. Finn's surgery is far more serious.'

'Still…' Evie attempted.

'Hey, I spend the next couple of hours in here, or back on the ward with Veronica.' She rolled her eyes. 'My mother-in-law.'

'Don't you get on?' Evie was dabbing her eyes now. For all her tears she was much calmer today than Ava had been last night. Evie was a tough thing really, Ava thought. Though she'd probably had to be, given the family she'd come from.

'Not really,' Ava admitted. 'I don't think I've fulfilled the role of James's wife very well in her eyes. By now I should be a stay-at-home mum and have given her at least two little Carmichaels.'

'Don't you want children?'

And Ava had her lists of answers for that one, as if

printed out in her mind so she could reel off the one that suited best. *Not for ages* or *Maybe someday* or *Not you too!* Or, said with a wry laugh to her more feminist friends, *I'd have expected better from you.* But today she didn't have the list handy. Today she was aching inside, today she was touched too, that from the innocence of Evie's question she knew Finn really had never told anyone about that time. And maybe it was time to be honest.

'We'd have loved to have had children,' Ava said. 'It just didn't work out that way.'

'Ava!'

'Evie, please.' Ava put her hand up. 'Can we talk about you and Finn, because I can't break down today, I truly can't— I don't want to go in to see James all upset. I'm sure he's worried enough as it is without me breaking down on him.' Oh, God, how easily she could—she could kick the wall in this very minute because yet again another block had been put in their path to parenthood.

'What did Finn say when you said goodbye?' Ava asked instead as she filled a glass of water from the sink and drained it and then managed to turn around and play calm.

'He said, "Bye, princess."' Evie gave a very watery smile. 'He calls me that, sometimes nastily...' Ava could imagine. Evie's father had donated so much to the hospital and everyone had once assumed that Evie had had some sort of free pass in the hospital so it was a bit of a nickname around the place and she could well imagine Finn using that barb.

'But he didn't say it nastily today. I know Finn can be a complete bastard…'

And had Ava not sat on the stairs and spoken with him last night, she might have inwardly agreed, except… 'There's a lot more to Finn than that,' Ava said. 'And this operation is just huge. I can't imagine what he's going through.'

'We're not going to know the outcome for ages,' Evie said. 'He's asked me not to visit. How am I supposed to stay away?'

'I don't know,' Ava said. 'Maybe…' Despite her best efforts she couldn't stop thinking about James, couldn't stop comparing the two men, which was ridiculous as they were completely different. 'Maybe just give him space,' she advised, but her heart wasn't in it because she could not stand that now for James and herself—and maybe sometimes it was better to admit the truth.

'I don't know, Evie. I don't know what to suggest. I think you just have to get through this bit for now.'

It was terribly hard to take her own advice, though.

'How much longer?' Veronica was pacing when Ava came down.

'It shouldn't be much longer now,' Ava said.

'And then the real wait begins.' Which it did, because they'd have to wait to find out for sure what they were dealing with.

'I know it's hard.'

'No, Ava, you don't,' Veronica said. 'He's my son.'

Ava tried not to take it personally but, hell, it felt personal and terribly so, as if unless she was a mother she didn't really know love, and of course Veronica hadn't meant that, but it stung, that was all.

'He's all I've got,' Veronica said, and it took all Ava's might to bite her tongue, to not point out that at least she'd had a child. There was a froth of anger inside her, like the type that washed up on the beach after a filthy storm, and Ava hated what the last days had done, not just to James but also to her.

'I'm just going up to Theatre to get him.' Lily popped her head around the door. 'I shouldn't be long.'

She wasn't. About ten minutes later Ava and Veronica stood outside in the hall again as James was transferred back to his bed, and then they waited outside while Lily did his obs and made him comfortable. Finally they were allowed in.

'Hey.' She bent her head and he was too groggy to turn his face away this time. She could smell the fumes of the anesthetic and she was so pleased to see him back. 'How do you feel?'

'Tired,' James said, and promptly went back to sleep.

And Veronica had been right, because now the real wait started, and time seemed to be moving terribly slowly. When his next set of obs were done half an hour later, Veronica gave in to a headache and said that she would go but would be popping over to the apartment that evening. 'Do you need me to bring anything?'

'We're fine,' Ava said. 'I'll text you when we get home.'

And there were more obs and he woke up and was sick once, and he got annoyed with her and told her to go. Then he woke up again and was more like James.

'You might as well go.' James said it a lot more nicely this time. 'I'll be a few hours yet.'

'I'm not going anywhere,' Ava said. 'Well, I might go and get a drink and I'll text people, let them know you're okay.'

'Get some lunch,' James suggested.

She did, except she didn't have it in the canteen. Instead, Ava bought a salad sandwich and a bottle of water and sat outside in the sun. It was nice to be outside, Ava realised. She didn't do this nearly enough. Most of her lunches she took in her office.

She looked out at the water. They hadn't been on the water in ages. They used to get the ferry, just hop off wherever and get breakfast when James had a weekend off. She would love to do it this weekend, but of course he wouldn't be able to, but maybe next, Ava decided, or maybe the weekend before he went back to work.

If they weren't over by then.

She felt like a fighter pilot, scrambling for a plan when already it was too late, but she sat in the sun, making lists in her mind of all the things they would do. They'd play Scrabble, and talk, or she'd just lie on the bed beside him and read. And, please, God, that the results weren't too bad, because there were so many things James had to do and so many things she wanted to do with him, and it was simply too hard to think like that today, so she stood and binned her half-eaten sandwich and then headed back to the ward.

When she returned the door was closed and as Ava walked in, Lily called from behind a drawn curtain and asked Ava to wait outside as she was just checking James's wound. That just seemed stupid to Ava—she'd seen it all before!—but she turned around obediently and went out to the corridor.

'Won't be long.' Lily popped out but closed the door behind her, and as she headed off to the supplies trolley she gave Ava a smile. Perhaps a bit rudely Ava didn't return it. Instead, she stood bristling in the corridor as Lily returned, holding a couple of medical packs.

She was being petty, Ava knew that. She and Lily shared a mutual love of horses and at Christmas dos and the like they sort of gravitated towards each other. Today she had been nothing but nice but Ava could not return her smile.

'Blake's going to come down and see him,' Lily said.

'Why?' Ava snapped, because Blake was an oncologist like James and this operation was being dealt with by the surgical team.

'He just wants to check in on him,' Lily explained.

'And then we can go home?' Ava checked, because she wanted so badly to be home with him, alone with him. Maybe when they got there she could ring Veronica and say that James was asleep and not to worry about coming over. But instead of answering her question, Lily gave that noncommittal smile that nurses did so well and disappeared back into the room, leaving Ava still standing in the corridor, tears stinging in her eyes.

She couldn't help it. She was jealous of Lily—her pregnancy, her happy marriage and healthy husband. She'd dealt with not being able to have a baby of her own, but today everything felt so raw that she was even jealous that it was Lily in with her husband now. So jealous of Lily, who would no doubt trot and canter her way through a textbook pregnancy.

Oh, God, what was wrong with her? Why was she thinking such horrible things?

Ava didn't know how she felt.

She hardly managed a smile when Blake appeared.

'I'm just going to take a look at him, Ava.' And after a few moments she was called into the room and she still didn't know how she felt as she stood there.

'The surgeons say that everything went really well today,' Blake said. 'However, he's still got some considerable pain and is nauseous, so we're going to keep him in overnight.' Blake confirmed what she'd guessed was happening—knew the little powwow he and Lily had had behind that closed door. 'He should be fine to go home tomorrow morning.'

'Thanks, Blake.' James shook his hand from his bed and then Blake left the room.

'I'll come back with your injection shortly,' Lily said, and left them alone.

'You didn't say you were in a lot of pain.'

'I didn't want to moan,' James replied. 'You might as well go home.'

'I can stay.'

'There's no point,' James said. 'I'll just be sleeping once I get the needle. When you get home can you ring Mum and tell her that they're keeping me in?'

'You know she'll just want to visit,' Ava said.

'Of course she will,' James said. 'I'm her son.'

'Here's your injection, James.' Lily came back in carrying a little kidney dish and she was going to swoosh that curtain any second, Ava knew it, and ask her to step outside, but it was James who spoke next.

'I'll see you, then, Ava.' And she knew that she was being dismissed. Ava didn't bother with the kiss good-bye for appearances' sake. Sure, he probably was in pain, but at the bottom of her heart Ava knew, and she knew that Lily knew, that James had told her and Blake that he'd prefer hospital to home.

She rang Veronica and told her of the development and, of course, Veronica informed her that she was heading back soon. 'I might take him in some dinner.'

Ava didn't bother with dinner—she was, in fact, exhausted.

She had a shower and climbed into bed, weary with fatigue, but her brain was going at a hundred miles an hour, and when her phone bleeped a text she jumped up, wondering if it was the hospital, hoping it was James, and then felt a little guilty when she saw that it was Evie, because she'd completely forgotten about Finn.

Finn out of Theatre and Recovery and now on ICU.

Way too early to say how it went but thankfully operation over.

It was a group text, Ava knew that. She'd sent one of her own to their family and friends when James had been returned to the ward. As nice as it was that people were thinking of them, the multitude of replies and questions had been somewhat overwhelming, so Ava did Evie a favour and didn't reply.

Just closed her eyes, relieved for Finn, scared for Finn.

Relieved for James, scared for James.

Scared for herself too.

CHAPTER SIX

JAMES texted in the morning and asked if she could bring up a coffee when she picked him up, so she stopped at the kiosk and waited while it was being made and noticed that her hand was shaking as she handed over the money.

She was nervous about seeing him and she didn't want to be.

'Oh, hi, Tom.' She turned as someone came up beside her, and because Tom was blind Ava introduced herself. 'It's Ava.'

'Ava!' Tom smiled. 'I've just come over to have coffee with Hayley—and to bring Sasha to see her mum. Hayley's on call all weekend.'

She glanced over to where Hayley, who was a surgeon, sat engrossed in her baby.

'How are you?' Tom asked.

'Good.' Ava said, because Tom must be the only person who didn't know, but he worked over at the university, and she simply didn't have the energy to talk about it today, and they seemed to be taking for ever to froth the coffee. *Oh, please,* Ava thought, *just hurry up.*

'And James?' Tom added, because he couldn't see the desperation in her eyes.

'Yeah, he's not bad,' Ava said, and did her best to keep her voice light and smiled as the cashier handed her her change, except she dropped all the coins on the floor. 'Sorry.'

She scrabbled to the floor and saw Tom's dog, Baxter, and wanted to weep onto him as she picked up her change. Instead, when she'd collected the coins she stayed kneeling for a moment and stroked his beautiful head.

'Ava.' Tom's voice came from a long way off. 'You can't pat Baxter.'

'Of course. Sorry.' She pulled her hand away and stood.

'While he's got his harness on, he's not to be patted,' Tom explained, and he was right, of course. Baxter was working, she'd simply forgotten, and Tom was only being nice, only saying what he must have to about a hundred times a day, yet it felt like a snub. Of course it wasn't a snub, but she was so prickly and raw that everything hurt a little more.

'I'll bring your coffees over, Tom,' the cashier said when she took his order, and Ava said goodbye as he headed back to his family. A little later as she took her coffee she saw Hayley speaking with Tom, saw Tom wince, knew that now Hayley was telling him.

Blake was there with James when she got up to the ward and so too was Lily. She looked tired today, but she was all smiles when Ava came in as Blake finished off giving his discharge instructions. Ava stood there as Lily hauled over a wheelchair and Ava wondered what on earth she was doing working. Her husband was a consultant after all…

And then she stopped herself, because so was hers and she'd worked, she believed in women working. She was just being horrible, jealous and vile and bitter, and— She didn't know how she felt.

'And Lily has given you all the after-care instructions.' Blake finished up as Ava struggled to concentrate on what was being said.

'I've got everything,' James broke in. 'And I'm not being wheeled down.'

'No choice.' Lily beamed. 'It's a long way to the foyer.'

As James took a reluctant seat Ava handed him his coffee.

'Thanks,' he said.

'Thanks, Blake,' Ava said. It felt strange to be speaking with him in this way—normally she only saw Blake at social events, sometimes when he came with his wife, Joan, to the apartment for dinner. 'I guess we now just have to wait till we get the results.'

'Yes.' James was clearly itching to get out of the hospital. 'Give me a ring as soon as you get *my* results.'

'Of course,' Blake said, and as his eyes briefly met Ava's, she felt a dull flush spread up her cheeks and it refused to go. There were tears at the back of her eyes too as the porter wheeled James down, Lily walking alongside. That blasted flush stayed on her cheeks as she went and got the car, and as she realised she'd forgotten her swipe card to get out of the staff car park the tears started trickling.

But she'd got into the car park, she told herself, so it had to be here, and she rummaged through her bag to look for it. She settled for a tissue instead and wept into it for a moment.

'Stop it, Ava.' She said it about four times. She should have done this at home, last night. 'Not here.'

And she dragged in a breath and rubbed some powder on her face and found her stupid swipe card and drove to where James was waiting with Lily, who was chatting easily with him.

And she knew how she felt then.

Knew the word she'd been searching for these past days.

Excluded.

Excluded from everything.

'I can manage.' He refused her help, just climbed into the passenger side, and he would have driven himself home if he'd been allowed to, Ava realised.

'Thanks.' She tried to smile at Lily, except her mouth wouldn't move.

'You're welcome.' Lily patted her arm. 'We'll catch up soon, Ava.'

They hardly said a word during the short drive home, and there was Veronica waiting at the door as he limped out of the lift.

Excluded.

That was how she felt as Veronica made James's lunch and suggested Ava go to the store and get some more ice for James's ice packs.

And he was the last mummy's boy on earth, but he did love his mum enough to *let* her look after him.

He slept for most of the afternoon then got up and had some dinner, cooked by Veronica, then stood up and declared he was going back to bed.

'Thanks.' He gave Veronica a kiss. 'Go home, Mum.'

'You're sure?'

'I just want to go to bed. Thanks for everything.'

Ava saw her out and then headed back to the lounge but James had already gone to the bedroom and was pulling back the sheets.

'Did you need anything?'

'I just want to go to sleep.'

'Sure,' Ava said. 'I'll bring you in a fresh ice-pack when I come to bed.' She went to head out, didn't want his words to catch her before she closed the door, but it was as if James had been waiting for them.

'Ava. I really appreciate you giving up *your* bed for a couple of nights.'

'James, please.' Ava swallowed. 'Let me come to bed.'

'You can do what you want, but if you get into this bed I swear I'll get straight out and check into a hotel.'

'James, I don't want you in a hotel.' She didn't and she didn't want something else too. 'I don't want a divorce. Can you just listen?'

'No, you listen!' he broke in. 'It was *your* miscarriages, *your* babies, *your* grief, you made it that way— well, it's *my* cancer. And do you know what I don't need now? I don't need to be one of your clients in this, I don't want you telling me that you can't feel the difference in my balls, or your patronising understanding when I'm so scared or drugged up that I can't get it up. Neither do I want sympathy sex, or any of it. The same way I didn't want you in there when I was getting my dressing changed. You didn't want any of it when I was well...'

She couldn't even cry.

'And—' he hadn't finished yet '—I heard you saying to Mum that you had taken a week off. Well, you can untake it, because I won't be able to rest or relax with you in the flat. What was it you used to say when I tried to give you a cuddle or, heaven forbid, a kiss? What was it you used to say when I tried to talk? Oh, I remember: "I need space." In your own words, Ava!'

CHAPTER SEVEN

JAMES was closed.

There might as well have been a sign around his neck—'Not back in five minutes, not open again soon.'

He was completely closed.

He'd done a similar thing when his dad had died, a week after his teeth had been knocked out. He'd just shut her off, only for a couple of days, but by the funeral, when all the bruises had looked brown and yellow, they had been together again, close again, making love again. Not that he'd ever really broken down about his dad—not once in their relationship had James cried, not even when she'd lost the babies. He just didn't do tears, and he wasn't doing them now—if anything, as the weekend passed, more and more he seemed quietly cheered.

He rang friends for chats, he sat on the computer for an hour on Sunday and bought about fifty books for his ereader and then, before he went back to bed, he ordered a pizza.

And, no, Ava noted, he didn't offer her a slice, but, then, why would he when she'd always refused before?

It was incredibly uncomfortable on the sofa and she'd forgotten to put her clothes out the night before, but he didn't wake up as she rummaged through her wardrobe early on Monday morning, neither did he wake up when she showered and did her hair.

Or maybe he was pretending to be asleep.

And then she felt the stab of regret as she qualified it—maybe he was pretending to be asleep, just as she had.

'What are you doing back?' he asked later that day, when she popped back on her lunch break. He was sitting in bed on the phone, but hung up when she came in.

'I just thought I'd check how you were.'

'I'm fine.' He had a computer game on, and if anything seemed to be treating it as a holiday. He hadn't shaved since they'd found the lump, and he was looking like he did whenever they had time off, sort of scruffy and rumpled and actually, impossibly perhaps, happy.

Unlike Ava.

'And there was some news on Finn I thought you might want to hear.'

'Yeah, I heard.' He nodded to the phone on the bed beside him. 'They didn't cut my ears off, Ava.'

And it was so James that if she'd paused for a moment, she might even have laughed, except there was nothing to laugh about today. It wasn't good news about Finn and she ached to speak with James about it. There was shrapnel they hadn't been able to reach and the attempts at removal had made things worse. Right now he was ventilated and in spinal shock. However, she pressed on with a conversation James didn't want.

'It doesn't look good for Finn,' she offered, but James just shrugged and went back to his game.

'Early days,' he said.

'I'll stop and get something nice for dinner,' Ava attempted, 'maybe take-away?'

'If you want,' James said, 'but not for me. I've got a freezer full of stuff from Mum.' And to prove his point he swung his legs out of bed and, much more easily now, walked over to the fridge and grabbed some herbed chicken and stir-fried rice, which was his favourite. Veronica had made loads, of course, and he popped his individual serving, which would feed a horse, into the microwave.

Yet for all his unhealthy eating he looked, and she really shouldn't be noticing such things, fantastic.

He had some bruising down his thigh and had a support on, but over that was new underwear, really sexy, modern underwear—from his shopping trips in Brisbane, Ava reminded herself.

Except she wasn't jealous at the moment, and she wasn't even upset. She was just looking at him, not at his eyes but at his chest and then down to his thigh and that bruise and then up to his flat stomach. Then she met his gaze and he snapped his eyes away, and she didn't know the hows and whys but if it had been another day, another time, they'd have already been on the floor, and she knew he knew it. He sort of grimaced a little bit and moved his support as he walked across the kitchen and his muscles were rippling as he reached into the fridge and pulled out a milk carton, and as if to defy her, because it was one of the few things she really *was* closed-minded on, he drank straight from the carton, then burped and drank again. When the microwave pinged he took his chicken and milk back to the bedroom with him and closed the door.

Maybe it was only she who had wanted to make love, then, Ava conceded.

Maybe he *was* happy it was over.

She stood in the kitchen, and faced the impossible truth.

Maybe he was simply relieved.

She went to walk out, opened the front door and stood a moment, and then closed it, because they had to talk, because, no, he couldn't be happy, he couldn't be relieved. She knew them better than that, knew how good they were, how good they had been. She could not live this a single moment longer so she drew in a breath, tried to gather the strength to just walk in the bedroom and force him to listen, except she could hear the blips as, assuming she'd gone out, he dialled a number on the phone and then came his voice.

'Yeah, sorry, Steph… It's okay, she's gone back to work. Nearly got caught there! Now, where were we?'

CHAPTER EIGHT

'I'M SORRY about this, Donald.'

'It's not a problem,' Donald said as Ava sat on a chair on the other side of his desk, pulling tissues from his box. 'Ginny has cancelled your clients for the afternoon.'

'Thanks.'

His office was so different from hers, his style, his stance the complete opposite of hers, yet *his* patients adored him. His brusque, direct approach was one that appealed to some, though Ava wasn't particularly grateful for it now, not grateful that he tutted and tsked as she poured out a little more of what was going on. 'You shouldn't have come in this week,' Donald said. 'You've got far too much going on to be sensible at work.'

'I know that,' Ava shrilled. 'But James doesn't want me at home. What am I supposed to do, spend the day walking on the beach?'

'You could ask him,' Blake said. 'Ask him if he's seeing someone else.'

'I could,' Ava said. 'And whether you believe me or not, if he didn't have this diagnosis hanging over him

I would.' She held her breath at the impossibility of it all. 'That's a whole lot of arguing to cram in between now and next week when he gets his results. Can I forgive him?' She didn't know. Sometimes she thought she could, sometimes she knew she never could. They needed time, time to thrash things out, but time was the commodity they'd frittered away so foolishly and now suddenly it was running out.

'Maybe check yourself into some hotel like he's threatening to.' Donald smiled. 'Spend the day in bed, getting room service.'

Ava was surprised to find herself smiling back. 'That's worryingly tempting.'

'Do it, then.' Donald shrugged.

'That's no answer.'

'Well, you're probably not getting much rest on that sofa.' He took a breath. 'Ava, you know James will be feeling scared, he'll also be angry…'

'He's not, though.'

'Ava?'

And she closed her eyes and thought about it, because Donald was right, James must be feeling those things, but then Donald pushed things too far. 'And he'll be feeling protective of you.'

'Of me?' Maybe Donald was from another planet after all.

'Of course he is. Even if your relationship was perfect at the moment, he'd still be behaving like this to some extent—he knows what's coming up better than anyone, maybe he doesn't want to put you through it too. Especially—'

'That's ridiculous—'

'Especially,' Donald spoke over her, 'if he thought the marriage was over anyway.'

'So what do I do?'

'What the man said,' Donald said. 'Give him some space. Give yourself some space too. Go home tonight with a take-away for one, and a movie and a pile of work. Let him get his own dinner, he's clearly capable. Buy a carton of milk and write your own name on it.

'But for now I'd suggest you go into that scruffy office of yours, take the phone off the hook, pull down the blinds and have a sleep.'

So she did.

She could hear the noises from the overhead loudspeaker and the murmur of Ginny on the phone, and for the first time since cancer had invaded, for the first time in a very long time, she slept.

And it helped.

And, to Donald's credit, his other suggestions actually helped too.

She shouted hi when she came in from work late, after seven, having stopped at her take-away, and she sat on the couch and ate noodles *with* chopsticks—from the box. James had always found that a bit pretentious. What the hell was the point when you had a drawer of forks and spoons? he would say. Well, James was in his room, so she used her chopsticks but ended up getting a spoon for the sauce at the bottom. She put on a movie, a movie that didn't involve guns, or worlds ending, or murder investigations, so there was no way it was a ploy to get him on the couch, and when he padded out a little bit later, she did hear a small laugh as he opened the fridge and must have seen 'Ava's milk'.

There was a pause.

Just a pause, and for that, after the days she'd had, she was terribly grateful.

CHAPTER NINE

JAMES knew the time lab results came in during the evening.

He knew too that things were being rushed through.

And though he'd told Ava and everyone else not to expect results till the middle of next week, on the Thursday evening after his surgery, just in case, he tried to log in and pull up his file, but Blake had locked him out and the lock remained.

He waited half an hour and then caved in, texted Blake to see if there was any news.

Out with Joan for wedding anniversary—will let you know as soon as I can.

He didn't say no. And James knew then that the next day he would know his results, that decisions would be made for the journey he was about to begin.

'Hi!' Ava walked in as he stood looking out of the window and as he turned to say hi, Ava smiled, but she was giving him the space he'd insisted on because she went straight through to the kitchen and poured herself a drink of water.

How could he put her through all this? James wondered.

He knew what lay ahead—knew as well as anyone who hadn't been through it all what lay ahead.

And for what?

James knew the statistics better than anyone, knew the odds were in his favour, that Donald was right, a future probably awaited him, but what if not?

He'd seen what losing the babies had done to Ava; he'd seen his vibrant, happy wife slowly go downhill to the point where their marriage was over.

A marriage that had, for a very long time, been such a good one.

And instead of staring out of the window, or slumping on to the couch or going back to his bedroom, when Ava went to the kitchen this time he followed her through.

'How was work?'

'Slow!' Ava said, opening the fridge, but there was nothing she fancied and she didn't want another takeaway. 'Two patients cancelled. I'd have come home earlier except I went for a coffee with Evie.' She saw his vague frown as she turned round. 'We've sort of become friends.' And it just sort of underscored how little they spoke, so she asked after him. 'How are you doing?'

'I'm bored,' James said, which wasn't strictly true. His mind had never been so restless, but he wanted distraction very badly. 'I can't stand another week of this. I think I'm going to go back to work next week.'

'You haven't even been out of the flat,' Ava pointed

out. 'You could go for a walk.' She said. 'Or we could, it's a nice—'

'I have been going for walks.' James said, and he sort of, almost, smiled. 'There was no choice, given there wasn't any milk.'

'There is milk…' Ava started, and then she sort of almost smiled too. 'If you want to get out a bit further than the corner shop, I could drive you to the beach.' She knew he'd say no, knew he'd just shake his head and head back to the bedroom that was his this week, except he didn't give the answer she was expecting. Instead, he nodded and walked out of the kitchen. 'I'll just get changed.'

She knew that James hated being driven so Ava was a little bit surprised, as they approached their local beach, when James suggested they drive on a bit further.

'How about the other beach?' James suggested. 'We haven't been there for a while.'

It had been their regular beach many years ago. James had been renting a large house along with some fellow students just a few hundred metres or so from the beach when she had first met him and as they drove past the house she saw James crane his neck for a glimpse of the house he had once lived in and the one she had also moved into.

'It still looks like a bombsite,' James said. It really was a renovator's delight, or maybe the whole thing would be better pulled down because from the front gate to the chimney work needed to be done, but they had known so many good times there. 'Its probably still being rented out to students.'

Ava parked the car as close as they could get to the beach and headed down the once familiar route. The sun was low on the water and the beach busy, with joggers and teenagers and couples like them, or people walking alone, just taking time to indulge, and the silence wasn't awkward, more pensive. It was James that broke it.

'Thanks for this. I think I was getting cabin fever.'

'It's nice to get out,' Ava agreed, because it really was. 'We used to go walking in the evenings a lot.' She gave him a nudge. 'Before you got all important.'

She was talking about his promotion a couple of years ago and instead of snapping back a smart retort as to how home hadn't actually been a bundle of laughs to race back to, James was silent for a moment as he walked on and thought about what she had said, because it was all so much more complicated than that. Feelings and events were so intricately intertwined that it was almost impossible to separate them, but on a night like tonight—when tomorrow everything changed— James did.

'Sorry about that.' She glanced over at his unexpected apology. 'I don't like rushing people,' James continued. 'I tried to put the difficult patients towards the end of the day, so I wasn't putting everyone else behind. You try and juggle it, to get the balance right.' He'd never really tried to explain it before. 'Like last week, when I found the lump, Blake moved his whole morning. And when my results come back I won't want just a ten-minute consultation.' Then he gave a wry laugh. 'Well, I might.'

He wanted a ten-minute incredulous apology from Blake actually, for Blake to tell him that they'd got it all completely wrong, that pathology had found nothing, nothing at all, and the blood tests were a complete mix-up, and Ava even smiled when he told her.

'I just hate pushing people through. I know I can't always take the time I'd like to, but seeing them later in the day…' He gave an uncomfortable shrug. 'It cost us, though, didn't it?'

'It wasn't just that,' Ava said, because they could have worked around that had things been better between them, then she saw him grimace. 'Are you okay?'

'Walking on the sand is harder than I thought,' James said, and he looked on ahead to a place that had once been theirs, where a much younger James and Ava had found out just how much they liked each other one night after a student party. But it was a place that seemed just a little bit too far away to get to this evening and as they turned and walked back towards the car, Ava wondered if James even remembered.

'Are you looking forward to the summer break?' James had asked.

They had wandered away from the party, the excuse being that it was too noisy to talk. Exams had finished and the summer had stretched ahead. Ava had lied when she'd answered him—after all, she couldn't really admit that she couldn't stand the thought of nearly three months of not seeing him. She'd had a crush on him for ages, they had spoken a couple of times, but now, just when they were really talking, just when it seemed things were starting to move on, she wouldn't see him for ages.

But of course she hadn't told him that. Instead she'd said that, yes, she was looking forward to it.

Then he'd asked, 'What plans have you got?'

'Well, it's my birthday in January and Mum and Dad have offered to get me a flight up to Queensland to go and visit my cousin.'

'A return flight, I hope?'

'I should check that, actually.' Ava had smiled as they'd sat down. 'I wouldn't put it past them.'

And she halted, because she really didn't want to talk about her parents, about how really every holiday for as long as she could remember she had been sent away, either to an auntie's or grandparent's, and now that she was older, the supposed gift was just another way to ensure she didn't get in her parents' way.

'I think I'll just ask them for the money instead. I'm going to be looking for a flat…' She really didn't fancy flat-sharing, but living at home wasn't working, and on her waitressing wage it was all she could afford.

'What about you?' Ava asked. 'Are you looking forward to it?'

'That depends,' James said, 'on whether or not I've got your phone number.'

Her breath seemed to burn in her lungs as he voiced what she had been thinking and her face was on fire as he moved towards her. And at eighteen, close to nineteen, she had her first kiss. Not that he knew it was her first, she hoped, and it certainly wasn't his, because James's mouth knew exactly what to do.

He stroked her lips with his and she felt his hand steady her head as he increased the pressure, as she tried to work out how to breathe with the man she had been thinking so much about finally close, and he simply didn't let her be clumsy or awkward, he just kissed her nervous lips till they gave in to the bliss, and just as her mouth accustomed to another on hers there was the shock of her first taste of tongue and another layer of bliss was exposed to her by him.

She struggled to contain it, to not simply melt beneath him as his lips pressed her down towards the sand. She was about to halt him, to stop him, except her mind asked her why, when it felt so nice with him over her.

His lips dragged from her mouth, to her cheeks, to her ear, and the feel of his hot breath there should surely not be so nice, or was it the words that had her unfurl?

'Don't go to Queensland,' James breathed. 'Spend the summer here.'

She could spend for ever here in his arms being kissed. Then there was a bombardment of new sensations, his hand moving up from her waist, warm fingers sliding up beneath her T-shirt, and she knew she should halt him, that perhaps she was giving him the wrong idea about where this was leading.

She could feel the solid press of him against her sand-dusted thigh, and still, dangerously, she kissed him back, and as his hand found her breast she wanted it to stay there. James knew that, for she moaned into his mouth and then she pulled back from him, looked up at him, and he felt her sudden tension—her hands on his shoulders and a flash of uncertainty in her eyes— and James removed his hand and went back to simply kissing her.

All he'd done that night was kiss her. He'd spent the entire summer gradually taking each barrier down, dismantling each insecurity, taking things slowly, acting patiently as she drove him wild.

And he wondered if she even remembered.

'It doesn't look good for Finn,' James said as they headed back to the car, and they spoke for a bit about Finn, about how hard it was on Evie.

'She's still working,' Ava said. 'But any minute she's not she's either with him on ICU or asleep on the on-call room there.'

'Finn wouldn't want that,' James said.

'Well, while Finn's got a tube down his throat, he doesn't exactly have much say in things.'

And James wouldn't want that either, and he tried not to think of a time when it might be Ava catching some shut-eye in a camp bed by his side. Ava spoon-feeding him, Ava running herself ragged through the 'Till death us do part' bit. He was being ridiculous, he tried to tell himself for the hundredth time this evening because, yes, the statistics were good.

But the glass was resolutely stuck on half-empty— he simply couldn't get it to half-full.

They got back to the car and once there he looked up

at the house he had once lived in, looked at the room that had once been his, had been theirs, but it ached to remember that time, so he climbed into the car and they drove the length of the beach that they had used to come to so often. He didn't want it to be tomorrow, didn't want to get his results, even though he was desperate to hear them. He knew too much about what lay ahead, knew how hard it would be not just on him but also on them. All that he would put Ava through, and for what?

He looked over at Ava. Her face was pale from the strain of the last few days but, then again, it had been pale the day he'd come home from Brisbane. The strain of the last two years was taking its toll—he'd promised to make her happy and clearly hadn't been doing a very good job.

'Do you want to get something to eat?' James suggested. 'Maybe go to Pete's?'

'Sure,' Ava said, a little taken back at his suggestion. 'I hope I'm not banned.'

'Banned?'

And she told him, well, not all of it, but about how she'd been upset and had dashed off without paying for her wine.

'They'll have your photo up at the bar.' James smiled, but it was a pale one—he'd been trying to get her to go to Pete's for the last two years, but now that he had cancer his wish was her command. Suddenly everybody was treating him just a little bit differently—as they walked into the bar they ran into Lexi and Sam, casual friends from the hospital, but the conversation was forcibly jovial and he wanted things the way they had been before.

'That was awkward,' James said as he steered Ava to their regular spot by the window.

'Lexi has got a lot on her mind,' Ava said. 'She's probably really worried about Evie.' Lexi was one of Evie's sisters and even if they hadn't been so friendly then, Ava recalled when their younger sister, Bella, had had a lung transplant and how neither she nor James had known how to broach it in conversation. It was hard being in the medical profession at times like this, when you knew perhaps more than a friend should.

'Remember how awkward it was when Bella had her surgery? We didn't know what to say to Lexi then.'

'I guess.' James shrugged as he looked through the menu 'I might get pizza,' James said, only it wasn't to annoy her this time. It was what they used to share when they had first moved here, a family-sized mozzarella, and he'd have far more than half of it. 'And a beer,' he added, because no matter what these results were tomorrow, he was going on a health kick. Good news or bad, he was going to take a lot better care of himself from now on, he just needed this one last night.

'I'm going to have a steak.' Ava was suddenly hungry.

'You need to add a glass of wine to the bill.' James smiled as the waiter came over and he relayed their orders, adding 'medium-rare' to her steak and salad when the waiter asked what her side order was, because he knew how she liked things. 'She has a tendency to run off without paying.'

And as it turned out, the waiter did remember her, and he laughed as he told her that the other couple had picked up her bill.

It was actually a really nice evening. Ava couldn't quite work out James's mood, but they chatted a lot about old times and they certainly weren't maudlin. Well, maybe a little bit, because they were at their old table and by mistake, about half an hour into their time there, the waiter brought over a bottle of champagne they hadn't ordered.

'Sorry!' He smiled when James said with a slightly wry note that they weren't celebrating. 'Wrong table.'

And they sat for a moment and neither said a word to each other. In fact, both looked away, but both surely remembered.

'I can't drink!'

They'd been almost deranged with excitement at the prospect of being parents, their hair still wet from the showers because as soon as she'd told him they'd started kissing and then ended up making love, and afterwards they'd decided to go out to Pete's to celebrate.

'You can have one glass.'

'No.' She'd been adamant, and so too had he, because he'd gone ahead and ordered a bottle and they'd sat holding hands and just grinning at their secret.

'When can we tell people?' James had asked.

'Twelve weeks,' Ava had said.

'That's ages,' James had moaned. 'Then again…'

he'd rolled his eyes '…my mum is going to go crazy, you do know that? She's been waiting years for this.'

James would have had children straight away as soon as they were married had Ava wanted to. He adored kids, was a favourite with the children in his extended family. He couldn't wait for a family of his own, but Ava had really wanted to be established in her career first. Sexual dysfunction had never been her intended specialty—in fact, she had intended to be a GP—but somehow she had drifted towards that area, and it had only been when she'd got to thirty that she'd felt ready to make that commitment, but once ready she'd embraced it wholeheartedly.

The waiter popped the champagne and poured it.

'To twins.' James grinned.

'Please, no!' Ava said, and she did have a tiny taste as they clinked their glasses and said 'Cheers'.

It had been their last perfect night, really, and the last time she'd tasted champagne.

By the next morning she hadn't been pregnant any more.

James suggested they leave the car where it was parked outside Pete's and instead walk the short distance home. She wished he'd at least take her hand, longed for the days when he'd kissed her against a wall or all the way up in the lift were long gone now.

She wanted them back, so badly she wanted them back.

When they got home James put on a movie, not a crime show for once, and neither was it one Ava would have chosen. In fact, it was science fiction, of all things, with subtitles. It was a movie she'd didn't even know that they had.

'I've seen this before, I think.'

'I found it at the second-hand market,' James said, and he sat on the sofa beside her, just not close enough to touch.

She was sure she had seen it, or maybe not. It was the maddest film, but there was a certain sense of déjà vu to it, or at least there was for a little while, but halfway through she was lost.

'No.' Ava shook her head. 'I haven't seen this.' And then she frowned because she'd been quite sure she had.

She never had found a flat before the start of her first semester. She had arrived one night at the house, in tears after her parents had had a blistering row. James had been on his way out with his housemates, but had waved them off and they had stayed behind and gone where they'd always gone—to his room. And though they had done an awful lot of things, they hadn't quite done that.

'I'm sorry about this.'

'Sorry about what?' James had asked. They'd been lying on the bed just talking and kissing, they'd given up trying to make sense of her parents, of trying to work out if her mother actually was leaving her father this time.

'You were going out.'

'Now I'm staying in.' His hand crept up her leg and she didn't wriggle away. Instead her hands found him and more and more she moved him closer to where he stroked her with his fingers, and they almost had a few times before, and he wasn't sure he could play that game again, except he wasn't stroking her now with his fingers, and her hands were up at his shoulders and he was almost there and it killed to not be inside her.

'Ava?'

She looked up into green eyes and there was not a doubt in her mind and she nodded, resumed their kiss because she'd made up her mind.

'Hold on.' He went to get a condom, sure she'd insist on it—she'd even made him have blood tests and things, and only for Ava would he do that—but as she so often did, she surprised him. 'I've gone on the Pill.'

'Yeah, but...' He almost shrank from the responsibility, for about one tenth of a second, and then her hands slid over his back and down to his buttocks and he felt her mouth on his shoulder as he lowered himself and edged his way in, and she sobbed out at the delicious agony and there was a nip of her teeth on his shoulder that almost took him over the edge and then he met Ava, the real Ava that he'd unleashed, her kisses fervent, her words enticing, and his kisses and words were too.

It was sex that was worth waiting for. It was more than just sex that night in his bed.

'God, Ava...'

She heard him moan and she had to come, she could feel the urgency. She could not believe then the noise and the passion and the feel of him inside her, and she knew she'd take for ever, knew because she always had, except he was thrusting inside her, his entire body suddenly rigid, and she was the one uncoiled beneath him. She could hear her own moans, her own shouts, her own collapse into silence, and then back to the real world.

She lay in his arms, watching some strange foreign science fiction film on his television that had started, neither wanting to get up from their haven, happy to read the subtitles, at least until his mouth found her shoulder again.

They never had got to see the end…

''Night, Ava.'

He yawned and stood up at about halfway through the movie, and tonight James did bend to kiss her, not her mouth, but the top of her head, and she felt his fingers in her hair and for a second they lingered, but even as she turned her head to him, he lifted his and headed to bed, and as she heard the door click closed behind him she knew what had happened, thought about it quite logically for a moment, and then she cried.

That walk on the beach, the trip to Pete's and now the film.

He'd been saying goodbye.

CHAPTER TEN

'It's your mother on the phone.' Ginny had rung through.

Ava was about to tell Ginny that she was in with a client, but instead she asked that she be put through. 'You might as well go now, Ginny. I've just got a quick phone consultation and then I'm heading home,' Ava said, then took a breath and took the call from her mum.

'Hi, there,' Ava said.

'Hi, Ava.' Fleur wasn't really one for chatting. 'Any news on James?'

'Nothing yet,' Ava said, because they weren't expecting the results till next week and she wasn't sure that they were even going to make it to next week. She had been on the edge of tears between every patient, had the most appalling feeling in her stomach and all she wanted was to go home.

'Well, let your father and I know when you hear.' There was a slight pause. 'How are you?'

'I've been better,' Ava admitted. 'Actually, Mum...' And then she stopped herself because she was not going to discuss this with her mother and, anyway, Fleur wouldn't understand—her parents' marriage was so liberal and open, she could never understand what Ava was grappling with, aside from James's illness.

Still, maybe she could do with a dose of liberality, Ava thought, maybe she could try talking with her mum. Her mum wouldn't turn a hair if she told her she thought James had had an affair, was still having one.

Turn a blind eye would be her mother's advice. It was strange really, everyone thought Ava was so open-minded, so liberal, except she only was with James. She really did believe in love and was so proud of the couples that came to see her and worked through things. Yes, maybe she did need some of her mum's rather more open views. 'I was thinking I might come over and see you this weekend.'

'Oh!' She could hear the surprise in her mother's voice. 'Is he up and about, then?'

'Not with James,' Ava said. Perish the thought, James didn't exactly like her parents, had said in some rows how they'd messed her up, and the thought of them together with tensions so high didn't particularly appeal. 'Just me. I'll see how the next couple of days go and let you know.'

'Well, ring first,' Fleur warned. 'I don't want you driving all that way if I'm out.'

She was thoughtful like that, Ava reflected darkly, putting down the phone and resting her head in her hands. For all Veronica irritated her at times, at least she was there. All the Carmichael clan had been around and had it been Ava they would have done the same. Well, maybe it would be a slightly diluted version and maybe the fridge would be more full so that James wouldn't starve while she was incapacitated, but at least they would have stepped up.

Her mother hadn't so much as sent a card or even spoken to James.

Ava had never been close to her mother, or her father. The only person in her life she'd been really close to had been James.

'Ava.' There was a knock at the door and she looked up at his voice. Oh, God, he was wearing those grey linen pants and that black shirt and he'd shaved and he had on that cologne and he looked more beautiful than he ever had, more beautiful than the man she had married even, and she was gripped tighter with the fear that was ever-present these days. Because he couldn't be sick, he just couldn't be, and Ava knew why he was there but she asked just the same.

'What are you doing here?'

'Blake got my results in.'

'Already? That is really quick. When are you seeing him…?' Her voice trailed off, knew it was pointless, knew that James wasn't there to ask her to come along with him to find out the news.

'It's good news,' James said, and he went a bit technical for a moment. Yes, it was good news, it just wasn't quite as good as he had hoped, not quite as contained, but it was still stage one. As he explained, her mind couldn't keep up with him and he toned it down. 'I've gone through it all with Blake and I'm going to have a course of chemo. I want to know that it's gone.'

It wasn't a discussion, but that was fair enough, it was James's field after all. 'I'll still be working, I'll just have to schedule around it…' And he spoke a little more about what was involved and there was thin relief because the news could have been so much worse. But there was also a sense of fear of the unknown too, because so much had changed in such a short space of time.

'We'll get through it,' Ava said.

And he shook his head and she knew, really knew, why he was there, and a fear of the known closed in.

She'd known since last night that this was coming.

'I'm moving out.' He said it just like that. 'I'm going round to Mum's now to give her the results and to tell her that I've walked out.'

'Please, don't.' She knew that he meant it, knew he had made up his mind, could feel him slipping away, or rather that he had been slipping away for ages but now, at this moment, he was completely out of her grasp. 'James, please. This isn't the time to be making these sorts of decisions.'

'It's done,' James said. 'I've got a serviced apartment; I've just been and picked up the keys.'

'You're not supposed to be driving.'

'Yeah, well, I was looking on the internet and I found out that there were these yellow things called taxis…'

She hated it when he did this, when he just blocked her out.

'I want to be with you. I want to help you get through it.'

Except she'd blocked him out too, and he told her as much. 'Do you think I didn't want to be with you?' James said. 'Relationships are supposed to be a two-way street, but not ours. Your grief was too private, too deep to share with me—well, you can't just suddenly decide now that you want to be all open and touchy-feely.'

And she stood in her office where she fixed and she healed, where she let couples discuss and say the words that hurt to hear but needed to be said. Except with James it was final. James didn't want to be in here. Unlike her couples, James didn't want it fixed.

'I've taken what I need for now. I'll sort out the study and stuff when I can lift and things, but I'll arrange a time that's suitable with you.' He walked over and put his key on the table and he made it sound so terribly simple, except it was far from that. And then he took off his ring.

Well, she wasn't taking off hers.

'I'm not getting a lawyer,' Ava said. 'I don't want a divorce.'

'Of course you don't,' James said. 'It would be a bit of a stupid thing to do now.'

'Sorry?'

'All the life insurance and everything.'

'Oh, for God's sake...' She was so angry. 'You can be such a bastard.'

And he didn't try and stop the row this time, neither did he lean over to kiss her. He just headed for the door.

'You could go to your mum's.' She was frantic. Anything was better than a serviced apartment. She couldn't stand for him to go through this alone, but she knew him too well, knew his answer almost before it came.

'I don't want to go to my mum's. I don't want anyone near. I want the dignity to puke in private.'

CHAPTER ELEVEN

'How are you doing, James?'

It was two weeks later and he was sitting in a reclining chair, rather than standing beside it, as Harriet,
one of the nurses he knew well, ran through the forms.

James hated paperwork, completely loathed it, but it
had never dawned on him that the patients felt the same.
He'd answered the same questions over and over, five
minutes apart at times.

And always the answers had been the same.

Today, though, a few were different and as he
skimmed through the form with Harriet, before he had
his first round of treatment, he paused.

'My emergency contact has changed.'

'Oh.'

'It's Veronica Carmichael—my mother.' He made
a thin joke. 'But only ring her if I'm dead—she worries a lot.'

And he had to change his home address too and de-
lete his home phone number to bit by bit extract himself from Ava's life.

He'd seen Harriet many times all gloved and gowned

up, but it felt very different to be sitting a reclining chair, getting his treatment. She'd done his obs diligently throughout and had chatted a little, but things *were* different. He found it very hard to pinpoint—his patients had spoken to him often about it and now he fully understood. There was this air of sympathy, of forced normality in almost every exchange he had these days, and James couldn't stand it. Sure, he preferred that Harriet wasn't flirting now, it had been awkward at times, but it wasn't about Harriet, it was about everyone. Well, almost everyone. There were still some people with whom he could relax.

'When you said you'd be beside me, whatever I decide...' James turned at the sound of Richard's—his teenage patient's—voice and gave a wry smile as he chatted on. 'This really is going above and beyond the call of duty.'

'I do my best,' James quipped back. 'Well, I guess you got your answer as to what I'd do if it was me.' He smiled at his patient and peer. 'Sorry I missed your appointment.' He really was. He knew how disappointed Richard would have been.

'No problem,' Richard said. 'I actually came back a couple of days after we spoke. I'd decided that I couldn't stand just waiting to see what happened. Blake said you weren't well—he didn't say what was wrong.' Richard looked him right in the eye. 'I'm really sorry.'

And they spoke about their results and their treatments.

'This is your second?' James glanced up to the bag

that was dripping its contents into Richard's arm. 'How was it?'

Richard pulled a face. 'Not as bad as I thought,' Richard said, 'but I've heard it gets worse.'

They spoke for a bit then Richard put his headphones on and listened to some music and when James got sick of the nurses chatting behind the glass—first about him. Did they know he and Ava had broken up? Later about Finn, how much he'd improved, but his arm was practically numb and there was some weakness in one of his legs. But he was insisting on being discharged apparently. He watched a DVD, a war one because he was sick of all the inspirational ones that people kept pressing on him. Still, even if it was a good movie, he couldn't really concentrate and instead he thought about many things as he tried not to think about Ava.

The cleaner was coming to the apartment today, but he'd told her not to come for the next three. He'd had his hair cut really short, because he didn't want to scare her when it all fell out. He thought about the gym and how pleased he was that he was a bit fitter than if it had happened a few months ago, but he wished too he'd eaten better. He'd ordered some frozen meals, healthy ones, the ones that got delivered—but he felt like a fighter pilot scrambling when it was already too late.

'James!' Cleo, the charge nurse, had come in for her late shift and the second she saw him she was over as Harriet removed his IV. 'How are you doing?'

'I'm fine. Just about ready to go home.'

He didn't feel fine, actually. He knew everyone reacted differently but, in fact, for the first time since he'd found that lump he felt ill, as if they'd administered an IV labelled fatigue straight into him.

He had some tea and sandwiches and was ready now to go home, or rather to return to the serviced apartment, but he couldn't stop thinking about the apartment at Kirribilli, about the fridge there that made ice cubes and the bed that was his, and he was still trying not to think about Ava.

'Did you want me to ring through to Ava and tell her you're ready for the off?' Cleo asked, and he saw Harriet's cheeks pink up

'No.' James shook his head. 'I just rang my mum and she's picking me up.' He'd had his anti-emetics, all the drugs dispensed, and he just wanted this over with.

'Ava and I broke up, Cleo.'

'Oh!' He watched as she struggled for a response. 'But you're at your mum's tonight?'

He didn't need a babysitter and they didn't need to know.

'Here she is.' James stood as Veronica entered. He saw the frantic look that had been on his mother's face since he'd first broken the news and he hated that he had put it there. 'Hey, Mum. Ready to go?'

Ava's mum wasn't worried. 'I'm not with you, Ava!' She'd done what she had said she never would and had gone to her mum's one lunchtime in the hope of advice. 'Ava, you haven't been sleeping together, you've been living separate lives, and now you're "devastated" that it's over?'

'You don't understand.'

'It's guilt, Ava.' Fleur was adamant. 'James had his chemo today and the martyr in you feels you ought to be there.'

And Ava listened, but not really, because her mum, she realised, just didn't do love.

'And whatever you do,' her mum said as she saw her to the car, 'don't even think about getting a divorce. No, don't look at me like that, Ava. I'm just being practical—you'd be mad to divorce him now, wouldn't you?'

Ava knew James had chemo today, and the day had stretched for ever, which was maybe why she had gone to her mum's. Sometimes she saw him at work, not often, but she'd started to have lunch in the canteen because so too had James. He'd had his hair cut short, in anticipation of the drug side effects, no doubt, but for now he looked as if he was brimming with health. He ignored her whenever he saw her, and one time she'd seen him sitting chatting with one of the nurses. Previously, she'd have just walked right on over, but instead she'd sat brittle and jealous, bobbing around in limbo—separated not divorced. Married but apart.

She walked through the car park, tried to focus her mind back on work, but really she would have preferred to go home and to bed and just pull the covers over her head. She had never felt more tired in her life.

It had been two weeks since he'd left her, and in those weeks Ava had grimly continued on as if it hadn't happened, as if James hadn't left. Desperately trying to convince herself that telling others would be premature—that any day now James would change his mind, that he'd ring and say he was on his way back home, or that she'd come out of the lift to find him waiting at the front door.

Apart from her mother this lunchtime, Ava hadn't told anybody. Amazingly for SHH, whose grapevine was legendary, word didn't seem to have got out yet. People were still asking her how James was doing, and after all she was still wearing her ring, and maybe James hadn't told anyone either. Maybe he was going to come back to her.

Ava forced herself to keep busy. She swam in the morning and rode most evenings, her time on the horse the only time her head felt calm, and then it was back to the flat that was too empty without him and a night spent resisting the urge to call.

Tonight would be even harder. She could not stand that he would be going through this treatment without her, and then she saw him, at the other end of the corridor and walking towards her. He looked the same as he had the last time she'd glimpsed him. Only Ava could see his exhaustion as James and Veronica neared. It was the first time in all of this that he actually looked unwell, or was it stress that marred his features? She truly didn't know.

At first he pretended not to have noticed her and Ava did the same, walking towards him with her heart hammering in her chest, pretending to check her phone, wondering how she should greet him. Veronica didn't look so well either—she seemed to have aged a decade since James had found the lump.

'Ava.' He nodded by way of a greeting, and she opened her mouth to speak to him to ask him how it had been, how he was feeling, except James wasn't in the mood for conversation and had already walked on.

'Hi, there, Ava.' Ginny gave her a smile as she walked past the desk and with supreme effort she gave her one back. 'Is everything okay?' Ginny asked. 'You're ever so pale.'

'I'm fine,' Ava said when she felt like screaming, and somehow she made it to her office.

Somehow she made it through the afternoon, but for once her mind could not quite focus on her patients. She did her best, of course, maybe they didn't notice, but in truth her mind was with James and her body ached to sleep.

She should be in bed this minute beside him, for she knew that that was where he would have headed, and it was as if her body was insisting, as if it was demanding that that be where she should be too.

'See you, Ginny.' For once she left on the stroke of five, hitched up her bag and said goodnight.

'Oh!' Ginny looked up from whatever she was doing. 'See you, Ava…' Except it was Ginny who forced the smile this time and Ava knew then that she knew.

That word was out.

That James and Ava's marriage was over.

Yes, there was guilt, but it was only a part of how

she felt as she headed for home, as she stood in the lift, which was working tonight, then let herself in the door.

Even if she'd lived alone for three months, it had still been James's home. There had still been the *chance* that he'd come home, but now it just felt empty.

Now would come the appalling silence from friends while they worked out what best to say. She and James had been guilty of that when Donna and Neil had split up.

'Ring him,' Ava had pushed.

'Ring her,' James had pushed.

They'd worried so much as to whom to ring first, in the end she'd gone into the bedroom and James to his study and they'd both rung at the same time on their mobiles and then met back in the lounge for a good old gossip.

She wasn't ready yet to smile at the memory. Smiling felt a long way off—at least in her personal life—and she knew it was pathetic to hope when there was a knock at the door, except she did.

'Oh, Ava.' It was Evie at her door

'You've heard the happy news, then.' She pulled the door open and let Evie in.

'I don't know what to say,' Evie admitted. 'I've been banging on about my problems and all this time...'

'Don't worry about that,' Ava said. 'It's nice of you to come over—it's been pretty chilly at the hospital this afternoon.' She made them both a drink, this time, though, it was for Ava to compose herself for a moment.

'So what's the gossip?' Ava asked when they were both sitting down. 'What's everyone saying?'

'Just that you two have split up. I actually heard something last week, but I just ignored it. I mean I know how hap—' She halted herself. 'I thought you two were so happy, it's just assumed that you are really,' Evie said. 'And what with James being sick, it seemed ridiculous. I knew you'd never...' She felt Evie glance at her wedding-ring finger, the ring still firmly there.

'He left me,' Ava said, but she knew that probably wasn't what was being said. 'Anyway, I don't have to defend myself.'

'Of course you don't.'

'I don't mean to you.' Ava shook her head, couldn't believe the mess her life was. 'We've been having problems for a long time.' Ava let out a little of what for so long she had been holding in. 'It isn't completely out of the blue. It just feels that way, though,' Ava admitted. It was actually nice to have Evie over, she was far easier to talk to than her own mother, and it was a relief to find out a bit about James.

'He's taking the next couple of days off, I think,' Evie said. 'The courses of chemo are three weeks apart, well, that's what I've heard.'

'I don't know anything,' Ava admitted. 'I don't know how bad it's going to be.' They chatted for a while about James and then Ava warmed them both a frozen meal for one and she asked after Finn.

'It doesn't look great,' Evie said. 'Not that I'm allowed to know.'

'He's still not letting you visit?'

'He's not letting anyone visit,' Evie said. 'You know he had some swelling after the operation and that's subsided, but...' Ava felt as if she were looking in a mirror. She could see the lines of tension around Evie's eyes, see the set of her lips as she struggled to stay positive. 'Well, things aren't great, but he's going home tomorrow and there's talk of scheduling another operation...'

They both stopped as they heard noises from above, like an angry ghost of Finn, because they were talking about him, but then Evie laughed.

'That's Luke and Lily,' Evie said. 'Luke prised his key off him and they're sorting out things there tonight, you know, fitting a shower chair and things...' Ava could see the sparkle of tears in Evie's eyes. 'He'll hate that.'

'Better than a wheelchair,' Ava said.

'I think Luke's gone and got another key cut so he can keep an eye on him, and they're stocking up the fridge,' Evie said, 'hiding the Scotch.'

Ava glanced up at the almost full bottle still sitting on the bench and thought about that night. For all they said about Finn's reckless ways, he could be very sensible too. 'He'll just bribe Gladys if he wants some.' Ava smiled. 'Finn's gong to be okay.'

'You don't know that,' Evie said.

But she did. Somewhere deep inside, she just felt that Finn would be okay. She just wished she had the same feeling about James.

Evie went up to help Lily and Luke, but Ava simply couldn't handle any more company or sympathy tonight and after she said farewell to Evie she took a long shower. She was too tired to blow-dry her hair so instead she did the hardest thing.

Took off her ring for the first time in seven years.

She'd felt Evie looking at her ring finger and now she thought about it, Ginny had too. She felt like the relatives days after an earthquake, still insisting the emergency workers keep looking, still demanding there was hope, when it had all but faded. Except she couldn't leave it there by the sink, so she added it to the chain she wore around her neck and she crawled into bed and lay there wondering how he was feeling tonight.

She didn't even try not to think about James.

The first wave of nausea hit at 5:00 a.m.

Just this violent wave, the type that jolted you awake and propelled you out of bed, and then a frantic dash to the bathroom and the chill of cold sweat as you knelt in the dark because you didn't have time to switch on the light.

Ava clung to the toilet bowl and held on for dear life, wondering if she was having sympathy nausea with James, because she hadn't vomited since...

She closed her eyes as another wave hit and then she started to cry because she simply couldn't be pregnant. They'd had sex once, for God's sake. She was on the Pill, except she hadn't taken it the morning they found the lump, and perhaps not the morning after that too.

Ava was terrified she was pregnant.

Refused to be.

She had gastric flu, she decided, and for the first time in a very long time she rang in at eight and used some of her sick leave, made a cup of tea and went back to bed.

Then she woke up at ten-thirty and couldn't dress quickly enough in her haste to find out. She walked down to the chemist, which had once been her regular walk—a monthly walk where she'd buy two pregnancy kits that each contained two pregnancy tests, because if it was negative she'd want to do it again the next morning and the morning after that too, and if it was positive, she'd be taking the test again and again just to be sure.

She bought one that morning.

One single one and then walked back to the flat, cursing her timing because there were Luke and Lily trying to hold back as a very thin and dishevelled Finn dragged himself on a cane towards the lift, his arm hanging limp and useless beside him.

'Morning.' She gave Lily and Luke an attempt at a smile and was completely ignored by Finn.

She felt as if they had X-ray vision and could see through the paper bag she was holding but knew that, in truth, they were thinking of Finn.

'Ava.' Lily returned her smile. 'I was going to call you.' She was just a little bit awkward and who could blame her? 'We should catch up…'

'Sure,' Ava replied, relieved when the lift door opened and she let herself into the flat and raced to the loo. She waited, desperate for the first time for the result to be negative.

She couldn't do this again.

Not now.

Not alone.

And how could she put James through it too?

She cried so hard when she saw that cross and she truly didn't know what to do. Except he had to know, he deserved to know, surely. And now there was a legitimate reason to see him too.

She drove to his serviced apartment and knocked on the door, bracing herself to be honest, to talk it out as she told all her clients, except it was Veronica who answered the door and her face was savage.

'What the hell do you want?'

'My husband,' Ava said.

'He's been up all night, ill,' Veronica said. 'He's told me that if you come to the door that you're not to be allowed in.'

'Look, Veronica.' Ava tried to keep her voice even. 'I need to speak to him.'

'Well, James doesn't need to speak to you, he doesn't need the stress…' Veronica said, and then she took her out into the hall and closed the door behind her. 'What sort of woman would leave her husband at a time like this?'

'He left me!' Ava reminded her, but she knew it was hopeless, knew the gossip around the hospital, and it was the same here—she was the shrew who couldn't stand by her man, who had got out when the going got tough.

'He stood by you through all those miscarriages,'

Veronica hissed. 'Whatever your problems were, could you not have put them on hold?'

'I just need to talk to him.'

'Well, the last thing he needs right now is you,' Veronica said. 'And I mean it, Ava. I bought him some DVDs and we've just been watching them. The best thing, they say, is to stay positive—James needs to be concentrating on himself not trying to repair a marriage that's been over for more than a year.' She must have seen Ava's already pale face turn to chalk. 'Just let him concentrate on himself.'

And she had to put it on hold, Ava realised, not just the marriage but the pregnancy too—she could not add to the pressure that James was under right now.

What was she supposed to tell him? *Oh, darling, I'm pregnant!* She knew the hell that would cause him, the confusion and fear, that James would know what she was going through, that somehow he would feel that he had to support her too as he did his best to get through his treatment.

And how could she tell him tomorrow or next week or next month that she'd lost it? How could she add to it all?

'If I were you—' Veronica broke into her trance '—if you care about him at all, you will just leave him well enough alone.'

CHAPTER TWELVE

It was hell to see him suffer from a distance.

He dragged himself to work, and over the weeks he lost weight, of course, but actually bald suited him. He carried right on working and sometimes she saw him laughing and chatting with colleagues, but only once did he meet her eyes. She was buying a coffee in the canteen and looked up to his and he didn't tear them away. Instead, he made his way over.

'I need to get a few things.'

'Sure.' She felt as if everyone in the canteen was watching them. 'When did you want to come over?'

'Tonight,' James said. 'Unless you're busy?'

'Tonight's fine.'

And, though tonight might be the time to tell him, she knew she wouldn't, for while it *was* hell to see him suffer from a distance, there was also a sense of relief too.

He had enough to deal with and it was better that he wasn't burdened with the worry about the pregnancy, that he wasn't walking on eggshells and worrying about her and how she'd be if she lost it. It actually felt easier for Ava, too, because she wasn't worrying about how disappointed he'd be when she did.

Except she didn't.

And it was starting to show.

So she pulled on leggings and a big sloppy jumper, not that she was really showing, but she was rounding out a bit and she worried he might notice.

He came over as arranged at eight.

Ava had wondered if it would be four mates and a truck, but it was just James.

'It's just mainly books that I came for,' James said, noting her attire, just a little bit annoyed that she hadn't made any effort at all. 'And clothes...' His were hanging off him. 'I've got some jeans from before I put on weight.'

'I threw them out.'

'Well, that didn't take long.'

'I threw them out years ago,' Ava said. 'You couldn't have worn them anyway—they would be totally out of fashion!' She hauled open the wardrobes and found some of his old black jeans that were a couple of sizes smaller and James took some T-shirts and then he went to the study.

'Do you want something to eat?' Ava offered.

'No, don't go to any trouble,' he called.

'It's no trouble,' Ava called back as she walked to the study. 'I could ring out for pizza.'

Except he'd given up pizza, was trying so hard to stick to the promises he'd made to himself deep into the night.

'No, really, I'm fine.'

'Coffee, then?'

She'd laugh if he told her he was drinking green tea.

'A glass of water would be great.' And she thought he was snubbing her while he thought of the fridge that pumped cold water and the sound of ice cubes as they hit the glass and wondered if he'd be pushing things if he asked for custody of the fridge.

'Here.' She handed him the glass and as he drank it down she forced conversation. 'How have you been doing?'

'Oh, you know,' James said. 'Chemo has its fun side.'

'Such as?'

'I can't think right now.' He was at his sarcastic best. 'How annoying is that? Oh, but it's right there on the tip of my tongue.'

'That bad, then?'

He just shrugged and carried on filling a box, and then he was done and their wedding photo was still sitting on the study desk. He hadn't added that to the mix.

'Donna came over,' Ava said. 'She rang for a chat last weekend and then got annoyed that I hadn't told her.' Ava rolled her eyes. 'Honestly, I need a to-do list!'

'Neil rang,' James said. 'Donna must have told him. I think he thought we'd be hitting the clubs together, he wasn't too impressed when he found out about the cancer.' Then he looked over. 'How was Donna?'

'Still talking about Neil.' Somehow they laughed. 'Still *moaning* about Neil. I wanted to put my hand up and stop her,' Ava said. 'I wanted to say, er, my marriage *just* broke up, yours ended years ago…'

And it shouldn't concern him, it was none of his business really, but he did want to know. 'How did your parents take it?'

'Oh,' Ava answered. 'Mum suggested I moved into my old bedroom so she could mother me a bit, you know…' And he stood and he looked because she didn't need to say she was being sarcastic, and even if his own mum drove him crazy at times he couldn't stand the way Ava's family were with her. It would be so easy now to wrap his arms around her, to stay, to just give in, but pride was a wall he couldn't get through.

'I think that's everything.'

He walked out into the living room and he could see the hospital and see the harbour and the view he knew and it smelt like home and he didn't want to go back to the serviced apartment and to sheets that smelt vaguely of bleach. He wanted to go right now and lie down in the bedroom that had once been theirs and just close his eyes, or even just rest on the sofa, except he had another treatment due soon, and it didn't exactly make for tender reunions. And, after all, she hadn't wanted him when he was well.

'If there's anything else you want…?'

'The fridge,' James said.

'Ha, ha.' She tried to laugh as he walked to the door and then she said what was true. 'I miss you.'

And he couldn't not ask. 'How are you doing?'

'I don't know,' Ava admitted. She truly didn't know.

She wasn't teary any more, she was glad he wasn't worrying about her and the pregnancy on top everything else. And she only thought about his cancer for fifty-five minutes of every hour now, which was an improvement on the previous week. It was funny how with James she could sometimes be her most honest. 'I'm tired,' Ava said. 'I'm the most tired I've ever been.'

'And me.'

He was, and always had been the only person who could ever really comfort her, not all the time, of course, because too often she hadn't let him, but tonight she did. He put down the box and he pulled her into his arms and let her rest there for a little while, and he rested there too.

'Come back, James,' she said to his chest.

'I can't,' James said to her hair that smelt of lavender and somehow, in the hallway, not looking, just holding, he was able to be honest, the most honest he had been with anyone since he'd found that lump. He knew that he was too proud for his own good, knew that he could be stubborn at times, but he felt as if he'd been given a golden ticket. Only it was one he didn't want, one that excused all previous behaviour, resolved all rows, that now he was sick, only now was he wanted. And he didn't want a marriage built on her guilt, didn't want to drag her along for the appalling ride when they'd already been about to get off.

'I can't come back, Ava. Let me do this myself.' But, yes, so badly he missed her and it wasn't just pride that stopped him. There was something else too. His mortality had been rammed home to him, and while the statistics were good…

Better to lose him this way, the dark nights told him.

Better that she get over him now, because surely Ava did not deserve another loss. And he found himself kissing her and she kissed him back. A deep, lingering kiss that neither of them wanted to end because then they'd have to confront it, so they just carried on kissing and let their mouths speak a language that was safer than words at the moment. When it ended she put her face back against his chest, a bit embarrassed and confused at the want that was still in them.

'I've got to go,' James said, still holding her.

And she didn't fight it, because she understood that he did.

But it was nice to hold on to each other for a moment.

CHAPTER THIRTEEN

SOMETIMES, Ava now realised, talking *was* impossible.

In fact, as the weeks went on she revised one of her well-worn theories, not just for herself but for her patients too.

'It's good to see you again,' she said as she stepped into the waiting room to call her next patients in.

It really was a joy to see George and Elise—to see all of her patients, in fact. She loved her work, no matter how Veronica or others might sniff or nudge; she loved seeing the difference she made.

Today it was a visible difference as she stepped out into her waiting room and saw Elise smiling and George walking into her office, of course a little awkward, but she'd heard them talking and laughing as she'd gone for their file. She knew before they had even sat down how much better things were for them—it was evident in their body language, in the smiles that greeted her.

And during the consultation she found out she was right.

Right in several ways, in fact!

'I just wish we'd come to see you sooner,' Elise said.

'Well, a lot of couples say that,' Ava admitted. 'They struggle on their own for a very long time, not realising that there's help available.'

'I just wish George had told me all he was going through. I could have helped…'

'Maybe George needed to do that by himself,' Ava said gently. 'Maybe he needed to work things out on his own.'

'But you say we should talk…'

'I know I do,' Ava said, 'but sometimes, when talking doesn't help, all you can rely on is time to heal and your history to hold you together while things sort themselves out. George had a lot of things to deal with, a lot of things to get straight in his own mind before he was able to share. And now look at you—your relationship seems better than it was even before the accident.' And it seemed strange that from something so terrible any good could come, but with George and Elise it had. 'I'd like to see you both again in three months. I also just want to check your medication, George, and I do want to see you again on your own, say, in another month?'

George nodded. He was going back to work in a couple of months, and Ava wanted to make sure he was ready for it.

'Well, it's been lovely to see you both again.' Ava saw them to the door.

'It's been lovely to see you too, Ava!' Elise gave her a smile, a knowing smile perhaps? 'You're looking very well.'

'Thank you.' Ava went a bit pink and she felt as if Elise knew.

Maybe Elise did. After all Ava had a white shirt on that was straining just a little at the top buttons, her waist was getting thicker, and just this morning she hadn't been able to do up her skirt. There was certainly a roundness there, and her bottom was a bit bigger too— the first subtle changes of pregnancy becoming more evident now. She was also further on than she had ever been, which was bizarre. She was swimming, working, stressing, crying, she hadn't even seen a doctor—after all, it hadn't helped in the past, but now... Ava knew that she ought to. She was taking vitamins, looking after herself, but she really ought to get checked.

Her phone rang and she was about to let it go to messages and get some lunch, but she reached for it instead.

'Ava Carmichael.'

'Ava, this is Marco, I am working today in outpatients.' A rich Italian accent came down the phone as he introduced himself—but of course she knew who he was. The dashing Italian obstetrician who was married to Emily, a midwife here. Serendipity, Ava thought with a wry smile, but of course he was ringing to discuss a patient.

'She is four months pregnant through IVF, her husband is paraplegic—they are the most delightful couple, but on speaking to them today, I feel there is not enough information for them. They are both from the country so there is not much help available. Could I arrange for you to see them, or one of your colleagues?

Of course I will write a referral, but I worry that if I make them wait...'

'Strike while the iron's hot, you mean?'

'Scusi?'

Ava smiled. He clearly didn't understand what she was saying. 'I'll come over now.'

After meeting with the young couple, she was actually thrilled that Marco had phoned her and a bit appalled at the lack of information the pair had been struggling with. Barry's accident had happened when he was twelve and there was a whole lot he hadn't been informed about. A shy couple, they had at first been terribly reluctant to speak—but once they had started, a full hour had flown by, and she rang Ginny to make an appointment to coincide with their next antenatal visit, delighted to have been able to help.

'Ava!' She smiled when she saw Bella in the waiting room.

'Look at you!' Ava said, because Bella was looking very glamorous. 'How's the studying going?'

'I'm wearing it today,' Bella said. She was studying fashion and looked gorgeous and happy, having recently married. 'So what are you doing here?' Bella nudged.

'Working!' Ava grinned. 'What about you.'

'Just here to find out a few things. I'm waiting for Charlie but I got here a bit early.' She gave a little blush. 'We're thinking of starting a family and given all my medications and things, we just need to find stuff out. So please don't go gossiping!'

'As if!' Ava rolled her eyes.

'I heard about you and James,' Bella said. 'Felt sick when I heard.'

'Thanks,' Ava said, because she felt sick about it too. 'Anyway, I've got to go, I just need to pop in and thank Marco, but you take very good care of yourself. I hope today goes well.'

'You take care of yourself too, Ava,' Bella said, and as Ava headed to Marco's room and saw the door open she knew that Bella was right, and she knocked and popped in and introduced herself.

'Marco, hi, it's Ava, from the sexual dysfunction clinic.'

'Ah, Ava.' He gave her a very nice smile.

'Thank you for the referral. I've had a long talk with them and I'll be seeing them again. I think it's been really helpful.'

'No. Thank you,' Marco said. 'I was very pleased to have this resource, it was very confident of them to speak.'

He meant courageous, but confidence, courage, it was all the same in a way and it was exactly what she needed to summon now.

'Can I speak to you?' She stepped into the office, closing the door behind her. 'About me.'

'Of course.'

'Off the record?'

Marco gave a nod.

'Your wife's a midwife here.'

'Your husband is an oncologist who is undergoing

chemotherapy.' Marco said. 'I know what this place is like and you can rest assured that you are speaking only with me.'

'I'm pregnant,' Ava said, and it was a relief to say it. 'But the thing is…' she swallowed '…my husband doesn't know—we're separated.'

'It's his?' Marco checked.

'Oh, yes.' Ava nodded. 'And I know I should have told him—it's just that I've had four miscarriages and it's been hell. We were already separated when I found out and I couldn't stand to do it to him again when I knew it was going to end up the same way…'

'But it hasn't?'

'No.'

And she explained about her previous pregnancies and the investigations that had taken place. 'There was nothing to explain it—all the tests came back as NAD…'

'How far along did you get?'

'Ten weeks was the longest.' Ava said. 'We decided, or rather I decided, that I didn't want to get pregnant again. It was just too hard to go through.' It was such a relief to talk and Marco didn't rush her. 'It put an incredible strain on our marriage…'

'I can imagine.'

'I thought that by going on the Pill…' She could feel tears welling, and really she didn't want to start crying but was grateful when he peeled off some tissues and handed them to her.

'I'm sorry.'

'Please don't be—I see many tears here every day. Do you know how far along you are?

She gave him the date of her last period and he checked on his calendar.

'That puts you at fourteen weeks,' Marco said. 'Into your second trimester. Let's have a look, shall we?'

She went over to the examination table and he took her blood pressure and then he took it again. 'It's at the higher end of normal.' Marco gave her the numbers.

'I'm a bit tense.'

'Of course, and I've taken that into consideration, but I'd like to keep an eye on that. I don't want it going any higher if we can help it.' Then Marco felt her bump and she had a bump, not a big one but certainly there was a small bump.

And then he put a disc into the scanner. 'Let's make a recording.'

And she looked and wished so badly that James was here, because there was their baby on the screen and it really was a baby and she was very scared to look because she knew she'd fall in love.

'It looks every bit as good as I could hope,' Marco said. 'The placenta is nice and high, the measurements are spot on and the heart rate is good.' He went through everything as she lay there, not really sure how she felt, and then he helped her up and she went and sat down at his desk. They spoke for a few minutes about antenatal care and she confessed to two swigs of whisky and a glass of wine and horse riding before she'd found out, but Marco just smiled.

'I don't recommend women take up horse riding when pregnant, but if you are a competent rider, many women ride all the way through, and if it relaxes you...' He reached for his pen. 'We should do some bloods too.'

'Can they wait?' Ava said, and maybe she was being paranoid but she didn't want it documented till she had shared things with James.

'Of course,' Marco said. 'But can I suggest you don't wait too long.'

'I've been taking vitamins—'

'Ava,' Marco interrupted, 'I'm not worried about your bloods at the moment. The fact is, maybe I am a little more perceptive about these things than most men, but I knew you were pregnant as soon as you walked in—your husband will be perceptive in this too. He'll see for himself in a week or two.'

And then he spoke some more and he mentioned something that James had on several occasions, something she had baulked at, something that had caused the most terrible rows.

'I haven't been depressed,' Ava insisted. 'I've just been dealing with a lot.'

'Of course—you have been dealing with many things,' Marco said. 'But depression is something I like to speak openly about, especially with women who have suffered losses.'

Ava nodded in all the right places and then thanked him for his care and told him that soon she would be in to see him formally, then headed down to the canteen, still clutching the DVD Marco had made for her.

She bought her lunch and then saw James walking in.

She watched as he moved his tray along the counter, and felt as if the world was watching as he sat at a table far from her. He looked better than he had for a while, but that only meant he had a treatment due soon then, because just as he seemed to pick up and get some colour, he was soon wiped out again.

How did she tell him?

She had the DVD on the table beside her. Maybe she should just walk over now, maybe she'd just give it to him and let him watch it in private. Let him work out himself how he felt, just as she was trying to do.

She watched as a nurse went and sat with him.

That cow, Ava thought, when things like that had never once troubled her.

'Hi, there.' Ava looked up at a smiling Lily.

'Mind if I join you?' Lily asked.

'Sure.' Ava gave an awkward smile. Lily was rather more pregnant than the last time she'd seen her. She was glowing, in fact, and Ava felt awful for her horrible thoughts on the day of James's operation. Not that Lily would know.

'How are you?' Lily asked.

'I've been better,' Ava admitted. 'I just feel as if everybody's watching us, everybody's wondering how I can not be with James as he goes through this.'

'Nobody's thinking that,' Lily said. 'If anybody's saying anything, it's just how awful it must be—for both of you.'

'Thanks,' Ava said, not that she really believed it—

oh, maybe their friends thought that, but gossip could be so vicious and Ava hated it. 'And, Lily, I have to apologise—I wasn't very nice to you when James had his surgery.'

'What?' Lily clearly had no idea what Ava was talking about.

'I wasn't very friendly.'

Lily just laughed. 'I'm sure you had far more on your mind than worrying about being friendly to the nurse.'

'I know.' Ava shook her head. She should just let it go, but Lily was being so nice and she wanted to apologise properly. 'I was just in a horrible place that day. I was jealous that James had clearly spoken to you about his pain and…' she gave an awkward shrug '…that he had told you he wanted to stay in hospital rather than go home.' Lily said nothing, neither confirmed nor denied, just leant over and gave Ava's hand a squeeze.

'It was just everything—and with you being pregnant as well. I knew my marriage was over and the thing is, we lost some babies…' She was starting to tell people, but it was still so difficult. 'Hard to explain.'

'Easy to understand,' Lily said, and Ava gave a smile of thanks, grateful for Lily's kind words. 'You should come out to the farm, get away from everything for a bit,' Lily suggested.

Ava was about to shake her head, to decline as she always did these days. She was just too low to talk to anyone and too scared that if she did, she might reveal her secret before she told James, except getting away for a bit sounded so tempting. Lily and Luke had a gorgeous farm less than an hour away, she'd been to their wedding there and it had been glorious, and it was terribly tempting, and they had always said they should catch up.

'Luke's on call so it will just be us. Come for the weekend if you want.'

She wouldn't go for the weekend, Ava decided, but she did go over the next day.

First, though, she stopped by at Finn's.

She was sick of ignoring him, sick of pretending they'd never talked, so she bought a fresh filled roll from the baker's and two chocolate éclairs and then headed up to him.

'Finn.' She knocked at the door. 'It's Ava.' She knocked again, feeling awkward because clearly he didn't want to see her, or maybe he was out, maybe he was over at Evie's, so she ate the roll and packed up the éclairs, made the forty-minute drive to Luke and Lily's. It was so nice to get away from the hospital and the lonely flat.

Lily had made a picnic—a huge chicken, avocado and mango salad—and then packed it all into a basket with sparkling water and Ava's éclairs. They walked for a while and then sat down and basked in the lovely sunshine as they ate lunch. Lily was marvellous, just let her ramble a bit, because she'd found out that James *did* have another round of treatment on Monday and, of course, she was worried about that. As much as they talked, the two women said nothing at times too—just lay back on the grass after lunch. Lily's eyes closed, her lovely bump moving, and Ava's eyes open, wondering if she'd ever have a bump that moved too, wondering how James would take it when she told him.

But she couldn't now, could she?

Couldn't land this on him when he had a round of chemo booked.

'Do you want to walk?' Ava was suddenly panicked, but Lily just grinned and said sure, and they walked in the sun. Ava calmed a little and, yes, it was good to get away. 'Luke's uncle Tom has a property over there...' Lily pointed out the landmarks as they walked around late afternoon. 'He's wonderful.'

They turned into the stables and it was surely the most beautiful place on God's earth, because just the sounds and the smells had Ava relaxing.

'You've met Glenfiddich,' Lily said, and Ava stroked his mane. He was absolutely beautiful. 'He's the one I rode for the wedding.'

'He's gorgeous.'

'Luke thinks he's too spirited, but he's a baby really. We could go riding,' Lily suggested.

'You're still riding?' Ava asked, because Lily must be seven months pregnant now.

'I'd go mad if I didn't,' Lily said as they walked to the next stable. 'I've had all the lectures from Luke but I've told him that riding keeps my blood pressure down.

'This is Checkers.' Lily gave the old boy a kiss. He was huge—big and black with a white blaze—and Lily told her he had been Luke's when he was a kid. 'He's such a gentle old thing,' Lily said. 'We had some children visiting the other day who had never seen a horse before and Luke put one of them on him. He'd never startle—would you, Checkers?' And though she hadn't said, somehow Ava knew that Lily knew too. 'It's a privilege to ride you, isn't it, baby?' Lily crooned to Checkers.

'Can I?' Ava asked.

It didn't feel brave or risky to be back in the saddle— it felt right. In fact, Ava was quite sure that had there been a blood-pressure cuff attached to her arm now, the numbers would be tumbling down—she felt her heels push down and her pelvis move, felt the strength and the trust in the horse beneath her, and they walked on, mostly in silence, as Checkers did what horses did for Ava—cleared her head.

And she *did* end up staying the night. She and Lily watched a girly movie and ate chocolate as only two pregnant women really could. And they went riding again early in the morning and she cleared her head further still. Finally Ava was ready—to go home.

To think.

To be honest.

Not with James. First she had to be honest with herself.

James had been right and Marco too had been right to flag it.

Depression was such a cloaked thing and, no, she hadn't wanted to have it, hadn't wanted to face it, had refuted it when James had suggested she might be, had got angry when he had insisted she was.

And then she'd given up.

She'd given up so many things. They'd even eaten different meals, hers rich in folate and no raw fish or soft cheese, *just in case*, and she'd hated it when he'd shoved a Camembert in the oven and eaten it all melted. He'd done it the night after her last miscarriage, the night she'd thrown him out of her bed, the night he'd taken residence on the sofa and there he had stayed.

And she looked at those times through his eyes now.

He'd been trying to comfort her, making her a food that she loved, that they could cuddle up on the sofa and share. He just hadn't got how much it had hurt, how unpregnant that cheese had made her feel that night.

She looked through their wedding photos and through loads of albums, watched as her smile disappeared, oh, not in public, of course, but there were little clues in the images. James with his arm around her there at Lily and Luke's wedding. She was just so rigid beside him, and as she sat on the sofa, she recalled the terrible row of the night before. And she'd been so awkward that day because Finn had been best man and the miscarriage had happened just a few weeks before.

And there was Mia and Luca, so clearly besotted with each other as she and James stood slightly apart. She turned the pages and every one was a fresh memory. There she was with Hayley and Tom, and Ava actually smiled when she saw the photo, because he'd told her that day too not to pat the dog, and yet it hadn't felt like a snub then.

And there was Teo and Zoe's wedding photo, taken

on the beach in Samoa, Teo so proud of his bride and loving Zoe's daughter as if she were his own.

James had tried to talk to her about fostering, adoption, but she'd been too scared of being let down.

She looked at her friends, saw Lexi and Sam unashamedly kissing. Those days had long since gone for James and herself.

She'd made it that way.

Ava knew that.

She'd refused to do the one thing she always told her patients they should.

To talk, to be honest, to get help if required. But then, James hadn't been honest either. James had kept it all in too, he'd just been this rock when she'd wanted his pain, and he'd hated it so much when she'd wept. He was an oncologist, for God's sake. He should be used to grief, used to pain.

Not hers, though…

She saw it then, that just as she wasn't the fabulous sex therapist at home, like everybody assumed, James was a different person at work too.

They knew what they were doing at work—it was the relationship part where they'd got lost.

And she wanted him home.

So badly.

Wanted to ring him, but didn't know what to say, didn't know where to start, wondered if he was in bed now, having his mind taken off things by this mysterious Steph woman, if she'd flown down from Brisbane…

She truly wondered if she'd left it too late.

There was a frantic thumping at the door and she ran to it. There was urgency in the knock, need, she was sure he could feel it, sure that finally it was James.

'Ava…' It was Gladys, the cleaner, her face ashen. 'I need help. It's Finn, I've just found him on the floor.'

CHAPTER FOURTEEN

GLADYS was too slow to wait for and Ava charged up the stairs.

She knew Gladys dropped in on Finn a lot and especially since he'd been out of the hospital.

'Oh, Finn.' She was appalled by what she saw—his breathing was terrible, rasping and rapid, and as she rolled him onto his side she could feel the heat from his clammy skin, saw the scar down his neck was angry and infected. How long had he been lying here? She cursed herself for yesterday morning. She should have kept knocking, or maybe rung Luke, but that was ridiculous. The last thing Finn wanted was a caretaker.

'Have you called an ambulance, Gladys?' Ava checked as the old lady puffed in.

'I didn't know what to do so I came and got you.'

'Okay, well, pass me the phone.'

Some doctor she was! She punched in the numbers and spoke to the operator. She didn't even have a bag, well, not one with anything that would help Finn at this moment! He was severely dehydrated and very, very ill, and the wait for the ambulance was interminable, especially with the hospital so close.

'I rang him earlier,' Gladys said. 'I'd made a nice roast and I thought I'd bring some for him, he's been losing so much weight.' She was beside herself. 'He didn't answer and I got all worried. I was nervous to let myself in…'

'Thank God that you did,' Ava said.

'What do you think is wrong with him?'

'He's got a wound infection,' Ava said. 'And a chest infection too by the sound of it.' She was furious with Finn, angry with this stubborn, proud man who just refused all help. 'There's nothing we can do till the ambulance gets here. Go down and get the lift ready for them.'

She thought of Evie, thought of how terrible it would be for her to have Finn come in in this condition if she was on duty tonight, and she used the phone again and asked to be put through to Emergency and then to the nurse in charge.

'No, I need to speak to the nurse in charge now.' She pulled rank. 'It's Dr Carmichael and it's about a patient that's being brought in.'

And the charge nurse, when she came to the phone, was lovely, she got it completely when Ava told her that the patient coming in soon was Finn.

'We'll get set up for him and I'll go and speak to Evie now,' the charge nurse said. 'Thanks so much for letting me know.'

The paramedics were marvellous. They put in two

drips and poured fluids into him and gave him oxygen too, and by the time they had moved him down and the cool night air hit, Finn was coming around just a little. She sat in the back of the ambulance with him for the short trip to SHH.

'Evie…' She knew he was worrying about the same thing as she had.

'She knows, Finn.' She'd never tried to be soft with him and she wouldn't start now, and anyway he wouldn't appreciate it. So she didn't hold his hand and make soothing noises. Instead she watched through the darkened window as the ambulance sped through the night and she was cross with Finn, so, so cross with him, and when he was better she'd tell him—in trying to save Evie from the burden, he'd just hurt her a whole lot more, Ava could see that.

Could see many things as they turned in to the approach for the hospital.

No matter how difficult it might make things, James really did need to know now.

She went to James's apartment straight from the hospital.

Finn was already improving, but Ava still felt faint at the thought of him lying on that floor all night because had Gladys not dropped in, he simply might not have been holding on by morning.

She wanted James, not just to tell him about the baby, not just to fight for them, but because tonight had been horrible and James was the only person who would understand the fright she'd had. She wasn't used to dealing with acute patients. It had been awful to feel so helpless.

Except he wasn't home, and she thought about ringing him, but sometimes you just needed face to face, so she waited it out all night and then in the morning she headed up to the oncology floor, prepared to wait in his office if she had to. To just close the door and have this out. But as she walked along the corridors she saw Evie. She didn't want to stop, but Evie clearly did.

'Ava! Thank you for last night.'

'It's no problem. Thank God for Gladys...'

Ava went to move on but Evie was still talking. She didn't want to hear about Finn, she wanted James. 'He's been treating the wound infection at home, can you believe it?' Evie was furious. 'Hasn't told anyone.' She let out a hiss of frustration as on and on she went when all Ava wanted was James. 'He's refusing to see anyone. Hayley wants to take him to Theatre for debridement, but he's refusing and he's told them to cancel the next operation. He wants to lecture instead of operate—'

'Evie...' Ava interrupted. She didn't want to hear about anyone else, she just wanted James. 'I'm sorry but I have to go.' She was almost running. She just wanted to see her husband. She took the lift to Oncology, except the lift let her out on the wrong floor, on the surgical ward, and just as she was about to go back in when she changed her mind because as desperately as she wanted to see James, there was something about the lifts not working and Finn, something inside her that made her feel brave, made her angry, made her right.

'Can you tell me where Finn is?'

'He's not taking visitors.' The nurse looked up as Ava strode over.

'He's taking this one!' Ava said, and she looked the nurse straight in the eye.

'Sorry, he's made it very clear…'

Ava turned to Hayley, who walked over, and asked again, but Hayley shook her head.

'Ava, he's not seeing anyone.'

'Go and tell him that Ava Carmichael is here and that if he refuses to see me then I'll tell everybody exactly what went on between us in the stairwell the night before his surgery.'

She stood there, cheeks flaming as she was the victim of yet more curious looks. The whole ward seemed to have stopped, even the domestic had stopped mopping, but actually Ava's cheeks were flaming in anger. She was past caring what the lot of them thought as she waited till Hayley returned.

'Has he said that he will see me?' Ava asked.

'Unfortunately, yes.' Hayley smiled. 'I was dying to find out what happened! Room four. Go on through.' Hayley caught Ava's arm as she walked past and then her voice was serious. 'Good luck.'

'Well, here she is!' Finn was at his most toxic—unshaven, the curtains drawn, he jeered as she walked into the room. 'The woman who left her husband in the middle of chemotherapy, her one-balled husband,' Finn added. 'The woman who had drunken sex in the stairwell…' Ava just stood there as he insulted her, just knew, as Evie did, that it wasn't really Finn. 'That's what they'll all be saying now, you realise.'

'I don't care what they're saying.'

'Did we?' Finn asked. 'I've had so many drugs since admission, you know, I can't really remember that night.'

'Oh, you can remember,' Ava said. 'You can remember how scared you were and how badly you wanted Evie. You just don't want to remember, you just don't want to admit it. Well, here's a bit of advice, Finn— you can push people away, you can shut them out, you can deal with everything on your own, and then one day you might have to live with the consequences.' She faced him.

'I'm aware of the consequences, thank you.'

'Are you?' Ava asked. 'Are you quite sure about that? Because one day you might find out that Evie needs you, one day it might be her that's sitting on the oncology ward with a bag of poison going into her arm, and you've pushed so far, you've left it so long, that *he's* dealing with things on his own…'

'I thought you were here to see me…not talk about James.'

'I'm talking about you,' she shouted back—and she was.

Sort of.

'I'm talking about us both, but I'm *telling* you, one day something might happen and you might find yourself the one locked out of Evie's life—when, wheelchair or not, you could've been supporting her. Think about that as you wallow in your self-pity.'

'Get out!' he roared.

'I'm leaving already.'

She did. She had too much adrenaline and was far too angry to take the lift. She ran up the stairs and onto the oncology floor and, when he wasn't in his office, she found out where he was and spoke for several moments with a nurse, the one she'd seen him with in the canteen, in fact, before donning a gown and gloves and being allowed in.

James didn't look up.

He'd been dreading this morning, had made a grim joke to Harriet that he'd considered ringing in sick, and then she'd told him that Richard had, and in all honesty, James didn't blame him. And then he'd heard the nurses start talking.

'What's this about you and Finn on the stairwell?' He was flicking the remote for a DVD.

'Well, that didn't take long.' Ava rolled her eyes.

'Someone really ought to tell the nurses that that glass they stand behind isn't soundproof. Though don't,' James quickly added. 'I kind of like hearing what's going on.'

'Nothing happened between Finn and I except for a long conversation.'

'It's not my concern.'

'Maybe not,' Ava said. 'The same way I understand if you've been seeing someone…' She loved him so much that she spoke the truth. 'I know that I've been hell to live with. I promise you, I understand if there was someone else, but I'm not giving up on us without a fight.'

'Someone else? Er…' He gave her a very strange look. 'I'm not exactly living the single life at the moment.'

'I meant before,' Ava said, 'before we broke up.'

'I was never unfaithful.'

'Oh, please,' Ava said. 'I'm not stupid—we hadn't slept together in more than a year.'

'I know that,' James said, 'but there wasn't anybody else.'

'Don't lie about this, James,' she begged. 'We can't start again if we lie.'

'Ava, why would I sleep around when I'd been trying to save us?'

'So who were you ringing after your operation? I came back to talk and you were on the phone.' She could hear her jealousy, but she swallowed it down and misquoted him. '"Sorry about that, she's gone back to work now—we were nearly caught! Now where were we, Steph?"'

'I was trying to sort out the serviced apartment.' He had the audacity to laugh. 'Steph was very helpful, she's used to men planning on moving out and not telling their wives—though my situation was a touch more complicated. I wanted an end apartment, with the toilet furthest away from the adjoining wall…' She shook her head in impatience at his detail. 'Didn't want to upset the other guests.' He went back to his TV.

'So who were the linen trousers for? The posh new

cologne? I mean it, James. I don't care… I mean, I understand if you…'

'They were for you.' He turned his head and there was so much anger in his green eyes she almost believed him.

Almost, but she knew him too well and he knew her too well too.

'Liar,' she said. 'You know I don't care about things like that.'

'I told the marriage counsellor the same thing.' Ava couldn't believe what she was hearing.

'You went to a marriage counsellor?'

'When I was in Brisbane. Three months of it, telling her everything, and she still didn't get it—I mean, how do you explain us?'

'I don't know,' Ava admitted.

'Like I told her that you eat healthily and that you moaned about the way I ate and she said that maybe I'd let myself go a bit.'

'That wasn't what upset me,' Ava said. 'I just want you to take care of yourself.'

'Well, she said that maybe you wanted me to make more of an effort…'

'No!' She laughed. 'Well, you did look nice.'

'It was for you,' James said, and her heart seemed to squeeze in her chest. 'I joined a gym. I was out running every morning, bought new clothes, shaved, put on cologne, hell…' She could see the hurt and rejection right there on his face, and she winced at the recall of her reaction to him, or rather her complete lack of it. 'And I came home and you didn't give me a second glance.'

'I thought…' Oh, God, she really had thought it was for someone else. 'I thought you'd done it for someone else. And then I got the flowers. I thought you felt guilty, you never send me flowers.'

'Yeah, well, I did feel guilty. I was having a session with the counsellor when you rang, I got all flustered.' Guilty eyes looked up at her. 'I'd just told her we hadn't had sex in, like, for ever, and then you rang. It was as if you knew I was talking about us.'

'Oh, James.'

'She heard what I said, that I'd call you back, and she said that I handled the conversation all wrong, that I should send flowers. I said you didn't appreciate them. Still, it was worth a go…' She could not believe it, that James, her James, would sit and pour his heart out to a stranger, and she told him so. 'Two hundred dollars a week.' James was incredulous. 'The appointments had to be after hours, so it was two hundred dollars! What a damn waste.'

'It wasn't a waste.' She looked at him and could not believe all he had done to save them—how hard he had worked. And what had she done?

'Come home.' She saw him close his eyes. 'I want you home.'

'Ava.' He was so tired, too tired to fight and too tired to refuse, but also too tired to hurdle over this huge mound of pride. 'You don't have to feel sorry for me. I've only got a couple more rounds to go.'

'I don't want you back because I feel sorry for you. I want you back because I love you, because I can't stand us being apart. James, I do know how you feel.'

'No, Ava, you don't.'

'You think that I want to be there for all the wrong reasons. That if we get back together it will be because we have to rather than we want to? Well, guess what? I feel the same too.' She saw him frown. 'Watch this,' she said, handing him a DVD.

'Not more feel-good schmaltz,' James groaned. 'I don't need a single bit more inspiration…'

Ava said nothing as she put the DVD in. She watched his expression as he watched it.

'I'm fourteen weeks pregnant, James. Actually…' she did the maths '…I'm nearly fifteen.' And she watched him frown, watched him try to take it in. 'And in case you do ever wonder, nothing happened on the stairwell.'

'I know that,' James said, and he looked at his wife. 'Because I know you'd tell me if it did.'

'I would,' Ava said. 'And I don't have to because it didn't. We shared some whisky, spoke about Evie and I came inside and then I called you.'

He looked back at the screen, at their baby, and he rewound it and played it again.

'You should have told me.' She knew he wasn't talking about Finn. 'How could you not tell me?' Now he was angry. 'You didn't even try.'

And she opened her mouth to speak, to defend herself, to say that she had been to the serviced apartment to try, but she halted, because this was about them and nobody else needed to be included.

'How could I?' she asked, and it was up to him whether or not he would forgive her for keeping quiet. 'I might lose it,' Ava said. 'But I promise you this, if I do I will cry and I will sob, but I will grieve with you this time, and you will cry too, if you want to, and then I promise you that I will move on, because whatever happens I am so grateful because this baby make me see sense…'

He still wouldn't give in, so she told him the truth. Was as direct with James as she'd been with Finn. 'That's your daughter or son there, and if this pregnancy does last…' They'd let things go so far, she just didn't know if they could claw back from it—but they had to.

'Do you just want access visits, James? Alternate weekends?' And it must have hit him somewhere inside, because he put his hand up to stop her, but she continued. 'I'll have Christmas mornings, please, and then you can take it to your mum's for lunch, or to your girlfriend's, or whatever…'

'Stop it.'

'No!' She would not stop. 'Because that's how it will be.'

'No.' And she watched her proud, strong man start crying, and it was the first time she had ever seen him cry, not held-back tears, not angry tears, just tears, and he was too tired to even wipe them away. He just sat in the chair so, so defeated, and she could see him bald and thin and yet still so proud and just perhaps the most honest and beautiful she had ever seen James, and she couldn't simply hold him and kiss away his tears, so instead she stood in gown and gloves and she stayed strong.

'Or you can come back to me today and I'll never really know if you're just coming back for the baby. I've got the golden ticket, haven't I?'

And she thought the same as he did, James realised, felt the same as he did, was simply a part of him. 'I've got the reason for you to come back…'

'Ava, all I want is to be with you, baby or no baby, that's all I ever wanted.' And she was scared to believe him too.

'Should you be here?' She smiled when he said it, when he looked up at the drip, because he was as terrified as her. 'I mean, with the chemo…'

'I spoke to the nurse when I came in. I have to be careful with your body fluids for the next forty-eight hours, but I'm upping it to seventy-two hours…' She gave him a little wink, but she was terrified of that part too—of chemo and the effects on the baby—but she couldn't live like that any longer, couldn't kill her marriage again.

'I've had whisky, though of course I didn't know I was pregnant then and Marco said not to worry, I probably needed a bit of sedation that night. And I'm swimming…' she looked at him '…and riding.'

'Before you found out?' James said, because he knew how she was.

'No.' She shook her head. 'Yesterday I went horse

riding and I went riding the day before too and for the first time since you found that lump, for a couple of hours I felt great, and the baby is still here and holding on…'

'Are we?'

'Yes,' she said. 'Yes.' She said it again and she was crying now too, and because she couldn't kiss him, instead she took that weary face she loved so much into her gloved hands. She hadn't touched his face in so long—it was relief, sheer relief to hold him, and the relief was mixed with frustration because she could only wipe away his tears through the rubber gloves.

And Ava, once practical, the moment she held him again believed, in kindred spirits and angels and a love that was meant to be. And James, who thought you just died and were buried, believed just a little too as he held her again, because it felt like nothing he could explain.

Not stir-fried rice and chicken and unconditional love, but this danger that came with the woman in his arms. And yet there was a sense of safety too.

She knew him.

She was the only person he wanted to be with and he didn't want to do this alone any more.

'I know you won't believe me,' James said, 'I know you think I'm just saying it, but that morning before I found it, I was thinking about you, I wanted you to come into the shower with me but I thought that might be pushing it so I was going to come out and talk. I wanted us to maybe try again.'

'James.' She didn't care about the nurses behind the

glass partition. Let them hear, she thought, let them see, because she loved him so much she was fine if the whole world knew it. 'What did you think I was coming into the shower for?' She saw him frown and she started to laugh, because the truth was so obvious now. 'I could hear you, you big idiot. You're not exactly quiet when you get it on!'

She saw him smile, she could hear her baby's heartbeat on the screen as the two of them remembered the night that it was made, and she told him her truth, a truth that had been lost in the pain of these past weeks.

'What do you think I was coming into the bathroom for, James? I was coming in to be with you.'

CHAPTER FIFTEEN

AND they tumbled into bed.

Except it didn't happen.

She wanted that.

Knew he did too.

Except it was more private than that for both of them. More difficult than, even in her job capacity, she had ever understood.

He puked his way through the first three days after chemo and she tried not to hover at the door, and he shouted to her once not to come in when she went to, because he didn't want her holding his head, but he did love the endless flannels she soaked in ice, and he conceded and drank her protein shakes when he could keep things down and ate Brazil nuts because Ava believed they would help.

She cooked for two.

Different sorts of meals from before, but this time they ate the same—because she'd been trawling the internet and was obsessed with his diet now instead of hers. And she got now how Veronica had needed to cook, needed to feed him, needed to do something, and

she smiled and chatted much more graciously when
Veronica came round. They had a baby to talk about so
that made things easier too. Then, one evening James
was called in for a patient. 'Richard,' he told Ava, because he told her more about his work now. Richard
had come back for his treatment yesterday but had been
admitted because he was febrile and James, of course,
was straight out of the door. Instead of scuttling off,
Veronica actually hung around and they chatted awkwardly for a moment and then Ava made tea.

'That time you came around…' Ava's hand was shaking as she pulled out the teabag as Veronica asked the
question… 'Did you know you were pregnant then?'

'I'd just found out,' Ava said.

'You'd come to tell him?' Veronica swallowed as Ava
nodded. 'James would never forgive me if he found out.'

'And he never will find out,' Ava said. 'And you're
wrong, James would forgive you.'

'Can you?'

'I did ages ago,' Ava said, because she'd done an
awful lot of thinking—about how hard it must be for
Veronica at times to be the one left to carry on. 'It didn't
feel like it at the time, but being apart…' She closed her
eyes for a moment because it was so hard to explain it
and she never wanted to be apart from him again, but
just as she had said to George and Elise, from something so awful good things had come. She'd been with
James since she was eighteen, had only ever been with
James, and had relied on his love perhaps a little too
much. Now she knew that if she had to she could make

it on her own and so could James. And in their uncertain worlds it brought them both comfort, and Ava knew also that she would never take his love for granted again. 'We're stronger for it.'

And the two women just tried harder, because they had one thing in common at least—they both loved James.

And he loved Ava, so he let her add the blueberries to his oat bran and he cut down on carbs, but he still insisted on sugar in his coffee, and at night they cuddled sometimes and other times slept on their own sides of the bed, and for the next couple of weeks they sort of learned how to share their lives again.

Just not that part.

Oh, they were sharing a bed now and sometimes she woke up in his arms, but they just hadn't got to where they fell asleep like that. She lay in bed this morning and all she wanted was a kiss. They'd had a couple, but sort of awkward ones, and she stared up at the dark and went through her faults.

Yes, she was practical at work but completely neurotic at home, and then she thought some more, went over their rows before they'd got back together, went over the one where he'd admitted that he was scared, and she grimaced as she recalled his words.

I'm patronising. She groaned in her head.

I am—she reluctantly concluded—*he was completely right.* If they had been together when he'd been diagnosed she'd have been terribly efficient about sex and so, so annoyingly understanding.

She actually made herself laugh as she thought about it, just lay in the dark and let out a giggle because, yes, at times she could be a right royal pain.

Maybe she should get up and have a shower.

Except she'd run out of conditioner *again*, but she'd bought some last week, she was quite sure of it.

'Don't look at me,' James said when she'd accused him last night of pinching her expensive stuff. 'What would I need conditioner for?'

She was disorganised too, Ava decided.

And then she felt something—something she'd been chasing, something that it felt like she'd been waiting for for ever, and it came the moment it wasn't on her mind.

This flutter in her stomach.

So fleeting, so vague, and of course it must be wind.

Except she felt it again.

Like a tiny mouse scratching from the inside.

'It moved.'

Her fifth pregnancy and she'd never felt her baby move, and she was now completely certain that it was.

'What?' Already woken by her mad, morning laughter James rolled over to face her on his side.

'The baby...'

He put her hand to her stomach and of course he couldn't feel the little mouse scratching.

'I felt it.'

'I know,' James said, because, well, Ava didn't say things that hadn't happened—she was far too practical with her body for that. So he held his hand on her tummy for a full sixty seconds and, no, he couldn't feel it, and got a bit bored maybe waiting, because all by it-self his hand wandered…

It just did.

Over a body that was changing, and his hand traced her stomach and then dusted down—it said hello to her thighs, but didn't greet her knees before it worked its way back up.

She felt each stroke and then she felt his caution, the wait for her say no, or for her to say she was tired, or needed space, or a panicked reminder about the *baby*! But instead she felt his mouth on her breast and, God, she loved his mouth, and she let her thighs relax and felt his fingers explore, and as controlling as she was, it was his fingers that controlled her then.

'Ava…'

He slipped his fingers in where she lay, loose-legged, and the very solid nudge of him every now and then told her that he was just as fine as she was. She lay there and didn't think about saline balls, or chemo, or that he was bald, or that she had a baby on board and a womb that could collapse at a moment's notice. She just thought about the lovely things he was doing to her and the lovely things she was doing to him too.

And she listened to their noise.

And James was usually noisy, but this morning it was she, moaning and groaning and giving Kirribilli Views their wake-up call of old.

'I'm going to come.' She said it in panic, because she should surely be the calm, reassuring one, insisting on taking things nice and slowly, except she couldn't.

'Come,' he said as his fingers brought her closer. 'I want to watch.'

And her books went out of the window; she should be so much more laid back, so much more...*thoughtful*.

Except she wanted him. Was she terrible that that was all she wanted?

'Come inside me!'

He was inside her in a minute.

He moved over her, split her apart with his thighs and there he was on top, her hands grabbing at shoulders, thinner than she remembered at uni but so much stronger their union now, and this was their glorious moment, because eyes never changed.

Green eyes gazed at her.

Loving her as together they came.

James.

Ava.

Worth fighting for.

EPILOGUE

'You'd turned them off.'

James gave a wry smile as he walked into the room.

Right at the end of her labour, when things had suddenly become tense, Ava had remembered that she might have left her hair straighteners on. Actually, she was quite sure she had, because she'd been straightening her hair for her antenatal appointment when all the drama had started, trying to tell herself that the contractions she was having were nothing to get excited about, they were probably Braxton-Hicks. Marco had warned her that her baby was a big one, and was today going to talk about inducing her, or even recommend she consider a Caesarean, which Ava definitely didn't want. Except that as she'd stood there pondering how soon he might induce her, and just how much bigger she could possibly get, her waters had broken and things had moved surprisingly quickly from then on.

'James?'

He'd heard her voice from the bathroom and even before he'd walked in there he'd known.

And he'd known how terrified she was too.

And he had been terrified as well, but not for a moment had he shown it, especially when by ten minutes later she was already two heavy contractions in, and four heavy contractions in by the time he'd been put through to Maternity to tell them they were on their way.

'Ring your mum!' Ava had ordered as they'd headed for the door, because Veronica had asked to be kept up to date with all news.

'She'll want to come,' James had said as she'd doubled up at the door. 'We'll ring her afterwards.'

'By the time she gets there,' Ava gritted, 'it will be afterwards.'

She was almost right.

There was something about Finn and lifts because as they stepped inside he was on his way down, dressed in a suit and on his way to work, his last day at work before his operation next week.

And after a brief good morning he suitably ignored them, because there were certain times you didn't want to be seen—except the lift wasn't moving and it was James rather frantically pushing the buttons and then there was nothing prim about Ava, Finn noted as she cursed like a navvy and pressed the buttons herself, because she was not going down by the stairwell and she was not having her baby here. But thankfully the lift started moving and as Finn got out at the ground floor while they headed down for the car in the basement, he had the decency to simply step out.

Emily, who was quite pregnant herself, examined her on arrival.

'We might just see about getting the doctor down.' She'd given Ava the nicest smile and had called out to a colleague and then quietly set up for delivery as Ava bore down.

'It's too fast...' Ava begged, because her mind couldn't catch up with the speed of things, and it was then she remembered the hair straighteners and that she might have left them on.

Marco, when she said it again, had told her to forget such things.

'Ava, don't worry about that now.' He said it very calmly. In fact, had she not been his wife, Emily might not have noted the slight tension in his voice, and she looked down to where the head that was almost out, and then it retracted. It was called 'turtle sign' and indicative of shoulder dystocia. Emily noted that James was a big guy, with very broad shoulders, and she saw James watching too, saw the dart of nervousness in his eyes, and Emily took a calming breath as Ava ranted about the hair straighteners, and her patient did not need to know what was happening yet, she was terrified enough.

'Nice slow breath, Ava,' Emily said. 'Let that thought go. Your baby's nearly here and then James can go home and check on those straighteners for you. Now, let's bring your legs right up.' She took one leg and James the other to open up the pelvis some more, and James told her that, yes, soon he'd go home, that she could stop worrying about that now.

And that helped her to stop terrifying herself, convincing herself, in fact, that as she laboured on, the flat was burning down, which meant the contracts wouldn't go through on the house they had bought.

Yes, they had a house.

The one she'd imagined James walking into, with kids hanging off him and clearly at peace with his saline ball, except she hadn't been walking past with frozen meals and vegetables and cat food. Instead, she had been sitting on the veranda, watching her family be.

And it was the house of her dreams. She simply hadn't recognised it then. It was the house where they had first made love. It had come onto the market three weeks after they'd got back together and everyone had said they were crazy, that they had far too much on their plates without buying an old bomb.

Except they'd fallen in love with it.

And Ava had co-ordinated the renovators and now, if not quite finished, they were ready to move in and the contracts for the flat were going through this week.

It would be there that they brought home their baby.

'You're doing great, Ava,' James said, his voice strong and calm, even though fear ripped through him at the potential precariousness of the situation as he watched his baby struggle to be born. Just for a second he wondered why things had to be so hard for them, wondered just how much more they could take, and then almost instantly he shoved that thought aside because life, too, had been wonderful to them and they could take whatever it sent them.

'Just relax a moment before the next one, Ava.' And she did as he said and relaxed just a little, just breathed for a moment, and the rest of the room breathed too as her pelvis opened that necessary fraction more, and then in a moment her new family was there, her baby being lifted onto her stomach, and there was this breeze of joy and relief and love that swept into the room.

James cut the cord and shook hands with Marco and nothing was said—because today she really didn't need to know, but, yes, if there were to be any more baby Carmichaels then it would be a Caesarean next time.

No, today Ava didn't need to know what a close call it had been for a moment.

Today she just had to concentrate on being a mum.

And so, after they'd cuddled their son and just marvelled at him, they had opened the door to Veronica, and there had been cuddles and kisses all around. Ava thought it was nice to have her there, nice to share the joy, nice to be happy but a little bit wistful too.

'I wish your dad was here.'

'So do I,' James admitted, and again Ava understood Veronica a bit more.

'What did your parents say?' Veronica asked. 'They must be beside themselves.

'They will be when they pick up their voicemail,' Ava said, understanding her own parents a little less, and she felt James's hand squeeze her shoulder just a bit tighter. And just as she was being moved to her room,

James had felt her tense and in the end had given her a kiss and popped home to check that she had turned the straighteners off.

And, yes, just as they hadn't at the start of their relationship, no longer did those sorts of things annoy him.

Well, maybe very occasionally, but they knew what was important now.

'I'm going to buy you the sort that turn off themselves,' Veronica offered when James came back and gave the inevitable all-clear.

'Well, can you buy her an iron that turns itself off as well, then,' James said. 'Oh, and an oven that turns itself off when you close the front door...' He looked at their new surroundings. 'Nice room.'

It was a wonderful room, with an amazing view—a view that so often had soothed her, a view that was there patiently waiting to see her through good times and bad, and she was infinitely grateful for it.

'Here!'

He handed her flowers.

Pale flowers with hardly a trace of scent. Iceberg roses from the bushes she had planted in their new garden.

Her very favourite kind.

'Teo's just giving him the once-over,' Ava said, as the paediatrician turned and gave James a smile.

'He's perfect.' Teo finished examining him and handed Baby Carmichel to James. 'Welcome to the sleepless-nights club,' he said.

'Yep,' James shook his hand while with the other he held his son. 'I hear you're a recent member.'

'Zoe came home yesterday.'

And when Teo had gone and the lunches were being brought out, Veronica did the most amazing thing.

'Well, I'm going to head home.' Ava nearly fell off the bed.

'Stay!' she offered, and peered at a very unappetising beef stroganoff. 'James can go out and get something nice for lunch…'

'That rabbit food you two eat?' Veronica frowned. 'No, thanks.' But then she did give Ava a smile because, after all, James was doing very well on it—even if Ava was convinced he was cheating an awful lot of the time. 'Anyway, I've got a lot of phone calls to make. I'll come in this evening, though—if that's okay?'

'That'd be great.'

'Do you need anything? Anything you want me to bring in?'

'Some of your chicken and fried rice maybe?' Ava said, because they'd cheat together tonight. 'And champagne.' She grinned.

'Already in the fridge,' Veronica said, and gave her grandson just one more cuddle before she was gone.

Not that they were alone for long.

Word had got out and the gift shop must be running hot because the domestic kept ferrying in balloons and bunches of flowers

'We take them out at night,' she assured them.

Well, they weren't taking out her iceberg roses, Ava decided.

And James read the cards out to her as she fed their son.

*George was in to see Donald and we heard the
news!*
So happy for you both.
George and Elise
(Playing lots of Scrabble) xxx

'Who are George and Elise and why are they playing lots of Scrabble?' James frowned and then stopped
frowning as he got it, because sometimes now she did
bring her work home with her, even if he didn't know it,
and they were playing lots of Scrabble too—and walking on the beach and, yes, lots of talking and, yes, things
would remain fine.

They'd both see to it.

'Oh, and I texted Richard with the news...' James
said, because, given all they had been through, Richard
had become far more than a patient, 'He rang straight
back, he's thrilled, and,' James added, 'he's got some
news of his own. We've got an engagement party to go
to in a few weeks.'

And then he went to read out another one but he just
stopped and laughed.

'Who's it from?' Ava asked.

'Guess.' James grinned.

Welcome to Baby Carmichael
Remembering the stairwell fondly,
*Finn (Actually it's Evie, he'd never think to send
flowers) xxx*

'Well, that's going to silence the rumour mill.' James laughed and then it faded, because the gift shop was going to be extra-busy in the next few days too. 'I hope his surgery goes well for him.'

'It will,' Ava said.

'You don't know that,' James said, because now he did stress a little, well, he always had, as it turned out, he'd just not told her.

And now he did.

'It's a big gamble,' James said. 'All or nothing this time…'

'Well, whatever the outcome, Finn will deal with it,' Ava said. 'And we'll all be there for him—whether the grumpy old goat wants it or not.'

And she looked down at her son, whose eyes seemed to reach into her heart.

'He's huge.' He had a squashed-up face like a boxer's and was sucking hungrily on his fist despite having been fed twice, and somehow he reminded her so much of his dad that it made her laugh.

'If there is a next time, I'm having a Caesarean.' She caught his eyes and he knew that she knew, but sometimes you didn't need to go over things.

'Yes, Ava,' James said. 'You are.'

And then she looked back at her baby and couldn't quite believe he was here. She peeled off the little beanie that was on his head and tufted the pale brown hair. 'He's got more hair than you.'

'Not for long,' James said, because it was growing

back, and he looked at his wife and climbed up on the bed beside her.

'He looks like an Eddie,' Ava said, and James looked at his son who looked like him, and he thought of his own dad and he smiled.

'Text your mum his name,' Ava said, 'so she can tell everyone.'

And James did, texted a photo of his son to his mother, so she could forward the image of Edward James Carmichael to the people she couldn't wait to tell.

And then the Emily stopped by on her way home and told her how well she had done.

'Thanks so much,' Ava said. 'And Marco too—you were both great.'

'I'm on in the morning.' Emily smiled. 'I'll come in and we can go through your labour,' she said, because by tomorrow or maybe the next day Ava would want to, but for now she needed to rest, just as her son was.

'Do you want me to put him in his crib?' Emily offered, and when Ava nodded she took a not so little Eddie and popped him in his crib and then suggested she could close the curtains and turn the lights down and, given the traffic from the gift shop, maybe a 'no visitors' sign on the door.

'Please,' Ava said, because she loved them all and everything, but there would be time for that tonight, time to share their good news with everyone. She just wanted to be with her husband now and, yes, the view was to die for, but it would still be there when she needed it. She needed some time with James more.

He was clean-shaven, wearing those grey linen trousers and he smelt just a little of cologne as he pulled her into him, and it was all for her.

'Fancy a second honeymoon?' James said. 'Just us three?'

'Yes, please.'

'Beach?'

Ava closed her eyes and shook her head.

'Mountains?' She shook her head again.

'Home,' she said. 'Let's honeymoon at home.' And she thought of their house and their garden that was waiting and the man who lay beside her and just how far the two of them had come, how much deeper their love now was, and she simply couldn't be happier.

'Let's enjoy every precious day.'

* * * * *

SYDNEY HARBOUR HOSPITAL: EVIE'S BOMBSHELL

BY
AMY ANDREWS

This book is dedicated to all the loyal
Medical Romance fans who always look for our books
and love a good series!

PROLOGUE

EVIE LOCKHEART BELTED hard on the door, uncaring if the whole building heard her. Loud rock music bled out from around the frame so she knew he wasn't asleep. 'Open up now, Finn Kennedy,' she yelled, 'or so help me I'm going to kick this fancy penthouse door right in!'

She glared at the stubbornly closed object. It had been two weeks since he'd been discharged from hospital after the less than stellar success of his second operation. Two weeks since he'd said, *Get out. I don't want you in my life.* Two weeks of phoning and texting and having one-sided conversations through his door.

And it was enough.

She was sick of Finn shutting her out—shutting the world out.

And if she didn't love him so much she'd just walk away and leave him to rot in the cloud of misery and denial he liked to call home.

But memories of the infection he'd picked up after his first operation and the state he'd got himself into as he'd tried to self-treat were never far from her mind and she was determined to check on him whether the stubborn fool wanted her to or not.

She was about to bash on the door again when the lift

behind her dinged and Gladys stepped out. She'd never been happier to see Finn's cleaner in her life.

'Gladys, I need Finn's key.'

The older woman's brow crinkled in concern as she searched through her bag. 'Is he all right? Is he sick again?'

'No,' Evie dismissed. Gladys had found Finn collapsed on the floor overwhelmed by his infection and still hadn't quite got over the shock. 'He's probably fine but I'd like to see it with my own two eyes.' *Then I'm going to wring his neck.*

Gladys stopped her frantic search. 'He was fine yesterday,' she hedged.

Evie had to stop herself from knocking the dear sweet little old lady, who also happened to clean her apartment along with many others at *Kirribilli Views*, to the ground and forcibly searching her bag.

'He told you not to give me the key, didn't he?'

Gladys looked embarrassed. 'I'm sorry, Evie. But he was very firm about it.'

Evie suppressed a scream but she stood her ground and held out her hand. 'Gladys, I'm begging you, one woman to another, I need to see him. I need the key.'

Gladys pursed her lips. 'You love him?'

Evie wasn't surprised that Gladys was in the gossip loop, given how long rumours about she and Finn had been floating around Sydney Harbour Hospital and how many of its staff lived at Kirribilli Views. She nodded, depending on the incurably romantic streak she knew beat inside the old cleaner's chest.

'Yes.' Although God knew why. *The man was impossible to love!*

Gladys put her hand in her bag and pulled out a set

of keys. 'He needs someone to love him,' she said, holding them out.

'He needs a damn good spanking,' Evie muttered, taking the keys.

Gladys grinned. 'That too.'

'Thanks,' Evie said.

'I'll leave his apartment till last today,' the elderly woman said, and turned back towards the lift.

Finn glared at her as the door opened and Evie felt the glacial chill from his ice-blue eyes all the way across the room, despite the darkened interior from the pulled-down blinds. 'Remind me to sack Gladys,' he said as he threw back the amber contents of a glass tumbler.

Evie moved towards where he was sitting on the couch, noticing how haggard he was looking. His usual leanness looked almost gaunt in the shadows. His regular stubbly appearance bordering on scruffy. His dark brown hair messy as if he'd been constantly worrying at it with agitated fingers. The light was too low to see the streaks of grey that gave him that distinguished arrogant air he wore so bloody well.

How could a man look like hell and still cause a pull low and deep inside her? And how, *damn it all*, could he stare at her with that morose belligerence he'd perfected and still not kill off her feelings for him?

Finn Kennedy was going to be the death of her. God knew, he'd already ground her pride into the dust.

The coffee table halted her progress and she was pleased for the barrier as the urge to shake him took hold. 'You're drunk.'

'Nope.' He poured himself another finger of Scotch from the bottle on the coffee table. 'Not yet.'

'It's three o'clock in the afternoon.'

He raised his glass to her. 'I appreciate this booty call, but if you don't mind I have a date with my whisky glass.'

Evie watched him throw it back, despairing how she could get through to him. 'Don't do this to yourself, Finn. It's early days yet.' She looked down at his right arm, his lifeless hand placed awkwardly on his thigh. 'You need to give it time. Wait for the swelling to subside. Rupert's confident it'll only be temporary. You'll be back operating again before you know it'

Finn slammed his glass down on the table. 'Go away, Evie,' he snapped.

Evie jumped but refused to be cowed. He'd been practically yelling at her and telling her to go away for their entire relationship—such as it was. But there'd been other times—tender moments, passionate moments—and that was the real Finn she knew was hidden beneath all his grouchy, arrogant bluster.

She understood why he was pushing her away. Knew that he didn't want to burden her with a man who would be forever less in his eyes because he might not ever again be the one thing that defined him—a surgeon.

But surely that was her choice?

'No. I love you and I'm not going anywhere.'

'I don't want you to love me!' he roared.

Evie came around to his side of the table until she was standing right in front of him. 'Well, you don't always get what you want in life Finn—*not even you*.' She shoved her hands on her hips. 'If you want me to leave then you're going to have to get your butt off that lounge and make me.'

'Oh, I see,' he said, his lip curling. 'This *is* a booty call.'

She endured a deliberately insulting look that raked over her body as if she was sitting in a window in Amsterdam.

'What's the matter, Princess Evie, feeling all horny and frisky with nowhere to put it? *Been a while, has it*? You really needn't have dressed for the occasion. Us one-armed guys can't afford to be choosy, or hadn't you heard?'

Evie had just come from lunch with her sisters and as such was dressed in a pencil skirt that came to just above her knee and a satiny blouse that buttoned up the front and fell gently against her breasts. Her hair was loose and fell around her shoulders.

She ignored him. She would not let his deliberate insults deter her from her goal. 'Let me help you, Finn. Please.'

His good hand snaked out and snagged her wrist. He yanked and she toppled forward, her skirt pulling tight around her thighs as she landed straddling his lap, grabbing at his shoulders for stability.

'Is this what you wanted?' he demanded. 'You want to see how I do this with one hand?' He groped a breast. 'Or this?' he persisted, letting his hand slide down to where her skirt had ridden up, pushing his hand up beneath the fabric, gliding it up her thigh, taking the fabric with him until it was rucked up around her hips and her legs were totally exposed, his hand coming to rest on the curve of one cheek.

Evie felt the drag of desire leaden in her belly as she fought against the seductive allure of her erect nipples and the quivering flesh in his palm. The heat in his gaze burnt into her with all the sear factor of a laser.

'You want to help me feel like a man again?' he sneered, his breath fanning her face. 'You want to take a ride on the one thing I have that *is* fully functional? You want to *screw*, Evie?'

Evie steeled herself against his deliberately crude taunts. He was lashing out. But she wasn't going to respond with the venom his remark deserved.

Because that's what he wanted.

'I just want to love you, Finn,' she said quietly, refusing to break eye contact even though she knew he was trying to goad her into it. Her pulse roared in her ears and her breath sounded all husky and raw. 'Let me love you.'

Evie watched as all the fight went out of him. His hand dropped from her bottom and then he looked away. 'I can't even touch you properly, Evie.'

She grabbed his face and forced him to look at her, his stubble almost soft now it was so long—more spiky than prickly. 'You have this,' she said, her thumb running over the contours of his mouth. 'Which, when it isn't being vicious and cruel, can melt me into a puddle.'

She grabbed his left hand with her right hand and brought it up to her breast. 'And this,' she said, her nipple beading instantly. 'Which knows its way around a woman's body as well as the other.'

Evie saw his pupils dilate as he dropped his gaze to look at his hand on her breast. He stroked his thumb across the aching tip and she shut her eyes briefly.

'And,' she said, dragging herself back from the completely wanton urge to arch her back, 'this.' She tucked her pelvis in snugly against his and rubbed herself against the hard ridge of his arousal.

'And I can do the rest.'

She put her hands between them and her fingers felt for his button and fly and in that instant Finn stopped wrestling his demons. His mouth lunged for hers, latching on and greedily slaking his thirst as his good hand pulled at her blouse then yanked, popping the buttons.

He grunted in satisfaction, his mouth leaving hers, as her hand finally grasped his erection. His grunt became a groan as he blazed a trail down her neck, his whiskers spiky and erotic against the sensitive skin. He yanked her bra cup aside and closed his hot mouth over a nipple that was already peaked to an unbearable tightness.

Evie's eyes practically rolled back into her head and there was no coherent thought as she mindlessly palmed the length of him and cried out at the delicious graze of his teeth against her nipple.

She wasn't aware his hand had dropped, distracted as she was by the combined pleasure of savage suction and long hot swipes as his tongue continually flayed the hardened tip in his mouth. She wasn't aware of him pushing her hand out the way, of him shoving her underwear aside, of him positioning his erection to her entrance, until it nudged against her thick and hard, and then her body recognised it, knew just what to do and took over, accepting the buck and thrust of him, greedily inflaming and agitating, meeting him one for one, adjusting the tilt of her pelvis to hit just the right spot.

It was no gentle coupling. No languid strokes, no soft caresses and murmured endearments, no long, slow build. It was quick and hasty. Just like their first time. Parted clothes. Desperate clawing at fabric, at skin. At backs and thighs and buttocks. Hitting warp speed instantly, feeling the pull and the burn from the first stroke.

Except this time when Finn cried out with his release, his face buried against her chest, he knew it was goodbye. That he had to get away. From Sydney. From the Sydney Harbour Hospital. From Evie.

From this screwed-up dynamic of theirs.

But for now he needed this. So he clutched her body to his and held on, thrusting and thrusting, prolonging the last vestiges of pleasure, finding a physical outlet for the vortex of grief and pain that swirled inside.

Holding on but saying goodbye.

CHAPTER ONE

Five months later

'WHERE IS HE, Evie?' Richard Lockheart demanded of his daughter. 'Prince Khalid bin Aziz wants Finn Kennedy and only Finn Kennedy to do his quadruple by-pass and he's going to donate another million dollars to the hospital to show his appreciation. Sydney Harbour Hospital needs him, Evie. Where is he?'

'I don't know,' Evie said staring out of her father's office window at the boats sailing on the sparkling harbour, wishing she was riding out to sea on one and could leave all her troubles behind her.

'Evie!'

She turned at the imperious command in his voice. 'What makes you think that I know where he is?' she snapped at her father.

'I'm not stupid, Evie. Do you think hospital gossip doesn't reach me all the way over here? I know you and he have a…had a…thing. A fling.' He shrugged. 'Whatever you want to call it. I'm assuming you've kept in touch.'

If Evie needed any other proof of how out of touch her father was with her life, or with life in the trenches generally, she'd just found it. If he knew Finn at all he'd know that Finn wasn't the keeping-in-touch type.

In the aftermath of their frenzied passion five months ago she'd hoped there'd been some kind of breakthrough with him but then he'd disappeared.

Overnight. Literally.

Gladys had told her the next day that he'd gone and handed her a note with seven words.

Goodbye Evie. Don't try and find me.

After all they'd been through—he'd reduced their relationship to seven words.

'Evie!' Richard demanded again, at his daughter's continuing silence.

She glared at her father, who was regarding her as if she was two years old and deliberately defying him, instead of a grown woman. A competent, emergency room physician.

'The state of play between Finn and I is none of your damn business.'

'*Au contraire,*' he said, his brows drawing together. 'What happens at this hospital *is* my business.'

Richard Lockheart took the *business* of Sydney Harbour Hospital very seriously. As its major benefactor he worked tirelessly to ensure it remained the state-of-the-art facility it was, carrying on the legacy of his grandfather, who had founded the hospital. Sometimes she thought he loved the place more than he'd ever loved his wife and his three daughters.

Evie sighed, tired of the fight already. She was just so bloody tired these days. 'Look,' she said, reaching for patience, 'I'm not being deliberately recalcitrant. I really don't know where he is.'

She turned back to the view out the window. His

brief impersonal note had been the final axe blow. She'd fought the good fight but there were only so many times a girl could take rejection. So she'd made a decision to forget him and she'd navigated through life these past five months by doing just that. By putting one foot in front of the other and trying not to think about him.

Or what he'd left behind.

But there'd only ever been a finite amount of time she could exist in her state of denial and the first flutterings this morning had brought an abrupt end to that. She couldn't deny that she was carrying his baby any longer.

Or that he deserved to know.

She turned back to her father. 'I think I know somebody who might.'

Evie had spent the last three afternoons pacing back and forth outside Marco D'Avello's outpatients rooms, waiting for his last expectant mother to leave, summoning up the nerve to go in and see him then chickening out each time as the door opened to discharge a patient.

Today was no different. It was five o'clock, the waiting area was empty and his door opened and she sprang from the seat she'd not long plonked herself in for the hundredth time in half an hour and headed for the lift.

'Evie?'

His rich, beautifully accented voice stopped her in her tracks. Evie had to admit that Emily, his wife and a midwife at the hospital, was an exceptionally lucky woman to wake up to that voice every morning. Not to mention the whole dark, sexy Italian stallion thing he had going on.

Just waking up with the person you loved sounded pretty good to her.

He walked towards her. 'I have been watching you outside my door for three days now.' His voice was soft. 'Would you like to see me?'

Evie dithered. She wasn't sure what she wanted. She didn't know what an obstetrician could tell her that she didn't already know. And yet here she was.

'Come,' he murmured, cupping his hand under her elbow.

Evie let herself be led. Why couldn't she love someone like Marco? Someone who was gentle and supportive?

And capable of love.

She heard the door click behind her and sat in the chair he shepherded her towards. 'You are pregnant. Yes?' he said as he walked around to his side of the desk.

Evie startled gaze flew to his. 'How did you...?' she looked down at her belly, placing her hand over the bump that was obvious on her spare athletic frame if she was naked but not discernible yet in the baggy scrubs she wore at work.

Marco smiled. 'It's okay, you are not showing. I'm just a little more...perceptive to this sort of thing. I think it goes with the job.'

Evie nodded, her brain buzzing. She looked at him for long moments. 'I'm sorry. I don't know why I'm here.'

He didn't seemed perturbed by her strange statement. She was pregnant. He was an obstetrician. It was where she should be. Where she should have been a lot earlier than now.

He just seemed to accept it and waited for her to talk some more.

'I haven't told anyone. No one knows,' she said, trying to clarify.

'How many weeks?'

'Eighteen.'

Marco frowned. 'And you haven't seen anyone yet?'

'I've been…busy.' Evie felt her defences rise, not that Marco seemed to be judging her. 'It's always crazy in the emergency department and…time gets away…'

She looked down at her hands still cradling her bump because what excuse was there really to have neglected herself, to have not sought proper antenatal care?

She was a doctor, for crying out loud.

'You have been well?'

Evie nodded, dragging her gaze back to Marco. 'Disgustingly. A few weeks of vague nausea in the beginning. Tired. I've been really tired. But that's it.'

She'd expected the worse when she'd first discovered she was pregnant. She'd figured any child of Finn's was bound to be as disagreeable as his father and make her life hell. But it had been a dream pregnancy to date as far as all that went.

Which had only made it easier for her to deny what was really happening to her body.

'We should do some bloods,' Marco said. 'Why don't you hop up on the couch for a moment and I'll have a feel?'

Evie nodded. She made her way to the narrow examination table and lay staring at the ceiling as Marco palpated her uterus then measured the fundal height with a tape measure. 'Measurements seem spot on for eighteen weeks,' he murmured as he reached over and flipped on a small ultrasound machine.

'No,' Evie said, half sitting, pulling down her scrub top. 'I don't want to…I don't want an ultrasound.'

She didn't want to look at the baby. Not yet. She'd made a huge leap forward today, finally admitting the pregnancy to someone else. She wasn't ready for a meet and greet.

And she knew that made her all kinds of screwed up.

'I'm sorry,' she apologised. 'That's probably not the reaction you're used to.' She couldn't explain why she didn't want to see the baby—she just knew she didn't. Not yet.

Marco turned off the machine and looked down at her and Evie could tell he was choosing his words carefully. 'Evie…you have left it too late to…*do* something about the pregnancy.'

Evie struggled to sit up, gratefully taking Marco's proffered hand as she sat cross-legged on the narrow couch. She had thought about termination but as with everything else pregnancy related she'd shoved it determinedly to one side.

She'd spent the past eighteen weeks not thinking about the baby—her body aiding and abetting her denial by being virtually symptom-free.

She looked at Marco. 'I know. I don't want to.'

She stopped. *Where had that come from?*

Termination had been an option and one, as a doctor and a woman, she firmly believed should be available, but suddenly she knew deep down in the same place that she'd known she loved Finn that she loved his baby too. And that nothing would come between them.

He may not have let her in, let her love him, but there would be no distance between Finn's child and her.

She gave Marco a half-smile. 'I'm sorry. I don't think

I really accepted until the baby moved a few days ago that I was actually pregnant. I'm still trying to…process things.'

He smiled back. 'It's okay. How about we listen to the heartbeat instead and get some bloods done as a first step?'

Evie nodded and lay back and in seconds she was listening to the steady whop-whop-whop of a tiny beating heart. Her eyes filled with tears. 'There really is a baby in there.'

Marco smiled at her gently and nodded. 'Your baby.'

Evie shut her eyes. *Finn's baby.*

Finn Kennedy eased his lean frame into the low squatter's chair and looked out over the vista from the shaded serenity of the wide wraparound veranda. He liked it here in this rambling old house perched on a cliff top overlooking the mighty Pacific Ocean. He gazed over acres of deep blue sea to the horizon, the constant white noise of the surf pounding against the rocks far below a wild serenade.

He liked the tranquillity. For too long he'd been keeping himself busy to block out the pain, drinking to block out the pain, screwing around and pushing himself to the limit to block out the pain.

Who knew that stopping everything and standing still worked better than any of that?

His muscles ached but in a good way. The hard physical labour he'd been doing the last five months had built up his lean body, giving definition to the long smooth muscles in his arms and legs. He felt fitter and more clear-headed than he had in a very long time.

He clenched and unclenched his right hand, marvelling in the full range of movement. He formed a pincer with his index finger and thumb and then tapped each finger in turn onto the pad of his thumb, repeating the process over and over. To think he'd despaired of ever getting any use of it back. It was weaker than his left hand for sure but he'd come a long way.

'As good as a bought one.'

Finn looked up at the approaching form of Ethan Carter, with whom he'd served in the Middle East a decade ago. 'I doubt I'll ever be able to open jam jars.'

Ethan shrugged, handing Finn a beer. 'So don't open jam jars.'

Finn snorted at Ethan's typical Zen-like reasoning as he lowered himself into the chair beside Finn's. Ethan, a Black Hawk pilot, had trained as a psychologist after his discharge from the army and *Beach Haven* had been his brainchild. An exclusive retreat for injured soldiers five hundred kilometres north of Sydney where they could rest, recover, rehabilitate and refocus their lives. Only partially government funded, Ethan worked tirelessly to keep up the very generous private funding that had come Beach Haven's way.

Neither of them said anything for a while, just looked out over the ocean and drank their beer.

'It's time, Finn.'

Finn didn't look at Ethan. He didn't even answer him for a long moment. 'I'm not ready,' he said eventually.

Prior to coming to *Beach Haven*, Finn would have thought being away from Sydney Harbour Hospital, from operating, was a fate worse than death. Now he wasn't sure if he ever wanted to return.

Dropping out and becoming a hermit in a beach

shack somewhere was immensely appealing. Maybe he'd even take up surfing.

'Your arm is better. You can't hide here for ever.'

He turned to Ethan and glared at him with a trace of the old Finn. 'Why not?'

'Because this isn't who you are. Because you're using this to avoid your issues.'

'So I should go back to facing them in a high-stress environment where people's lives depend on me?'

'You've healed here, Finn. Physically. And mentally you're much more relaxed. You needed that. But you're not opening up emotionally.'

He shrugged and took a slug of his beer. 'I'm a surgeon, we're not emotional types.'

'No, Finn. Being a surgeon is what you do, not who you are. Beyond all those fancy letters after your name you're just a man who could do nothing but sit and cradle his dying brother while all hell was breaking loose around you. You couldn't help him. You couldn't save him. You couldn't stop him from dying. You're damaged in ways that go far beyond the physical.'

Finn flinched as Ethan didn't even try to pull his punches. In five months they hadn't once spoken about what had happened all those years ago. How Ethan had found a wounded Finn, peppered with shrapnel, holding Isaac.

'But I think you find some kind of emotional release in operating. I think that with every person you save, you bring back a little bit of Isaac. And if you're not going to open up about it, if surgery is your therapy of choice, then I think you should get back to it.'

More silence followed broken only by the pounding of surf.

'So you're kicking me out,' Finn said, staring at the horizon.

Ethan shook his head. 'Nope. I'm recommending a course of treatment. You're welcome to stay as long as you like.'

Finn's thoughts churned like the foam that he knew from his daily foray to the beach swirled and surged against the rocks with the sweep and suck of the tide. He knew Ethan was right, just as he'd known that this reprieve from the world couldn't last.

But his thoughts were interrupted by the crunching of tyres on the gravel drive and the arrival of a little red Mini sweeping into the parking area.

'Are we expecting an arrival today?' Ethan frowned.

'Not as far as I know,' Finn murmured.

They watched as the door opened and a woman climbed out. 'Oh, crap,' Finn said.

Ten minutes later Evie leaned against the veranda railing, looking out over the ocean view, the afternoon breeze blowing her loose hair off her shoulders. It ruffled the frayed edges of her denim cut-offs and blew the cream cotton of her loose, round-necked peasant blouse against her skin. She breathed the salt tang deep into her lungs.

'Wow,' she said, expelling her breath. 'This is a spectacular view.'

'It's all right,' Finn said, irked that he was enjoying the view of her perky denim-clad backside a hell of a lot more than the magnificent one-hundred-and-eighty-degree ocean view.

Since he'd slunk away in the night after their explosive session on his couch he'd thought about Evie a lot. Probably too much. Some of it R-rated. Most of it involving her big hazel eyes looking at him with love and compassion and pleading with him to let her in.

Up here he'd managed to pigeonhole her and the relationship she'd wanted so desperately as a bad idea. Standing a metre away from her, the long, toned lines of her achingly familiar, he had to clench his fists to stop from reaching for her.

Once upon a time he would have dismissed the impulse as a purely sexual urge. Something he would have felt for any woman standing here after five months of abstinence. A male thing. But solitude and time to think had stripped away his old defence mechanisms and as such he was forced to recognise the truth.

Evie was under his skin.

And it scared the hell out of him. Because she wouldn't be happy with half of him. She would want all of him. And as Ethan had not long ago pointed out, he was damaged.

And it went far beyond that awful day ten years ago.

He didn't know how to love a woman. He doubted he'd ever known. Not even Lydia.

'How did you find me?'

Evie turned to face him, amazed at this version of Finn before her, lounging in a chair, casually knocking back a beer.

Had he ever been this chilled?

Okay, there had been a wariness in his gaze since she'd arrived but this Finn was still a stark contrast to Sydney Harbour Hospital Finn. The old Finn was a serious, driven, sombre professional who oozed energy and drive from every pore. His mind was sharp, his tongue even more so, and his pace had always been frenetic.

His drink of choice was seriously good Scotch.

This Finn was so laid back he may as well have been wearing a Hawaiian shirt and a flower behind his ear. His body was more honed, spare, and his skin had been kissed to a golden honey hue. A far cry from the haggard shadow he'd been when last she'd seen him.

Had he been surfing all this time?

The incredible blue of his eyes, so often frigid with disapproval, were like warm tropical waters amidst the golden planes of his stubbly face. And she wanted to dive in.

She'd been nervous that he'd take one look at her and know she was pregnant. Which was ridiculous given that it would be at least another month, maybe more, before it was obvious to anyone. But she really needn't have worried. This Finn didn't look like he'd be bothered if she'd turned up with his triplets.

Something rose in her chest, dark and ugly. It twisted and burned and she realised she was jealous. This was the kind of Finn she'd longed for, had known was there somewhere. The one he'd never shown her.

'Daddy get a private detective?' he goaded.

His voice had an edge that she recognised as the old Finn and she found herself responding accordingly. She was like Pavlov's dog, still salivating over the slightest crumb.

She cleared her throat as emotion lodged like a fist in her trachea. 'Lydia.'

'Lydia?' Finn sat up. '*Lydia* told you I was here?' Isaac's widow, the woman he'd had a seriously screwed-up co-dependent relationship with in the aftermath of his brother's death, had been talking to Evie?

He frowned. '*You know Lydia?*'

Evie nodded calmly. Well, she'd met her anyway—
she still had no clue as to their relationship. 'I met her
outside your apartment a couple of days after you left.
She came to pick up some stuff for you. Told me you
were okay. That you needed space. Time… She gave
me her card.'

Finn shut his eyes and leaned back into the canvas
hammock of the squatter's chair. Trust Lydia to interfere. He opened his eyes to find her looking at him.

'Your arm is better, I see.'

Finn looked down at it. He clenched and unclenched
his fingers automatically, still amazed that he could do
so. 'Yes.'

Evie pressed her butt hard into the railing. She
wanted to launch herself at him, throw herself into his
lap, hug him to her, tell him she'd known it would get
better, that he'd just needed a little faith and a lot of patience. But he didn't look so laid back now and memories of what had happened last time she had been in his
lap overrode everything else.

There was even more between them now than there'd
ever been—more than he certainly knew—and she
couldn't think about any of it until she had him back
in Sydney, until after he'd operated on their celebrity
patient, until after she'd told him about the baby…

'You must be very relieved,' Evie murmured.

Finn didn't want to make small talk with her. His
mind had been clear ten minutes ago and now it was
all clouded up again.

Seeing Evie after five months' break made him realise how much he'd missed her wide hazel eyes and her
interesting face. How much he'd taken her presence for
granted when they'd worked in the same hospital, when

she'd been there for him during his ops. How much he'd come to depend on seeing her, even though he'd pushed her away at every turn.

He'd been able to ignore all of that five hundred kilometres away from her—out of sight out of mind. But it was impossible to ignore now. She made him want things he didn't know how to articulate.

And he wanted her gone.

So he could go back to ignoring her and all the stuff that bubbled to the surface whenever she was around all over again.

'Why are you here?' he demanded.

Evie swallowed at his sullen enquiry. His gaze was becoming chilly again and she shivered. 'Prince Khalid bin Aziz.'

Finn frowned at the name from his past. Several years ago he'd revived a man who had collapsed in front of him on the street a couple of blocks from the hospital. He'd had no way of knowing at the time that the man was a Saudi oil prince. There'd been no robes, no staff, no security. He'd just been another heart to start and Finn's medical training had taken over.

But it had certainly worked out well for the hospital, which had benefited from a huge donation.

'What does he want?'

'He wants you.' *Not as badly as she did, however.* 'He needs a quadruple bypass and he wants you *and only you* to perform it.'

Finn gripped his beer bottle harder as Evie opened a door he'd shut firmly behind him and a surge of adrenaline hit him like a bolt from the blue. He could almost smell the chemical cleanliness of the operating room, hear the dull slap as an instrument hit his gloved hand, feel the heat of the overhead lights on the back of his neck.

He shook his head, quashing the powerful surge of anticipation. 'I'm not ready to come back.'

Evie's looked down at him as he absently clenched and unclenched his right hand. Her heart banged loudly in her chest. *What on earth was he talking about?* Finn was a surgeon. The best cardiothoracic surgeon there was. He had to come back. And not just for the amir.

For him. For his sanity. For his dignity. The Finn she knew *needed* to work.

'You look physically capable,' she said, keeping her voice neutral.

Finn pushed up out of the chair as the decision he'd been circling around for five months crystallised. He walked to the railing, keeping a distance between them, his gaze locking on the horizon. 'I don't know if I'm going to come back.'

Evie stared at his profile. 'To the Harbour?'

Finn shook his head as he tested the words out loud. 'To surgery.'

Evie blinked, her brain temporarily shutting down at the enormity of his admission. Quit being a surgeon? *That was sacrilege.*

She turned around slowly so she too was facing the horizon. Her hand gripped the railing as the line between the earth and the sky seemed to tilt. 'My father will not be pleased,' she joked, attempting to lighten the moment while her thoughts and emotions jumbled themselves into an almighty tangle.

'Ah, yes, how is the great Richard Lockheart?'

Evie would have to have been deaf not to hear the

contempt in Finn's voice. It was fair to say that Finn was not on Team Richard. But, then, neither was she.

'Already counting the pennies from the big fat donation Prince Khalid has promised the hospital.'

Evie wondered if Finn remembered that it was through Prince Khalid's misfortune that she'd first met him. At the gala dinner that the prince had thrown in Finn's honour the first time he'd donated one million dollars to the Sydney Harbour Hospital's cardiothoracic department.

Finn had been as unimpressed as she to be there.

He snorted. 'Of course. I should have known there would be money involved.'

Evie had never heard such coldness in Finn's voice before. Not where his work was concerned, and it frightened her. She was used to it regarding her and anything of a remotely personal nature. But not his job.

She'd never thought she'd have to convince him to come back to work. She'd just assumed he'd jump back in as soon as he possibly could.

Just how long had his hand been recovered for?

'So don't do it for him,' she said battling to keep the rise of desperation out of her voice. 'Or for the money. Do it for the prince.'

'There are any number of very good cardiac surgeons in Sydney.'

'He doesn't want very good. He wants the best.'

Finn turned to face her, propping his hip against the railing. 'No.'

Evie turned too, at a complete loss as she faced him. 'Please.'

She seemed to always be asking him for something he wasn't prepared to give. Saying, *please, Finn, please*. And she was heartily sick of it. And sick of being rejected.

And if she wasn't carrying his baby she'd just walk right away. But she was. And he needed to know—whatever the fallout might be.

She opened her mouth to tell him. Not to bribe him into doing what she wanted but because she could see his mind was made up, and before he sent her away for the last time, he had to know.

But Ethan striding out onto the veranda interrupted them. 'Finn—' Finn looked over Evie's shoulder. 'Oh… sorry…I thought I heard the car leave,' Ethan said, smiling apologetically at Evie as he approached.

'It's fine,' Evie murmured.

'What's up?' Finn asked, dragging his gaze away from Evie's suddenly pale face.

'What's the name of that agency you were telling me about?'

Finn frowned. 'The medical staffing one? Why?'

'Hamish's father-in-law had a heart attack and died two hours ago. He's taking two weeks off. I've been ringing around everywhere but no one's available and I can't run this place without a medico on board, it's a government regulation.'

'For God's sake, Ethan,' Finn said, his voice laced with exasperation, having had this conversation too many times before. *'I'm* a doctor.'

Ethan shook his head firmly. 'You're a client.'

Finn shoved his hand on his hip. 'These are extenuating circumstances.'

Ethan chuckled. 'No dice, buddy. Them's the rules.'

'You never used to be such a stickler for the rules.'

Ethan clapped him on the back. 'I wasn't running my own business back then.'

Evie was surprised at the obvious affection between the two men. Surprised even more at the spurt of jealousy. Finn wasn't the touchy-feely kind. He maintained professional relationships with his colleagues and he'd been known to sit at the bar over the road from the hospital and knock back a few whiskies with them from time to time but he was pretty much a solo figure.

He and Ethan, a big bear of a man with a grizzly beard and kind eyes, seemed to go back a long way.

'Problem?' she asked, at Finn's obvious frustration.

Finn shook his head then stopped as an idea took hold. He raked his gaze over her and knew it would probably be something he would come to regret, but choices were limited in the middle of nowhere.

Maybe the current pain in his butt could be Ethan's silver lining. 'Evie can do it.'

'What?' she gaped, her pulse spiking. 'Do what?'

Ethan smiled at Evie apologetically. 'I'm sorry. He's not very good with social nuances, is he?'

'She's a fully qualified, highly trained, *very good* emergency doctor,' Finn continued, ignoring Ethan's remark.

'You can't just go springing jobs on people like that and acting like they have no choice but to take them,' Ethan chided, his smile getting wider and wider. 'Not cool, man. Maybe you should try asking the lady?'

Finn turned to Evie, his palms finding her upper arms, curling around her biceps. 'I'll come back and do Khalid's surgery. But only if you do the two weeks here first.'

Ethan crossed his arms. 'That's not asking.'

Evie felt her belly plummet as if she'd just jumped out of a plane. She wasn't sure if was due to his snap decision, his compliment over her medical skills or his touch but she couldn't think when he looked at her with need in his eyes.

Even if it was purely professional.

'C'mon, Princess Evie,' Finn murmured, trying to cut through the confusion he could see in her hazel eyes. 'Step outside your comfort zone for a while. Live a little.'

'You suck at asking,' Ethan interjected.

Evie swallowed as she became caught up in the heady rush of being needed by Finn. Not even the nickname grated.

Why not?

It would kill two birds with one stone—Khalid got his op and she bought herself some time. And her father had told her to do *anything* to get Finn back.

'Okay,' she said, hoping her voice didn't sound as shaky as it felt leaving her throat.

Finn nodded and looked at Ethan. 'You've got yourself a doctor.'

Ethan looked from one to the other, his bewildered look priceless. Like he couldn't quite believe that in less than a minute his major problem had been settled.

Neither, frankly, could Evie.

CHAPTER TWO

EVIE CLIMBED ONTO the back of the four-wheeler behind Ethan the next morning for the grand tour. *Beach Haven* retreat covered a couple of hundred acres and wasn't something that could be quickly traversed on foot. Finn, who had disappeared shortly after he'd bribed her into staying for two weeks, was still nowhere to be seen. She didn't ask Ethan where he was and he didn't tell her.

Her father hadn't been happy with the two-week delay but as the prince's blocked arteries had been found on a routine physical and hadn't been symptomatic, the surgery wasn't urgent.

Their first port of call was the clinic. It could be seen from the homestead and she'd be able to walk easily to and from along the track, but as it was just the first stop of many today Ethan drove them across.

It looked like an old worker's cottage from the outside but had been renovated entirely on the inside with a waiting area, a couple of rooms with examination tables and a minor ops room. A small dispensary with common medications, a storeroom, a toilet and a kitchenette completed the well-equipped facility. Thought had also been given to disabled access with the addition of ramps, widened doors and handrails.

'Clinic starts at ten every morning. First come first

served. There's rarely a stampede. They usually come to see me.'

Evie cocked an eyebrow. 'For therapy?' He nodded. 'I wouldn't have thought you'd have any takers.'

Ethan shrugged. 'It's a pre-req for a place here. Weekly therapy—whether they like it or not.'

She thought not liking it would be the predominant feeling amongst a bunch of battle-weary soldiers. 'Does that include Finn?'

He nodded. 'No exceptions.'

Evie absorbed the information. Maybe that was why he seemed so chilled? But…surely not. The Finn she knew wasn't capable of talking about his issues. 'I don't imagine those sessions would be very enlightening.'

Ethan laughed. 'He's pretty guarded, that's for sure. But…' he shrugged '…you can lead a horse to water… I can't force him or anyone else to open up. I just hope like hell they do. In my opinion, there's not a man who's seen active duty who couldn't do with some therapy.'

'Is that why you opened this place?' Evie asked. 'A ruse to get soldiers into therapy?'

He laughed again and Evie found herself wondering why it was she couldn't fall for someone like Ethan. He was attractive enough in a shaggy kind of way with a ready smile and an easy manner.

'Kind of,' he said, his voice big and gruff like the rest of him. 'Returned soldiers have issues. Those who have been physically injured even more so. It's too easy for them to slip through the cracks. Succumb to feelings of uselessness, hopelessness and despair. Here they're able to continue their rehab, contribute to society and find a little perspective.'

'And you're the perspective?' she asked, smiling.

Ethan looked embarrassed but smiled back. 'Anyway...' he said, looking around, 'clinic is done by twelve and then your day is your own as long as you stay on the property and have your pager on you in case an emergency arises.'

'Does that happen very often?'

Ethan shook his head. 'The last one was a couple of months ago when there was an incident with a nail gun.'

She raised an eyebrow. 'Do I want to know?'

He grinned and shook his head. 'Nope.'

Evie nodded slowly, also looking around. 'So, that's it? A two-hour clinic and the odd nail-gun emergency?'

Ethan nodded. 'Think you can cope?' he teased.

Compared to the frenetic pace of a busy city emergency department Evie felt as if Ethan had just handed her the keys to paradise. And there was a beach to boot! 'I think I can hack the pace,' she murmured. 'In fact, I think I may just have died and gone to heaven.'

He grinned. 'C'mon, I'll show you the rest.'

Ten minutes later they pulled up at what appeared to be a massive shed that actually housed an Olympic-sized indoor swimming pool and a large gym area where she caught up with Bob, the physiotherapist she'd met last night. He was in the middle of a session with two below-knee amputees so they didn't chat.

From there it was another ten minutes to a series of three smaller sheds. The side doors were all open and the sounds of electric saws and nail guns pierced the air as Ethan cut the bike engine.

'This is where we build the roof trusses I was telling you about last night,' Ethan said as they dismounted.

With a noticeably absent Finn over dinner last night, Ethan had filled her in on the flood-recovery project the retreat participants contributed to during their stay. Several extreme weather events had led to unprecedented flooding throughout Australia over the previous two years and demand for new housing was at a premium. Roof trusses were part of that. It was a small-scale project perfect for Ethan's ragtag band of clients, which aided both the flood and the soldiers' recovery.

It was win-win.

They entered the nearest workshop, which was a hive of activity. The aroma of cut timber immediately assailed Evie and she pulled it deep into her lungs. One by one the men stopped working.

'I suspect,' Ethan whispered out of the side of his mouth, 'you may well see an increase in visits to the clinic in the next few days. Just to check you out. Not a lot of women around here.'

Evie smiled as all but one lone nail gun pistoned away obliviously. It stopped too after a few moments and the owner turned and looked at her.

It was Finn.

Evie's breath caught in her throat. He was wearing faded jeans and an even more faded T-shirt that clung in all the good places. A tool belt was slung low on his hips. Used to seeing him in baggy scrubs, her brain grappled with the conflicting images.

Her body however, now well into the second trimester and at the mercy of a heightened sex drive, responded on a completely primitive level.

Tool-Man Finn was hot.

A wolf whistle came from somewhere in the back.

'Okay, okay back to work.' Ethan grinned. 'Don't scare our doctor away before her first day.'

One by one they resumed their work. Except Finn,

who downed his nail gun, his arctic gaze firmly fixed on her as he strode in her direction.

'Uh-oh,' Ethan said out of the corner of his mouth. 'He doesn't look too happy.'

Evie couldn't agree more. She should be apprehensive. But he looked pretty damn sexy, coming at her with all that coiled tension. Like he might just slam her against the nearest wall and take her, like he had their first time.

'I don't think happy is in his vocabulary.'

Finn pulled up in front of Ethan—who seriously should know better than to bring a woman into an environment where most of the men hadn't seen one in weeks—and glared at his friend. *Who had clearly gone mad.*

'What is *she* doing here?' he demanded.

Ethan held up his hands. 'Just showing the lady around.'

'She only needs to know where the clinic is,' Finn pointed out.

'Well, apart from common courtesy,' Ethan murmured, his voice firm, '*Evie* really should know the lie of the land in case of an emergency.'

Finn scowled at his friend's logic. 'Now she knows.' He turned and looked at Evie in her clothes from yesterday, her hair loose. 'This is no place for a woman,' he ground out.

Having been in the army for a decade and here for almost five months, Finn knew these men and men just like them. Even hiding away, licking their wounds, sex was always on their mind.

Evie felt her hackles rise. Had she slipped back into the Fifties? She glared at him, her gaze unwavering. 'You ought to talk,' she snapped, pleased the background noise kept their conversation from being overheard. 'What kind of a place is this for a surgeon, Finn? Wielding a nail gun when you should be wielding a scalpel!'

Finn ignored the dig. 'Get her out of here,' he said to Ethan.

Finn scowled again as Ethan grinned but breathed a sigh of relief when Evie followed Ethan out, every pair of eyes in the workshop glued to her butt.

His included.

On their next leg, they passed a helipad and a small hangar with a gleaming blue and white chopper sitting idle.

'Yours?' she asked.

He nodded. 'Handy piece of transport in the middle of nowhere.'

They drove to a large dam area, which had been the source of the silver perch they'd eaten last night. Above it evenly spaced on a grassy hill sat ten pre-fab dongas.

'Each one has four bedrooms, a bathroom, a kitchen and common area,' Ethan explained, as he pulled up under a shady stand of gumtrees near the dam edge and cut the engine. 'They're not luxurious but they're better than anything any of us slept in overseas.'

'So your capacity is forty?'

'Actually, it's forty-five if you count the homestead accommodation,' Ethan said, dismounting and walking over to inspect the water. 'That's over and above you, me, Bob and Finn.'

Evie nodded, also walking over to the water's edge. The sun was warm on her skin and she raised her face to it for long moments. She could hear the low buzz of insects and the distant whine of a saw.

Ethan waited for a while and said, 'So…you and Finn…'

Evie opened her eyes and looked at him. 'What about me and Finn?'

'You're…colleagues? Friends…?'

Evie considered Ethan's question for a while. She didn't know how to define them with just one word. Colleagues, yes. Lovers, yes. Soon to be parents, yes. But friends…?

She shrugged. 'It's…complicated.'

Ethan nodded. 'He's a complicated guy.'

Evie snorted at the understatement of the century. 'You've known him for a while?'

Ethan picked up a stone at his feet and skipped it across the surface. 'We served together overseas.'

'You know his brother died over there?'

'I know.'

'It's really messed with his head,' she murmured.

Ethan picked up another stone and looked at it. 'You love him?' he asked gently.

Evie swallowed as Ethan followed his direct question with a direct look. She thought about denying it, but after five months of denying it it felt good to say it to someone. 'Yes.' She gave a self-deprecating laugh. 'He's not exactly easy to love, though, you know? And God knows I've tried not to…'

Evie paused. She had a feeling that Ethan knew exactly how hard Finn was to love. 'I think what happened with his brother really shut him down emotionally,' she murmured.

She knew she was making another excuse for him

but she couldn't even begin to imagine how awful it would be to hold Bella or Lexi in her arms as they died. The thought of losing her sisters at all was horrifying. But like that?

How did somebody stay normal after that?

How did it not push a person over the edge?

Ethan looked back at the stone in his hand, feeling its weight and its warmth before letting it fly to skim across the surface. 'Yes, it did. But I think Finn had issues that predated the tragedy with Isaac,' he said carefully.

Evie snapped to attention. 'He told you that?'

Ethan snorted. 'No. This *is* Finn, remember. He's always been pretty much a closed book, Evie. At least as long as I've known him. And we go back a couple of years before what happened with Isaac. He's been much, much worse since then but he wasn't exactly the life of the party before that. Part of it is the things he'd seen, the injuries, the total…mayhem that is war. A person shuts themselves down to protect themselves from that kind of carnage. But I think there's even more than that with Finn, stuff from his distant past.'

Evie stilled as the enormity of what she faced hit home. If Ethan was right she was dealing with something bigger than his grief. She looked at Ethan helplessly, her hand seeking the precious life that grew inside her, needing to anchor herself in an uncertain sea. 'I don't know how to reach him through all that.'

Ethan shrugged. 'I don't know how you do it either but I do know that he's crying out for help and after that little performance in the workshop, I think you're the one woman who can do it. I have never seen Finn so… emotionally reactive as just now.'

Evie cocked an eyebrow. 'Is that what you call it?'

He grinned. 'Don't give up on him, Evie. I think you'll make a human being out of him yet.'

Ethan had been right—word had got out. Evie's clinic was bustling that first morning with the most pathetic ailments she'd ever treated. But it felt good to be able to practise medicine where there was no pressure or stress or life-and-death situations and the men were flirty and charming and took the news of her pretend boyfriend waiting back home for her good-naturedly.

She and Bob had lunch together on the magnificent homestead veranda serenaded by the crash of the surf. She yawned as Bob regaled her with the details of the nail-gun incident.

'Sorry,' she apologised with a rueful smile. 'It must be the sea air.'

Bob took it in his stride. 'No worries. You should lie down and have a bit of a kip, love. A siesta. Reckon the Italians have that right.'

Evie was awfully tempted. The pregnancy had made her tired to the bone and by the time she arrived home after manic twelve-hour shifts at Sydney Harbour she was utterly exhausted. She already felt like she was in a major sleep deficit—and the baby wasn't even out yet! She fantasised every day about midday naps and she could barely drag herself out of bed on her days off.

But it didn't seem right to wander off for a nanny nap in broad daylight—was that even allowed?

'Go on,' Bob insisted as she yawned again. 'There's nothing for you to do here and you have your pager.'

Evie hesitated for a moment longer then thought, What the hell?

She pulled the suitcase off her bed—it must have been delivered while she'd been working that morning. She'd tasked Bella with the job of packing two weeks' worth of clothes for her because, as a fashion designer, Evie knew her sister would choose with care. Her youngest sister Lexi, on the other hand, who was thirty-two weeks pregnant and time poor, would have just shoved in the first things that came to hand.

As her head hit the pillow her thoughts turned to Finn, as they always did. Should she tell him, shouldn't she tell him? When to tell him? Here? Back in Sydney? When would be a good time?

But the lack of answers was even more wearying than the questions and within a minute the sound of the ocean and the pull of exhaustion had sucked her into a deep, deep sleep.

Evie woke with a start three hours later. She looked at the clock. She'd slept for three freaking hours?

She must have been more tired than she'd thought!

She certainly hadn't felt this rested in a long time. Maybe after two weeks here she'd have caught up on the sleep she needed.

She stretched and stared at the ceiling for a moment or two, her hand finding her belly without conscious thought.

'Well, baby,' she said out loud. 'Should I track your father down and tell him right now or should I wait till we're back in Sydney and he's done the op?'

Evie realised she should feel silly, talking to a tiny human being in utero who couldn't respond, but she'd spent so much time avoiding anything to do with the life inside her that it suddenly seemed like the most natural thing in the world—talking to her baby.

'Move now if you think I should tell him today.'

Again, quite silly. If she was going to rely on airy-fairy reasoning to inform her critical decisions, it'd probably make more sense to flip a coin.

But then the baby moved. And not some gentle fluttering, is-it-or-isn't it, maybe-it's-just-wind kind of movement. It was a kick. A very definite kick. As if the baby was shaping up to play soccer for Australia.

Crap. The baby had spoken.

Twenty minutes later she'd changed into a loose, flowing sundress that she'd never seen before but which fitted her perfectly. Bella had attached a note to say, 'Designed this especially for you. xxx.'

It was floaty and feminine with shoestring straps—perfect for the beach and the warm September day. And exactly what she needed to face Finn.

Finn couldn't be found around the homestead but Ethan came out as she was standing at the veranda railing, contemplating the horizon.

'Good clinic this morning,' he said.

Evie smiled. 'I've never known a bunch of tough guys see a doctor for such trifling complaints.' Ethan laughed and she joined him. 'I don't suppose you know where Finn might be?' she asked, when their laughter petered out.

'I'd try the beach.' He inclined his head towards the well-worn track that lead to the safety-railed cliff edge and the two hundred and twenty stairs that delivered the intrepid traveller straight onto the beach.

They were not for the faint-hearted…

'He normally swims everyday around this time.'

'Am I allowed to go that far away?' she asked.

Ethan laughed. 'Of course. It's not that far. And even though it isn't a private beach, we kind of consider it as within the property boundaries.'

She smiled. 'Thanks.'

Halfway down she stood aside to let a buff-looking guy in boardies and a backpack run past, his below-knee prosthesis not seeming to hinder him an iota. He nodded at her as he pounded upwards and she turned to watch him as he scaled the stairs as if they were nothing.

Her gaze drifted all the way up the sheer cliff face to the very top. She was dreading *walking* back—running just seemed insane.

Her foot hit the warm sand a few minutes later and her gaze scanned the wide arc of yellow, unpatrolled beach for Finn. She couldn't see him but as she walked closer to the thundering ocean she could see a towel discarded on the sand and she looked out at the water, trying to see a head amongst the continually rolling breakers.

Her heart beat in sync with the ocean as she searched in vain through the wild pounding surf and a hundred disaster scenarios scuttled through her head. She calmed herself with the knowledge that he was a strong swimmer and ignored the ominous power of the surging ocean. Then she spotted his head popping up out of the water. He was quite a distance out but she could see his wet hair was sleek, like a seal's pelt, and his shoulders were broad and bare.

She sat on the sand next to his towel and waited.

* * *

Finn was aware of Evie from the minute she'd set foot on the beach. Some sixth sense had alerted him and he'd watched her advance towards the shoreline, obviously looking for him.

And, of course, she looked utterly gorgeous in a dress that blew across her body, outlining her athletic legs, her hair whipping across her face, the shoestring straps baring lovely collar bones and beautiful shoulders.

Just looking at her made him hard and he was grateful for the cover of ocean.

It had been so long since he'd touched her. He wanted to stride up the beach, push her back into the sand and bury himself in her. But he hated the feelings she roused in him and the loss of control he exhibited when he was with her.

Besides…it would just put them back at square one when he'd tried so hard—and succeeded—at putting distance between them.

He could tell, though, even from this distance, she was here to chat. And, God knew, he didn't want to chat with her. Right now the only thing he wanted to do with her involved being naked and he was going to stay right here until he'd worn the impulse down.

He swam against and with the strong current until he was chilled to the bone and his arm ached. A part of him hoped she'd get sick of waiting and just leave. Or maybe her pager would go off. But she sat stubbornly staring out to sea, watching him until finally the chill was unbearable and, admitting defeat, he strode from the surf.

She handed him his towel as he drew level with her and he took it wordlessly, rubbing vigorously at his body. When he was done he wrapped it around his waist and threw himself down next to her, taking care to leave a gap. She didn't say anything to him as they both sat and watched the ocean for a while, the sun's rays beginning to work their magic on the ice that seemed to penetrate right down to his bones.

Although the ice around his heart was as impenetrable as always.

'I hear you have a boyfriend,' he said after a while.

Evie, her brain still grappling with the perfect words to tell Finn he was going to be a father and her stupid pregnant hormones still all aflutter from his sexy Adonis-rising-from-the-ocean display, didn't register the terseness in his tone.

'A cosmetic surgeon who owns a Porsche and comes from North Shore money,' he continued.

Evie bit back a smile at the ill-disguised contempt in his voice. When choosing her fake boyfriend she'd deliberately chosen all the attributes Finn would despise. 'Well, I figured if I was going to have a make-believe boyfriend I might as well go all out.'

Finn wasn't mollified. 'He sounds like a tosser.'

Evie smiled at the ocean. 'Because he does lips and boobs or because of the Porsche?'

Finn glared at her as she continued to stare at the horizon. 'Is that what you want, Princess Evie? Some blue-blooded prince to keep up your royal lineage?'

She turned to look at him, her nostrils flaring as the scent of sea salt and something her hormones recognised as quintessentially Finn enveloped her. 'I think you know who I want.'

And suddenly the roar of the ocean faded as the pounding of her pulse took over. The fact she was supposed to be telling him about their baby also faded as her heart drummed a primitive beat perfectly at home in this deserted windswept landscape. The world of the beach shrank until there was just him and her and the sun stroking warm fingers over their skin, lulling her common sense into a stupor. His bare chest and shoulders teased her peripheral vision, his sexy stubble and wet, ruffled hair taunted her front and centre.

'I've only ever wanted you, Finn,' she murmured, her breath rough as her gaze fell to his mouth. Wanting to feel it on hers. To feel it everywhere. 'And right now all I can think about is how good we are together.'

Finn shut his eyes, images of how good they were rolling through his brain as seductively as her voice, like a siren from the sea. He opened them again and her hazel eyes were practically silver with desire. 'Evie...'

Her breasts grew heavy at the rawness of his voice. Longing snaked through her belly, hot and hard and hungry as she lifted her hand to his face, ran her fingers over his mouth. 'I've wanted to kiss you every day for five months,' she murmured.

Finn gently grabbed her wrist, intent on setting her away, but the breeze blew the scent of her shampoo, of her skin right into his face, enveloping him in a cloud of memories, and he knew he wasn't strong enough. Not after five months of denial.

'Oh, hell,' he half muttered, half groaned as he slid his hand from her wrist into her hair, pulling her head close and lowering his mouth to hers.

He'd lain awake at night thinking about her kiss. And it was as good as he remembered. Better. She opened to him on a sigh, moved into the shelter of his arms as if she belonged there and he felt the last of the cold disappear from his bones as an intense heat roared and raged through his marrow.

And then he was hot everywhere.

Their tongues tangoed as he pressed her back onto the sand, his thigh instantly pushing between hers, his hand automatically stroking down her neck, across her shoulders before claiming a breast, firmer and rounder even than he remembered, the nipple beading instantly beneath his palm.

Evie moaned as she arched her back, pushing herself into his hand more, the ache of the aroused tip mirroring the ache between her legs. She rubbed against his thigh to relieve it but he only pushed harder against her, stoking the need higher.

And then with a muffled curse against her mouth he was over her, on top of her, and she revelled in the pressure of him pushing her into the warm sand, the imprint of each grain against the backs of her calves, the feel of the naked planes of his back dry and warm from the sun beneath her hands.

Her head spun from his kiss, her breath was short and choppy and her belly dipped and tightened with every thrust and parry of his tongue. And if it hadn't been for a lone seagull landing practically on top of them and startling them both out of their stupor, Evie had no doubt they would have gone all the way, oblivious to everything but the primitive imperative of their bodies.

Evie broke off their kiss as sense invaded their bubble and she became aware they were making out on a beach and anyone with two eyes and a pair of binoculars could be watching them from the cliff top. Not to mention anyone coming down the stairs from the retreat copping an eyeful.

Finn uttered another curse and rolled off her, flopping onto his back, his chest heaving, his pulse battering his temples, his erection throbbing painfully.

'Finn.' She reached for his arm but he vaulted upright abruptly and she knew he was already regretting what had happened.

'I'm sorry,' he said. 'That shouldn't have happened.'

Evie sighed as she too sat, her body still zinging from their kisses. 'Why not?' she asked. 'We're both adults, Finn.'

Finn shook his head vehemently. 'We're not going down this road again, Evie,' he said.

Evie smoothed her dress over her knees. *Tell him.* Tell him they were on the road together whether he liked it or not. 'Would it be so bad?'

'I lose my head when I'm around you and I don't like it.'

'That's a shame,' she said, trying to lighten the moment. *Tell him!* 'I like it when you lose your head.'

'Damn it, Evie,' he barked, looking at her, her lips full and soft from his ravaging. 'I don't. I don't like it. I almost had you naked on your back on this beach.'

She placed her hand on his forearm. It felt warm and solid in her palm and she never wanted to let go.

Tell him!

But she couldn't. She didn't want to use the baby to win him. 'Finn…I've known you for five years and I've never seen you so relaxed. So why don't you just…relax and see where this takes us?'

Finn shrugged her hand away. 'You want more than I'm prepared to give. And you deserve it, too.' He stood and looked down at her. 'We've got two weeks here together. Let's just stay away from each other, okay?'

He didn't give her a chance to reply as he turned on his heel. The baby thumped around inside her as she watched him stride off. No doubt it was trying to make her feel guilty for not accomplishing what she'd come to the beach to achieve.

'Sorry, baby,' she whispered. 'Not going to happen. I'll tell him when we get to Sydney—promise.'

CHAPTER THREE

AND STAY AWAY from each other they did. At least, Finn steered clear of her anyway.

Painstakingly…

His distance reminded her of how they had co-existed for years at the hospital. Aware of each other, of what might have happened that first night they'd met at the gala in Finn's honour had her father not come along and given her away as a Lockheart. Aware of something bubbling beneath the surface but neither crossing the professional divide—junior doctor and consultant.

Even her catastrophic relationship with Stuart now seemed a desperate attempt to cling to someone she could have, to distract herself from someone she couldn't.

But despite all that, their mutual attraction—subversive, unspoken—had simmered away until it had flared out of control one day and little by little she'd wedged herself into his life. He hadn't liked it, he didn't like it now, but it was simply too big to ignore.

Although she had to give it to Finn, the man did denial better than anyone she knew.

So Evie did what she had been raised to do from an early age by a father who'd prized her social skills above her brains and talent—she fitted in.

Schmoozed.

She got to know the gang. Mingled with the guys as they went about their day-to-day business—despite Finn's scowls. Took quad lessons with whoever was around to teach her. Helped Tom out at the gym and in the hydrotherapy pool. Became a sounding board for Ethan over a couple of the guys he was worried about.

And she slept in and read a book a day from the extensive library at the homestead and ate the delicious food cooked by Reginald, an ex-army chef, and soaked in the sea air and the sunshine like a giant sponge. She felt good—fit and healthy—and knew from the mirror that the tired smudges beneath her eyes had disappeared and that her skin was glowing and her hair shone.

She'd also taken to swimming after her clinic each day. She tagged along with a group of the guys and lolled in ankle-deep waters as they ran drills on the beach. Despite being a strong swimmer, she was never quite game enough to go out too far, preferring the gentler push and pull of the shallows. Such a desolate wind-swept section of the coastline, dominated by sheer cliffs and rocky outcrops, needed to be respected.

After a couple of hours of swimming and soaking up the sun they'd head back again. Oftentimes Finn would be on his way down. The men would greet him enthusiastically and if any of them thought Finn's reserved response was odd they never commented. They seemed to respect him and his personal space and if it made Evie sad to think that Finn came to the beach alone when he could have had company, she was obviously the only one.

Two weeks flew by so fast and Evie couldn't believe it was her last day as she dressed for her final sojourn to the beach. Thoughts of how relaxing it had been here filled her head as she rounded the side of the veranda and literally ran smack bang into Finn.

'Sorry,' she apologised as he grabbed her to steady her from their impact.

For the briefest moment their bodies were pressed together and neither of them moved as heat arced between them. Then Finn set her back and stepped away.

'Going down for your daily flirt, I see?' he said through stiff lips.

He looked her up and down as if she was wearing a skimpy bikini instead of a very sensible pair of boardies and the un-sexiest sun shirt ever made. Apart from the fact the shirt was tight around her bust due to the pregnancy, everywhere else pretty much hung and Evie was grateful for the extra layers of fabric as her bump seemed to become more and more noticeable to her by the day.

She decided to ignore the jibe. 'Have you packed up all your stuff for the trip home tomorrow?'

Her time in paradise was over—Hamish would be back tonight and she and Finn would return to Sydney tomorrow. A flutter wormed its way through her belly at the thought of going back. Part of her wanted to stay—hole up here and forget the world. With the pound of the ocean below, it was incredibly tempting. But she was a fighter, not a hider. And real life beckoned.

The thought of being in a car with Finn for five hours, of having him back in Sydney, of telling him what she knew she must, made her pulse trip.

But it had to be done.

'Nothing to pack—I still have my apartment with everything I'll need,' he said. 'And I'll be coming straight back here after Khalid's discharge.'

Evie blinked. 'You're coming back?'

Finn gave a curt nod. 'Yes. I'm done with surgery.' He hadn't been sure when she'd first arrived but two weeks back in her company had crystallised his decision.

Evie stared at him blankly for a moment then allowed the bubble of laughter rising in her throat an escape. He seriously thought he could just waltz in and do a one-off and not be sucked back into a world he'd thrived in?

Even she knew being a surgeon was like oxygen to him.

'You know as well as I do that you'll change your mind the minute you step foot in your old operating theatre.'

Finn hated how her laughter trivialised something he'd grappled with for a long time.

And that that she knew him so well.

It had been hell having her around the last two weeks. Hearing her voice and catching glimpses of her everywhere. Reminding him of them. Of his old life. Watching the guys flirt with her and then talk about her—*Evie this and Evie that.* The calm that he'd found here over the last months had well and truly evaporated and he desperately wanted it back.

The sooner he fulfilled his end of the bargain, the sooner he could find it again.

But he was scared. Scared that her prediction would come to pass. That he'd pick up a scalpel and find the salvation he'd always found there. The concentration, the focus, the intensity.

That he'd never want to leave.

Scared that he'd say yes. To surgery. To her.

And Finn didn't like feeling scared. It reminded him too much of the perpetual fear he'd lived with during his fractured childhood—for him, for Isaac. Trying to keep him safe, to keep them together.

Fear that he'd conquered a long time ago.

And frankly it pissed him off.

'Don't think you know me,' he snarled, 'because you don't. You think because we rutted like animals...' he saw her flinch at his deliberate crudity but his adrenaline was flowing and he couldn't stop '...a few times that you know me? Read my lips.' He shoved his face close to hers and watched her hazel eyes widen. 'I don't want to be a surgeon,' he hissed. 'I don't want to work at your father's precious hospital. *I don't want to be anywhere you are.*'

Evie felt like he'd taken a bloody great sword and cleaved it right through her middle, leaving her mortally wounded. A surge of white-hot bile rose in her chest as a blinding need to strike back took hold.

'You're a liar, Finn Kennedy,' she snarled. 'And a coward to boot. And to think you once called yourself a soldier!'

Finn took a step back at the disdain and contempt in her voice. No one had ever called him a coward before. No one. And he was damned if he was going to legitimise her accusation with a response.

Evie drew in a ragged breath as Finn stormed away, her insides shaking at their exchange. At her terrible insult. At the venom in his voice. Anger she'd expected—God knew, he pretty much existed in a perpetually angry state—but vitriol? That had been cutting. A block of tangled emotions rose to mingle with the acid in her chest and her legs started to shake. The urge to crumple into a heap undulated through her muscles but she refused to succumb to it.

Not here on the veranda, at least.

On autopilot she slung her hold-all over her shoulder, found the stairs, pounded down them. Hurried down the track, his angry words chasing her, nipping at her heels. And it didn't matter that she'd given as good as she'd got, that her words had been just as harsh, it was his voice that ran through her head.

Rutted like animals.

Your father's precious hospital.

I don't want to be anywhere you're at.

It was a little early for her rendezvous with the guys—it didn't matter, she had to keep moving, do something other than think, get away from his words.

Rutted like animals.

The ocean, more rolling than pounding and surprisingly calm in some areas beneath the leaden sky, lay before her and she knew it was what she needed. To cleanse herself. Let the ocean wash the ugliness of his words away.

Rutted. Rutted. Rutted.

She took the stairs two at a time, her breath choking and catching in her throat, shaking her head to jam the audio playing on continuous loop.

Her foot hit the sand, her lungs and throat burning as breath and sob fought for the lion's share of each inhalation. She ran down to the shoreline, dropped her bag and kept going, running into the water, not registering the cooler temperature or the depth she quickly reached.

She just threw herself into the waves and struck out against the ocean. Heaving in oxygen through her nose, pulling armfuls of water behind her as she freestyled like she had a rocket attached to her feet.

Getting away from Finn. Away from his words.

Away from his rejection.

She swam and swam, not looking up or around, just hitting out at the waves as her anger grew to match his.

Finn Kennedy was a jerk of the highest order.

He was a misogynist. A masochist.

Bloody-minded. Arrogant. Bastard.

And she was much too good for him.

So she swam. She swam and she swam until she couldn't swim another stroke. And then she stopped.

She had no idea how long she'd been swimming. All she knew was her arms, legs and lungs were screaming at her and the beach seemed a very long way away. And the thought of having to swim all the way back was not a welcome one.

Damn it. Now look what he'd done.

He'd chased her right out into the middle of the bloody ocean. She sighed as she prepared to swim back.

Finn stood on the cliff top, his anxiety lessening as Evie came closer to land. Stupid fool to go out swimming by herself. The water might look calm to the untrained eye but the swell often made swimming very hard going and the tide was on the turn—always a more dangerous time to be in the water. From this vantage point he could see a rip forming close to the shore before his eyes.

And Evie was swimming right into it.

'Evie!' he called out, even though he knew it was futile all the way up here, with the wind snatching everything away.

He hit the stairs at a run, his gaze trained firmly on

Evie, watching as she started to go backwards despite her forward stroke. Seeing her lift her head, her expression confused when she realised what was happening. Noting the look of panic and exhaustion as her desperate hands clawed at the water as if she was trying to gain purchase.

Thank God his raging thoughts had brought him to the cliff edge. That he'd sought the ocean to clear his head after their bitter exchange.

'Evie,' he called out again as his foot hit the sand. Still futile but coming from a place inside that kicked and burned and clawed, desperate to get the words out. 'Evie!'

It took Evie long seconds to figure out she'd been caught in a rip. And even longer seconds to stop fighting the pull at her legs and push at her body. No matter how much she kicked and bucked against the current, bands of iron seemed to pull tighter and just would not give.

Over the pounding of her heart her sluggish brain tried to remember what every Aussie kid growing up anywhere near a beach had been taught from the cradle.

Don't fight it.

Lie on your back and go with it.

Wait until it ebbs then swim parallel to the beach.

Conserve your energy.

Evie felt doomed immediately. She was already exhausted—where on earth would she find the energy to swim back again once this monstrous sucker had discharged her from its grip? She opened her eyes to glance wistfully at the rapidly receding shoreline.

And that's when she saw him.

A shirtless Finn running into the ocean, looking

right at her, his mouth open, calling to her maybe? She couldn't hear the words but just the sight of him made her heart sing. Half an hour ago she could have cheerfully murdered him but right this second he was what he'd been since that night she'd plonked herself down next to him at the gala—her everything.

She was tired and cold but suddenly she felt like everything was going to be okay and she finally relaxed and let the current sweep her along, her gaze firmly fixed on him as he threw himself into the rip and headed her way.

Her numb fingers found her bump and she whispered, 'Daddy's coming, baby.'

Finn caught up with her five minutes later as the rip swept them closer and closer to the rocky headland that divided this bay from the next.

Her lips were a pale purple and her teeth were chattering but she essentially looked in one piece and the tight fist around his heart eased a little. They weren't exactly out of the woods but she wasn't taking on water.

'You okay?' he shouted above the crash of the waves on the nearby rocks.

Evie nodded, smiling through lips that felt frozen to her face. The man didn't even have the decency to look out of breath. 'C-cold,' she whispered.

Finn knew it would be impossible to warm her up in the water. 'I think it's weakened enough now that we can swim back. That'll get the blood flowing again.'

Evie kicked into a dog paddle and managed a feeble smile. 'Yay.'

'Are you going to be able to manage the swim?' Finn asked.

Evie looked at the distant beach and thought about her baby—their baby—depending on her to manage. 'Guess I'll have to,' she said, knowing every arm movement, every leg kick would feel like swimming through porridge.

Finn could hear her exhaustion and wondered just how far she'd make it in the swell. He scanned around. They were situated between the two bays now, with the rip spitting them out directly in front of the rocky headland—the nearest piece of terra firma.

Waves thundered where the sea met rock and Finn knew they'd be smashed mercilessly, their bones as insignificant as kindling. But the bay on the other side seemed much more sheltered and he could see a couple of areas where they might be able to gain purchase on this calmer side of the headland and pull themselves out of the water.

It would certainly be quicker and less energy-sapping than the arduous swim back to shore.

'There.' He pointed. 'We should be able to get onto those rocks. Go. I'll follow you.'

Evie felt tired just looking at the waves sloshing against the rocks. He didn't consult with her or seek agreement from her. Typical Finn—used to everyone jumping when he demanded it.

Finn frowned at her lack of activity. 'C'mon, Evie,' he said briskly. 'You're cold, you need to get out of the water.'

Evie looked back at him, his unkempt jawline and freaky blue eyes giving him a slightly crazy edge. Like he conquered rough seas and rocky headlands every day.

'Evie!' he prompted again.

Evie sighed. 'Okay, okay,' she muttered, kicking off in a pathetic type of dog paddle because anything else was beyond her.

Two slow minutes later they were almost within reach and Finn kicked ahead of her, looking for the best purchase. Finding a smooth, gently sloping rock that was almost like a ramp into the water, he reached for it. A breaker came from out of nowhere and knocked him against the surface, his ribs taking the brunt of the impact. Pain jolted him like a lightning strike and cold, salty water swept into his mouth as his breath was torn from his lungs.

Evie gasped. 'Finn!'

'I'm fine,' he grunted, gripping the surface of the rock as pain momentarily paralysed his breathing. He lay for long moments like a landed fish, gasping for air.

'Finn?'

Finn rolled on his back at an awkward angle, half on the rock, half in the water. 'I'm fine,' he said again as his lungs finally allowed the passage of a little more air. 'Here,' he said, half-sitting, the pain less now. Still, he gritted his teeth as he held out his hand. 'Grab hold, I'll pull you up.'

Evie did as she was told and in seconds she was dragged up next to him and they both half wriggled, half crawled onto flatter, water-smoothed rocks back from the edge, away from the suck and pull of the ocean.

They collapsed beside each other, dragging in air and recovering their strength. Evie shut her eyes against the feeble breaking sunlight and wished it was strong enough to warm the chill that went right down into her bones. The wind didn't help, turning the flesh on her arms and legs to goose-bumps, tightening her nipples.

Finn lay looking at the sky. His ribs hurt—for sure there was going to be a bruise there tomorrow—but now they were safe he wanted to throttle her for scaring ten years off his life. He sat up. 'Let's go.'

Evie groaned. Despite how cold she was, she just wanted to lie there and shut her eyes for a moment. 'Just a sec.'

'No,' he said standing up. 'Now. You're hypothermic. Walking will help.'

And if he stayed here with her he was going to let the adrenaline that had surged through him have free rein and it was not going to be pretty. His brain was already crowded with a hundred not-so-nice things to say to her and given that he'd already dumped on her earlier, she probably didn't need another dressing down.

He crouched beside her and grabbed her arm, pulling firmly. 'Now, Evie!'

Evie opened her eyes at the distinct crack in his tone—like a whip. She knew she should be grateful, she knew she should apologise for calling him a coward when the man had jumped into a rip to help her, but she wasn't feeling rational. She wanted a hot shower and a warm bed.

Normally she'd fantasise about snuggling into him in that bed too but he was being too crabby and today was not a normal day.

'Okay, okay,' she said, letting him drag her into a sitting position and going on autopilot as she assisted him in getting her fully upright. She leaned heavily against him as her legs almost gave out.

He cursed. 'You're freezing.'

Evie frowned at his language but nodded anyway, her teeth chattering for good measure. 'Cold,' she agreed. 'Tired.'

'Right,' he said briskly. 'Let's go. Quick march. Up and over the rocks then onto the sand then up the stairs.'

Evie groaned as her legs moved, feeling stiff and un-coordinated as if they'd had robotic implants. 'Oh, God, those bloody stairs,' she complained as Finn dragged her along.

'You'll have warmed up by then,' he said confidently.

'Oh, yes,' she mocked. 'I'll be able to sprint right up them.'

It was on the tip of Finn's tongue to snap that she'd made her own trouble but he was afraid that once he started, the fear that had gripped his gut as he'd raced down those stairs would bubble out and he'd say more stuff that he regretted, like he had earlier today.

So he didn't say anything, just coaxed, bullied and cajoled her every step over the headland, gratified to see her become more co-ordinated and less irrational as her body warmed up. When they reached sand he jogged ahead of her to where her bag had been dis-carded on the beach, took out her fluffy dry towel and jogged back to her, wrapping her in it.

'You must be cold too,' Evie protested as she sank into its warm folds.

'I'm fine,' he dismissed.

Somehow they made it to the top of the stairs and into the homestead and Finn was pushing Evie into the bathroom and turning the hot shower on and ordering her in. She'd never been more grateful for Finn being his bossy, crabby self.

Thirty minutes later Evie was tucked up in her bed and drifting off to sleep on a blissfully warm cloud when Finn barged in, carrying a tray.

'Drink this,' he ordered plonking a steaming mug of something on her bedside table along with a huge slab of chocolate cake on a delicate plate with a floral border. 'Reginald insists,' he said.

Evie struggled to sit up, every muscle in her body protesting the movement. 'Well, if Reginald insists…'

She propped herself against the headrest, drawing her knees up as she reached for the mug. The aroma of chocolate seduced her, making her stomach growl and her mouth fill with saliva, and she was suddenly ravenous.

She sighed as her first sip of the hot sweet milk coated the inside of her mouth and sent her taste buds into rapture. Finn, dressed in a T-shirt and jeans, prowled around the end of her bed, slapping the tray against his legs, and she tried her best to ignore him as she reached for the cake.

Finn paced as Evie ate, reliving their moments in the ocean, still feeling edgy from the hit of adrenaline. He'd tried not to think of the hundred things that could have gone wrong when he'd been in the water and trying to get her back to the house, but the minute the bathroom door had shut and he'd known she was truly safe, reaction had well and truly set in.

They'd been lucky. *She'd* been lucky. He wondered if she had a clue how close she'd come to being a drowning statistic. The thought sent a chill up his spine.

As much as she was a pain in his butt, the thought of her not being around was unthinkable.

Did she not realise how precious life was?

Had growing up with that damn silver spoon in her mouth blinded her to the perils mere mortals faced every day?

Bloody little princess!

His ribs grabbed and moaned at him with every foot-fall, stoking his anger at her stupidity higher and higher.

Evie had eaten half of the cake before his silent skulking finally got on her last nerve. 'Why don't you just say it, Finn?'

Finn stopped mid-pace and looked at her. Her hair was still damp from her near-death experience in an unfriendly ocean and despite her obvious exhaustion she looked so damned imperious and defiant he wanted to put her over his knee and spank her. He threw the tray on the bed.

'What the devil were you doing, swimming by yourself? You could have been swept out to sea, dashed on the rocks, drowned from exhaustion, frozen to death or been eaten by a bloody shark!'

Evie blinked at the litany of things that could have befallen her. They'd lurked in her mind as the current had dragged her further and further away from the shore but she'd tried not to give them any power. Trust Finn to shove them in her face.

Did he really think she needed them spelled out?

Did he think she hadn't collapsed on her butt in the shower, shaking from head to toe at the what-ifs? That she hadn't thought about how she'd not only put her life at risk but the life of their unborn child? She'd never been more grateful to feel the energetic movements of her baby as she'd stripped off her clothes in the shower.

'I know,' she said quietly

But Finn had started pacing again and was, apparently, on a roll. 'And none of us would have known. You'd just suddenly be missing, just…gone.' He clicked his fingers in the air. 'And there'd be hundreds of people everywhere out there, looking for you. Combing the bush and the ocean, and your sisters would be frantic and your father would want to shut this place down and wouldn't rest until Ethan—' He stopped and glared at her. '*A good man doing good things* was nailed to a wall but what would you care? You'd be dead.'

Evie dragged in a rough breath at the passion of his mesmerising speech and his heated gaze that swept over her as if he could see down to her bones.

And what about you, Finn? How would it make you feel?

It hadn't been her goal to scare an admission out of him but his tirade gave her a little hope. Would he be this het up about someone he didn't have feelings for?

'I'm sorry,' she apologised.

'Well, that's not enough!' He twisted to resume his pacing but the abrupt movement jarred through his injury and he cursed under his breath, movement impossible as he grabbed automatically at his ribs with one hand and the wooden framework at the foot of the bed with the other.

Evie sat forward. 'Finn?' He didn't answer, just stood sucking in air, his eyes squeezed shut, his hand splinting his chest. 'Finn!'

'I'm fine,' he snapped.

Evie peeled back the cover and crawled to the end of the bed on her hands and knees. 'You are not,' she said as she drew level with him. 'Let me look,' she said, reaching for his shirt.

Finn stood upright, batting her hand away. 'I said I'm fine, damn it!'

She was wearing a baggy T-shirt and loose cotton shorts that came to just above her knee and she smelled fresh and soapy from the shower and she was so close he wanted to drag her into his arms and assure himself that she really was okay.

But he also wanted to kiss her hard and lose himself in her for a while, and he was more than pleased there was a wooden bed end as a barrier between them.

'Finn, I'm a doctor, remember?'

'So am I.'

She nodded. 'Which is exactly why you shouldn't be diagnosing yourself.'

'It's just a bruise,' he dismissed.

She reached for his shirt, laying her hand against his chest. 'Why don't you let me be the judge of that?' she murmured.

Her palm print seared into his chest and shot his resolve down in flames. He knew he should step back, walk away, but she was lifting his shirt and she was safe and well and so very close, looking like Evie and smelling like her and reminding him of all the times he'd seen her in the hallways at the Harbour looking at him with that aloofness that didn't fool him and making him want her even more and he couldn't make himself resist her.

Not after today.

Evie gasped at the ugly blue black bruise on his side, her fingers automatically tracing its ugly outline. 'Bloody hell, Finn,' she murmured.

But already her fingers were becoming methodical, prodding, shutting her eyes as she fell into a familiar routine. She pushed gently all around the injured area, feeling Finn's abdominal muscles tense, hearing the harsh suck of his breath.

'Sorry,' she murmured, opening her eyes, her own

breath catching at their proximity, at the intensity in his gaze. 'Can't feel or hear any crepitus,' she said, her voice unsteady.

'That's because they're not broken,' he said.

Evie nodded, her breath thick in her throat as her fingers lightly stroked the bruised tissue, exploring the dips of his ribs. 'You should get an X-ray tomorrow when we get back to the Harbour.'

Finn nodded as the light caress of her cool fingers soothed and inflamed all at once. 'Maybe.'

Evie smiled. She guessed his ribs *must* be bad for him to sort of comply so easily. She dropped her hand but he didn't move away and she didn't want him to. They were close enough for her to lay her head on his chest, have him put his arms around her.

Close enough to tell him about the baby.

The silence stretched but she just couldn't get the words out. And she needed him to come back to Sydney. Not disappear.

But she had to say something. Because if she didn't she was going to kiss him and then they'd be on the bed because a kiss was never enough with Finn and he'd find out then for sure.

'Sorry for calling you a coward,' she murmured. 'You're not. Not in the physical sense, anyway. You certainly proved that today.'

Finn grunted. Only Evie could call him an emotional coward and couch it as a compliment. 'I'm sorry for what I said too. I…'

He broke off. He what? He did want to be a surgeon? He did want to be near her? The truth was he'd spoken his mind. But he'd never wanted to hurt her with it. To throw his words at her like they were poisonous darts.

'You what?' she prompted as his unfinished sentence hung in the air.

Finn shook his head, his gaze dropping to Evie's mouth. 'You drive me crazy.'

Evie pulled her bottom lip between her teeth. 'I know.'

Finn felt the movement jolt all the way down to his groin. 'Damn it,' he muttered, reaching for her, sliding his hand under her damp hair at the back of her neck, pulling her head closer as he closed the gap from his side, claiming her mouth on a tortured groan.

'Damn it, damn it, damn it,' he muttered against her lips, as she whimpered and the urge to hurdle the barrier between them took hold and he pushed his other hand into her hair and her mouth opened as his moved against hers and he kissed her hard and deep and hungry, every ragged breath tearing through his ribcage.

A loud knock thundered against her door and he pulled away, gasping. They both were.

'Evie? Evie? Are you okay?'

Finn clutched his chest again as he took a step back, every nerve ending on fire, every cell begging him to get closer, to get looser, to get naked.

His gaze never left her face as he slowly backed even further away, her moist mouth and glazed expression slugging him straight in the groin, begging him to come nearer.

His back bumped gently against the door. 'She's fine, Ethan,' he called.

Then he turned the doorhandle and admitted his friend. And a massive slice of sanity.

CHAPTER FOUR

ON MONDAY MORNING at eight-ten precisely Finn picked up the scalpel and knew Evie was right.

He couldn't not be a surgeon.

He'd been wasting his time, his talent, his future at *Beach Haven* when his true calling was right here— surgery.

Damn it!

As he worked methodically through the steps of the quadruple bypass, as familiar to him as his own breath, the fact that the man on the table was one of the world's richest men faded to black.

Everything faded to black.

It was just him, an open chest and a beating heart. Cutting into the pericardium, harvesting the veins, putting the patient on bypass, clamping the aorta, starting the clock, stopping the heart, grafting the veins beyond the coronary artery blockages, restarting the heart, closing up.

One hundred per cent focused. One hundred per cent absorbed.

Coming out of the zone as he stood back and peeled his gloves off, a little dazed still, as if he'd been in a trance. Registering again the smell of the mask in his nose, the trill and ping of machinery, the strains of Mozart which had been Prince Khalid's music of choice. The murmur of voices around him as they prepared to transfer the patient to ICU.

'Thanks, everyone,' he acknowledged, surprised momentarily that he hadn't been alone.

Nothing had touched him as his fingers and brain had worked in tandem. Evie had been forgotten Isaac had been forgotten. The gnawing hunger of a crappy childhood forgotten.

Just him and the knife.

Taking it all away. Centring him.

And as the outside world started to percolate in through his conscious state, he knew he needed it again.

Damn it!

Finn was surprised to see Evie at the canteen half an hour later when he dropped by to get something to eat on his way to check on Khalid in ICU. Surprised who she was with, anyway. She was sitting with Marco D'Avello and they looked deep in conversation. Marco reached out and touched her hand and Finn was annoyed at the quick burn of acid in his chest. Marco was married—happily married—to Emily and they'd not long had their first child.

What the hell was he doing, touching Evie in the middle of the canteen where everyone could see them?

He hadn't pegged Marco as the straying kind.

Or Evie as a home-wrecker, for that matter.

And even though he knew that wasn't what was going on because he *knew* Evie, it irritated him nonetheless. And not everyone sitting in the canteen would be so forgiving.

He turned away as he placed his order but a sudden short burst of laughter from Evie had him looking back, and suddenly she was looking up and in his direction and her smile died, and for a moment they both just looked at each other before Evie stood up and headed his way.

The woman behind the counter handed Finn his sandwich and drink and he headed for the door.

He didn't want or need any Evie Lockheart chit-chat.

'Finn,' Evie called as he walked out the door, her legs hurrying to catch up. Drat the man—she just wanted to ask him about the surgery. 'Finn. Wait!' she called again as she stepped outside. She watched as he faltered and his shoulders seemed to fall before he slowly turned to face her.

She was in baggy work scrubs—her long, lean legs outlined with each step towards him, and he averted his eyes as he waited for her to catch him up before he resumed his trajectory.

'How'd it go?' Evie asked as she fell into step beside him.

'Fine.'

Evie waited for him to elaborate. He didn't. 'Prince Khalid came through it okay?'

He nodded. 'I'm just going to check on him now.'

They walked some more in silence and Evie could have gleefully strangled him. 'Well?' she demanded when she couldn't wait for him to be forthcoming any longer. 'How'd it feel?' she asked. 'Was it good to be back?'

Finn stopped and shoved his hands on his hips. 'Yes. Was that what you wanted to hear? That you were right? That it felt like I was coming home? Well, it did. And after I've been to the ICU I'm heading up to Eric

Frobisher's office to get myself back on the OR schedule. Eric, who is an arse and will make a huge song and dance over the *inconvenience* of it all, even though he knows I'm the best damn cardiothoracic surgeon in the country, just because he can. Are you satisfied?'

Evie wanted to be satisfied. Her heart was tapping out a jig and emotion, light and airy, bloomed in her chest. If he was here then maybe there was a chance for them. Maybe with the baby in the mix, Finn would eventually admit what she knew was in his heart.

But she didn't want him to feel trapped.

'I'm glad that you're staying. But I don't want you to be miserable.'

'Well, you can't have it both ways, Princess Evie. You can have me here doing what I do best, what I need to do, but if you want me to be whistling in the corridors and singing to bluebirds as they land on my shoulder, that isn't going to happen.'

He dropped his hands and started walking again towards the lifts.

'You don't have to work here,' she called after his back. What was the point if he just came to resent her more? 'You could do this anywhere. You could walk into any hospital in this country and name your price.'

It was a startling reality for her but Evie knew that a man like Finn had to operate. Even if it meant doing it somewhere else. Didn't they say if you loved someone you had to set them free?

Finn turned again. He knew that. He'd done nothing but turn the conundrum over and over in his brain for the last half an hour. He'd trawled through his many options but had discarded each one. Partly because Sydney Harbour Hospital had the best cardiothoracic department in the country, partly because Evie was here and he just didn't seem to be able to stay away, but mostly because it felt like home. It was the longest he'd ever stayed anywhere and deep down Finn was still an eight-year-old boy desperate for the stability of the familiar.

'I only work at the best,' he said impatiently, knowing it was only a half-truth and feeling like a coward as she looked at him with her clear hazel gaze. 'Sydney Harbour Hospital is the best.'

He marched to the lift and pushed the button. She followed. The empty lift arrived promptly. He got on.

She followed.

And because he was angry that she was still right beside him and that she was always going to be around as long as he was here, smoothing away at his edges and his resistance like bloody Chinese water torture, he lashed out at the first thing that entered his head.

'I didn't realise you and Marco D'Avello were such pals.'

Evie frowned at the slight accusation in his voice, nervous that he might connect the dots. 'I'm sorry?'

'You need to be careful. You know how easily gossip starts in a place like this.'

Evie blinked as his implication became clear. Clearly no dots to worry about! 'Don't be ridiculous,' she spluttered.

Finn held up a hand in surrender. 'I really don't care what you do, Evie, or who you do it with,' he lied, 'but maybe you might like to consider his wife and their newborn baby and how gossip might affect them.'

Evie was momentarily speechless. Which turned to outrage pretty quickly. She wasn't sure if it was because of what he was suggesting or the fact that he really didn't seem to give a fig if it was the truth or not.

That she might actually be sleeping with Marco D'Avello.

Who was married!

The lift pinged as they arrived on the third floor and the doors opened. 'Is that what you think?' she asked as he walked out. She stepped out too just as two nurses appeared, grabbing the lift as the doors started to shut. 'That Marco and I are…having some kind of affair?' she hissed as the doors shut behind them.

Finn sighed at the injury in her voice and quashed the little niggle of irritation that had pecked at his brain since he'd witnessed the canteen hand squeeze. 'Of course not, Evie. But in this place, where gossip is a second language, you can bet that others will…that's all I'm saying.'

Evie glared at him. Wanted to tell him he was being preposterous but she knew it to be true. How much gossip had she heard about herself over the years? In her first year it had been about what a stuck-up cow she was, breaking poor Stuart's heart, thinking she was too good for him even though he'd broken her heart when she'd discovered he only wanted her for her family name and connections.

And in this last year or so endless reams of gossip about her and Finn.

Evie felt herself deflate like a balloon as all the fight oozed out of her. 'Yes. People do like to talk, don't they?'

Finn shrugged. 'Well, they're going to talk anyway. Best not to feed them too much ammunition—that's my philosophy.'

Evie blinked. 'You've done nothing but feed them ammunition the entire time you've been here. Sleeping with any pretty young thing that batted her eyelashes at you.'

Even her. Not that she'd ever batted her eyelashes.

He grinned. 'It stopped them talking about my injury, though, didn't it?'

Evie grinned back at his unashamed admission—she couldn't help herself. He suddenly seemed years younger than his trademark stubbly jawline portrayed and it was rare to share such a moment with him. He was always so intense—to see him amused was breathtaking.

Suddenly Evie felt back on an even keel. Enough to begin a dialogue about the subject she'd been avoiding. 'Do you think we can find some time this week to talk?' she asked tentatively.

Finn felt the bubble of happiness that had percolated from nowhere burst with a resounding pop. *A talk* sounded as inviting as root-canal treatment.

He eyed her warily. 'I don't like to talk.'

Evie nodded. 'I've noticed.'

'Nothing's changed just because I'm back, Evie.'

She steeled herself against the ominous warning. It would do her well to take heed.

Finn Kennedy was one hard nut to crack.

'I know,' she rushed to assure him. 'It's not about that. About us.'

Not strictly speaking anyway.

She crossed her fingers behind her back. 'It's... something else.' She stopped and wondered if it sounded like the complete hash it was. 'It's to do with work...'

It was. *Sort of.* Her career was going to have to take a back seat for a while. His would be affected too if he wanted to be involved with the baby.

She watched his frown deepen. Why did she have to fall for a man who was always so suspicious? 'Look, it's complicated, okay? Can you just say yes? Then I'll promise not to bother you again.'

Finn wasn't keen on *a talk*. In his experience women's talks involved rings and dresses and happily ever afters. But it was work related…and the payoff sounded pretty damn good to him.

Never being bothered by her again was an opportunity he couldn't pass up.

It was a futile hope, of course, because he dreamed about her too bloody much to ever fully realise that blissful state of Evie-lessness and every time he saw her a very distinct, very unevolved, caveman urge seemed to overcome him.

But if she could do her bit then he could master the rest. He was used to it.

'After Khalid's discharge?' he suggested. 'A few days? At Pete's?'

Evie slowly exhaled her pent-up breath. 'Thank you.'

Finn nodded. 'I'll let you know.'

He didn't wait for her to answer. Just turned away, his mind already shifting gears.

After some rhythm complications, it was Friday afternoon before Khalid was discharged to a penthouse suite at one of the city's most luxurious hotels. It was top secret but Finn knew and Khalid had his number. Along with round-the-clock private nurses, Finn was confident the prince would have a very nice convalescence with a world-class view.

He'd seen Evie around over the intervening days—with just one VIP patient on his books, he wasn't exactly flush with things to do. In fact, glimpses of her here, there and everywhere were driving him more than a little nutty. And always, it seemed, she was deep in conversation with Marco. By the end of the week he was starting to wonder if perhaps there *was* something going on with them after all.

His idleness was driving him spare—giving him too much time to think. At *Beach Haven* it had been what he'd needed—but back in amongst the rush and hurry of *the Harbour* he needed to be busy. Eric, the CEO, had been the superior jerk he'd predicted and had refused to put Finn back on the surgical roster until after their VIP had been discharged.

But, as of Monday, he was back. Which would give him a lot less time to wonder about what Evie and Marco were up to.

To wonder about Evie full stop.

The prospect of *the talk* had kept her front and centre all week—with no surgery to do and just Khalid to see, there'd been nothing else to occupy his brain. He pulled his mobile phone out of his pocket as he made his way to his outpatient rooms. It was time to get it out of the way.

Check it off his list.

Start the new week with a clean slate.

And it was an opportunity to lay down some ground rules with Evie. They couldn't go on the way they had been prior to him leaving. He was different now—his injury was healed. He didn't need anyone's sympathy or pity or to cover for his lapses.

If they were going to co-exist peacefully in this hospital he had to start as he meant to go on.

Without Evie.

Evie breathed a sigh of relief as the electronic noise of the monitor grew fainter as the last patient from the pile-up on the motorway was whisked off to Theatre. They'd been frantic for hours and between the adrenaline buzz, the noise pollution and the baby dancing the rumba inside her she had a massive headache.

She could hear the soft plaintive beep of another alarm in the empty cubicle and it nibbled at her subconscious like fingernails down a chalk board. 'Where the hell is that coming from?' she asked irritably as her stomach growled and the baby kicked.

She looked around at the electronic gadgetry vital in a modern emergency department. The alarm wasn't one she was familiar with as she approached the bank of monitors and pumps.

'It's the new CO_2 monitor,' Mia di Angelo, her ex-flatmate and fellow emergency physician, said. 'It can't be on charge.'

Evie scanned the machines for an unfamiliar one. She hated it when they got new equipment. It was great to keep their department up to date and stocked with the latest and greatest but it was hell assimilating all the new alarms and buttons.

When she located the unfamiliar piece of equipment with its little yellow flashing light she followed the cord at the back and noticed it trailing on the floor instead of being plugged into the power supply at the back of the cubicle. She squeezed in behind, not such an easy job any more, and the baby let her know it did not like being constricted by a swift one-two jab.

She sucked in a breath, her hand automatically going to her belly in a soothing motion as she bent over, picked up the plug from the floor and pushed it into the socket.

Instead of the instant peace she was hoping for, a loud sizzle followed by some sparks and the pungent smell of burnt electrical wiring rent the air. The point where her fingers touched the plug tingled then burned, a painful jolt cramped up her arm and knocked her backwards onto her butt.

'Evie!' Mia gasped rushing to her friend's side. 'Are you okay?'

Evie blinked, too dazed for a moment to fully understand what had happened. All she was aware of was a pain in her finger and the sudden stillness of the baby.

'What's wrong?' Evie heard Luca's voice. He was Mia's husband and head of the department.

'Help me get her up,' Mia said. 'She got an electric shock from the pump.

Evie felt arms half pulling, half guiding her into a standing position. 'Evie, talk to me. Are you okay?' Mia was saying, inspecting the tiny white mark on Evie's index finger.

'Let's get her on a monitor,' Luca was saying as his fingers palpated the pulse at her wrist.

Suddenly she broke out of her daze. 'No.'

She shook her head. The baby. It was so, so still. She needed to see Marco. She had to know if the shock had affected the baby.

She had to know now.

'I'm fine,' she assured them, breaking out of their hold. 'Really I am.'

Mia frowned and folded her arms. 'You just got a zap that knocked you on your butt. You should be monitored for a while.'

Evie shook her head again and forced a smile onto her face even though it felt like it was going to crack into a thousand pieces as concern for the baby skyrocketed with every single stationary second. 'I'm fine. I'm in the middle of a hospital. If I start to feel unwell, I'll let you know.'

Luca nodded. 'Her pulse is steady.'

Mia grabbed Evie's hand. 'This could do with a burns consult in case it's worse than it looks. It'll definitely need dressing.'

Evie thought quickly. 'Yes. Good idea. It's burns clinic today, right? I'll pop in and see if they can squeeze me in.'

'I'll come with you,' Mia said.

'Status epilepticus two minutes out,' a nurse said to them as she dashed past.

And then the distant strains of a siren, a beautiful, beautiful siren, made itself known, and Evie had never been more grateful to hear the wretched noise.

'You can't,' Evie said. 'You're needed here. You both are. I'll be fine,' she assured them again, a surge of desperation to get away, to get to Marco, making her feel impotent.

'Okay,' Mia acquiesced. 'But I want to see you after you get back.'

Evie nodded. 'Absolutely.'

By the time she scurried up to the outpatient department ten minutes later Evie was frantic. The baby hadn't moved and an ominous black cloud hovered over her head. When she'd been hypothermic in the middle of the ocean her brain had been too sluggish to think of the implications for the baby. But today all her mental faculties were intact and totally freaking her out as all the horrible possibilities marched one by one through her mind.

She was on the verge of tears when she finally located Marco, who wasn't in his rooms but was chatting to a midwife in the long corridor that ran behind the outpatients department.

'Marco,' she called.

He looked up and smiled at her, his joy quickly dying as he saw the distress on her face. He strode over to her.

'Evie,' he said with that lovely lilt of his, his hands grasping her upper arms, a frown marring his classically handsome face. He could see she was about to crumple and led her away from the busy thoroughfare into the nearby cleaning closet. It wasn't very roomy and the door was chocked open but it was more private than outside. 'What is wrong?'

'I think the baby might be dead,' she whispered, choking on a sob as she buried her face in his chest.

Finn scrolled through his contacts on his phone as he stepped out of the lift and headed for the outpatients department. He wanted to spend some time looking at the case notes for his theatre list on Monday. He found Evie's number and hit the button as he entered the department.

His gaze wandered across to the corridor on the far side as he waited for her to pick up and that's when he spotted them. Evie and Marco alone in some kind of supply cupboard—embracing. He fell back a little, shocked by the image, watching them from just outside the department as they pulled apart slightly and Evie fumbled in her scrubs pocket and pulled out her phone.

'Hello?'

Finn didn't say anything for a moment, trying to decide how he should play it. 'It's me,' he said, watching her as she stayed in the shelter of Marco's body, his arm around her shoulder. 'I'm free for that talk now.'

Evie looked up at Marco as she grappled with a vortex of emotions

Now? He wanted to talk now?

'Er…I can't right now… I'm busy.'

Finn raised an eyebrow. Icy fingers crept around his heart and he leant against the nearby wall. 'Emergency a little crazy at the moment?'

Evie nodded, grabbing the excuse he had thrown her with glee. 'Certifiable.'

The fingers squeezed down hard. 'I could come down there and wait for you,' he suggested.

Alarm raced along Evie's nerve endings. 'No, no,' she said. 'I'll give you a ring when it settles and I can meet you across at Pete's.'

'Okay,' he murmured.

'Bye.'

Finn blinked at her hasty hang-up and to torture himself a little further he watched as Marco drew her against his chest and hugged her again before walking her to his rooms, his arm firmly around her waist.

He had absolutely no idea what the hell was going on with those two but he had every intention of finding out! She'd been pretty convincing in her mortification at his inference that she and Marco were *sleeping together* a few days ago but maybe she was protesting too much? Maybe there was more to Marco and Evie than she was letting on?

His heart pounded as bile burned in his chest and acid flowed through his veins. He pushed off the wall and headed in their direction.

'Finn Kennedy, well, I'll be. I heard you were back.'

Finn stopped in mid-stride to greet Sister Enid Kenny, nurse in charge of Outpatients for about a hundred years and a true Sydney Harbour Hospital icon. She was large and matronly and no one, not even the great Finn Kennedy, messed with Enid Kenny.

If she wanted to chat, you stopped and chatted.

Unfortunately for him, as he looked over her shoulder at the closed door of Marco's office, she was in a very chatty mood.

Evie was so relived she'd agreed to the ultrasound as she watched her baby—her baby boy—move around on the screen. Marco had been trying to convince her to have one all week but part of her had wanted to break the news to Finn before having an ultrasound, which she'd been hoping he would want to attend.

But after her scare just listening to the heartbeat wasn't going to cut it. She needed to see him. To watch him move. To reassure herself fully. To count his fingers and toes, to see the chambers of his heart, the hemispheres of his brain.

To know everything was perfect.

Marco was very thorough doing measurements and pointing out all the things any radiographer would have and Evie felt the gut wrenching worry and the threatening hysteria ease as her little boy did indeed seem perfect.

'Can I hear the heartbeat one more time?' Evie asked.

Marco chuckled. 'But of course.'

He flicked a switch on the ultrasound machine and the room filled with the steady *whop, whop, whop* of a robust heartbeat.

Neither of them expected the door to suddenly crash open or for Finn to be standing there, glowering at them and demanding to know what the devil was going on.

Evie was startled at the loud intrusion. 'Finn,' she whispered.

Marco turned calmly in his chair. 'Welcome, Dr Kennedy. You're just in time to meet your son,' he said.

It took Finn a moment or two to compute the scene before his eyes. The lights down low. Evie lying on the examination bed, her scrub top pulled up, a very distinctive bump protruding and covered in goo. Marco's hand holding an ultrasound probe low down on Evie's belly. A grainy image of a foetus turning somersaults on the screen.

And the steady thump of a strong heartbeat.

Finn looked at Evie and shoved his hands on his hips. 'What the hell...?' he demanded.

Marco looked at Evie as he removed the probe and reached for some wipes. 'I think I should leave you and Finn to talk, yes?' he murmured as he methodically removed every trace of the conduction gel.

Evie sat up, dragging her top down as she did so. Finn stood aside as Marco passed him, flipping on the light as he went and shutting the door after him.

'You're pregnant?' he demanded, his own heartbeat roaring through his ears at the stunning turn of events. He'd half expected to barge in and find she and

Marco doing the wild thing on the desk. He'd never expected this.

Evie nodded. 'Yes.'

Her quiet affirmative packed all the power of a sucker punch to his solar plexus. 'This is what you wanted to talk about?'

'Yes.'

He shook his head as all the control he'd fought for over the years started to disintegrate before him, unravelling like a spool of cotton.

His breath felt tight. His jaw clenched. His pulse throbbed through his veins, tapping out *no, no, no* against his temple.

'No.'

He couldn't be a father. He just couldn't. He was selfish and arrogant and egotistical. He was busy. He was dedicated to his job. He hadn't grown up in any home worth a damn and the one person who'd been entrusted to his care had died in his arms.

He was damaged goods. Seen too much that had hardened him. Made him cynical. Jaded.

Not father material.

Most days he didn't even know how to be a normal, functioning human being—he was just going through the motions.

How on earth could he be a decent father?

He looked at her watching him, wariness in her hazel eyes. But hope as well. And something else. The same thing he always saw there when she looked at him—belief.

She had no idea who he really was.

He steeled his heart against the image that seemed

to be ingrained on his retinas—his baby on an ultra-sound screen.

'You have to get an abortion.'

Evie flinched at the ice in his tone. It wasn't anything she hadn't thought about herself in those days when she'd lived in a space where denying the baby even existed had been preferable to facing the truth. But she'd felt him move now, seen him sucking his thumb on the screen just a few minutes ago, and even if she hadn't already decided against it and it had been possible at this advanced stage in her pregnancy, she knew she could never do what Finn was asking.

'I'm twenty-one weeks.'

Finn opened his mouth to dispute it but the evidence of his own eyes started to filter in. The size of her belly and the size of the baby on the screen and then some quick maths in his head all confirmed her gestation.

He groped for Marco's desk as the import of her words hit home.

There could be no abortion.

There would be a baby.

He was going to be a father.

'Why didn't you tell me?'

Evie swung her legs over the edge of the couch. 'Because you went away and I spent a long, *long* time in denial. And, honestly, I think because part of me knew you'd demand what you just demanded and even though I'd thought about it myself, a part of me wanted to put it beyond reach. For both of us. And then the longer you go...' she shrugged. '...the harder it gets.'

'You've just spent two weeks with me at *Beach Haven*. You could have told me then.'

'I almost did but...' She looked at him staring at her

like she'd just been caught with state secrets instead of a bun in the oven. 'You're not very approachable, Finn.'

He looked at her for a long moment. 'I don't know how to be a father.'

Evie sucked in a breath at the bleakness in his blue eyes. He suddenly looked middle-aged. 'You think I know how to be a mother?' she asked. 'My mother was an absent alcoholic. Not exactly a stellar role model.'

Finn snorted. She had no idea. Her poor-little-rich-girl upbringing had been a walk in the park compared to his. 'I think you'll figure it out.'

'I think you will, too,' she said, feeling suddenly desperate to connect with him. To make him understand that she knew it was daunting. But they could do it.

Finn's pager beeped and he was grateful for the distraction as he absently reached for it and checked the message on the screen. It was Khalid.

'I have to go,' he said.

He needed to think. To get away. Life events had robbed him of a lot of choices and now even the choice not to burden some poor child with his emotionally barren existence had been snatched away.

'Okay.' She nodded, pushing down the well of emotion that was threatening as she watched him turn away from her.

He needed time and she had to give him that. It had taken *her* months to adjust and accept and she wasn't Finn. A man who didn't express emotion well and never let anyone close.

She had to give him space to come to terms with it.

So she sat there like a dummy as he walked out the door, despite how very, very much she wanted to call him back.

CHAPTER FIVE

Finn woke up at nine on Saturday morning, his head throbbing from one too many hits of his very expensive malt whisky the previous night.

It had been a good while since he'd overdone the top-shelf stuff. For years he'd used it to dull the physical pain from his injuries but since his recovery and his move to *Beach Haven* he'd only ever indulged in the odd beer or two.

He'd forgotten how it could feel like a mule had kicked you in the head the next day. Which might actually be worth it if it had come with some sort of clarity.

It hadn't.

Just a thumping headache and the very real feeling that he'd woken up in hell.

He stared at the ceiling as the same three words from last night repeated in his head—*Evie is pregnant*. Each word pounded like a battering ram against the fortified shell surrounding his heart with a resounding boom.

Evie. *Boom!* Is. *Boom!* Pregnant. *Boom!*

He was going to be a father. Some tiny little defenceless human being with his DNA was going to make its arrival in four short months. He was going to be *Daddy*.

Whether he liked it or not.

And it scared the hell out of him. Being a parent—*a*

good parent—required things life just hadn't equipped him with. Like compassion, empathy, love.

There'd been so little love in his life. From the moment his mother had abandoned him and Isaac to a childhood in institutions to his regimented life in the army, ruled by discipline and authority, love had been non-existent. Sure, he'd loved and protected Isaac and Isaac had loved him, but it had been a very lonely island in a vast sea of indifference.

Add to that the slow fossilising of his emotions to deal with the horror and injuries witnessed in far-flung battlefields and the death knell to any errant tendrils of love and tenderness that might still have existed when Isaac had died in his arms and the product was the man he was today.

Ten years since that horrifying day and still he felt numb. Blank. Barren.

Emotionally void.

He hadn't loved Lydia, his brother's widow, with whom he'd had a totally messed up affair and who had needed him to love her no matter how screwed up it had been at the time.

He operated with the cold, clinical precision of a robot. Always seeing the part, never seeing the whole. Totally focussed. Never allowing himself to think about the person whose heart he held in his hands or the love that heart was capable of. Just doing the job. And doing it damn well.

He hadn't felt anything for any of the women he'd slept with. They had just been pleasant distractions. Something different to take to bed instead of a bottle of Scotch. A momentary diversion.

Apart from Evie. Whom he'd pushed and pushed and pushed away and who knew what he was like but refused to give up anyway. Who could look right past his rubbish and see deep inside to the things he kept hidden.

Evie, who was having his baby.

A baby he didn't know how to love.

A sudden knock at his door stomped through his head like a herd of stampeding elephants and he groaned out loud. He wanted to yell to whoever it was to go away but was afraid he might have a stroke if he did. If he just lay here, maybe Evie would think he'd already gone out.

Because that knock had the exact cadence of a pissed-off woman.

It came again followed by, 'Finn? Finn!'

Lydia? Wrong pissed-off woman.

'Finn Kennedy, open this bloody door now. Don't make me get my key out!'

Finn rolled out of bed. It wasn't the smoothest exit from his bed he'd ever executed but considering he felt like he was about to die, the fact he could walk at all was a miracle.

'Coming,' he called as the knock came again, wincing as it drove nails into his brain.

He wrenched open the door just as he heard a metallic scratching from the other side. His brother's widow, a petite redhead, stood on the doorstep glowering at him, hands on hips.

'You look like hell,' she said.

He grunted. 'I feel like hell.'

'Right,' she said, striding past him into his apartment. 'Coffee first, I think. Then you can tell me what happened to get you into this state.'

Finn was tempted to throw her out. But he really, really needed coffee.

* * *

Fifteen minutes later he was inhaling the aroma of the same Peruvian Arabica beans Lydia had brought him the last time she'd come for a flying visit and he hadn't touched since. Grinding beans was way too much trouble, no matter how good they were. He took a sip of coffee and shut his eyes as his pulse gave a little kick.

His home phone rang from the direction of his bedroom and he ignored it as he felt the coffee slowly reviving him. Khalid only had his mobile number and everything else could just wait.

Lydia waited until he'd taken a few more sips before pinning him with that direct look of hers. She'd come a long way since the broken woman he'd comforted a decade ago. In his own grief and in the midst of their screwy relationship he had judged her harshly for that, for what he'd perceived as weakness, but she had come out the other side a much stronger person.

'Spill,' she said.

Finn thought about playing dumb but the truth was that Lydia was one of the few people who really understood how he ticked. She'd been the one who'd moved on from their half-hearted affair when she'd seen it had been perpetuating an unhealthy co-dependence. The strange mix of relief and regret at its ending had confused him but she'd never left him completely and as his one tangible link to Isaac he'd been grateful for her watchful eye and bossy persona.

'Evie's pregnant.'

Lydia blinked. 'Oh.'

Finn took another sip of his coffee. 'Indeed.'

'It's yours?'

Finn nodded. It wasn't something he'd questioned for a moment. 'A little boy.'

'Oh,' Lydia said again, hiding a smile as she sipped at her coffee.

Finn frowned. 'Are you smiling?'

Lydia shook her head, feigning a serious expression. 'Absolutely not.'

'This is not funny.'

Her shaking became more vigorous. 'Not funny at all.'

Finn plonked his mug on the coffee table and raked his hands through his hair; his chest felt tight and his heart raced. He blamed the coffee rather than what he suspected it actually was—sheer panic.

Lydia didn't understand.

Except she did.

His hands trembled as he looked at her with bleak eyes that had seen too much hate. 'I'm too damaged for a baby, Lyd.'

Lydia's smile disappeared in an instant and she reached out her hand to cover his. 'Maybe this is just what you need to help you heal?' she murmured.

He shook her hand away—how could he gamble that on the life of an innocent child? 'I never wanted a baby. This wasn't my choice.'

'Well, we don't always get what we want in life, do we, Finn? You know that better than anyone. So you didn't get a say? Too bad—it's here, it's happening. And guess what, you do get a choice about what you do now.'

Finn stared at her incredulously. 'What? *Be a father*?'

'Yes,' she nodded. 'Be a father.'

Finn shook his head as his chest grew tighter, practically constricting his chest. 'No.'

'Be the father you always wanted.'

Finn shook his head. 'I never wanted a father.'

Lydia gave him a stern look. 'Isaac told me, Finn. He told me how you wished every night for a father to come and take you both away from it all. That you'd tell him stories about him picking you up and taking you to Luna Park for the day and a ferry on the harbour and then back to his house by the sea. You can't go back and fix that, but you do get a chance to start over.'

Lydia stood, swooping his empty mug off the table. 'You want your son to not have a father either? To miss out on such a vital ingredient in his childhood? To dream every night of you coming and taking him out to Luna Park and for a ride on the ferry and to live by the sea? A boy needs a father, Finn.'

'He needs a mother more.'

She shook her head. 'No, he needs a mother *as well*.'

Finn chewed on his lip. Why did Lydia always make so much sense? But the nagging, gnawing worry that spewed stomach acid and bile like a river of hot lava inside his gut just wouldn't let up.

He looked at Lydia. A woman who had needed him to love her. A love he'd been incapable of giving. 'What if I...?' He could barely even bring himself to say the words. 'What if I don't love him?'

Lydia gave him a sad smile. 'You already do, Finn. Why else are we having this conversation? Just *be* a father. The rest will follow.'

By the time Lydia had ordered him to take a couple of headache pills and have a shower then dragged him to Pete's for brunch, Finn was feeling more human again. She'd nattered away about the weather and her job and the football scores and other inane topics, for which he was grateful, and by midday he was back at his apartment alone, with Lydia's wise words turning over and over in his head.

He wasn't utterly convinced by any of them but he had started to think that being part of his child's life was a responsibility he shouldn't shirk.

How many times as a boy had he vowed to do it different when he became a father? Back in the days before all hope for his future had been quashed. When he'd believed that his life could still be normal.

Lydia was right. A boy needed a father.

A stable, committed presence.

God knew, he and Isaac could have done with one instead of the bunch of losers that had drifted in and out of their mother's life until one had stuck and they'd been pushed out of the nest.

He could do stable and committed.

The light was flashing on the answering-machine from the call earlier and he hit the button to listen to the message.

'Finn…its Evie. I didn't really want to tell this to your machine but…what the hell…it might just be easier all round. I just wanted you to know that I know it's a lot for you to comprehend and I didn't want to tell you to…get something out of you. I'm not after money or any kind of…support. It's okay…you don't have to have anything to do with him…the baby… I just think you deserved to know, that's all. I'm happy to do it all. I'm fine with you never being a part of his life. I don't need that from you. So…that's all really. I just wanted you to know that you're off the hook…if that's what you want. Okay…bye.'

Beep...

Finn stared at the machine. *He was off the hook? If that's what he wanted?*

It should have been what he wanted. He wasn't capable of anything else—he'd just been telling Lydia the same thing. But a surge of anger welled up in his chest, washing over him with all the rage and power of a tsunami.

I'm fine with you never being a part of his life.

You don't have to have anything to do with him.

Like his own father.

Evie was going to raise *his* son by herself. Without his money. His input. His support.

Without him.

It was what he should want. It made sense. She'd love him and nurture him and provide all the things he needed.

Physically and emotionally.

Comfort and security. A real childhood. Aunties, uncles, grandparents. Birthday parties, trips to the beach, photos with Santa.

It should make him happy but it didn't. The anger dissipated quickly, replaced by something that felt very much like…craving. It slid like a serpent through his gut and whispered.

Be a father.

Damn Evie and her independence. Her grand plans. Her *happy to do it all*. Lydia was right—he did have a choice. And he'd be damned if his son would grow up without a father.

Stable and committed trumped absent any day.

An hour later Evie was examining a patient's foot in cubicle two when the curtain snapped back with a harsh screech. She blinked as Finn stood there, glaring at her with his laser gaze, looking all scruffy and shaggy and very, very determined.

'I need to talk to you Dr Lockheart,' he said. 'Now, thank you.'

His imperious tone ticked her off even as her hormones demanded she swoon at his feet in a puddle of lust. Luckily the baby gave her a hefty kick, as if to remind her she had a backbone and to use it.

'I'm busy,' she said, smiling sweetly for the benefit of the elderly lady, who looked startled at his intrusion.

But not as startled as she was!

Finn smiled at the patient as he strode into the cubicle and put his hand under Evie's elbow. 'Important cardiac consult,' he said to the grey-haired woman. 'It won't take a minute.'

'Oh, of course, dear,' the lady said. 'Off you go. Hearts are more important than my silly broken toe.'

Finn smiled at her as he firmed his grip on Evie. 'Let's go,' he said, pulling insistently against her resistance.

Once outside he dropped his hand and stalked down the corridor, naturally assuming she'd just follow him. Evie had a good mind to walk in the opposite direction and force him to come looking for her again but they did need to talk. In fact, she was a little surprised he was willing to do so this early. She'd assumed he'd be thinking about her little bombshell for a while longer.

Which meant he'd probably got her phone message.

So she followed him, glaring at his broad shoulders and the way his hair curled against his collar until both of them disappeared into the on-call room. She steeled herself, taking a moment before she entered. It had taken all her guts to make that phone call this morning when every cell in her body had been urging her to say the opposite.

But she'd meant it. She'd cope if he didn't want a bar of them. *It would hurt, but she'd cope.*

She took a deep breath and pushed through the door. He was standing waiting for her on the opposite side, his arms folded impatiently across his chest.

'You look awful,' she said.

She'd seen Finn in varying states of disarray. Angry, inebriated, in pain, high on pain pills, in denial, unkempt and hungover.

This was about as hungover as she'd ever seen him.

'Trust me, this is an improvement on a few hours ago.'

'Did it help?' she asked, trying to keep the bitterness out of her voice but not really succeeding.

Finn shook his head. 'Nope.'

Evie folded her hands across her chest. 'I left a message on your machine this morning.'

Finn gave a curt nod. 'I got it.'

'Oh.' Evie's hand dropped automatically to her belly, feeling the hard round ball of her expanding uterus. A nurse that morning had joked that she was 'looking preggers' and Evie knew that her baggy scrubs weren't going to help for much longer. 'I mean it, Finn. I don't need you to be part of this.' *I want you to, though, with every fibre of my being.* 'Plenty of kids grow up in single-parent families and they do just fine.'

Finn thought about his own dismal childhood. *Plenty of kids didn't do just fine as well.* And although he'd always thought being a father was the last thing on earth he wanted, he suddenly realised that was wrong.

His child being fatherless was the last thing he wanted.

Didn't *his* son deserve the very, very best? Everything that *he* hadn't had and more? A happy, settled, normal family life? Two people who loved him living and working together to ensure that his life was perfect?

A father. And a mother.

And a puppy!

'I think we should get married,' he said.

Every molecule inside Evie froze for long seconds as his startling sentence filtered through into suddenly sluggish brain cells. 'What?' she asked faintly when she finally found her voice.

Finn wondered if he looked as shocked as she did at the words that had come from nowhere. They hadn't been what he'd been planning to say when he'd practically dragged her into the on-call room but he knew in his bones they were the right words.

His child was growing inside her and, no matter what, he was going to be present. He was going to *be a father*. Conviction and purpose rose in him like an avenging angel.

'You can move in with me. No, wait, I'll buy a house. Somewhere by the harbour, or the northern beaches. Bondi or Coogee. He can join the Nippers or learn to surf.'

Evie's head spun, trying to keep up with Finn's rapid-fire thinking. 'A house?'

'I think kids should grow up near a beach.'

Having been dragged from one hot suburban shoebox to the next, he wanted his son to have the freedom of space and a sea breeze and the rhythm of the ocean in his head when he went to sleep instead of rock music from the bikie neighbours or the blare of the television in the next room.

Finn's thoughts raced in time with his pulse. He was going to *be a father.*

'I'll look into celebrants when I get home.'

Evie stared at him incredulously. He had them married and living at the beach with their surfing son all without a single mention of love.

'We'll do it just after the baby's born. No need to inconvenience ourselves until necessary.'

Evie felt as if she'd entered the twilight zone and waited for eerie music to begin. He didn't even want to get married until the baby had arrived—to inconvenience himself. Could he make it any clearer that this sudden crazy scheme had no basis in human emotion? That it wasn't a love match?

Evie had grown up in a house where her parents had been strangers and she was never, *ever* going to subject herself *or her child* to a cold marriage of convenience.

'No,' she said quietly.

Finn shrugged. 'Well, maybe just before then?'

Evie blinked. Oh, when she was as big as a house and needed to get married in a tent? Was he for real? Did he *not* know how important a wedding was to a woman? Even one who wasn't into sappy ceremonies or big flouncy affairs? Didn't he know that most women wanted declarations of love and commitment when they were proposed to?

If that's what this was…

No, of course he didn't. Because, as with everything in his life, Finn just assumed that she'd jump to do his bidding when he asked.

Wrong.

'I'm not marrying you, Finn.'

Finn dragged his attention back to Evie and her softly spoken rebuttal. He snorted. 'Don't be ridiculous, Evie. This is what you wanted, isn't it?'

More than anything. *But not like this.* 'No. I told you, I can raise this baby without your help.'

Finn shoved a hand on his hip. 'Evie…come on…I know how you feel about me…'

She gave a half-laugh at his gall. 'I always forget how capable you are of breathtaking arrogance. Silly of me, really.'

'Evie,' he sighed, desperate to get on with plans now he'd made up his mind, 'let's not play games.'

Evie felt his impatience rolling off him in waves. 'Okay, fine, let's lay our cards on the table. How do *you* feel about *me*?'

Finn felt the question slug him right between the eyes, which were only just recovering from their brush with the whisky. How he felt about Evie was complicated. But he knew it wasn't what she wanted to hear.

'You want me to tell you that I'm in love with you and we're going to ride off into the sunset and it's all going to be hunky-dory? Because I don't and it isn't. Not in a white-picket-fence way anyway.'

Evie moved to the nearby table and sank into a chair. She'd known he didn't love her but it was still hard to hear.

Finn shut his eyes briefly then opened them and joined her, taking the seat opposite. 'I'm sorry, Evie. It's not you. It's me. There's a lot of…stuff in my life…that's happened. I'm just not capable of loving someone.'

Evie nodded even as the admission tore through all the soft tissue around her heart. Had Isaac's death and the other stuff that Ethan had hinted at really destroyed Finn's ability to love?

'Well, that's what I want,' she said quietly. 'What I need. Love and sunsets and white picket fences. And I won't marry for anything less.'

Finn's lips tightened. This had seemed so easy in theory when the marriage suggestion had slipped from his mouth. She'd say yes and the rest would fall into place. It hadn't occurred to him that Evie would be difficult.

In fact, if anything, he'd counted on those feelings she always wore on her sleeve to work in his favour.

'Not when there's a perfectly good alternative,' she continued. 'I'm happy…really, really happy…that you want to be involved, Finn. But we're going to have to work out a way to co-parent separately because I'm not marrying a man who doesn't love me.'

Her words were quiet but the delivery was deadly and Finn knew that she meant every single one. 'Contrary to what you might think, growing up without two parents kind of sucks, Evie. *Trust me on that.*'

Evie shivered at the bitterness in his words. 'Is that what happened to you?' she murmured. Had Ethan been right about Finn's emotional issues extending further back than Isaac's death?

She watched his face slowly shut down, his eyes become chilly. 'We're not talking about me.'

Evie snorted. 'You tell me to trust you, demand that I marry you, but you clam up when I try to get close? Well *trust me,* Finn, growing up with two parents who hate each other kind of sucks too.'

'At least you had a stable home life,' he snapped.

So he hadn't? 'It wasn't stable,' she said through gritted teeth. 'My father just had enough money to buy the illusion of stability. Ultimately my mother was a drunk who came and went in our lives while my father put nannies in the house and mistresses in his bed.'

Finn's mouth twisted. 'Poor little rich girl.' So Evie's life hadn't been perfect—it had still been a thousand per cent better than his had ever been.

Evie shook her head. He really could be an insensitive jerk when he put his mind to it. 'I won't be with a man who doesn't love me.'

She reiterated each word very carefully.

'You seemed to be with Stuart long enough,' Finn jibed, 'and Blind Freddie could have seen he didn't love you.'

Evie gasped at his cruel taunt, the humiliation from that time revisiting with a vengeance. 'At least he'd pretended to care. I doubt you're even capable of that!'

'You want me to pretend? You want me to lie to you? Okay, fine, Evie I love you. Let's get married.'

She stood, ridiculously close to tears and tired of his haranguing. If he thought this was the way to win her over, he was crazy. 'Go to hell, Finn,' she snapped, and stormed out of the room.

Finn's brain was racing as he took the fire stairs up to his penthouse apartment half an hour later. The lifts were being temperamental again and, frankly, after missing his daily ocean swims he could do with the exercise and the extended thinking time. He was breathing hard by the time he got to the fifth floor and stopped by the landing window to catch his breath and absently admire a large slice of the harbour.

Kirribilli Views apartments had certainly been blessed by the location gods.

The door opened and he turned to find Ava Carmichael entering the fire escape. She looked momentarily surprised and then grinned at him. 'We really must stop meeting like this.'

Finn grunted, remembering their last meeting in this stairwell when he'd come upon Ava crying over her broken marriage. Actually, they'd been through a lot together, with him helping her the day she'd miscarried in the lift and then she and Gladys finding him collapsed from a major infection after his first operation.

Not that they'd ever talked about those things. Ava was like that. For a therapist, she was very non-intrusive. Mostly anyway. There had been an occasion or two where she'd spoken her mind but even then she'd given it to him straight. Hadn't couched anything in vague psychological terms.

He liked that about her.

It was good to know that things had improved for both of them since. He had fully recovered from his injury and she and James had reconciled, having had their first baby just before his second operation and his desertion to *Beach Haven*.

'It's not too late,' Finn said, forcing himself to keep things light. 'We can still make out in the stairwell and no one would know.'

Ava laughed at the rumour she'd threatened to start to blackmail him into seeing her the day after he'd scared the daylights out of all of them with his infection. He'd been in an absolutely foul mood but she'd served him up some home truths anyway.

Not that he'd taken them on board.

He was a stubborn, stubborn man. But she had a soft spot for him because he'd never tried to offer any advice or interfere or make things better when things with James had been going to hell in a hand basket. Unlike others. And she'd appreciated that.

'I heard you were back and fully recovered. Although…' she squinted and inspected his face a little closer '…you don't look so good at the moment.'

Finn almost groaned. Did every woman find it their duty today to tell him he looked like hell? 'What are you doing here? Didn't you move to your white-picket-fence house in the burbs?'

'Just visiting the old stomping ground,' she said.

Finn turned to look back out the window and Ava knew she had been dismissed, that it was her job to walk on down the stairs and leave him to his obvious brooding, but there was something achingly lonely about Finn and they'd been pretty frank with each other in the past.

Still, she hesitated. She knew that Finn was an intensely private man. But then Finn turned his gaze towards her. It was so incredibly turbulent, almost too painful to look at.

'You're a therapist, right?'

Ava laughed. 'I'm a *sex* therapist, Finn.'

He shrugged. 'But you *do* have a psychology degree?'

Ava nodded. 'Is there something you want to talk about?'

Finn shook his head. He wanted to talk to Ava Carmichael about as much as he wanted to become a father but…she'd always given it to him straight and he could do with some insight into the female psyche right now.

'Evie's pregnant. I suggested we get married. She said no. I need her to say yes.'

Ava blinked at the three startling pieces of information. She and Evie were friends, not bosom buddies and they certainly hadn't seen much of each other since her own baby had been born, but she knew more about Finn and Evie's relationship than Finn probably realised.

People told her stuff—it was an occupational hazard.

She knew Evie loved Finn. She knew Finn was a hard man to know and an impossible one to love. She knew that if Evie had turned him down it had been for a pretty good reason.

'Okay...' she wandered closer to him, propping her hip against the window sill. 'So when you say you *suggested*? What did that entail exactly?'

'I said I thought we should get married.'

Ava nodded. 'So, let me guess...you didn't get down on one knee and do the whole big proposal thing? You kind of...presented it as a fait accompli?' Finn looked away from her probing gaze. 'Am I warm?'

He looked back again, glaring. 'It was more of a... spontaneous thing. Us getting married isn't about any of the hoopla. It's about being practical. About giving our child a normal family with a mother and father living under the same roof. And Evie isn't the kind of woman that goes for all that romantic rubbish.'

Ava arched an eyebrow. 'And how do you know that, Finn? Have you ever really even tried to get to know her?'

He looked away again at the view. 'I know she loves me, Ava. Why be coy about it? Why pretend this isn't what she wants?' He looked back at her. 'This way she gets what she wants and I get what I want.'

'What? A man who doesn't love her?'

Finn wanted to smash the window at her gentle insight. 'Look, Ava...it's complicated. I grew up in a single-parent household and then...' He shook his head.

He couldn't tell Ava, no matter what degree she had. He didn't talk about his issues—he just left them behind in the past, where they belonged. Where they couldn't touch him any more. 'I don't want that for my kid.'

Ava pitied him. Finn was a man on the edge and he was the only one who didn't know it. 'Tell *her*, Finn. Not me.'

He shook his head. He was so used to burying it inside he doubted he even knew how to access the words. 'I can't.'

Ava's heart squeezed at the bleakness in his eyes. 'I do recall telling you that this would happen one day, Finn. That by pushing Evie away and not letting her in that one day something would happen and you'd find yourself locked out of Evie's life.'

Finn nodded miserably. She'd said exactly that. Yelled it at him, actually, when he was being rude and stubborn and difficult, refusing to see Evie after he'd been hospitalised with the infection.

'Seriously?' he said. 'You're going with an *I told you so* now? Where'd you get that degree?' he grouched. 'In a cornflakes packet?'

Ava smiled. 'Coco Pops, actually.'

Finn gave a half-smile before turning back to the window. 'Fine. How do I fix it?'

'Maybe it's time to stop pushing her away. To open yourself up.'

Finn pressed his forehead against the glass. She may as well have told him to stand in the middle of the hospital naked. 'What? No pill?'

Ava shook her head. 'I'm afraid not.'

'You're a lousy therapist,' he muttered.

She laughed. 'What do you expect for free?'

CHAPTER SIX

A MONTH PASSED and it was business as usual at Sydney Harbour Hospital. Finn was back on board, being his brilliant, arrogant, grouchy self. Anyone who'd thought that with him now fully recovered from his injury his mood might have improved had been sorely mistaken. Evie's recalcitrance had taken over from the pain and restrictions that had made him notoriously moody, resulting in a crankier than ever Dr Kennedy.

But given that Prince Khalid's cheque had made the hospital one million dollars richer, no one was about to call him on it. Those on his team just knew—you did your job with skill and competence and stayed the hell out of Finn's way.

Even Finn and Evie's relationship had gone back to that of polite detachment, which was causing an absolute buzz on the grapevine. At twenty-five weeks Evie could no longer hide her pregnancy and with everyone knowing Finn was the baby-daddy, speculation was rife.

Were they together?

Would they get married?

Were they already married and keeping it a secret?

Why couldn't they barely say two words to each other?

Did they even like each other?

Everything from the hows and wheres of the baby's conception to a potential wedding and the custody arrangements were red-hot topics.

Everything about Finn and Evie were red-hot topics—like they were freaking royalty.

The fact that both of them were tight-lipped with answers to any of the questions being asked didn't help.

And in the absence of truth there was gossip.

Evie soldiered on regardless of the whispers. Finn stayed away and she alternated between being mad and glad. But mostly she just wished she knew what the hell was going on inside his head and where they went from here. Sooner or later they were going to need to talk but she was damned if she was going to instigate it.

As far as she was concerned, the ball was firmly in his court!

Evie was late arriving at Pete's—the pub that had stood across the road from the hospital for twenty years—on Saturday afternoon. Bella and Lexi were already seated and deep in conversation.

Pete smiled at her from behind the bar and mouthed, 'The usual?' at her. She nodded, the usual these days being sparkling water instead of a nice cold bottle of beer.

Not that abstaining from drinking for nine months was a hardship but she did miss it occasionally after a long day on her feet—and it had been a very hectic day.

She joined her sisters, pushing into the cubicle next to Bella to give Lexi some room. Two pregnant women on one side of a booth was one pregnant woman too many, especially given Lexi's about-to-pop status.

'How's it going?' Evie asked her sister as Pete

brought her water over in a wine glass. Bless him, at least she had the illusion she was drinking something fortified.

Lexi grimaced. 'This baby is sitting so low I feel like my uterus is going to fall out every time I stand up.'

Evie and Bella laughed. They both knew that Lexi and Sam, a transplant surgeon, were ecstatic about the fast-approaching due date. Their relationship was stronger than ever now after their years apart. 'Pretty sure that's not possible,' Evie said.

Lexi laughed too. 'There's always a first time.'

They chatted for a while about baby things, both of her sisters being careful to avoid the F word even though she could tell they were dying to ask her about the latest with Finn. But what was there to say? There was no latest.

The baby kicked and Evie grimaced.

'What is it?' Bella asked. 'Did he kick?' Evie nodded, her hand smoothing over the spot where the baby was busy boogying. 'Can I feel?' Bella asked, her hands automatically gliding over Evie's belly to where her hand was, exclaiming in awe when the baby performed right on cue.

Evie noticed the wistful look on her younger sister's face as she enjoyed the show. 'I'm sorry, Bells, this must be hard for you.'

Bella had cystic fibrosis and Sam had performed a double lung transplant on her less than a year ago. She and Charlie, an orthopod the hospital, desperately wanted a baby but there were risks that neither of them was willing to take on Bella's health, not to mention the sceptre of any baby also having CF.

'It's fine. I'm just pleased neither of you carry the gene so my lovely little niece and nephew will be fine.'

She smiled at them both but Evie could tell it took a huge effort. Poor Bella had already had so much taken from her in life.

'Besides,' Bella continued, 'I get to be the cool aunty, who fills them up with lollies and ice cream and lets them watch scary movies till midnight and teaches them to drive.'

'And designs fabulous couture for their proms and weddings from your latest collection,' Lexi added.

'That right,' Bella agreed. Her new lungs had given her more freedom to make her fashion design dream a reality. 'And you can organise fabulous parties for them,' Bella said.

Lexi, an events planner, grinned. 'Starting with your baby shower,' she said to Evie.

Evie laughed. 'Steady on, there's plenty of time to be worrying about that. Just you concentrate on getting this little one…' she patted Lexi's belly '…out. We'll worry about my baby shower a few months down the track.'

Lexi shifted uncomfortably. 'Deal.'

'So, Bells,' Evie said, as Pete plonked another wine glass of sparkling water in front of her, 'tell us about your course. What are you working on?'

They nattered away for the next hour and Evie felt lighter and happier than she had in weeks. Between Finn, the gossip and the baby, she'd had a lot on her mind. It was fabulous to leave that all beyond for a while and be pulled headlong into girly, sister stuff.

Or at least it was until Finn showed up in jeans and a T-shirt, looking all rugged and stubbly and very determined. She'd seen that look before and went on instant alert despite the flutter in the region of her heart.

'Evie,' he greeted her, with a quick nod of his head to Lexi and Bella.

Evie frowned at him. 'Is there something wrong?'

He shook his head. 'I have something I'd like to show you. If your sisters can spare you…of course.'

Finn's face ached from being polite when all he really wanted to do was snatch her up and throw her over his shoulder. The refined, educated side of him was horrified by the prehistoric notion but the rampaging Neanderthal he'd become since she'd turned him down quite frankly didn't give a damn at the spectacle that would ensue should he follow through on his impulse.

'Finn…' Evie sighed. She didn't have the energy to fight today.

'Please, Evie.'

Evie blinked. Finn wasn't one for saying 'please'. Not even when he'd *suggested* they get married had he thrown in a 'please'.

'Where exactly are you taking her?' Bella asked, placing a protective hand on her sister's arm.

Bella didn't like the way he'd been treating Evie, especially his silence this last month. If she were pregnant there was no way Charlie would treat her so abysmally. He'd wrap in her cotton wool, which was no less than any woman deserved. Especially Evie, who'd been the Lockheart family rock for ever and worked such long, punishing hours.

'It's a surprise,' Finn hedged.

'Is it a good surprise?' Bella demanded. 'Will she like it, Finn Kennedy, because I don't care how much money you bring into the hospital's coffers or how brilliant everyone says you are, frankly I think you can be pretty damn obtuse.'

'Bella,' Lexi said reproachfully.

But Finn gave a grudging smile. Trust another Lockheart to tell him like it was. Bella had been pretty easy to dismiss due to being sickly most of her life but those new lungs had certainly given her a whole lot of breath! 'Yes,' he conceded, 'it's a good surprise.'

Evie's pulse fluttered at her wrist and tap-danced at her temple as Bella removed her hand. He didn't look any softer but his words were encouraging. Maybe they were going to have an adult conversation about the way forward?

'Fine,' she said, dropping a kiss on Bella's cheek before she eased herself out of the booth. Finn stepped aside for her and Evie was excruciatingly aware of the sudden rabid interest—some subtle, some not so subtle—directed towards them as she gave Lexi a quick peck.

She turned to Finn, ignoring the speculation she could practically feel coursing through Pete's like an electrical current. 'Lead on,' she said.

She breathed a little easier once they'd got out of the pub and were walking to his car, parked at the kerb outside. It was black and low with only two seats—the ultimate status symbol—and it surprised her. She'd never seen Finn's car. He walked to work as everyone who lived at Kirribilli Views did, and like everyone else at his professional level and with his abrasive personality didn't have a social life that really required one.

She supposed the women he'd dated probably thought it was hot and cool. Good-looking doctor—check! Racy car—check! But all she could think as the engine purred to life was, *Where was he going to put the baby seat?*

'So what's the big surprise?' she asked as Finn negotiated the late-afternoon traffic.

'Patience,' he said, his eyes not leaving the road. 'Patience.'

So they didn't talk for the fifteen minutes it took to get where they were going. Evie looked around bewildered as they pulled up at a house in Lavender Bay, not far from the hospital or the harbour. In fact, as she climbed out of his car—something that would probably be impossible at nine months—she could see down to the harbour where the early evening light had laid its gentle fingers and across the other side to the tall distinctive towers of the SHH and further on to the large garish clown mouth of Luna Park and the famous bridge that spanned the harbour.

A breeze that smelled of salt and sand picked up her hair, blowing a strand across her face as she tracked the path of a yellow and green ferry. She pulled it away as she turned to face Finn, who was opening the low gate of the house where they were parked.

'Okay, so…what are we doing here?'

'All will be revealed shortly,' he said as he gestured for her to follow him up the crumbling cement path.

Evie frowned. Whose place was this? Did he want her to meet someone? Someone who might help her understand him? A patient? A relative? Lydia? However she fitted into the puzzle that was Finn. His mother? His grandmother? *Did he even have either of those?* He never spoke of them.

It had to be someone he knew, though, because he had a key and as she watched him walk up the three stairs and traverse the old-fashioned balcony covered by a Seventies-style awning he didn't even bother with knocking. Just slipped the key into the lock and pushed the door open.

He turned to her. 'Come,' he said as he stepped into the house.

Evie rolled her eyes. The man was clueless. Utterly clueless. But she followed him anyway because she was dying to know who lived in this gorgeous little cottage overlooking the harbour and what they had to do with Finn.

Maybe it was a clue to his life that he always kept hidden from her. From everyone.

She stepped inside, her heels clacking against smooth polished floorboards the colour of honey. The sound echoed around the empty house. The rooms, as she moved through, following Finn, were devoid of furniture, curtains or blinds and floor coverings. Soaring ceilings graced with decorative roses added to the cavernous echo.

He opened the back door and she followed him down the three stairs to the back entertaining area and then onto a small patch of grass, the back fence discreetly covered by a thick row of established shrubbery.

'Well?' he said, turning around with his arms splayed wide like a game-show host. 'It's beautiful, don't you think?'

He was smiling at her, a rare smile that went all the way to his eyes, lighting them up like a New Year's Eve laser display, and Evie's foolish heart skipped a beat. 'Yes,' she said hesitantly, smiling back.

'It's yours,' he said. 'Ours. I bought it. As a wedding gift. The perfect place to raise our son.'

Evie stared at him for the longest time as everything around her seemed to slow right down to a snail's pace. The flow of blood in her veins, the passage of air in her lungs, the distant blare of a ferry horn on the harbour. Then the slow death of her smile as realisation dawned.

'Is this another way of *suggesting* we get married?' she asked, her quiet voice sounding loud in the silence that seemed to have descended on the back yard.

Finn shook his head vigorously. 'Absolutely not. It's a proposal. I was wrong last time just…assuming. I should have asked you. I got the call this afternoon from the real estate agent that she was mine.'

Ours, she corrected silently knowing that the gesture, while grand, was empty. It was obvious he didn't think of it as theirs. That it was just another way of getting what he wanted.

He reached out and took her hand. 'What do you say, Evie? Let's get married. Let's raise our son together, here in this house with the harbour just there and everything he could ever want.'

Evie looked into his gorgeously shaggy, earnest face. A part of her whispered, *Do it*. Say yes. Take the fake marriage. Take whatever he's offering. You can make him love you with time and patience.

And it was, oh, so tempting.

But she couldn't. She just couldn't.

She wanted more than that. She wanted it all—the whole hearts and flowers catastrophe. If she'd learned anything from her own parents' marriage and years of navigating a fraught household, it was that you couldn't make someone love you if they didn't.

No matter how hard you tried.

And you had to start as you meant to go on.

She withdrew her hand from his. 'No.'

She refused to live on Finn's crumbs as her mother had on her father's. If they were going to enter into a marriage then she wanted all of him.

'Hell, Evie,' Finn said, shaking his head incredulously. 'I bought you a house. What more do you want from me?'

'I can buy my own house,' she snapped.

'Then what *do* you want' he demanded.

'You, Finn,' she yelled. 'I want you. I want you to open up to me. To know every secret, every ugly thought, every tear you've ever shed. I want to know about every sad, sorry day of your existence. And I want you to *want* to know about *mine*. I want to know about Isaac and the day that he died in your arms and about who the hell Lydia is and how she fits into your life and about your childhood and your time in the army as a trauma surgeon.'

Evie was breathing hard as she finished and she'd just scraped the surface of the things she wanted to know about the man she loved. 'That's what I want,' she said, ramming her hands onto her hips, pulling her shirt taut across her bump. 'Anything less is asking me to debase myself. And I deserve better than that.'

Finn reeled from her list. *She wanted too much.* She wanted stuff he'd never given to anyone. Not to Lydia. Not even to Isaac.

Finn steeled himself to be the practical one. Obviously the pregnancy was making level-headed Evie a trace emotional.

'None of those things are open to negotiation,' he said, his voice steely. 'Neither are they required to make a life together. I'm sure if we're both practical we can make it work, Evie.'

Evie's temper flared at his condescension. He truly thought he could just wear her down. She'd swallowed a lot of pride where Finn was concerned because she loved him and she'd known he'd been hurting and she'd seen the injured soul under the gruff and bluff but she drew the line here. She would not become his wife— give him her all—and end up married to a stranger.

'Okay, then,' she snapped. 'Tell me how it will work, Finn. How? We get married and have a committed normal relationship where you take out the rubbish and I hang out the washing and we argue over the TV remote and snuggle in bed on the weekends with the newspapers?'

She glared at him as she drew breath. 'Or is it just a name-only thing? Do we sleep in the same bed to keep up the ruse for our son? Or apart? Do we have some kind of open marriage where we discreetly see other people? Or do we just go without sex for the next twenty-ish years and you spend a lot of time in the shower and I run up an account at the sex shop we just passed?'

Finn blinked at her vehemence, lost for words, but she seemed to have paused for a moment and was looking at him like it was his turn to add to the conversation. 'I haven't really thought about the nitty-gritty, Evie.'

'*Bum-bah*!' she snorted. 'Wrong answer. Try again. You want me to accept this proposal?' She folded her arms. 'Convince me.'

Finn picked carefully through words and phrases in his head, hoping that he found the right ones to convince her. 'I assumed we'd be sharing the same bed. In the...' he searched around for a delicate way to put it '...fullest sense of the word.'

'Well, I just bet you did, didn't you? Works well for you, doesn't it, to have sex on tap. No need for all those showers then.'

Finn wondered if Evie was maybe becoming a little hysterical but he was damned if he was going to be made out to be the bad guy here because he wanted to have sex with his wife. 'No need for you to take out shares in sex-toy companies either,' he pointed out, his jaw aching from trying to stay rational.

'Well, I wouldn't count on that.'

It was Finn's turn to snort. 'You know well enough, Evie Lockheart, that I can make you come loud enough to scare nesting birds on the other side of the harbour.'

She shrugged. 'So can a little imagination.'

He quirked an eyebrow. 'It can't hold you afterwards.'

'Maybe not. But at least it's not going to break my heart a little more each time and slowly erode my self-respect.'

'Damn it, Evie,' he fumed as his control started to slip. '*This is not what I wanted.* I didn't want to be a father but it's happening and I'm here. Do you think you could at least meet me halfway?'

Evie grappled with her escalating temper. He was right. He was here. Even if he was being a total idiot about it. She took a calm, steadying breath.

'*This,*' she said, repeating his open-armed action from earlier as she indicated the house and yard, 'isn't halfway, Finn. *This* is full throttle. Halfway is agreeing to a parenting schedule. Talking about how it's going to affect our jobs and what we can do to lessen the impact on two households. It's talking about what schools he should go to and getting our wills in order.'

Finn shook his head. She seemed much calmer now but he could feel it all slipping away. This was not how he'd planned today would go. 'What about the house?' he demanded.

'It's fabulous,' she said gently. God knew, she'd move in tomorrow if things were different between them. 'And our son is going to love being here with you. But I'm not going to marry you, Finn. Not when you don't love me.'

'I don't want some modern rubbish arrangement for my kid,' he said stubbornly. He didn't want his son to be bouncing between houses—his whole childhood had been like that and he'd hated it. 'It'll be confusing for him.'

'He won't have known anything else,' she murmured, and then she shook her head. 'It's funny, I never picked you as a traditionalist.'

'Kids should be raised by their parents. Together.'

'Sure. In an ideal world. But what we've got here isn't ideal, is it, Finn? And I'm pretty sure I'm capable of doing my bit to raise our son.'

Her calmness was getting on his nerves. He knew for sure he wasn't capable of raising a child by himself. He needed her. He needed her to provide the love and comfort stuff. The nurturing. He could teach him to build a fire and climb a tree and how to fish. He needed Evie there to make up for the stuff he wasn't capable of in all the quiet, in-between times.

'Well, you haven't exactly done such a stellar job so far,' he lashed out. 'You've got yourself electrocuted, almost drowned and followed that up by a case of hypothermia.'

Evie gasped, her hand automatically going to her belly, as if to shield the baby from the insult. If she'd been a more demonstrative woman, she might just have slapped him. 'The baby is perfectly fit and healthy and completely unharmed,' she said, her voice vibrating with hurt.

His gaze dropped to where her hand cradled her belly and he felt the irrational surge of anger from the day she'd been caught up in the rip break over him again. 'Well, that was sheer luck, wasn't it?' he snapped.

Evie wanted to scream and rant and stomp her foot but it was useless and exhausting and getting them nowhere. Finn was being his usual pig-headed self and she should know better than to try and reason with him in this mood.

She shook her head at him, swallowing down all the rage and fury and sucking up his bad temper like she always did. The only thing she had was the high ground. And now seemed like a very good time to take it.

'Goodbye, Finn,' she said, turning on her heel and marching through the house.

He followed her, calling out to her about being reasonable and driving her back, but a taxi came along just as she was opening the gate and it pulled in when she waved, and she didn't look back as Finn told her to stop being ridiculous. She just opened the door and told the driver to go, go, go.

A week later Evie was lying in bed on her day off after five day shifts, too exhausted to get up to relieve her full bladder, which the baby was taking great delight in using as a trampoline. She hadn't heard boo from Finn all week. In fact, she'd only glimpsed him once, and she didn't know whether that had been his passive-aggressive way of agreeing to do it her way or if he was just off plotting his next grand gesture.

She suspected the latter, although right now she was too tired to care.

Another five minutes of baby gymnastics and she could ignore the need to go no longer. She rolled out of bed and did her business. She was heading back again when there was a knock on her door. She wistfully eyed the corner of her bed, which she could see through the open door.

It was probably just Bella, who had taken to dropping in all the time to check on her. She could probably just ignore it but the knock came again and she didn't have the heart to leave her sister on the doorstep.

Except it wasn't Bella when she opened the door. It was Lydia.

Evie blinked, feeling like an Amazon next to the tiny redhead. She tried to suck in her belly but that was no longer possible. 'Oh… Hi…Lydia?'

Lydia smiled at her as she checked out Evie's belly. 'Well, he's right,' she said. 'You're definitely pregnant.'

'Er…yes,' Evie said, struck by how truly bizarre this moment was. Not knowing Lydia's exact relationship with Finn made this meeting kind of awkward. For her anyway. Lydia didn't seem ready to scratch her eyes out—in fact, she seemed friendly—so maybe they didn't have that kind of history?

'Do you think I could come in?' Lydia asked. 'I've come on behalf of Finn.'

Evie groaned—Finn had sent an emissary? She was

too tired for this. 'Look, Lydia, if Finn's sent you to offer me some crazy incentive—money or diamonds or the goose that lays the golden eggs—I really need to let you know right off the bat that you're wasting your breath.'

Lydia pursed her lips. 'Oh, dear…the house,' she tutted. 'It's worse than I thought.'

Evie frowned. 'Huh?'

'Can I, please, just come in and explain?' Evie hesitated and Lydia dived in to reassure her. 'I've come on behalf of Finn but he doesn't know I'm here. *He'd be furious if he did.* But I haven't seen him this…bleak in a very long time and I can't bear it any longer.'

Evie could hear the woman's genuine concern and worry as she had that day Lydia had told her Finn's whereabouts. She got the sense that Lydia loved Finn and the spike of jealousy that drove into her chest almost knocked Evie flat. She reached for the door to steady herself, the overwhelming urge to slam it in Lydia's face warring with her curiosity.

Curiosity won out.

Part of Evie needed to know where Lydia fitted into Finn's life.

Evie fell back and ushered her inside. She played the perfect hostess, fixing Lydia a cup of coffee and some green tea for herself. They sat on opposite sides of the coffee table, sipping at their drinks for a moment or two, and then Evie voiced what she'd sensed from the beginning.

'You love him?'

Lydia nodded. 'Yes.'

Evie gripped the cup at the other woman's calm response, her pulse pounding in her ears. What must

Lydia think of her? Carrying Finn's baby. Did Finn love her back? Was that why he couldn't love her?

'I'm sorry, I didn't know...' She put a hand on her belly. 'I would never have...if I had known he was with you.'

Lydia frowned. 'What?' She made an annoyed little noise at the back of her throat. 'He hasn't told you about me, has he?' She reached across the coffee table and patted Evie's hand. 'Finn's my brother-in-law. I'm Isaac's wife. Widow, to be precise.'

Evie felt a rush of relief like a slug of Finn's whisky to her system. She let out a pent-up breath in a loud rush. 'His sister-in-law?'

Lydia grinned again. 'Yes.'

'Oh,' Evie said, lost for words as the high robbed her of her ability to form a complex sentence. 'That's good.' She smiled. 'That's good.'

Lydia nodded. 'Although in the interests of full disclosure we did have a...relationship. A very messed-up one for a few years after Isaac's death. I was a complete wreck...it was a very dark time... I think we both held on for much longer than we should have because we were each other's link to Isaac.'

'Oh,' Evie said again, still having trouble with sentences but this time because of Lydia's frankness. Finn and Isaac's widow had been lovers? 'Did he...did he love you?'

Lydia shook her head. 'Not in that way, no. I wanted him to...needed him to at the time...but he's been through a lot...seen a lot...he's a complex man. He doesn't love easily.'

Evie nodded slowly. 'Tell me about it.'

'You love him?'

'Yes.'

'And yet you won't marry him.' Lydia smiled. 'You have him quite riled up.'

Evie shrugged, looking into the bottom of her cup. 'He doesn't love me. And I'm not settling for anything less.'

'Good for you.' Lydia laughed. 'If it's any consolation, though, I think he does love you.'

She looked up at Lydia sharply, expecting to find her looking as flippant as the remark, but she seemed deadly serious. 'Well, I think he does too,' she said. 'But he has to say it. He has to admit it. To himself more than anything.'

Lydia nodded. 'Yes. For a man so bloody intelligent he can be exceedingly dim-witted.'

Evie laughed and Lydia joined her. When their laughter died Lydia suddenly sat forward and grabbed Evie's hand. 'Don't give up on him, Evie, please. He needs you.'

Evie was reminded of Ethan's words. It spoke volumes that Finn had people who loved and cared about him.

'I need him too,' she said. 'But I need all of him.'

Lydia let her hand go. 'Of course you do.' She sipped at her coffee. 'He showed me the house,' she said after a while.

'Ah,' Evie murmured. 'The house.'

'You don't like the house?' Lydia asked, her brow crinkling.

'I freaking love the house,' Evie muttered. 'But I don't want grand gestures from him.'

Lydia gave her a sad smile. 'You have to understand what that house means to Finn.'

'Oh, yes?' Evie asked, trying to keep the jealousy out of her voice. 'And what's that? Believe me, I'd love to know. But he doesn't tell me anything. He just wants to install me there like bloody Miss Haversham.'

Lydia pursed her lips again as if deciding what to say next. Evie hoped and prayed she'd say something, anything, that would give her some insight into the man she loved.

'Finn and Isaac grew up in the system,' Lydia said. 'Their mother abandoned them when Finn was eight. Isaac was six. It was…tough. They got passed around a lot. Finn fought to keep them together, which was hard when most families only wanted one troubled child and that was usually the much sunnier Isaac. There was a lot of rejection. A lot of…bouncing around. Finn would tell Isaac stories about their dad coming to take them away to Luna Park for the day and a ride on a ferry then bringing them back to his home by the sea.'

Evie sat for long moments, letting the import of Lydia's words sink in. Finn had bought his childhood fantasy home for his own son, the house he'd never known, with the hope of providing his child with an upbringing he'd never had.

She sat very still, moved almost to tears. And yet she was blindingly jealous too. Why had she had to hear this story from Lydia? Why couldn't he have told her himself? If he'd told her this the day he'd taken her to the house she might not have been so bloody angry all week.

'He told you all this?' she asked, looking up at Lydia.

Lydia shook her head with a wry smile. 'Good grief, no. Isaac did. Finn never speaks of it. I doubt he's ever told anyone.'

It shouldn't have made her feel better. The story was tragic and awful. But somehow it did. Somehow knowing that he hadn't told any woman about his younger years gave her hope. Hope that he would open up to her about it eventually.

Over time.

Which was what they had now. Time. Before the baby was born.

Maybe she could use it wisely to get them what they both wanted?

CHAPTER SEVEN

AVA HAD BEEN in her office for one minute on Monday morning when the door opened and Finn stormed in.

'What do women want?' he demanded.

Ava looked up from the mail she'd been opening. He was in his usual work attire of a carelessly worn suit, his tie pulled askew. 'And good morning to you too, Finn.'

Finn waved his hand dismissively. 'I bought her a house—*a goddamn house*—and she still turned me down.'

'You bought her a house because…you love her?'

He shoved his hand on his hip. 'This has nothing to do with love. I bought her a house so our son has a roof over his head.'

'Right…so you bought her a house but you don't love her? Goodness.' Ava tsked. 'That's a tad ungrateful.'

Finn glared at her. 'There's no need for sarcasm.'

Ava sighed as Finn prowled back and forth in front of her desk. 'Okay. Did she say why she turned you down?'

Finn stopped pacing. 'She said she could buy her own house.' He shot her an incredulous look. 'Like I'd offended her feminist principles.'

Ava nodded patiently. Of course Evie Lockheart could buy her own house. With or without the Lockheart fortune behind her. But years of being a psychologist told her there was a lot more to Evie's refusal than an affront to feminism.

'What else?'

'What?'

'Did she say anything else?'

Finn took up prowling again and Ava leaned back in her chair to wait him out.

'She wants me to *open up to her*,' he said eventually.

Ava suppressed a smile. Opening up was not something that Finn was known for. He made it sound as if Evie had asked for a sparkly unicorn or some other such nonsense.

'And you don't want to do that?'

'How does talking about my past have anything to do with raising our son together?' he demanded.

Ava swung slightly in her chair, watching Finn pace. 'Because it's what couples do?' she suggested.

'We're not a couple,' he snapped, coming to an abrupt halt.

She quirked an eyebrow. 'And yet you want her to marry you…?'

'None of that stuff is important to a successful future together.'

Ava knew he was dead wrong and she suspected that somewhere beneath all the injury and barriers he knew it too. But it wasn't her job to tell him he was wrong. 'Is it important what *you* think or what *she* needs?'

He glared at her. 'Goddamn it. Can't you just give me one piece of useful advice instead of answering every question with another question? You're a sex therapist, aren't you supposed to be full of practical ideas about making relationships work?'

Ava sighed. He was far from ready for practical exercises and she should be annoyed that he wanted her to give him a magic wand without doing any of the hard yards he obviously needed. But this was Finn, who wasn't a client, and for Evie's sake maybe she could help.

'Fine.' She folded her arms across her chest. 'Woo her, Finn.'

He frowned. 'Woo her? Are we living in Shakespearian England all of a sudden?' he scoffed.

Ava knew that good wooing took time and if Evie was smart she'd use it to her advantage. 'You wanted my advice.' She shrugged. 'You got it.'

'I've already got her pregnant—don't you think it's a little late for the wooing?'

Ava shook her head. 'It's never too late for wooing.'

Finn shut his eyes. *Bloody hell.* He'd bought her a house and now he was going to have to *woo* her as well?

He opened his eyes. 'Gee, thanks.'

Ava grinned at Finn's look of distaste. 'Don't mention it.'

Finn knocked on Evie's door that night in his suit, juggling some flowers and a bag of Indian takeaway. He knew she was on days off because he'd checked the emergency department's medical roster at lunchtime.

He'd been brooding about Ava's advice all day and by the time he'd finished his afternoon theatre list he'd decided it might be a worth a try. He had time, after all, and instead of rushing like a bull at a gate, which was what he had been doing, maybe a little subtlety *was* called for.

But it had better show dividends pretty quickly because, come hell or high water, they would be married by the time the baby was born.

The door opened and he suddenly felt awkward and unsure of himself standing there with flowers. Women usually came to him—flowers and that kind of thing weren't his style.

Evie blinked. 'Finn?'

'I have flowers,' he said, pushing them into her arms. He lifted up the plastic bag in his other hand. 'And Indian takeaway. Have you eaten?'

Evie shook her head, the aroma of yellow roses and oriental lilies enveloping her. 'I was just doing some… yoga.'

Finn noted her workout gear. Skin-tight Lycra knee-length leggings. An equally form-fitting top with a round neckline and spaghetti straps that bared her shoulders and stretched over her full breasts and rounded belly. Her hair had been scraped back into a messy ponytail.

'I see,' he said, exceedingly self-conscious as he tried not to stare. She seemed to get bigger every time he saw her.

'Come in,' she said, falling back to allow him entry.

Finn stepped inside and then followed her through to the lounge room. There was some low Gregorian chant playing from a sound system somewhere and he noted the yoga mat on the floor. He sat where she indicated on the three-seater lounge and started to pull the containers out while she took the flowers out of sight.

He heard water running, a fridge door opening then shuffling of crockery and tinkling of glasses as he pulled the lids off. He almost called out to just bring some cutlery but he supposed part of the wooing process was to eat off good plates rather than straight from the containers.

Evie, her brain busy trying to fathom what Finn was up to now, was back in the lounge room in a couple of minutes, balancing a tray and the vase of flowers. Finn, who'd taken off his jacket and tie, stood and relieved her of the tray as she placed the vase on top of the television cabinet and used a remote to turn the music off. When she turned back he'd unloaded the tray and her plate was waiting for her, the napkin a bright slash of red against the snowy white pattern.

He was pouring them both sparkling water and he smiled at her as he handed her the glass. A smile that went straight to her insides. She sat towards the end of the lounge, tucking a foot up underneath her, being careful to leave a cushion's distance between them as he asked her what she wanted then proceeded to plate it up for her, passing it and the napkin over when he was done.

She took it and sat unmoving for a few moments as he turned his attention to his own meal. When that was done he smiled at her again and then tucked in.

'Okay,' she said, placing her plate on the coffee table. 'What's going on?'

Finn, in mid-swallow, thought about feigning obtuseness as Bella had already accused him of being obtuse anyway. But he was a cards-on-the-table kind of guy.

He finished his mouthful and took a drink of water as the spicy lamb korma heated his mouth. 'Ava thinks I should woo you.'

Evie frowned. 'Ava? *Ava Carmichael?*'

Finn nodded. 'The one and only.'

'You're seeing Ava?'

'Yes. No. Not like that. We just…chat sometimes…'

Evie was lost for words. 'I…see…' What on earth could she say to such a startling revelation?

It was Finn's turn to frown. 'You don't like it.' He shook his head. 'I knew it was a dumb idea,' he muttered.

Evie shook her head. 'No, I just…' Just what? Was shocked, amazed, flabbergasted? That Finn Kennedy had not only asked a sex therapist for advice about their relationship but had also obviously taken it on board. 'It's sweet…really sweet,' she ended lamely.

'Great,' Finn grumbled, as he also put his plate down. 'Why don't you just pat me on the head and tell me to run along?'

Evie watched as he ran a hand through his hair. This was her chance to start making inroads into his reserve. If he'd finally dropped his bullying tactics and was willing to take others' advice he might just be open to doing things her way.

She leaned forward, resting her bent elbows on her knees. 'I don't want you to woo me, Finn.'

Finn gave a self-deprecating smile. 'Probably just as well. I obviously suck at it.'

Evie laughed. 'You were doing fine. I'm sure with a little practice you'll be perfect.'

He glanced at her. 'But it's not what you want?'

She shook her head slowly. 'How about I do you a deal? I *will* marry you *after* the baby is born if we spend these next few months getting to know each other first.'

Finn's heart started to pound in his chest. It was the same thing she'd told him she wanted at the house. Except she'd made a major concession—she was promising to marry him. 'You've changed your tune,' he said warily.

Evie nodded. 'I spoke to Lydia. She thinks you're worth a little perseverance.'

Finn felt every muscle in his body tense. 'Lydia?'

Evie almost shivered at the sudden drop in his tone. 'She told me a little about you and Isaac growing up in the care system and what the house at Lavender Bay symbolises for you. She asked me not to give up on you. So, by the way, did Ethan.'

Finn wanted to roar at the interference. How dared they talk about him behind his back? This stuff was deeply, deeply personal! 'Lydia *and Ethan,*' he ground out, 'should really learn to keep their big mouths shut.'

'They care about you, Finn,' she murmured. 'As I do. And I'm willing to meet you at this halfway you wanted, to marry you, but only if you're willing to meet me halfway. I want us to get to know each other, Finn. No holds barred. No topic off limits.'

Finn felt the slow burn of anger being doused by hope as the push and pull of emotions seesawed inside him.

He could have what he wanted.

But at what cost?

Was she hoping her amateur attempts at psychology would result in some breakthrough? 'Do you think me spilling my guts to you will make me love you somehow? Is that what you're hoping for, Evie? Because it's probably just going to make me resent you.'

Goose-bumps broke out on Evie's arms at the conviction in his voice. She shrugged. 'Well, I guess that's a risk I'm prepared to take. This isn't about making you love me, Finn.'

'Isn't it? Isn't it?' he demanded, his emotions swinging again. 'So when we get to the end of it all and you know all the sordid details of my life, especially the bit where I don't know how to love anybody because I grew up without any and I still can't give you the love you want, you're still going to marry me? Is that right?'

Evie swallowed at the stark facts he hadn't bothered to sugar-coat. 'Yes. That's right. I just want to know you better. Is it so wrong to want to know the man you're married to? The father of your child?'

Finn hated that she was so bloody rational. They were talking about his life and there was nothing rational about that. He stood and glared down at her. 'So you want to know how it felt to have Isaac die in my arms?' he demanded. 'And my awful childhood with a mother who abandoned us? You want to know all my dirty little secrets?'

Evie nodded, knowing it was vital to stay calm in the face of his consternation. She understood she was asking a *very big thing* of him. It was only fair for him to rail against it for a while.

'Yes,' she said quietly. 'I don't want you to tell me everything in one night. We can build up to the hard stuff but…yes, I want to know it all.'

Finn felt lost as the storm raged inside him. He'd thought she'd back down in the face of his outrage but she wasn't even blinking. He felt angry and scared and panicked as he contemplated what she wanted.

Cornered.

And then Evie slipped her hand into his and it was like the storm suddenly calmed and he had an overwhelming urge to tell her everything. Completely unburden himself. 'Sit down,' she said. 'Eat your curry. It's getting cold.'

Finn sat, his heart beating like a bongo drum as he raked his hands through his hair. She picked up his plate and handed it to him and he took it, eating automatically as his thoughts whizzed around and collided with each other like atoms on speed.

'What do you want to know?' he asked eventually after half his meal had been demolished and he couldn't stand the silence any longer.

'It's okay,' Evie said. 'We don't have to talk tonight. Just...tell me about your day.'

He frowned. 'My day?'

Evie gave a half-laugh at his bewildered expression. 'Yes. Your day. You know, the stuff married people talk about all the time.'

It was awkward at first but they were soon chatting about safe hospital topics—his theatre list tomorrow, how Prince Khalid was going, some new whizz-bang monitor he wanted for the cath lab and the new salads on the canteen menu. And before Evie knew it, two hours had passed and Finn was on his second cup of coffee.

Even he looked surprised when he checked his watch as he drained the dregs from his mug. 'I guess I'd better get going,' he said, looking at her, curiously not wanting to leave.

Evie nodded. It would be the easiest thing in the world to ask him to stay. He'd actually been acting like a human being for once and he looked tired and stubbly and masculine and it had been so long that she wanted to reach across the gap and sink into his arms. But she didn't want to mess with what she was trying to establish now.

Sex would just distract them.

Suddenly the baby gave a swift kick that stole her breath and she gasped involuntarily and soothed her hand over the action.

Finn followed the intimate action, struck by the notion that he'd put the baby inside her. That it was his son, his flesh and blood that blossomed in her belly. 'Baby awake?' he said, feeling awkward again.

Evie looked up, a grimace on her face, which died quickly. Finn was staring at her belly, or rather at the circular motion of her palm, and he seemed so alone and isolated, so untouchable, *so Finn*, way over the other side of the cushion, that it almost tore her breath from her lungs.

'Do you…?' She hesitated, unsure of how to broach the subject. 'Would you like to feel him moving?' she asked.

Finn mentally recoiled from her quiet suggestion even as his fingers tingled at the possibility. His pulse kicked up a notch. His breath thickened in his throat.

Lay his hands on her? Feel his son moving inside her?

He was used to touching women. Used to touching this woman. But as a prelude to something else. Not like this. Not in a way that bound them beyond just a physical need for release.

He would know his son soon enough. He didn't need to feel his presence to understand his responsibilities.

'Ah, no,' he said, standing, gathering his jacket and his tie and taking a pace back for good measure. 'I'm good.'

Evie tried not to take his rejection personally. They'd taken a big step tonight—she didn't want to scare him away by going all militant mummy on him. 'That's fine,' she said, plastering a smile on her face as she also stood.

They looked at each other, Finn avoiding her belly, Evie fixing on his collar. Finn cursed the sudden uncomfortable silence. The night had gone well—considering.

He cast around for something to say. It seemed only fair, given that he'd been the one to ruin the atmosphere. 'Do you want to have dinner with me tomorrow night?'

Evie blinked. She suddenly felt like a teenager being asked on her first date. 'Ah…yes.'

He nodded. 'I'll pick you up at seven.'

And that set the pattern for the next couple of weeks. Going out or staying in, keeping things light, getting used to just being together without arguing or tearing each other's clothes off. One night Evie pushed a little and asked Finn about his life as a trauma surgeon in the army, and for the longest moment as he hesitated she thought he was going to shut her down, but he didn't and she found herself asking a bit more about it each night. About the places he'd been and the people he'd met.

He was more close-lipped about the specifics, about the horrors he must have seen, but each time he gave away a little more and a little more, even mentioning Isaac's name a couple of times before he realised and then stopped awkwardly and changed the subject.

But for every backward step Evie felt as if they were inching forward and they had plenty of time. She was determined not to push him too far too fast.

Evie was almost twenty-eight weeks when Finn called one night to say he'd been delayed at the hospital and would miss their restaurant booking. 'How does a spot of telly and a takeaway sound?'

Like an old married couple, she almost said, but, already exhausted from her own full-on shift, she readily agreed.

'I could be a while yet,' he warned.

'Whenever you get here will be fine,' she assured him. She took great delight in kicking off her pregnancy jeans, which she hated, and her bra, which felt like a straitjacket around breasts that seemed to get bigger by the day, and getting into her sloppy pyjamas. The shirt had a tendency to fall off her shoulder and the legs were loose and light. One day soon it wasn't going to meet in the middle but for the moment the ensemble was holding its own.

That was one of the advantages of their unconventional relationship. There was no need to dress to impress. The man had already seen everything she had. She could sloth around in her daggy pyjamas with no bra and no real shape and he was prepared to marry her anyway.

Besides, she didn't think he found her pregnant body much of a turn-on. He'd studiously avoided looking, touching or getting too near her belly. He didn't refer to it, he never remarked about how big she was getting or comment when she rubbed it.

She knew that was partly to do with his issues but she had to face facts—she'd put on some weight, her breasts had doubled in size and her belly had well and truly popped out.

Hardly a sex kitten.

So there seemed very little point making an effort and there was something very comforting about a man

who was a sure thing so she threw herself down in front
of the telly, her feet up on the coffee table, and waited.

It was nine o'clock when Finn finally knocked and Evie
was almost asleep on the couch, but her belly rumbled
as she admitted him and she realised she was ravenous. For food and for him. There was something very
sexy about the total disregard with which Finn wore a
suit. The way he never bothered to do up the jacket so
it flapped open all the time or how he couldn't care less
about doing up the collar buttons on his shirt and how
his tie was always just a little skew. The whole look
said, I'd much rather be in scrubs.

Which pretty much summed him up.

He'd brought beer and pizza and they ate it out of
the box while he told her about the emergency thoracot-
omy he'd had to perform on an MVA that had come in
after her shift had ended and they watched TV re-runs.

Finn shook his head as Evie laughed at some ridiculous antic. 'I can't believe we're watching this.'

'Hey, I love this show,' Evie protested. 'The nanny
used to let us watch it if Lexi and I had done our homework.'

'What about Bella? Didn't she watch it?'

'Of course, but none of them made Bella do anything
because of her CF.'

'Poor Bella,' he mused. 'How did she feel about
that?'

Evie opened her mouth to give him a flippant reply
but it suddenly struck her that Finn was asking *her*
about *her* life, seemed interested in *her* life. After two
weeks of gently pushing his boundaries back with a
feather, he was actually taking an interest in her past.

It was beyond thrilling. She smiled at him. 'She played on it for all she was worth.'

An hour later, with Evie having fallen asleep on his shoulder and snuggled into his side, Finn decided it was time to leave. His arm was numb, which was the stuff his nightmares were made of, and frankly with a large expanse of her cleavage exposed to his view she was just too tempting.

He'd tried not to notice how her body had burgeoned over the last weeks. Tried to concentrate on her, on sticking to his side of the bargain, but her athletic body was developing some fascinating curves, which he'd need to be blind not to notice, given how much time they were spending together.

It was taking all his self-control not to reach for her. To remember she was pregnant. As her bump was getting bigger, it shouldn't have been that difficult but here, now, with her all warm and cosy and smelling fresh and soapy with her hair all loose and her shirt half falling off, exposing the creamy rise of most of one breast and the light from the TV flickering over her skin, it was very difficult.

Finn liked sex. And he was good at it. Even when he'd been practically crippled with pain and numbness in his arm, he'd been good at it.

He and Evie were especially good at it. He reached a plane with her that he'd never reached with anyone else. There'd always been something more than physical. Kind of like what they'd been sharing these last few weeks.

But she was pregnant and they were trying to build a relationship beyond what they already had so making a move on her right now, when things were going so well, was just plain stupid.

He tried to slowly ease away from her but she shifted and murmured and seemed to cling to him even more firmly, pushing her soft breasts into his side.

He prayed for patience, or deliverance.

Whichever came first.

'Evie,' he whispered, and shook her gently, trying really hard not to watch everything jiggling nicely. 'Evie.'

She stirred a little and murmured sleepily. 'Hmm?'

'I'm going to go,' he whispered, trying to ease away again.

Evie dragged herself back from the dark abyss of sleep towards the lure of Finn's whisper. Her eyes fluttered open and her gaze slowly fixed on his face as awareness filtered in. She'd crashed on his shoulder and was smooshed up against him like some crazy stalker.

She removed her hand from his biceps and sat back a little, snuggling her head against the couch instead of his shoulder. She gave him a sleepy, apologetic smile. 'Sorry,' she murmured. 'I'm perpetually tired these days.'

Finn felt the low note of her voice hum along his veins like a tuning fork. 'It's fine,' he said, also keeping his voice low and his gaze firmly trained on her face and not the view straight down her loose top.

'Thanks for the pizza.' She rubbed her belly. 'It was delicious.' The action pulled her shirt down a little more and Evie was surprised to see Finn's eyes widen slightly.

Finn looked. He couldn't help himself. Her breasts were so lush and so...right there. He grimaced as he looked back at her. 'I should...definitely go,' he murmured.

Evie felt her insides dissolve to mush at the look of naked lust she saw heating his gaze to a blue flame. Her hormones, suddenly not sleepy, roared to life. 'You don't have to go,' she said.

Finn sucked in a breath at the shimmer in her soft hazel eyes. 'Evie…'

Evie leaned forward, her breasts tight, her internal muscles quivering in anticipation. 'Stay,' she murmured, and pressed her mouth lightly to his. The beer on his breath was sweet and heady.

Finn, everything north of his groin burning up, groaned the second her lips touched his, ploughing his hands into her hair and deepening the kiss. He pulled back, pressing his forehead against hers as he sucked in air. He felt his control unravelling, as the urge to push her back against the lounge and ravage her pounded through his system. 'I want this too much,' he said on a husky whisper.

'Good,' she breathed, picking up his hand, placing it on her breast and muttering, 'So do I,' as she sought his mouth again.

Finn held her back. 'Wait,' he muttered. 'Not here.' Too many times they'd had rushed sex, hastily parted clothes and a dash to the finish line. Not tonight. Not in her state. He stood and held out his hand. 'Your bedroom.'

Evie would have been perfectly happy with the lounge or the wall or the floor but she was touched by his consideration. But once they hit the bedroom he swept her up and she felt his control shatter on a guttural groan as he kissed her deep and hard.

And then they were pulling at each other's clothes. Shirts and buttons and pants and zippers seemed to melt away as their hands sought bare flesh. And then they were standing before each other naked, his erection jutting between them. His hands brushed against her belly and he pulled away from her, looking down at it, looking down at where his baby was growing. He reached for it again, slid his hands over its rounded contours then slowly up over her breasts, fuller than he remembered, the nipples bigger.

He looked back at her face. 'You're beautiful,' he whispered.

Evie felt beautiful when he looked at her like that. When he touched her so reverently. 'So are you,' she murmured, pressing a kiss to both flat broad pecs.

She trailed her fingers where her mouth had been, trekking up to his shoulders, tracing the scars on his right shoulder before moving down to his biceps. Then slowly shifting, moving around his body until she was standing behind him, her fingers trailing over his back, finding the shrapnel scars she'd only ever felt before, each one breaking her heart a little more.

'Did you get these the day Isaac died?' she asked, dropping a kiss on each one, rubbing her cheek against the puckered skin of his back.

Finn shut his eyes as her kisses soothed and healed. It reminded him of the time she'd tried to offer him solace after he'd lost a patient on the table and for a moment in the operating theatre's change room they'd stood like this, fully dressed, her cheek to his back, him drawing comfort from her simple gesture.

'Evie…'

'I hate it that you were hurt,' she whispered, her lips brushing his skin. 'That you had to go through all that. That your brother was taken from you.'

He opened his mouth to tell her it was a long time ago but it felt as raw right now as it had back then. 'There wasn't anything I could do,' he murmured.

Evie squeezed the tears from her eyes. She'd expected him to say nothing, to clam up. The anguish in his voice was unbearable. She kissed his back. 'I know,' she murmured. 'I know.'

And then she circled back to his front and kissed him with every ounce of passion and compassion she'd ever owned. And then they were on the bed, stroking each other, caressing, kissing and teasing as if they were getting acquainted all over again.

And when they could take it no more Finn looked down at Evie, stroked her belly and said, 'I don't want to hurt you…'

And she hushed him, rolling up on top of him and Finn had never seen anything more beautiful than Evie pregnant with his child, her hair loose, her full breasts bouncing, her belly proud as they moved in a rhythm that was slow and languorous and built to a crescendo that was so sweet Finn knew the sight of Evie flying on the crest of her orgasm would be forever burned into his retinas.

She collapsed on top of him, spent, and he didn't know how long they lay there but at some stage she shifted and he pulled her close, fitting her back against his chest, curling around her, his hand on her belly, kissing her neck, all to the hum of a phenomenal post-coital buzz.

And then he felt the baby move.

And the buzz evaporated.

He waited for something. A bolt of lightning or a beam of light, a trill of excitement—but he got nothing. Life, his own DNA, moved and shifted and grew right under his hand and he felt…nothing.

Panic rose in him. Shouldn't he feel something?

Other than protective? And an overwhelming urge to provide?

Shouldn't he feel love?

Evie, oftentimes oblivious to the baby's movements due to their frequency and this time due to a heavy sexual fog, only became aware of them as she felt Finn tensing around her. She felt him about to withdraw and clamped his hand against her.

'It's okay,' she whispered. 'It's just the baby moving.'

But it wasn't okay and Finn pulled his hand away, eased back from her, rolled up, sat on the side of the bed, cradling his head in his hands.

Evie turned to look at his back, the scars affecting her as deeply as they had just moments ago. She scooted over to where he sat. Her fingers automatically soothed the raised marks and he flinched but didn't pull away, and she kissed each one again as she had earlier. 'What is it Finn? What are you worried about?'

Finn shut his eyes. He wanted to push her away but her gentleness was his undoing. 'Something died in me the day I got these scars, Evie. The day Isaac died. I don't think I'm capable of love.'

He heard her start to protest and forced himself to open his eyes, forced his legs to work as he broke away to stand and look down at her, gloriously naked, her belly full of his baby.

'I'm worried I'm not going to love him.'

Evie smiled at him gently. 'Of course you will. That's what parents do.'

Finn shook his head and the sadness in his eyes cut her even deeper than his scars had.

'Not all of them, Evie.'

CHAPTER EIGHT

EVIE DRAGGED HERSELF through the next few days. She hadn't seen Finn since he'd picked up his clothes and left the other night and there was a small part of her that was beginning to despair that she might never be able to reach him.

But after three punishing day shifts in a row she was too exhausted to care when she crawled into bed at eight-thirty and turned off the bedside lamp. Her feet ached, her back ached and she wanted to shut her eyes and sleep for a week.

She'd worry about Finn tomorrow.

Except that wasn't to be.

Evie woke from a deep, dark sleep with a start several hours later, a feeling of dread pushing against her chest. Her heart was racing. Something was wrong but for a moment she couldn't figure out what.

As she lay in the dark, the luminous figures on the clock telling her it was two-thirty a.m., she slowly became aware of a feeling of wetness. She reached down, her hand meeting a warm, wet puddle. Had she wet herself?

Before she could apply any logical thought process, a spasm that caused her to cry out and clutch at her belly, pulsed through her deep and low.

Was she bleeding?

The pain eased and panic drove her into a sitting position as she kicked off the sheet and reached for the light, snapping it on. The bed was saturated, clear liquid soaking into the sheets and mattress, her wet pyjama pants clinging to her legs.

Her pulse hammered madly at her temples as she tried to think.

Clear. Not blood. And a lot of it.

Not urine. Too much. She hadn't the bladder capacity for more than a thimbleful for what seemed for ever.

Another pain ripped through her and she gasped as it tore her breath away and she suddenly realised it was amniotic fluid in the bed.

Her membranes had ruptured.

And she was in labour.

The spasm held her in its grip for what seemed an age and Evie failed miserably at doing all the things she knew you were supposed to do during a contraction—stay calm, breathe deeply—by intermittently crying and then holding her breath to try and stop herself from crying.

She collapsed on her side, reaching for the phone on the bedside table as soon as she was able, quickly stabbing Finn's number into the touchpad. It rang in her ear and she hoped like crazy that he had the same special powers that every other doctor who spent half of their lives on call possessed—the ability to wake to a ringing phone in a nanosecond.

He picked up on the third ring but she didn't give him a chance to utter a greeting. 'Finn!' she sobbed. 'It's Evie. My membranes have ruptured. I'm contracting.' As if to prove her point the next contraction came and she almost choked as she doubled up, trying to talk and gasp and groan all at the same time. 'The baby… is coming…now!'

'I'll be there in one minute.'

But she didn't hear him as the phone slipped from her fingers and she curled in a ball, rocking and crying as the uterine spasm grabbed hold and squeezed so tight Evie felt like she was going to split open.

It was too early. The baby would be too small. She couldn't do this. She wasn't ready. The baby wasn't ready.

She heard Finn belting on her door a minute later and she cried out to him but the contractions were coming one on top of the other, paralysing her. She just couldn't get up and open it. She was conscious of a loud crash and Finn calling out her name, his voice getting closer and closer, and she cried out to him again and suddenly he was stalking into her bedroom.

Finn was shocked at the sight that confronted him. Evie—strong, competent, assured Evie—curled up in a ball on the bed, her pyjama pants soaking, her face and eyes red from crying, a look of sheer panic on her face.

He threw himself down beside her. 'Evie!'

'Finn,' Evie sobbed clutching at his shirtsleeve, her hand shaking. 'Help me,' she begged. 'It's too early. Don't let our baby die.'

The words chilled him, so similar to the words Isaac had used as he'd reached out a bloodied hand to Finn.

Finn! Finn! Help me. Don't let me die.

Words that had haunted him for a decade. The promise that he'd given haunting him for just as long. One he hadn't been able to keep in the middle of hell, injured as he'd been and with precious medical help too far away.

But he could make a promise right here and now that he could keep. Last time he'd been powerless to help.

But not this time.

'I won't,' he promised. 'I won't.' He was damned if he was going to let down another person he cared about.

He stood and dragged the light summer blanket that had fallen off the end of Evie's bed away from the mattress and wrapped it around her then scooped her up as she moaned in pain and sobbed her heart out.

There was no point in ringing an ambulance—he could be there in three minutes at this hour of night.

He strode out the door he'd damaged trying to get in and pulled it shut behind him—he'd get the lock fixed later. The lift arrived within seconds and a minute later she was ensconced in his car and he was driving out of the garage. He dialled the emergency department and got the triage nurse.

'This is Finn Kennedy. I'm three minutes out with Evie Lockheart, who has gone into premature labour at twenty-eight weeks. I need the neonatal resus team there stat.'

He hung up and dialled another number, zoning Evie's anguish out, doing what he had to do, drumming his fingers on the steering-wheel as he sped through a deserted red light.

The phone was picked up. 'Marco? It's Finn Kennedy. Evie's gone into labour. I'm two minutes out from the hospital. The baby is coming now.'

Whether it was that particular note of urgency one doctor recognised in another or the background noise of Evie's distress, Finn wasn't sure, but Marco's 'I'll be there in ten' was all he needed to hear before he hung up.

He glanced at Evie and reached for her hand. 'Everything's ready. The neonatal team will be there and Marco's on his way. We're a minute out.' He squeezed her hand. 'Hold on, okay?'

Evie squeezed back as contractions battered her body. She knew she was a snivelling mess, she knew she shouldn't be, that she should be calm and rational and confident in modern medicine and the stats on premmie births, but fear pounded through every cell, rendering her incapable of reason.

Right now she was a mother. And she was terrified.

Finn screeched into the ambulance bay fifty-five seconds later. Mia and Luca were there with two nurses and a gurney, and they had a hysterical Evie inside in a cubicle within a minute. The neonatal team was already there, a high-tech cot with its warming lamps on ready to accept the baby, and Finn suddenly felt superfluous as the team went into action around him.

He felt lost. Outside his body, looking down. Usually in an emergency situation in a hospital setting *he* was the one in control. But not now. Right now he could do nothing but just stand around helplessly and watch.

Just like with Isaac.

'Finn!'

Evie's wretched wail as she looked around for him brought him back to the present, to the trilling of alarms, to the hive of activity.

'I'm here,' he said, stepping closer, claiming a position near her head, reaching for her searching hand. They weren't in the dirt in the middle of a battle zone and she wasn't dying. They were at Sydney Harbour

Hospital with as good a medical team around them as anywhere in the world and she wasn't dying. 'I'm right here.'

The curtain snapped back and Marco entered, and Finn knew everything was going to be fine. 'Well, Evie,' Marco said in that accented way of his, 'this is unexpected but don't worry, you are in very good hands.'

Evie was grateful Marco was there but the feeling was swept away by a sudden overwhelming urge to push. She half sat forward, dislodging two monitoring electrodes and causing a cacophony of alarms to go off. 'I need to push,' she said, the noise escalating her panic to full-scale terror.

Marco nodded. 'Don't push, Evie,' he said calmly as he snapped on a pair of gloves. 'Pant. Let me just check you.'

Evie gritted her teeth. 'I…can't…' she groaned as her abdomen contracted of its own accord.

Finn leaned in close to her ear, kissed her temple and said, 'Yes, you can, Evie. Yes you can. Here, do it with me,' he said, as he panted.

Evie squeezed his hand harder, fighting against the dictates of her body, trying hard to pant and be productive and not let the panic win.

'Okay, the baby is crowning,' Marco said.

'No,' Evie pleaded. 'No, no, no.' She turned to Finn, clutching their joined hands to her chest. 'It's too soon, he's too small.'

'And he's in the best place,' Finn said, hoping it was the right thing to say, the thing she needed to hear. He wished he could take the fear and anguish from her eyes. That he could take her physical pain and bear it for her. 'And we're all going to fight for him.'

'Okay Evie, let's meet your son,' Marco said.

Evie cried and shook her head, still trying to stop it, to hold inside her the precious baby who needed more time, but the urge coming over her again couldn't be denied and although she didn't assist, she couldn't fight it either, and because the baby was so small he slipped out into Marco's waiting hands in one smooth movement.

'Got him!' Marco exclaimed, as he quickly clamped and cut the cord and passed the still newborn into the warmed sterile dressing towel held by the neonatologist.

'He's a good size,' Marco said, looking up at Evie.

Finn and Evie only vaguely heard him as they both held their breath, straining to hear a little cry through the rush and hurry around them.

'He's not crying,' Evie murmured.

Finn kissed her forehead as the suction was turned on. 'Give it a sec.'

But there was still no gurgling first baby cry. No annoyed, indignant wail at having a plastic tube shoved up its nose. They could hear terms like *bradycardic* and *low sats* and *starting compressions* and *get an IV* and *need to tube him* and Evie turned her face into Finn's shoulder and cried, quietly this time, as a scenario she'd been part of on many occasions played out.

Only this time it wasn't some anonymous person off the street—it was happening to her.

'He's going to be fine,' Finn said, his head close to hers. 'He's going to be fine.'

If he said it enough times, it might just be true.

Then he heard *I'm in* and he looked up as the tone of the sats monitor changed. *Sats improving. Heart rate picking up.*

He kissed Evie on the head. 'They've tubed him,' he whispered. 'He's improving.'

Evie looked up, the normal sound of the sats monitor like music to her ears. She turned her head towards the flurry of activity around the cot. 'How's he doing?' he asked.

The neonatologist turned around. 'He was a little flat. He needed some help with his breathing—not unusual at twenty-eight weeks. Hopefully we can get him straight on to CPAP. We'll put in an umbi line and given him some steroids down the ETT. We'll take him up to the unit now, it's the best place for him.'

Evie nodded vigorously. 'Of course, go, take him,' she urged. She wanted him in the best place, with the best people looking after him, but she couldn't deny how bereft she felt. She'd given birth to him but she hadn't even touched her little boy yet or seen his face.

Her arms ached to hold him. To be near him right now.

She turned to Finn. 'Go with them,' she said.

Finn frowned. 'What? No Evie, he's in good hands, I'll stay with you until you're settled upstairs and then I'll go and check on him.'

Evie, feeling strong now, dashed at the moisture clinging to her cheeks. 'I don't want him up there by himself, Finn.'

'He's going to be surrounded by people,' Finn said gently.

'No.' She shook her head vehemently. 'Not people who love him. That is our son up there and I want him to know that every second of every day we're right beside him. Go, please, please go. If you don't, Finn, I swear to God I will, placenta delivered or not.'

Finn caught the eye of Marco, who indicated with a quick flick of his head to hop to it. But he was torn. He wanted to be with his son, but he didn't want to abandon Evie either.

Evie grabbed his sleeve. 'I'm going to be fine,' she said. 'I'm sorry, I know I've been a mess tonight but I'm fine now. And I need you to do this. Promise me you'll stay with him until I can get there.'

Finn blinked at the zealous glow in Evie's eyes that turned them from soft hazel to a supernatural hue. He nodded, knowing it was another promise he could keep. 'I promise,' he murmured. 'But don't be long.'

Evie gave a half-laugh. 'I'll try. Now go!' she urged as the cot and the team headed out of the cubicle.

Finn stopped by Marco, who was pulling gently on the umbilical cord to deliver the placenta. 'I have my mobile. Call me as soon as you're done here.'

Marco nodded. *'Assolutamente.'*

Five hours later Ava strode into the isolation room they'd put little baby Lockheart in because there were some perks to being on staff and because they were quiet enough at the moment to allow it. Not that it was exactly isolated—large windows on three sides kept it fully visible to the entire unit.

She smiled at the nurse making notes on a computer console before spying Finn sitting in a chair beside the open cot, valiantly trying to keep his eyes open, his head bobbing up and down as he intermittently lost the battle before regaining control.

'Finn,' she said bending down to push her face closer to him when he didn't seem to register her presence.

He looked as if he'd been pulled through a hedge

backwards. His jeans had a stain down the front and his shirt looked like it had been crumpled in a ball in the corner for a week. His stubbly look was bordering on haggard. His feet were bare.

Finn shook his head as his name was called again and the figure in front of him came into focus. 'Ava.'

She pushed a takeaway coffee towards him. 'You specialise in looking like hell, don't you?'

He gave a half-smile, accepting her offering gratefully. 'Only for you.'

Ava looked at the cot, seeing more tubes than baby. 'Big night, I hear.'

Finn nodded. He stood and looked down at his son, who had rapidly improved in just a few hours and was now only on CPAP via the ventilator to lightly support his own breathing rather than the machine doing the breathing for him.

'This is just the half of it. Evie needed a manual removal of her placenta then part of it was left behind so she had to have a D and C as well. She only got back to her room at six.' He still felt sick thinking about the fist that had squeezed a handful of his gut when Marco had come to tell him the news personally.

Ava nodded. 'I know. I've just come from there.'

Finn looked up, eager for firsthand news of her. 'You have? How's she going?'

'She's sleeping. Bella's with her.'

Finn nodded. He had called Bella a couple of hours ago because he didn't want Evie to be alone. Lexi had been his first instinct but she was also dealing with a newborn and he figured she needed the sleep more. Bella had popped in briefly to see the baby, taken a picture, then gone to her sister.

'Evie made me promise not to leave him until she got here.'

Ava smiled. 'Of course she did. She's a mum now. And what about you? How are you feeling now he's here and it's all a little more real?'

Finn shook his head. 'More like surreal.' He looked down at his tiny son, just over one kilo, everything in miniature but all still in perfect working order. His chest rose and fell robustly despite his little bird-like ribcage and his pulse oximeter bleeped away steadily in the background, picking up the strong, sure beating of his heart.

'I'm scared. Worried. Petrified.'

'But he's doing well, yes?'

Finn nodded. 'But I keep thinking about all the possibilities. Immature lungs. Intracranial haemorrhages. Infection. Jaundice. Cardiac complications. I can't breathe when I think of all the things that can go wrong.'

'Well, that's one of the hazards of knowing just a little too much, I guess. But this little tyke is probably stronger than you think. He's a tough guy, just like his daddy.'

Finn felt his heart contract and then expand so much it felt like it was filling his chest, the cold bands that had clamped around it the day Isaac had died shattering into a thousand pieces. He gazed at his son. 'I love him more than I thought it possible to love anything.'

Ava smiled. 'Of course, you're a dad now.'

Three hours later Finn was watching his son take his first breaths off the ventilator. He'd done so well the team had extubated him and popped on some high-flow humidified nasal prongs. He'd fussed at first, his little hoarse squawk pinging Finn's protective strings, but with a couple of sleepy blinks he'd settled and was, once again, getting on with the business of breathing unassisted.

Finn was watching his son through the open cot's glass side panel when he heard some squeaking behind him and turned around to find Bella pushing her sister into the room in a wheelchair.

'Evie?' Finn stood, shocked by her pallor, covering the two steps separating them quickly, sinking to his knees in front of the wheelchair. She had dark rings under her eyes and her lips were dry. 'Are you okay? I don't think you should be out of bed.'

'She shouldn't be,' Bella agreed. 'But she threatened to pull her drip out and make a run for it if I didn't bring her.'

'I'm fine,' Evie dismissed. Nothing else mattered to her right now more than seeing her baby. The little boy who'd been impatient to make his entry into the world.

He'd been the first thing on her mind when she'd woken from her anaesthetic and after letting weariness, exhaustion and well-intentioned people fob her off for the last few hours, she'd made her stand.

'Push me closer, Bells,' Evie demanded, bouncing in her seat a little, trying to get a better view. If she'd thought she could walk and not faint, she'd have been by his side already.

Finn stood. 'Here. Let me.'

Bella stepped back. 'I'll give you two some privacy,' she said. 'Ring me, Finn, when Evie's ready to go back and I can take her, or I can sit with the baby for a while if you like so you can stretch your legs.'

Finn nodded his thanks and pushed Evie over to the cot side. 'Here he is,' he murmured. 'Master Impatient.'

Evie felt tears well in her eyes, overwhelmed by the fragile little human being they'd created dwarfed by the medical technology around him. He was wearing the tiniest disposable nappy Evie had ever seen and a little blue beanie. He looked like a doll and the mother in her wanted to scoop him up, clutch him to her breast, slay anyone who dared come near him, but the doctor knew he was better off right where he was for now.

She flattened her palm against the glass, too low in the chair to be able to reach in and too sore and weak to be able to stand but feeling the strength of their connection anyway. Their unbreakable bond.

'Hello, baby, I'm your mummy,' she whispered.

And she listened as Finn pulled up a chair beside her and recounted what had happened since they'd left her in the department. About how their son had improved in leaps and bounds and how incredibly stable his blood gases and body temp and sugar levels had been.

'He's done everything right, Evie.' Finn placed a hand on her knee. 'He's a real little fighter.'

Evie nodded, tears blurring her vision. 'Of course,' she said, placing a hand over his and giving him a squeeze. She looked at him. 'He's just like his daddy.'

Finn's heart almost broke at the shimmer of tears in her eyes. He never wanted her to hurt again. He'd watch her go through hell last night and then she'd gone through even more without him, and he didn't want to ever be away from her again. He wanted to wrap them both up and love them for ever.

Finn turned his hand over and intertwined their

fingers. 'According to your father, he has the Lockheart brow.'

Evie laughed. 'My father's been?'

Finn nodded. 'He and your mother called in briefly earlier. She agreed.'

'My mother?' They'd been making some inroads to their relationship in the last months since Bella had received her new lungs but Evie knew there was still a long way to go.

'Well, they're both wrong,' she said, gazing at her son's tiny face. Even all wizened, she could see the mark of Kennedy genes everywhere. 'He has *your* brow. *And* your chin. *And* your nose. I don't know about those fabulous cheekbones, though…'

Finn stared at them as he'd been doing for the last eight hours, trying not to remember why they were so familiar. 'They're Isaac's,' he whispered, finally admitting it. 'According to Lydia, Isaac had cheekbones that belonged in Hollywood.'

Evie glanced at him. His voice was tinged with sadness and humour and regret. 'I'm sorry he never got to see his nephew,' she whispered, holding tight to his hand.

Finn nodded. 'So am I. He'd have been a great uncle.'

And for the first time in a long time he remembered the happy times he and Isaac had shared instead of how it had all ended, and he could smile. How Isaac had always managed to find a baby to cuddle or a toddler to give a piggy-back ride to, wherever they'd ended up.

The baby squirmed, making a mewling noise like a tiny kitten and waving his little fists, no bigger than gumballs, in the air, dislodging a chest electrode and tripping an alarm. Evie's gaze flew to the cot, her pulse spiking as a moment of fear gripped her, suddenly understanding how nerve-racking it must be for her patients to be in an unfamiliar environment with strange machines that made alarming noises.

'It's okay,' the nurse said, unconcerned, as she pushed the alarm silence button. 'Just lost a dot.'

She located the AWOL chest lead and replaced it back just below a collarbone that looked to Evie as spindly as a pipe cleaner. 'There we go, little darling,' the nurse crooned. 'All fixed.' She smiled at Finn and Evie. 'Is there a name yet? Because we can call him little darling for ever but he might get teased when he goes to school,' she joked.

Evie looked at Finn and then back at the nurse. 'We hadn't got that far,' she said helplessly, already feeling like she'd failed her tiny little son twice. Once for not being able to keep him inside where he'd desperately needed to stay for a good while longer and now not having a name to give to him.

'Well, there's no rush,' she murmured. 'But a wee little guy like this needs a warrior's name, I reckon.'

Evie couldn't agree more and as the nurse fussed over the lines in the cot she knew with sudden clarity what to call him. 'Isaac,' she said to the nurse. 'His name's Isaac.'

The nurse smiled. 'Isaac,' she repeated. 'Ooh, that's good. Strong. Noble.' She looked down at the tiny baby in her care and said, 'Welcome to the world, Isaac.'

Evie smiled through another spurt of tears as the nurse bustled away. She turned to face Finn. 'Is that okay with you?'

Finn's chest was so tight he thought it might just implode from the pressure. He was shocked to feel moisture stinging his eyes and a lump in his throat that barely allowed for the passage of air. He forced himself to look at her instead of turning away or blinking the tears back, like he'd done for so many years. He couldn't even remember the last time he'd allowed himself to cry. Not even as the life had ebbed from his brother's eyes had he broken down.

He'd just shut down. Gone numb.

And it had taken this woman and this tiny scrap of humanity to bring him back.

'I think that would be quite wonderful,' he whispered, his voice thick with emotion.

'But could you hear it every day, Finn?' she probed, her voice gentle. 'Would it make you sad every day?'

Finn shook his head. 'No. I've spent a decade of my life trying to forget what happened and all I've managed to do is erase all the good things as well. I think it's time I remembered them also.'

Evie nodded, squeezing her hand. It sounded like a damn fine plan to her. 'Do you think Lydia will mind?'

Finn smiled. 'I think she'd be delighted.'

'Good,' Evie murmured. 'Good. Isaac it is.'

They smiled at each other for a long moment then turned to gaze lovingly at their son. Finn slid a hand onto Evie's shoulder. 'I've been such an idiot,' he said as he watched Isaac's little puffy breaths kick his rib cage up and down.

'You were grieving,' Evie dismissed, also watching her son, trying to absorb every tiny detail about him.

'I don't mean that. I mean about what I said the other night. After we'd…'

'Oh,' Evie said, glancing at his profile. 'That.'

'All I have to do is look at him and I feel this incredible surge of love rise in me.' Finn didn't take his eyes off Isaac's face. 'And I don't even know where it comes from or that I even had it in me but I do know that it's deep and wide and unfathomable and if I live to be a hundred I'd never get to the bottom of it.'

He looked at Evie then and she was watching him so intently, and he needed her to know, to understand so she could never, ever doubt that he loved Isaac. 'I was so, so worried that I wouldn't, Evie. I was terrified. But it's like…it's just there. It's suddenly just there.'

Evie felt his relief and wonder and even though she'd never really doubted that he would feel this way about his own flesh in blood he'd been so bleak, so convinced the other night when he'd left that she'd felt her first prickle of unease.

She smiled at him. 'I know.'

'It's like a…miracle.' He laughed. 'This love is like a bloody miracle. It's so different from anything I've ever felt before.'

Evie smiled but it felt forced in comparison to his obvious high. She was ecstatic that he knew what she'd always known—that he'd take to fatherhood, revel in it even. But part of her wished a little of that miracle was coming her way.

That he'd look at her and talk about the miracle of the love he felt for her. A very different love from what he was talking about now.

Because while Isaac needed Finn's love, so did she. The kind of love that would fill her soul and warm her days.

A man's love for a woman.

'And you,' Finn said, shaking his head, in awe of what she'd been through. 'You are amazing. Incredible. What your body has done is truly awesome.' He looked at his son, so small but so perfect. 'Isaac and I are so lucky to have you and I'm going to spend the rest of my life taking care of you. Nothing…nothing will be too good for the mother of my child. I love you, Evie,' he said, watching Isaac. 'I couldn't have picked a more perfect mother if I'd tried.'

Evie's breath caught at the words she'd been waiting to hear ever since they'd met at that hospital function five years ago. And they felt so empty.

He was on his daddy high and she was the mother of his child swept up in the raw newness of him coming inside after a long cold winter.

Suddenly she felt overwhelmingly tired.

CHAPTER NINE

AN HOUR LATER, after Evie had expressed for the first time and they'd watch one mil of milk disappear down the gastric tube Finn had insisted that Evie go back to bed. She looked exhausted, the black rings around her eyes had increased, her shoulders had drooped and she was sleep staring at everything with long slow sleepy blinks.

He made a mental note to check her haemoglobin with Marco when he saw him later.

'What about you?' she protested. 'You've been up since two with no sleep.'

'Yes, but I haven't given birth or had an emergency operation. I'll catch some sleep tonight in my office if everything stays stable.' He'd spent many a night on the surprisingly comfortable couch.

It felt wrong to leave Isaac but Bella and Lexi had eagerly volunteered to keep vigil while he pushed Evie back to her room and he had to admit it felt good to be out, stretching his legs.

She was quiet on the trip and his concern for her condition ramped up to another level. 'Are you okay?' he asked as he pulled the wheelchair up beside her bed, crouching down in front of her. 'Have you got pain? Do you feel unwell?' He placed his palm on her forehead, checking for a temperature.

Evie shut her eyes, allowing herself to lean into his hand for a few seconds. 'I'm fine,' she said, avoiding his gaze as she opened her eyes again. 'Just tired.'

He frowned as she seemed to evade eye contact. It seemed more than that. 'You need to be rested and well for your milk production.'

Evie blinked. As a doctor, she understood what he was saying was correct. She'd told many a patient exactly that and she had the pamphlet in her hand to back it up. But it wasn't what she wanted to hear him say. She wanted him to hug her, rub her back and tell her she was beautiful.

Which, of course, he wouldn't, first because he was Finn and, second, she really wasn't beautiful, more classically interesting, and last she doubted she'd ever looked worse. Although she guessed it didn't really matter what you looked like when you'd stopped being a woman and become the milk supply line for a premmie baby.

'I see you're going to be the milk police,' she said, her voice brittle.

Finn chose his words carefully to her irritable response. There *was* something bugging her. 'Colostrum is vital for Isaac's immune system.'

Evie took a steadying breath as despair and animosity battled it out inside her. This was typical Finn in tunnel-vision medical mode. All about the facts.

'Yes, I know,' she said, scooting him aside so she could crawl onto her freshly made bed. She almost groaned out loud as the crisp white sheets melted against her skin like snowflakes and all her cells sighed in unison.

Finn stood up and watched as Evie's eyes fluttered shut. He had the distinct feeling she was trying to block him out. 'Evie…?'

He hesitated, not really knowing how to voice his concerns to a woman who was probably experiencing a hormone surge not unlike Chernobyl's meltdown. Even if he did love her.

'You seem…down…and you know PND can start very early post-partum and it's particularly high in mothers with premmies.'

Evie sighed. *There he went with the facts again.* 'Finn,' she said sharply, opening her eyes and piercing him with her cranky hazel gaze. 'I've just given birth to a twenty-eight-weeker who's in the NICU and I'm two floors away. I feel like an utter failure and my arms *literally* ache to hold him. Yes, I'm *down*. No, I *do not* have postnatal depression.'

Finn sat on the side of the bed. 'Oh, Evie…' He reached for her hand.

Evie really did not want to be pitied so she evaded his reach. 'Look, just go, will you, Finn? Go back to Isaac. I'm tired and not thinking straight. I'm sure I'll feel a lot better after a sleep.'

Finn opened his mouth to say something but Marco entered the room, greeting them in his usual jovial way. 'How are you feeling, Evie?'

'Tired,' Finn murmured.

Evie glared at him. 'A little tired, otherwise fine.'

'What's her haemoglobin, Marco?' Finn asked.

'Ten point nine,' Marco said, not having to consult the chart in his hands. 'She lost very little blood,' he assured Finn, before turning to Evie and asking a couple more questions. 'I think we take down that drip now and discharge you tomorrow morning if everything goes well overnight.'

Evie nodded, feeling ridiculously teary again at the thought of going home without Isaac. 'I won't be going far,' she said.

'Which makes me even more comfortable with discharging you.' Marco smiled.

They chatted for a while longer, talking about Isaac, and Marco smiling over his own little one's antics before he noticed Evie yawn. 'I better get on,' he said. 'I'll see you in the morning.'

Finn stood and shook his hand. 'Thanks, Marco. You were brilliant last night.'

'Yes,' Evie agreed. 'You were fabulous. I'll never forget how you came in when you weren't on call.'

Marco winked at her. 'Anything for Evie Lockheart.'

Finn rolled his eyes. 'I bet you say that to all your mothers.'

Evie shut her eyes as Marco chuckled and Finn once again relegated her to a role instead of a person. Would he ever see her as a woman again? Love her as a woman? Or would he always just love her because she was the mother of his child?

'But thanks,' Finn continued. 'Evie's right. I owe you.'

Marco chuckled. 'I hope that is something I never have to collect on. My cholesterol is good and there is no cardiac history in my family.'

'Well, how about I buy you a beer at Pete's as soon as Isaac is home instead?'

Marco nodded. 'It's a deal. Although let's make it a red wine instead—just to be sure.'

Marco left and Evie faked a yawn. She had the sudden urge to bury her head under the covers and not come out. Maybe Finn was right. Maybe she was going through those baby blues a little early.

'I'll go too,' he said, satisfied to see her already look a little less exhausted around her eyes, even if she did seem to still be avoiding eye contact. He sat on the side of the bed again. 'Ring me after you've had a sleep and I can come back and get you.'

Evie nodded, a lump in her throat at the tenderness in his voice. Then he leaned forward and pressed a chaste kiss on her forehead. He stood and said, 'I love you, Evie,' before walking out the door.

Evie let the tears come then. She wasn't sure what had been more heartbreaking, his throwaway line about loving her or the kiss currently air-drying on her forehead. His declaration of love—his second—was about as heartfelt as that kiss. Something he might bestow on an aged great-aunt with whiskers growing out of her chin.

Asexual. Perfunctory. Expected.

Was that what she had to look forward to now she was a *mother*? Some idealised figure who was a nurturer. And nothing else?

Finn was going to put her on some bloody pedestal and turn her into something holy and untouchable.

After a full night's sleep Evie was almost feeling human again at barely five a.m. as she crept down to the NICU by herself to visit with her little man and do some more expressing. Finn was there, still maintaining his vigil beside Isaac's incubator, and for a moment she just stood in the doorway, watching him watch their son.

Her heart squeezed painfully in her chest at the sight. She could feel Finn's love for Isaac rolling off him in waves, encompassing the cot and the tiny little scrap of humanity inside it as if he was the most precious child that had ever lived. The area around the cot practically glowed with the force field of Finn's love.

It was exactly what she'd wanted. And yet she was suddenly incredibly jealous.

Which was selfish, hateful and greedy.

And she had to let it go because their son needed her to concentrate on him and his needs and the long haul ahead. Not on any insecurities over Finn. And this morning at least she was feeling more in charge of herself to do just that.

She shuffled forward in her slippers and slid her hand onto Finn's shoulder. He turned and looked up at her and he looked so weary and sexy she plastered a smile on her face.

'Morning,' she murmured. 'How's our little warrior?'

Finn smiled back, hopping out of his chair for her to sit in. 'He's doing well. They've reduced his oxygen. He's coping.'

'Did you sleep?' she asked.

'No,' the nurse piped up.

'I dozed on and off,' Finn corrected her.

Evie looked up at him standing beside her. He looked like he hadn't slept in a hundred years—his lines had lines. 'You look exhausted,' she said.

'I'm fine.' Finn brushed his tiredness aside. '*You*, on the other hand, look much, much better.'

'I feel a hundred per cent better,' she admitted.

Finn squeezed her shoulder. He'd been worried about her yesterday but she looked like the old Evie and he felt one of his worries lift. 'Good.'

'In fact…' Evie stood, gently reaching out and stroking Isaac's closest arm, the warm fuzz covering it tickling her finger '…I'm going to go and express then I'm going to come back here and stay until Marco's round at eleven for my discharge and then I'm coming straight back. So I want you to go and catch up on some sleep.'

Finn looked at the determined set to Evie's chin and felt that protective part of him that had refused to let him leave Isaac's side relax as it recognised the strength of Evie's protective instinct. 'Okay. I'll go to my office and have a couple of hours.'

Evie shook her head. 'Finn, you need a shower, a decent meal and a proper bed. Go home. Rest properly.'

He shook his head. 'I can't leave you sitting here all day. Not so soon after your discharge. You need the rest more than I do.'

Yeah, yeah. The milk. But she let it go, refusing to dwell on something that was fact anyway.

'It's okay. Bella and Lexi will be in and out fussing around all day, making me go for walks and feeding me well. And seeing as your theatre cases have been reassigned this week, I'll let you take the night shift again.'

Finn laughed. 'Why, thank you.'

He hesitated. The offer was tempting. He'd been in the same clothes for almost thirty-six hours. And they hadn't been clean to begin with. If it hadn't been for Ava persuading Gladys to let her into his apartment, he probably still wouldn't have shoes. He'd used the toothpaste and toothbrush from the care pack he'd been given by one of the NICU nurses.

A shower and his own bed did sound mighty tempting.

He looked down at Isaac and felt torn. What if something went wrong while he was away? He'd been rock-steady stable but Isaac was in NICU for a reason.

'I promise I'll call immediately if anything happens,' Evie murmured, sensing his conflict and knowing it intimately. How much had she fretted during the hours she'd spent away from him?

'Okay,' he said, giving in to the dictates of his utterly drained body. 'Thanks.'

Finn was back at three o'clock. He'd eaten, showered, slept like a log for two hours longer than he'd planned and zipped quickly into town to do something he should have done weeks ago. Then he'd left his car back at Kirribilli Views and walked to the hospital. It was a nice day and it gave him a chance to think things through, to plan. He stopped in at the canteen on his way to the unit and bought two coffees and some snack supplies for later tonight.

'Hi, there,' he said, striding into Evie's room.

She looked up from changing Isaac's nappy. It was the first time she'd touched him properly and even though it was a thick, black, meconium bowel motion, she was vibrating with excitement. Perfectly functioning bowels were another cause for celebration.

'Poo!' she announced to Finn. 'Who'd have ever thought you could be so happy about a dirty nappy!'

Finn caught his breath. Her eyes were sparkling and she looked deliriously happy. He didn't understand why it had taken him so long to figure out he loved her when just thinking about her now made his heart grow bigger in his chest.

He laughed, understanding an excitement that might seem bizarre to others. 'That's our boy,' he said.

Lexi, who was also in the room, shook her head and pronounced them nuts.

Evie finished up and Finn hovered nearby, talking to his son, whose eyes fluttered open from time to time indignantly as his sleep was disturbed. When she was done he passed her the coffee, gave his to Lexi and they filled him in on the day, including the news that the oxygen had been reduced even further.

'He's a little marvel!' Lexi exclaimed.

Finn couldn't have agreed more and to see Evie with her eyes glittering and her skin glowing was a sight for sore eyes.

'You're just in time,' Evie said. 'I was about to go and express. You can entertain Lexi.'

Finn glanced up. 'Actually, would you mind going solo for a bit, Lex? I wouldn't mind having a chat with your sister.' He looked at Evie. 'If that's okay with you?'

Evie felt her breath catch a little at the intensity in his blue, blue gaze. She'd forgotten with all the madness of the last couple of days and a side whammy of maternal hormones how it could reach right inside her and stroke her.

Was she okay with him watching her express? It should have been an easy answer—it wasn't like he hadn't seen her naked before. They'd made Isaac together, for crying out loud. But she hesitated anyway. It was pretty damn obvious he'd already relegated her to mother status—surely that would only enhance his opinion more?

Lexi noticed her hesitation. 'Why don't you let the poor woman and her leaking breasts be, Finn Kennedy? I won't bite and after she's done I'll stick around so you can take Evie outside and talk without the slurp and suck of a breast pump serenading you.'

Finn looked at Evie. He could tell she was relived at her sister's intervention and he didn't know what that meant exactly. He'd felt on the same page with her during their getting to know each other weeks but due to the rather dramatic interruption of Isaac's early arrival he wasn't sure about anything any more.

He was, however, grateful for a little bit of sanity from Lexi. What had he been thinking? Breast-pump music was not the ambience he was after.

'Of course.' He smiled. 'Good plan.'

Forty-five minutes later Finn and Evie were ensconced in a booth at Pete's. He'd chosen it over the canteen for its relative quietness at this time of the day. Week-day hospital staff didn't tend to arrive until after six o'clock so they had plenty of time to be uninterrupted. Unlike the canteen, where they'd have been swamped with well-wishers, their conversation stifled.

And he could do without their private life being aired on the grapevine—for once.

'So I was thinking,' Finn said as he placed a sparkling water in a wine glass in front of her and a Coke in front of him, 'that you should move into the pent-house with me while we're getting the Lavender Bay house set up.'

Evie, who had chosen that moment to take a sip of

her drink, almost choked as she half-inhaled it in shock. She coughed and spluttered for a while, trying to rid the irritation of sparkling water from her trachea.

'Is it that shocking?' Finn joked as he waited for her to settle.

'Yes,' she rasped, clearing her throat and taking another sip of water.

Finn reached across the table and covered Evie's hands with his. 'It makes sense to me. We'll be getting married as soon as Isaac is home and as we both live in the same building anyway, it seems silly to keep two places going.'

Evie looked down at their joined hands as the very practical reasons for her moving in with him sank in. 'Right,' she murmured. She had to admit he made good sense even if it had been thought about in that logical way of Finn's.

But...where was the emotion?

The *I can't live without you one more day.* The *I love you, never leave my side.*

She drew her hands out from under his. 'Finn...I don't think this is something we should be worrying about at the moment. I just want to focus on Isaac. On what he needs.'

Finn felt her withdrawal reach deep inside him. He knew she was right, that Isaac had to come first, but they also had to look after themselves. There was no point being run down from stress and lack of sleep when Isaac finally came home.

Home.

The word resonated inside him and settled easily, warming him from the inside out instead of echoing around all the lonely places as it always had.

He had a home. And a family to share it with.

'You still need a base, Evie. A place to have a quick shower and change your clothes, lay your head for a few hours maybe, collect your mail…that kind of thing.'

She nodded. 'Fleeting visits, yes. But I plan to spend as much time on the unit with Isaac as I can without totally exhausting myself. I can't bear to think of him there all by himself, Finn.' She took a sip of water as she felt a thickening in her throat. 'There certainly won't be any time to be shifting apartments.'

Finn nodded. There was no point reminding her that Isaac wasn't alone because he knew exactly how she felt. It felt wrong being away from him, leaving him in the care of strangers—no matter how excellent or vital it was.

He nodded. 'Okay, fine, but…' He put his hand into his pocket and pulled out a burgundy velvet box. 'I want you to have this.'

He opened it to reveal the one-carat princess-cut diamond—a princess for a princess. It sparkled in Pete's downlights as he pushed it across the table to her. 'I realised that I hadn't given you one yet and that was remiss of me. I want you to have it, to wear, so everyone knows we're going to be a family.'

Evie was rather pleased she wasn't drinking anything when he put the box on the table or she might well have choked to death this time. Her pulse thundered through her ears as she picked it up. The ring was exquisite in a platinum antique setting.

'It's beautiful,' she whispered. It was the kind of ring she would have picked out herself and just for a moment she wanted to hold it and look at it and marvel. 'It must have cost you a fortune.'

Finn shook his head. 'No price is too high for the mother of my child.'

Evie felt a hysterical sob rising in her throat and swallowed it down hard. Everything she had inside her wanted to take the exquisite piece of jewellery and put it on her finger and never take it off.

To be Finn's wife.

But she knew if she did, if she compromised what she needed from him, she'd lose herself for ever. With more self-control than she'd known she possessed, she snapped the lid shut and passed it back to him, keeping her gaze firmly fixed on the bead of moisture running down her glass. 'I'm not going to marry you, Finn.'

Finn frowned as a prickle of unease scratched at his hopes and dreams and he was reminded of how she hadn't been able to look at him yesterday. 'What?'

Evie fiddled with the straw in her glass. 'I know I told you I would but…that was before all of this.'

Finn put his hand over top of hers, stilling its swishing of the straw. 'Look at me, Evie,' he said.

Evie fleetingly thought of telling him to go to hell but this was a conversation that they might be better having now so Finn knew she couldn't be waited out, persuaded or bullied. So she looked at him and tried to keep the hurt from her gaze.

'What's really going on here?' he asked.

Evie sighed at the brilliant, clueless man in front of her. What would Lexi or Bella say to him? 'You suck at proposing, Finn.'

Finn snorted. She was having some kind of female hissy fit because he hadn't gone down on bended knee? 'I'm sorry I've been a little busy to organise a flash mob and a blimp.'

Evie felt tears well in her eyes and for an awful second she thought she was going to cry. Right here in the middle of Pete's. Wouldn't that be great for the gossips? 'I don't need grand gestures, Finn,' she said quietly. 'Not a flash mob or a blimp or even a bloody house. But I *do* need to hear three little words.' She paused and cleared her throat of its wobble. 'I'm not marrying you because you don't love me.'

Finn frowned. That was the most preposterous thing he'd ever heard. 'Yes, I do. Of course I do. I've told you that.' He had, hadn't he? More than once.

'Sure,' Evie said bitterly. 'Suddenly the love is flooding in for Isaac so much it radiates out of you and you're dragging everything nearby with you like some bloody comet, and I've been swept up in it too.'

He shook his head. 'No, Evie, that's not right.'

'Isn't it?' she demanded in a loud, angry whisper, sitting forward in her chair. 'I'm the mother of your child—of course you love me, you have to. You've got me all set me up as this esteemed mother figure. As this revered nurturer. The provider of milk and changer of nappies.'

If Finn could have kicked his own butt he would have. 'Of course you mean more to me than that. I love *you*, Evie.'

Evie felt as if he'd struck her with the words, so obviously an afterthought. 'Then why in hell do I get a ring pushed across the table accompanied by a *This was remiss of me*. If you loved me, really loved me, as a woman, not just as the mother of your child, then you would have told me that. That's what men who love the women they propose to do. But you didn't. And do you know why?' she snarled, uncaring who might be overhearing their conversation, 'Because it never oc-curred to you. Because it's not the way you feel. Well, I'm sorry, Finn,' she said, standing up, not able to bear the look of total bewilderment on his face. 'I need more than that. I know that you had a terrible upbringing and you need a home and a family and you've got this whole fantasy going on around that, and I thought I could live with just that. But I can't. I won't.'

She sidestepped until she was out of the booth. 'Do me a favour, give me an hour with Isaac before you come back.'

And she whirled out of the pub before the first tear fell.

Lexi was alarmed when Evie arrived back with puffy eyes and insisted she'd ring her babysitter to stay lon-ger, but Evie sent her on her way, assuring her she was fine, just Finn being Finn on top of the worry and stress over Isaac.

By the time Finn arrived back she had herself under control and was determined to stay that way. He looked at her tentatively and despite how he kept breaking her heart, she felt sorry for him. Finn was a man who'd shut himself down emotionally to deal with a crappy life. Opening up like this couldn't be easy for him.

'Evie, can we please talk—?'

Her quick, sharp headshake cut him off. 'Listen to me,' she said, her voice low so the nurse wasn't privy to their conversation. 'I do not want to talk about what happened today until after Isaac is home and we know he's safe and well. For the moment, for the foreseeable future, he is the *only* thing that's important. *The only thing that we talk about.* The only thing we concentrate on. *Just Isaac.'*

In the time she'd had to herself, looking down at the precious little bundle that connected her to Finn, Evie had decided she wasn't going to snivel about what had just happened. She'd drawn a line in the sand and that was her decision, and until Isaac was well enough to come home she wasn't going to think, cry or argue about it again.

'Can I have a commitment from you that you'll do the same?'

Finn opened his mouth to protest but Evie was looking so fierce and sure, and after the bungled way he'd managed the whole ring thing he wasn't keen to alienate her further. By his calculations, if everything went well Isaac would probably be discharged in a month or so once he hit a gestational age of around thirty-two weeks or a certain weight.

He could wait a month.

Live by her edict for another four weeks.

But after that she'd better prepare herself. Because he intended to propose properly and leave her in absolutely no doubt of how much he loved her.

He nodded. 'Fine. But once Isaac is home, *we will be revisiting this, Evie.'*

Evie shivered at the steel in his tone and the flicker of blue flame in his eyes. 'Fine.'

Four days passed. Four days of tag-teaming, polite condition updates and stilted conversation. Evie taking the days, Finn the nights. Four days where Isaac continued to grow stronger and put on weight and have most of his lines removed and Evie was finally allowed to have her first kangaroo cuddle with him.

As she sat in the low comfy chair beside the cot, a squirmy, squeaky Isaac held upright against her naked chest, both of them wrapped up tight in a warm blanket, Evie wished Finn was there. The nurse took a picture but it wasn't quite the same thing. This was the kind of moment that parents should share, watching their tiny premmie baby snuffling and miraculously rooting around for a nipple, even finding it and trying to suckle, no matter how weakly.

She felt teary but determinedly pushed them away. She'd been strong and true to her promise not to dwell on it—stress and exhaustion helping—and she wouldn't do it now, not during this simply amazing moment when she and her baby bonded, skin on skin.

On the fifth morning Evie woke early and couldn't go back to sleep, trying to decide if Finn would mind having his time cut short. Or at least sharing a bit of it with her. It made sense to go in—all she was doing was lying there thinking about Isaac anyway and she could feel her breasts were full.

May as well head to the hospital and pump.

Evie was being buzzed in through the main entry doors half an hour later. She noticed a group of nurses standing off to one side of the station and frowned. She smiled at them as she went past and they smiled back, indicating for her to hush and stay with them for a moment. Bemused, Evie turned to see what had them so agog. Her smile slipped as she realised they were watching Finn kangaroo-cuddling with Isaac through the isolation room's windows.

It was a touching, tender moment, stealing her breath and rendering her temporarily paralysed.

Her two darling boys.

'The great Finn Kennedy,' one nurse whispered.

'Who'd have thunk?' said another.

Evie left them to their amazement. Not that she could blame them. She doubted anyone, Finn included, would have ever thought he could be brought to his knees by a tiny baby.

She stood in the doorway for a moment, just admiring them from the back. Finn sitting in the low chair next to the cot, obviously shirtless if the bare shoulder blade just visible through the folds of the blanket was any indication, skin on skin with his son.

She swallowed hard against the lump in her throat, preparing to enter. But then she realised that Finn was talking quietly to Isaac and she hung back, not wanting to intrude on a father-son moment.

'There we are,' Finn said, 'I think we've got you comfortable now you've realised no matter how much you look for it, I'm just not your mummy. She'll be along later. She won't really talk to me because she's mad at me and she'll only have eyes for you anyway.'

Evie's ears pricked up at the conversation and she leaned in a little.

'My fault, I'm afraid, little mate. Totally stuffed everything up there. Take it from me, women may be complicated but in the end all they really want is for you to love them. I've never been good at that stuff, couldn't even tell your uncle Isaac I loved him until he was dying in my arms. You're a lot like him and I promise I'm going to tell you every day. And hopefully I'll get a chance to tell your mum as well. Trust me on this, matey, never make *I love you* sound like an afterthought. Stupid, stupid, stupid.'

Evie held her breath.

'And now she thinks I only love her because she's part of some package deal with you. That I only see her as *your* mother. And I can't tell her she's wrong, that's she's the sexiest, smartest woman I've ever met and I'm crazy about her because I promised her I wouldn't talk about it until you were home. So you need to hurry up and get home, you hear?'

Evie blinked back a threatening tear as she listened unashamedly now.

'Because the truth is I don't want to live a day of my life without her in it. I love you, little guy, and the same applies to you, but it's different with your mother. I want to hold her and touch her and kiss her and make love with her and do all those things that people in love do. You probably won't ever realise this because she's your mum, but she's one sexy lady.'

Evie blushed at the rumble in Finn's voice.

'And of course I love her because she's your mother and there are things she can give you that I can't, but I love her also because she can give *me* things that you can't—a different kind of love. And I never thought I'd hear myself say this but I need that. And I want to give her the love that you can't. I want to love her like a woman deserves to be loved. And I never want to stop.'

Evie let the tears come this time. She didn't try to stop them. She pushed off the doorframe and was at his side in five seconds. Bending her head and kissing him two seconds after that.

'Why,' she demanded face wet, eyes glistening, 'didn't you say those things in Pete's?'

Finn looked into her beautiful, interesting face made even more so by two wet tear tracks, his heart thudding in his chest. 'Because I'm emotionally stunted and incredibly stupid.'

She laughed and kissed him again. 'Do you really mean all those things? About loving me as a woman, not just as Isaac's mother?'

Finn smiled. 'Of course. You wouldn't let me tell you so I figured I'd tell him.'

Evie crouched beside him, peeking inside the blanket at Isaac snuggled up in a little ball against Finn's chest. 'I'm glad you did.'

'So am I,' Finn murmured, looking down into her face. 'I'm just sorry I got it so wrong for so long, Evie. I *do* love you. Just as you are. Evie Lockheart. No one's mother or sister or doctor. Just you. You helped me love again, feel again, and I need you in my life. All of you.'

Evie nodded, two more tears joining the others. 'And I love you.'

Finn dropped a kiss on her mouth and it was the sweetest thing Evie had ever known.

'Don't think you're off the hook for the flash mob and the blimp, though,' she warned as they broke apart.

Finn grinned. 'I'll consider myself on notice.'

And then a tiny little snuffly sneeze came from under the covers and they smiled at each other, brimming with love.

EPILOGUE

EVIE LOOKED UP from watching Isaac happily crawling around the back yard to see her husband approaching with a massive wrapped box.

Finn grimaced as he set the heavy box on the ground. 'Delivery for the birthday boy.'

Isaac turned at the interesting new arrival and crawled their way, gurgling happily. It was hard to believe a year had passed since the frantic night of his birth and while the doctors still corrected his age to nine months, it was still his *birth* day.

His milestones were behind, he was only just crawling and he was smaller than most kids his age, but he was bright and engaging and his parents were besotted with him.

Finn bent and picked his son up off the grass, kissing him on the head. 'What do you think about that?' he asked him.

Isaac kicked his legs excitedly and Finn and Evie laughed as they helped him pull the paper off the box and get it open. Inside sat the most exquisitely carved and decorated rocking horse Evie had ever seen.

'Finn,' she breathed reverently as he pulled it out and placed it on the grass. 'It's beautiful... Where did you get it?'

Isaac squirmed to get down and Finn obliged. 'It's not from me,' he murmured, upending the box and searching for a card. A piece of thick embossed card slipped out.

Finn read it. 'It's from Khalid,' he murmured.

Evie stared at it. A Saudi oil prince had sent Isaac a first birthday present. The sun shone down on the exquisite workmanship and they both admired it for a moment.

'Is that…gold leaf?' she asked.

Finn nodded. 'I think so.'

They looked at each other and laughed. Then they heard Isaac giggling too and looked down to find him peeking out of the box at them.

'But who needs gold leaf when you've got a box?' Finn smiled.

And Evie watched with joy and love in her heart as Finn pushed a giggling Isaac round and round the yard in his cardboard car.

* * * * *

MILLS & BOON®

Why shop at millsandboon.co.uk?

Each year, thousands of romance readers find their perfect read at millsandboon.co.uk. That's because we're passionate about bringing you the very best romantic fiction. Here are some of the advantages of shopping at www.millsandboon.co.uk:

* **Get new books first**—you'll be able to buy your favourite books one month before they hit the shops

* **Get exclusive discounts**—you'll also be able to buy our specially created monthly collections, with up to 50% off the RRP

* **Find your favourite authors**—latest news, interviews and new releases for all your favourite authors and series on our website, plus ideas for what to try next

* **Join in**—once you've bought your favourite books, don't forget to register with us to rate, review and join in the discussions

Visit **www.millsandboon.co.uk** for all this and more today!

MILLS & BOON®

Why not subscribe?
Never miss a title and save money too!

Here's what's available to you if you join the exclusive **Mills & Boon® Book Club** today:

✦ *Titles up to a month ahead of the shops*
✦ *Amazing discounts*
✦ *Free P&P*
✦ *Earn Bonus Book points that can be redeemed against other titles and gifts*
✦ *Choose from monthly or pre-paid plans*

Still want more?
Well, if you join today, we'll even give you
50% OFF your first parcel!

So visit **www.millsandboon.co.uk/subs**
to be a part of this exclusive Book Club!